Martin Pippin in the Apple Orchard

by

Eleanor Farjeon

The Echo Library 2007

Published by

The Echo Library

Echo Library
131 High St.
Teddington
Middlesex TW11 8HH

www.echo-library.com

Please report serious faults in the text to complaints@echo-library.com

ISBN 978-1-40686-366-6

FOREWORD

I have been asked to introduce Miss Farjeon to the American public, and although I believe that introductions of this kind often do more harm than good, I have consented in this case because the instance is rare enough to justify an exception. If Miss Farjeon had been a promising young novelist either of the realistic or the romantic school, I should not have dared to express an opinion on her work, even if I had believed that she had greater gifts than the ninety-nine other promising young novelists who appear in the course of each decade. But she has a far rarer gift than any of those that go to the making of a successful novelist. She is one of the few who can conceive and tell a fairy-tale; the only one to my knowledge—with the just possible exceptions of James Stephens and Walter de la Mare—in my own generation. She has, in fact, the true gift of fancy. It has already been displayed in her verse—a form in which it is far commoner than in prose—but Martin Pippin is her first book in this kind.

I am afraid to say too much about it for fear of prejudicing both the reviewers and the general public. My taste may not be theirs and in this matter there is no opportunity for argument. Let me, therefore, do no more than tell the story of how the manuscript affected me. I was a little overworked. I had been reading a great number of manuscripts in the preceding weeks, and the mere sight of typescript was a burden to me. But before I had read five pages of Martin Pippin, I had forgotten that it was a manuscript submitted for my judgment. I had forgotten who I was and where I lived. I was transported into a world of sunlight, of gay inconsequence, of emotional surprise, a world of poetry, delight, and humor. And I lived and took my joy in that rare world, until all too soon my reading was done.

My most earnest wish is that there may be many minds and imaginations among the American people who will be able to share that pleasure with me. For every one who finds delight in this book I can claim as a kindred spirit. J. D. Beresford.

CONTENTS

INTRODUCTION

In Adversane in Sussex they still sing the song of The Spring-Green Lady; any fine evening, in the streets or in the meadows, you may come upon a band of children playing the old game that is their heritage, though few of them know its origin, or even that it had one. It is to them as the daisies in the grass and the stars in the sky. Of these things, and such as these, they ask no questions. But there you will still find one child who takes the part of the Emperor's Daughter, and another who is the Wandering Singer, and the remaining group (there should be no more than six in it) becomes the Spring-Green Lady, the Rose-White Lady, the Apple-Gold Lady, of the three parts of the game. Often there are more than six in the group, for the true number of the damsels who guarded their fellow in her prison is as forgotten as their names: Joscelyn, Jane and Jennifer, Jessica, Joyce and Joan. Forgotten, too, the name of Gillian, the lovely captive. And the Wandering Singer is to them but the Wandering Singer, not Martin Pippin the Minstrel. Worse and worse, he is even presumed to be the captive's sweetheart, who wheedles the flower, the ring, and the prison-key out of the strict virgins for his own purposes, and flies with her at last in his shallop across the sea, to live with her happily ever after. But this is a fallacy. Martin Pippin never wheedled anything out of anybody for his own purposes—in fact, he had none of his own. On this adventure he was about the business of young Robin Rue. There are further discrepancies; for the Emperor's Daughter was not an emperor's daughter, but a farmer's; nor was the Sea the sea, but a duckpond; nor—

But let us begin with the children's version, as they sing and dance it on summer days and evenings in Adversane.

THE SINGING-GAME OF "THE SPRING-GREEN LADY"

(The Emperor's Daughter sits weeping in her Tower. Around her, with their backs to her, stand six maids in a ring, with joined hands. They are in green dresses. The Wandering Singer approaches them with his lute.)

THE WANDERING SINGER
Lady, lady, my spring-green lady,
May I come into your orchard, lady?
For the leaf is now on the apple-bough
And the sun is high and the lawn is shady,
 Lady, lady,
 My fair lady!
  O my spring-green lady!

THE LADIES
You may not come into our orchard, singer,
Because we must guard the Emperor's Daughter
Who hides in her hair at the windows there
With her thoughts a thousand leagues over the water,
 Singer, singer,
 Wandering singer,
  O my honey-sweet singer!

THE WANDERING SINGER
Lady, lady, my spring-green lady,
But will you not hear an Alba, lady?
I'll play for you now neath the apple-bough
And you shall dance on the lawn so shady,
 Lady, lady,
 My fair lady,
  O my spring-green lady!

THE LADIES
O if you play us an Alba, singer,
How can that harm the Emperor's Daughter?
No word would she say though we danced all day,
With her thoughts a thousand leagues over the water,
 Singer, singer,
 Wandering singer,
  O my honey-sweet singer!

THE WANDERING SINGER
But if I play you an Alba, lady,
Get me a boon from the Emperor's Daughter—
The flower from her hair for my heart to wear
Though hers be a thousand leagues over the water,
  Lady, lady,
  My fair lady,
    O my spring-green lady!

THE LADIES
(They give him the flower from the hair of the Emperor's Daughter, and sing—)
Now you may play us an Alba, singer,
A dance of dawn for a spring-green lady,
For the leaf is now on the apple-bough,
And the sun is high and the lawn is shady,
  Singer, singer,
  Wandering singer,
    O my honey-sweet singer!

(The Wandering Singer plays on his lute, and The Ladies break their ranks and dance. The Singer steals up behind The Emperor's Daughter, who uncovers her face and sings—)

THE EMPEROR'S DAUGHTER
Mother, mother, my fair dead mother,
They have stolen the flower from your weeping daughter!

THE WANDERING SINGER
O dry your eyes, you shall have this other
When yours is a thousand leagues over the water,
  Daughter, daughter,
  My sweet daughter!
    Love is not far, my daughter!

The Singer then drops a second flower into the lap of the child in the middle, and goes away, and this ends the first part of the game. The Emperor's Daughter is not yet released, for the key of her tower is understood to be still in the keeping of the dancing children. Very likely it is bed-time by this, and mothers are calling from windows and gates, and the children must run home to their warm bread-and-milk and their cool sheets. But if time is still to spare, the second part of the game is played like this. The dancers once more encircle their weeping comrade, and now they are gowned in white and pink. They will indicate these changes perhaps by colored

ribbons, or by any flower in its season, or by imagining themselves
first in green and then in rose, which is really the best way of
all. Well then—

(The Ladies, in gowns of white and rose-color, stand around The Emperor's Daughter, weeping in her Tower. To them once more comes The Wandering Singer with his lute.)

THE WANDERING SINGER
Lady, lady, my rose-white lady,
May I come into your orchard, lady?
For the blossom's now on the apple-bough
And the stars are near and the lawn is shady,
  Lady, lady,
  My fair lady,
    O my rose-white lady!

THE LADIES
You may not come into our orchard, singer,
Lest you bear a word to the Emperor's Daughter
]From one who was sent to banishment
Away a thousand leagues over the water,
  Singer, singer,
  Wandering singer,
    O my honey-sweet singer!

THE WANDERING SINGER
Lady, lady, my rose-white lady,
But will you not hear a Roundel, lady?
I'll play for you now neath the apple-bough
And you shall trip on the lawn so shady,
  Lady, lady,
  My fair lady,
    O my rose-white lady!

THE LADIES
O if you play us a Roundel, singer,
How can that harm the Emperor's Daughter?
She would not speak though we danced a week,
With her thoughts a thousand leagues over the water,
  Singer, singer,
  Wandering singer,
    O my honey-sweet singer!

THE WANDERING SINGER
But if I play you a Roundel, lady,
Get me a gift from the Emperor's Daughter—
Her finger-ring for my finger bring
Though she's pledged a thousand leagues over the water,
  Lady, lady
  My fair lady,
    O my rose-white lady!

THE LADIES
(They give him the ring from the finger of The Emperor's Daughter, and sing—)
Now you may play us a Roundel, singer,
A sunset-dance for a rose-white lady,
For the blossom's now on the apple-bough,
And the stars are near and the lawn is shady,
  Singer, singer,
  Wandering singer,
    O my honey-sweet singer!

(As before, The Singer plays and The Ladies dance; and through the broken circle The Singer comes behind The Emperor's Daughter, who uncovers her face to sing—)

THE EMPEROR'S DAUGHTER
Mother, mother, my fair dead mother,
They've stolen the ring from your heart-sick daughter.

THE WANDERING SINGER
O mend your heart, you shall wear this other
When yours is a thousand leagues over the water,
  Daughter, daughter,
  My sweet daughter!
    Love is at hand, my daughter!

The third part of the game is seldom played. If it is not bed-time, or tea-time, or dinner-time, or school-time, by this time at all events the players have grown weary of the game, which is tiresomely long; and most likely they will decide to play something else, such as Bertha Gentle Lady, or The Busy Lass, or Gypsy, Gypsy, Raggetty Loon!, or The Crock of Gold, or Wayland, Shoe me my Mare!—which are all good games in their way, though not, like The Spring-Green Lady, native to Adversane. But I did once have the luck to hear and see The Lady played in entirety—the children had been granted leave to play "just one more game" before bed-time, and of course they chose the longest and played it without missing a syllable.

(The Ladies, in yellow dresses, stand again in a ring about The Emperor's Daughter, and are for the last time accosted by The Singer with his lute.)

THE WANDERING SINGER
Lady, lady, my apple-gold lady,
May I come into your orchard, lady?
For the fruit is now on the apple-bough,
And the moon is up and the lawn is shady,
  Lady, lady,
  My fair lady,
    O my apple-gold lady!

THE LADIES
You may not come into our orchard, singer,
In case you set free the Emperor's Daughter
Who pines apart to follow her heart
That's flown a thousand leagues over the water,
  Singer, singer,
  Wandering singer,
    O my honey-sweet singer!

THE WANDERING SINGER
Lady, lady, my apple-gold lady,
But will you not hear a Serena, lady?
I'll play for you now neath the apple-bough
And you shall dream on the lawn so shady,
  Lady, lady,
  My fair lady,
    O my apple-gold lady!

THE LADIES
O if you play a Serena, singer,
How can that harm the Emperor's Daughter?
She would not hear though we danced a year
With her heart a thousand leagues over the water,
  Singer, singer,
  Wandering singer,
    O my honey-sweet singer!

THE WANDERING SINGER
But if I play a Serena, lady,
Let me guard the key of the Emperor's Daughter,
Lest her body should follow her heart like a swallow
And fly a thousand leagues over the water,
  Lady, lady,
  My fair lady,
    O my apple-gold lady!

THE LADIES
(They give the key of the Tower into his hands.)
Now you may play a Serena, singer,
A dream of night for an apple-gold lady,
For the fruit is now on the apple-bough
And the moon is up and the lawn is shady,
  Singer, singer,
  Wandering singer,
    O my honey-sweet singer!

(Once more The Singer plays and The Ladies dance; but one by one they fall asleep to the drowsy music, and then The Singer steps into the ring and unlocks the Tower and kisses The Emperor's Daughter. They have the end of the game to themselves.)

Lover, lover, thy/my own true lover
Has opened a way for the Emperor's Daughter!
The dawn is the goal and the dark the cover
As we sail a thousand leagues over the water—
  Lover, lover,
  My dear lover,
    O my own true lover!

(The Wandering Singer and The Emperor's Daughter float a thousand leagues in his shallop and live happily ever after. I don't know what becomes of The Ladies.)

"Bed-time, children!"
In they go.
You see the treatment is a trifle fanciful. But romance gathers round an old story like lichen on an old branch. And the story of Martin Pippin in the Apple-Orchard is so old now—some say a year old, some say even two. How can the children be expected to remember?
But here's the truth of it.

MARTIN PIPPIN IN THE APPLE-ORCHARD

PROLOGUE

PART I

One morning in April Martin Pippin walked in the meadows near Adversane, and there he saw a young fellow sowing a field with oats broadcast. So pleasant a sight was enough to arrest Martin for an hour, though less important things, such as making his living, could not occupy him for a minute. So he leaned upon the gate, and presently noticed that for every handful he scattered the young man shed as many tears as seeds, and now and then he stopped his sowing altogether, and putting his face between his hands sobbed bitterly. When this had happened three or four times, Martin hailed the youth, who was then fairly close to the gate.

"Young master!" said he. "The baker of this crop will want no salt to his baking, and that's flat."

The young man dropped his hands and turned his brown and tear-stained countenance upon the Minstrel. He was so young a man that he wanted his beard.

"They who taste of my sorrow," he replied, "will have no stomach for bread."

And with that he fell anew to his sowing and sighing, and passed up the field.

When he came down again Martin observed, "It must be a very bitter sorrow that will put a man off his dinner."

"It is the bitterest," said the youth, and went his way.

At his next coming Martin inquired, "What is the name of your sorrow?"

"Love," said the youth. By now he was somewhat distant from the gate when he came abreast of it, and Martin Pippin did not catch the word. So he called louder:

"What?"

"Love!" shouted the youth. His voice cracked on it. He appeared slightly annoyed. Martin chewed a grass and watched him up and down the meadow.

At the right moment he bellowed:

"I was never yet put off my feed by love."

"Then," roared the youth, "you have never loved."

At this Martin jumped over the gate and ran along the furrow behind the boy.

"I have loved," he vowed, "as many times as I have tuned lute-strings."

"Then," said the youth, not turning his head, "you have never loved in vain."

"Always, thank God!" said Martin fervently.

The youth, whose name was Robin Rue, suddenly dropped all his seed in one heap, flung up his arms, and,

"Alas!" he cried. "Oh, Gillian! Gillian!" And began to sob more heavily than ever.

"Tell me your trouble," said the Minstrel kindly.

"Sir," said the youth, "I do not know your name, and your clothes are very tattered. But you are the first who has cared whether or no my heart should break since my lovely Gillian was locked with six keys into her father's Well-House, and six young milkmaids, sworn virgins and man-haters all, to keep the keys."

"The thirsty," said Martin, "make little of padlocks when within a rope's length of water."

"But, sir," continued the youth earnestly, "this Well-House is set in the midst of an Apple-Orchard enclosed in a hawthorn hedge full six feet high, and no entrance thereto but one small green wicket, bolted on the inner side."

"Indeed?" said Martin.

"And worse to come. The length of the hedge there is a great duckpond, nine yards broad, and three wild ducks swimming on it. Alas!" he cried, "I shall never see my lovely girl again!"

"Love is a mighty power," said Martin Pippin, "but there are doubtless things it cannot do."

"I ask so little," sighed Robin Rue. "Only to send her a primrose for her hair-band, and have again whatever flower she wears there now."

"Would this really content you?" said Martin Pippin.

"I would then consent to live," swore Robin Rue, "long enough at all events to make an end of my sowing."

"Well, that would be something," said Martin cheerfully, "for fields must not go fallow that are appointed to bear. Direct me to your Gillian's Apple-Orchard."

"It is useless," Robin said. "For even if you could cross the duckpond, and evade the ducks, and compass the green gate, my sweetheart's father's milkmaids are not to be come over by any man; and they watch the Well-House day and night."

"Yet direct me to the orchard," repeated Martin Pippin, and thrummed his lute a little.

"Oh, sir," said Robin anxiously, "I must warn you that it is a long and weary way, it may be as much as two mile by the road." And he looked disconsolately at the Minstrel, as though in fear that he would be discouraged from the adventure.

"It can but be attempted," answered Martin, "and now tell me only whether I go north or south as the road runs."

"Gillman the farmer, her father," said Robin Rue, "has moreover a very big stick—"

"Heaven help us!" cried Martin, and took to his heels.

"That ends it!" sighed the sorry lover.

"At least let us make a beginning!" quoth Martin Pippin.

He leaped the gate, mocked at a cuckoo, plucked a primrose, and went singing up the road.

Robin Rue resumed his sowing and his tears.

"Maids," said Joscelyn, "what is this coming across the duckpond?"

"It is a man," said little Joan.

The six girls came running and crowding to the wicket, standing a-tiptoe and peeping between each other's sunbonnets. Their sunbonnets and their gowns were as green as lettuce-leaves.

"Is he coming on a raft?" asked Jessica, who stood behind.

"No," said Jane, "he is coming on his two feet. He has taken off his shoes, but I fear his breeches will suffer."

"He is giving bread to the ducks," said Jennifer.

"He has a lute on his back," said Joyce.

"Man!" cried Joscelyn, who was the tallest and the sternest of the milkmaids, "go away at once!"

Martin Pippin was by now within arm's-length of the green gate. He looked with pleasure at the six virgins fluttering in their green gowns, and peeping bright-eyed and rosy-cheeked under their green bonnets. Beyond them he saw the forbidden orchard, with cuckoo-flower and primrose, daffodil and celandine, silver windflower and sweet violets blue and white, spangling the gay grass. The twisted apple-trees were in young leaf.

"Go away!" cried all the milkmaids in a breath. "Go away!"

"My green maidens," said Martin, "may I not come into your orchard? The sun is up, and the shadow lies fresh on the grass. Let me in to rest a little, dear maidens—if maidens indeed you be, and not six leaflets blown from the apple-branches."

"You cannot come in," said Joscelyn, "because we are guarding our master's daughter, who sits yonder weeping in the Well-House."

"That is a noble and a tender duty," said Martin. "From what do you guard her?"

The milkmaids looked primly at one another, and little Joan said, "It is a secret."

Martin: I will ask no more. And what do you do all day long?

Joyce: Nothing, and it is very dull.

Martin: It must be still duller for your master's daughter.

Joan: Oh, no, she has her thoughts to play with.

Martin: And what of your thoughts?

Joscelyn: We have no thoughts. I should think not indeed!

Martin: I beg your pardon. But since you find the hours so tedious, will you not let me sing and play to you upon my lute? I will sing you a song for a spring morning, and you shall dance in the grass like any leaf in the wind.

Jane: I think there can be no harm in that.

Jessica: It can't matter a straw to Gillian.

Joyce: She would not look up from her thoughts though we footed it all day.

Joscelyn: So long as he is on one side of the gate—

Jennifer: —and we on the other.

"I love to dance," said little Joan.

"Man!" cried the milkmaids in a breath, "play and sing to us!"

"Oh, maidens," answered Martin merrily, "every tune deserves its fee. But don't look so troubled—my hire shall be of the lightest. Let me see! You shall fetch me the flower from the hair of your little mistress who sits weeping on the coping with her face hidden in her shining locks."

At this the milkmaids clapped their hands, and little Joan, running to the Well-House, with a touch like thistledown drew from the weeper's yellow hair a yellow primrose. She brought it to the gate and laid it in Martin's hand.

"Now you will play for us, won't you?" said she. "A dance for a spring-morning when the leaves dance on the apple-trees."

Then Martin tuned his lute and played and sang as follows, while the girls took hands and danced in a green chain among the twisty trees.

The green leaf dances now,
The green leaf dances now,
The green leaf with its tilted wings
Dances on the bough,
And every rustling air
Says, I've caught you, caught you,
Leaf with tilted wings,
Caught you in a snare!
Whose snare? Spring's,
That bound you to the bough
Where you dance now,
Dance, but cannot fly,
For all your tilted wings
Pointing to the sky;
Where like martins you would dart
But for Spring's delicious art
That caught you to the bough,
Caught, yet left you free
To dance if not to fly—oh see!
As you are dancing now,
Dancing on the bough,
Dancing on the bough,
Dancing with your tilted wings
On the apple-bough.

Now as Martin sang and the milkmaids danced, it seemed that Gillian in her prison heard and saw nothing except the music and the movement of her sorrows. But presently she raised her hand and touched her hair-band, and then she lifted up the fairest face Martin had ever seen, so that he needs must see it nearer; and he took the green gate in one stride, and the green dancers never observed him. Then Gillian's tender mouth parted like an opening quince-blossom, and—

"Oh, Mother, Mother!" she said, "if you had only lived they would not have stolen the flower from my hair while I sat weeping."

Above her head a whispering voice made answer, "Oh, Daughter, Daughter, dry your sweet eyes. You shall wear this other flower when yours is gone over the duckpond to Adversane."

And lo! A second primrose dropped out of the skies into her lap. And that day the lovely Gillian wept no more.

PART II

It happened that on an afternoon in May Martin Pippin passed again through Adversane, and as he passed he thought, "Now certainly I have been here before," but he could not remember when or how, for a full month had run under the bridges of time since then, and man's memory is not infinite.

But in walking by a certain garden he heard a sound of sobbing; and curiosity, of which he was largely made, caused him to climb the old brick wall that he might discover the cause. What he saw from his perch was a garden laid out in neat plots between grassy walks edged with double daisies, red, white and pink, or bordered with sweet herbs, or with lavender and wallflower; and here and there were cordons of fruit-trees, apple, plum and cherry, and in a sunny corner a clump of flowering currant heavy with humming bees; and against the inner walls flat pear-trees stretched their long straight lines, like music-staves whereon a lovely melody was written in notes of snow. And in the midst of all this stood a very young man with a face as brown as a berry. He was spraying the cordons with quassia-water. But whenever he filled his syringe he wept so many tears above the bucket that it was always full to the brim.

When he had watched this happen several times, Martin hailed the young man.

"Young master!" said Martin, "the eater of your plums will need sugar thereto, and that's flat."

The young man turned his eyes upward.

"There is not sugar enough in all the world," he answered, "to sweeten the fruits that are watered by my sorrows."

"Then here is a waste of good quassia," said Martin, "and I think your name is Robin Rue."

"It is," said Robin, "and you are Martin Pippin, to whom I owe more than to any man living. But the primrose you brought me is dead this five-and-twenty days."

"And what of your Gillian?"

"Alas! How can I tell what of her? She is where she was and I am here where I am. What will become of me?"

"There are riddles without answers," observed Martin.

"I can answer this one. I shall fall into a decline and die. And yet I ask no more than to send her a ring to wear on her finger, and have her ring to wear on mine."

"Would this satisfy you?" asked Martin.

"I could then cling to life," said Robin Rue, "long enough at least to finish my spraying."

"We may praise God as much for small mercies," said Martin pleasantly, "as for great ones; and trees must not be blighted that were appointed to fruit."

So saying, he unstraddled his legs and dropped into the road, tickled an armadillo with his toe, twirled the silver ring on his finger, and went away singing.

"Maidens," said Joscelyn, "here is that man come again."

Maids' memories are longer than men's. At all events, the milkmaids knew instantly to whom she referred, although nearly a month had passed since his coming.

"Has he his lute with him?" asked little Joan.

"He has. And he is giving cake to the ducks; they take it from his hand. Man, go away immediately!"

Martin Pippin propped his elbows on the little gate, and looked smiling into the orchard, all pink and white blossom. The trees that had been longest in bloom were white cascades of flower, others there were flushed like the cheek of a sleeping child, and some were still studded with rose-red buds. The grass was high and full of spotted orchis, and tall wild parsley spread its nets of lace almost abreast of the lowest boughs of blossom. So that the milkmaids stood embraced in meeting flowers, waist-deep in the orchard growth: all gowned in pink lawn with loose white sleeves, and their faces flushed it may have been with the pink linings to their white bonnets, or with the evening rose in the west, or with I know not what.

"Go away!" they cried at the intruder. "Go away!"

"My rose-white maidens," said Martin, "will you not let me into your orchard? For the stars are rising with the dew, and the hour is at peace. Let me in to rest, dear maidens—if maidens indeed you be, and not six blossoms fallen from the apple-boughs."

"You cannot come in," said Joscelyn, "lest you are the bearer of a word to our master's daughter who sits weeping in the Well-House."

"From whom should I bear her a word?" asked Martin Pippin in great amazement.

The milkmaids cast down their eyes, and little Joan said, "It is a secret."

Martin: I will inquire no further. But shall I not play a little on my lute? It is as good an hour for song and dance as any other, and I will make a tune for a sunny May evening, and you shall sway among the grasses like any flower on the bough."

Jane: In my opinion that can hurt nobody.

Jessica: Gillian wouldn't care two pins.

Joyce: She would utter no word though we tripped it for a week.

Joscelyn: So long as he keeps to his side of the hedge—

Jennifer: —and we to ours.

"Oh, I do love to dance!" cried little Joan.

"Man!" they commanded him as one voice, "play and sing to us instantly!"

"My pretty ones," laughed Martin Pippin, "songs are as light as air, but worth more than pearls and diamonds. What will you give me for my song? Wait, now!—I have it. You shall fetch me the ring from the finger of your little mistress, who sits hidden beneath the fountain of her own bright tresses."

The milkmaids at these words nodded gayly, and little Joan tip-toed to the Well-House, and slipped the ring from Gillian's finger as lightly as a daisy may be slipped from its fellow on the chain. Then she ran with it to the gate, and Martin held up his little finger, and she put it on, saying:

"Now you will keep your promise, honey-sweet singer, and play a dance for a May evening when the blossom blows for happiness on the apple-trees."

So Martin Pippin tuned his lute and sang what follows, while the girls floated in ones and twos among the orchard grass:

A-floating, a-floating, what saw I a-floating?
Fairy ships rocking with pink sails and white
Smoothly as swans on a river of light
Saw I a-floating?
No, it was apple-bloom, rosy and fair,
Softly obeying the nod of the air
I saw a-floating.
A-floating, a-floating, what saw I a-floating?
White clouds at eventide blown to and fro
Lightly as bubbles the cherubim blow,
Saw I a-floating?
No, it was pretty girls gowned like a flower
Blown in a ring round their own apple-bower
I saw a-floating.
Or was it my dream, my dream only—who knows?—
As frail as a snowflake, as flushed as a rose,
I saw a-floating?
A-floating, a-floating, what saw I a-floating?

Martin sang, and the milkmaids danced, and Gillian in her prison only heard the dropping of her tears, and only saw the rainbow prisms on her lashes. But presently she laid her cheek against her hand, and missed a touch she knew; and on that revealed her lovely face so full of woe, that Martin needs must comfort her or weep himself. And the dancers took no heed when he made one step across the gate and went under the trees to the Well-House.

"Oh, Mother, Mother!" sighed Gillian, "if you had only lived they would never have stolen the ring from my finger while I sat heartsick."

Above her head a whispering voice replied, "Oh, Daughter, Daughter, mend your dear heart! You shall wear this other ring when yours is gone over the duckpond to Adversane."

Oh wonder! Out of the very heavens fell a silver ring into her bosom. And if that night Gillian slept not, neither wept she.

PART III

In the beginning of the first week in September Martin Pippin came once more to Adversane, and he said to himself when he saw it:

"Now this is the prettiest hamlet I ever had the luck to light on in my wanderings. And if chance or fortune will, I shall some day come this way again."

While he was thinking these thoughts, his ears were assailed by groans and sighs, so that he wet his finger and held it up to find which way the wind blew on this burning day of blue and gold. But no wind coming, he sought some other agency for these gusts, and discovered it in a wheat-field where was a young fellow stooking sheaves. A very young fellow he was, turned copper by the sun; and as he stooked he heaved such sighs that for every shock he stooked two tumbled at his feet. When Martin had seen this happen more than once he called aloud to the harvester.

"Young master!" said Martin, "the mill that grinds your grain will need no wind to its sails, and that's flat."

The young man looked up from his labors to reply.

"There are no mill-stones in all the world," said he, "strong enough to grind the grain of my grief."

"Then I would save these gales till they may be put to more use," remarked Martin, "and if I remember rightly you wear a lady's ring on your little finger, though I cannot remember her name or yours."

"Her heavenly name is Gillian," said the youth, "and mine is Robin Rue."

"And are you wedded yet?" asked Martin.

"Wedded?" he cried. "Have you forgotten that she is locked with six keys inside her father's Well-House?"

"But this was long ago," said Martin. "Is she there yet?"

"She is," said Robin Rue, "and here am I."

"Well, all states must end some time," said Martin Pippin.

"Even life, sighed Robin, "and therefore before the month is out I shall wilt and be laid in the earth."

"That would be a pity," said Martin. "Can nothing save you?"

"Nothing but the keys to her prison, and they are in the keeping of them that will not give them up."

"I remember," said Martin. "Six milkmaids."

"With hearts of flint!" cried Robin.

"Sparks may be struck from flint," said Martin, in his inconsequential way. "But tell me, if Gillian's prison were indeed unlocked, would all be well with you for ever?"

"Oh," said Robin Rue, "if her prison were unlocked and the prisoner in these arms, this wheat should be flour for a wedding-cake."

"It is the best of all cakes," said Martin Pippin, "and the grain that is destined thereto must not rot in the husk."

With these words he strolled out of the cornfield, gathered a harebell, rang it so loudly in the ear of a passing rabbit that it is said never to have stopped running till it found itself in France, and went up the road humming and thrumming his lute.

On the road he met a Gypsy.

"Maids," said Joscelyn, "somebody is at the gate."

The milkmaids, who were eating apples, came clustering about her instantly.

"Is it a man?" asked little Joan, pausing between her bites.

"No, thank all our stars," said Joscelyn, "it is a gypsy."

The milkmaids withdrew, their fears allayed. Joan bit her apple and said, "It puckers my mouth."

Joyce: Mine's sour.

Jessica: Mine's hard.

Jane: Mine's bruised.

Jennifer: There's a maggot in mine.

They threw their apples away.

"Who'll buy trinkets?" said the Gypsy at the gate.

"What have you to sell?" asked Joscelyn.

"Knick-knacks and gew-gaws of all sorts. Rings and ribbons, mirrors and beads, silken shoe-strings and colored lacings, sweetmeats and scents and gilded pins; silver buckles, belts and bracelets, gay kerchiefs, spotted ones, striped ones; ivory bobbins, sprigs of coral, and sea-shells from far places, they'll murmur you secrets o' nights if you put em under your pillow; here are patterns for patchwork, and here's a sheet of ballads, and here's a pack of cards for telling fortunes. What will ye buy? A dream-book, a crystal, a charmed powder that shall make you see your sweetheart in the dark?"

"Oh!" six voices cried in one.

"Or this other powder shall charm him to love you, if he love you not?"

"Fie!" exclaimed Joscelyn severely. "We want no love-charms."

"I warrant you!" laughed the Gypsy. "What will ye buy?"

Jennifer: I'll have this flasket of scent.

Joyce: I'll have this looking-glass.

Jessica: And I this necklet of beads.

Jane: A pair of shoe-buckles, if you please.

Joan: This bunch of ribbons for me.

Joscelyn: Have you a corset-lace of yellow silk?

The Gypsy: Here's for you and you. No love-charms, no. Here's for you and you and you. I warrant, no love-charms! Ay, I've a yellow lace, twill keep you in as tight as jealousy, my pretty. Out upon all love-charms!—And what will she have that sits crouched in the Well-House?

"Oh, Gypsy!" cried Joscelyn, "have you among your charms one that will make a maid fall OUT of love?"

"Nay, nay," said the Gypsy, growing suddenly grave. "That is a charm takes more black art than I am mistress of. I know indeed of but one remedy. Is the case so bad?"

"She has been shut into the Well-House to cure her of loving," said Joscelyn, "and in six months she has scarcely ceased to weep, and has never uttered a word. If you know the physic that shall heal her of her foolishness, I pray you tell us of it. For it is extremely dull in this orchard, with nothing to do except watch the changes of the apple-trees, and meanwhile the farmstead lacks water and milk, there being no entry to the well nor maids to milk the cows. Daily comes Old Gillman to tell us how, from morning till night, he is forced to drink cider and ale, and so the farm goes to rack and ruin, and all because he has a lovesick daughter. What is your remedy? He would give you gold and silver for it."

"I do not know if it can be bought," said the Gypsy, "I do not even know if it exists. But when a maid broods too much on her own love-tale, the like weapons only will vanquish her thoughts. Nothing but a new love-tale will overcome her broodings, and where the case is obstinate one only will not suffice. You say she has pined upon her love six months. Let her be told six brand-new love-tales, tales which no woman ever heard before, and I think she will be cured. These counter-poisons will so work in her that little by little her own case will be obliterated from her blood. But for my part I doubt whether there be six untold love-tales left on earth, and if there be I know not who keeps them buttoned under his jacket."

"Alas!" cried Joscelyn, "then we must stay here for ever until we die."

"It looks very like it," said the Gypsy, "and my wares are a penny apiece."

So saying she collected her moneys and withdrew, and for all I know was never seen again by man, woman, or child.

My apple-gold maidens," said Martin Pippin, leaning on the gate in the bright night, "may I come into your orchard?"

As he addressed them he gazed with delight at the enclosure. By the light of the Queen Moon, now at her full in heaven, he saw that the orchard grass was clipped, and patterned with small clover, but against the hedges rose wild banks of meadow-sweet and yarrow and the jolly ragwort, and briony with its heart-shaped leaf and berry as red as heart's-blood made a bower above them all. And all the apple-trees were decked with little golden moons hanging in clusters on the drooping boughs, and glimmering in the recesses of the leaves. Under each tree a ring of windfalls lay in the grass. But prettiest sight of all was the ring of girls in yellow gowns and caps, that lay around the midmost apple-tree like fallen fruit.

"Dear maidens," pleaded the Minstrel, "let me come in."

At the sound of his voice the six milkmaids rose up in the grass like golden fountains. And fountains indeed they were, for their eyes were running over with tears.

"We did not hear you coming," said little Joan.

"Go away at once!" commanded Joscelyn.

Then all the girls cried "Go away!" together.

"My apple-gold maidens," said Martin Pippin, "I entreat you to let me in. For the moon is up, and it is time to be sleeping or waking, in sweet company.

So I beseech you to admit me, dear maidens—if maidens in truth you be, and not six apples bobbed off their stems."

"You may not come in," said Joscelyn, "in case you should release our master's daughter, who sits in the Well-House pining to follow her heart."

"Why, whither would she follow it?" asked Martin much surprised.

The milkmaids turned their faces away, and little Joan murmured, "It is a secret."

Martin: I will put chains on my thoughts. But shall I not sing you a tune you may dance to? I will make you a song for an August night, when the moon rocks her way up and down the cradle of the sky, and you shall rock on earth like any apple on the twig.

Jane: For my part, I see nothing against it.

Jessica: Gillian won't care little apples.

Joyce: She would not hear though we danced the round of the year.

Joscelyn: So long as he does not come in—

Jennifer: —or we go out.

"Oh, let us dance, do let us dance!" cried little Joan.

"Man," they importuned him in a single breath, "play for us and sing for us, as quickly as you can!"

"Sweet ones," said Martin Pippin, shaking his head, "songs must be paid for. And yet I do not know what to ask you, some trifle in kind it should be. Why, now, I have it! If I give you the keys to the dance, give me the keys to your little mistress, that I may keep her secure from following her heart like a bird of passage, whither it's no business of mine to ask."

At this request, made so gayly and so carelessly, the girls all looked at one another in consternation. Then Joscelyn drew herself up to full height, and pointing with her arm straight across the duckpond she cried:

"Minstrel, begone!"

And the six girls, turning their backs upon him, moved away into the shadows of the moon.

"Well-a-day!" sighed Martin Pippin, "how a fool may trip and never know it till his nose hits the earth. I will sing to you for nothing."

But the girls did not answer.

Then Martin touched his lute and sang as follows, so softly and sweetly that they, not regarding, hardly knew the sound of his song from the heavy-sweet scent of the ungathered apples over their heads.

Toss me your golden ball, laughing maid, lovely maid,
Lovely maid, laughing maid, toss me your ball!
I'll catch it and throw it, and hide it and show it,
And spin it to heaven and not let it fall.
Boy, run away with you! I will not play with you—
This is no ball!
We are too old to be playing at ball.
Toss me the golden sun, laughing maid, lovely maid,

Lovely maid, laughing maid, toss me the sun!
I'll wheel it, I'll whirl it, I'll twist it and twirl it
Till cocks crow at midnight and day breaks at one.
Boy, I'll not sport with you! Boy, to be short with you,
This is no sun!
We are too young to play tricks with the sun.
Toss me your golden toy, laughing maid, lovely maid,
Lovely maid, laughing maid, toss me your toy!
It's all one to me, girl, whatever it be, girl
So long as it's round that's enough for a boy.
Boy, come and catch it then!—there now! Don't snatch it then!
Here comes your toy!
Apples were made for a girl and a boy.

There was no sound or movement from the girls in the shadows.

"Farewell, then," said Martin. "I must carry my tunes and tales elsewhere."

Like pebbles from a catapult the milkmaids shot to the gate.

"Tales?" cried Jessica.

"Do you know tales?" exclaimed Jennifer.

"What kind of tales?" demanded Jane.

"Love-tales?" panted Joyce.

"Six of them?" urged little Joan.

"A thousand!" said Martin Pippin.

Joscelyn's hand lay on the bolt.

"Man," she said, "come in."

She opened the wicket, and Martin Pippin walked into the Apple Orchard.

PRELUDE TO THE FIRST TALE

"And now," said Martin Pippin, "what exactly do you require of me?"

"If you please," said little Joan, "you are to tell us a love-story that has never been told before."

"But we have reason to fear," added Jane, "that there is no such story left in all the world."

"There you are wrong," said Martin, "for on the contrary no love-story has ever been told twice. I never heard any tale of lovers that did not seem to me as new as the world on its first morning. I am glad you have a taste for love-stories."

"We have not," said Joscelyn, very quickly.

"No, indeed!" cried her five fellows.

"Then shall it be some other kind of tale?"

"No other kind will do," said Joscelyn, still more quickly.

"We must all bear our burdens," said Martin; "so let us make ourselves as happy as we can in an apple-tree, and when the tale becomes too little to your taste you shall munch apples and forget it."

"Will you sit in the swing?" asked Jennifer, pointing to the midmost apple-tree, which was the largest in the orchard, and had a little swing hanging from a long upper limb.

Close to the apple-tree, a branch of which indeed brushed its mossed pent-roof, stood the Well-House. It had a round wall of old red bricks growing green with time, and a pillar of oak rose up at each point of the compass to support the pent. Between the south and west pillars was a green door, held by a rusty chain and a padlock with six keyholes. The little circular court within was flagged, and three rings of worn steps led to the well-head and the green wooden bucket inverted on the coping. Between the cracks of the flags sprang grass, and pink-starred centaury, and even a trail of mallow sprawled over the steps where Gillian lay in tears, as though to wreathe her head with its striped blooms.

"What luck you have," said Martin, "not only to live in an orchard, but to have a swing to swing in."

"It is our one diversion," said Joyce, "except when you come to play to us."

"It is delightful to swing," said little Joan invitingly.

"So it is," agreed Martin, "and I beg you to sit in the swing while I sit on this bough, and when I see your eyelids growing heavy with my tale I will start the rope and rouse you—thus!"

So saying, he lifted the littlest milkmaid lightly into her perch and gave her so vigorous a push that she cried out with delight, as at one moment the point of her shoe cleared the door of the Well-House, and at the next her heels were up among the apples. Then Martin ensconced himself upon a lower limb of the tree, which had a mossy cushion against the trunk as though nature or time had designed it for a teller of tales. The milkmaids sprang quickly into other branches around him, shaking a hail of sweet apples about his head. What he could he caught, and dropped into the swinger's lap, whence from time to time he helped himself; and she did likewise.

"Begin," said Joscelyn.

"A thought has occurred to me," said Martin Pippin, "and it is that my tale may disturb your master's daughter."

"We desire it to," said Joscelyn looking down on the Well-House and the yellow head of Gillian. "The fear is rather that you may not arouse her attention, so I hope that when you speak you will speak clearly. For to tell you the truth we have heard that nothing but six love-tales will wash from her mind the image of—"

"Of whom?" inquired Martin as she paused.

"It does not matter whom," said Joscelyn, "but I think the time is ripe to confess to you that the silly damsel is in love."

"The world is so full of wonders," said Martin Pippin, "that one ceases to be surprised at almost anything."

"Is love then," said little Joan, "so rare a thing in the world?"

"The rarest of all things," answered Martin, looking gravely into her eyes. "It is as rare as flowers in Spring."

"I am glad of that," said Joan; while Joscelyn objected, "But nothing is commoner."

"Do you think so?" said Martin. "Perhaps you are right. Yet Spring after Spring the flowers quicken my heart as though I were perceiving them for the first time in my life—yes, even the very commonest of them."

"What do you call the commonest?" asked Jessica.

"Could any be commoner," said Martin, "than Robin-run-by-the-Wall? Yet I think he has touched many a heart in his day."

And fixing his eyes on the weeper in the Well-House, Martin Pippin tried his lute and sang this song.

Run by the wall, Robin,
Run by the wall!
You might hear a secret
A lady once let fall.
If you hear her secret
Tell it in my ear,
And I'll whisper you another
For her to overhear.

The weeper stirred very slightly.

"The song makes little sense," said Joscelyn, "and would make none at all if you called this flower by its right name of Jack-in-the-Hedge."

"Let us do so," said Martin readily, "and then the nonsense will run this way as easily as that."

Hide in the hedge, Jack,
Hide in the hedge!
You might catch a letter
Dropped over the edge.
If you catch her letter
Slip it in my hand,
And I'll write another
That she'll understand.

As he concluded, Gillian lifted up her head, and putting her hair from her face gazed over the duckpond beyond the green wicket.

"The lady," said Joscelyn with some impatience, "who understand the letter must outdo me in wits, for I find no understanding whatever in your silly song. However, it seems to have brought our master's daughter out of her lethargy, and the moment is favorable to your tale. Therefore without further ado I beg you to begin."

"I will," said Martin, "and on my part entreat your forbearance while I relate to you the story of The King's Barn."

THE KING'S BARN

There was once, dear maidens, a King in Sussex of whose kingdom and possessions nothing remained but a single Barn and a change of linen. It was no fault of his. He was a very young king when he came into his heritage, and it was already dwindled to these proportions. Once his fathers had owned a beautiful city on the banks of the Adur, and all the lands to the north and the west were theirs, for a matter of several miles indeed, including many strange things that were on them: such as the Wapping Thorp, the Huddle Stone, the Bush Hovel where a Wise Woman lived, and the Guess Gate; likewise those two communities known as the Doves and the Hawking Sopers, whose ways of life were as opposite as the Poles. The Doves were simple men, and religious; but the Hawking Sopers were indeed a wild and rowdy crew, and it is said that the King's father had hunted and drunk with them until his estates were gambled away and his affairs decayed of neglect, and nothing was left at last but the solitary Barn which marked the northern boundary of his possessions. And here, when his father was dead, our young King sat on a tussock of hay with his golden crown on his head and his golden scepter in his hand, and ate bread and cheese thrice a day, throwing the rind to the rats and the crumbs to the swallows. His name was William, and beyond the rats and the swallows he had no other company than a nag called Pepper, whom he fed daily from the tussock he sat on.

But at the end of a week he said:

"It is a dull life. What should a King do in a Barn?"

So saying, he pulled the last handful of hay from under him, rising up quickly before he had time to fall down, and gave it to his nag; and next he tied up his scepter and crown with his change of linen in a blue handkerchief; and last he fetched a rope and a sack and put them on Pepper for bridle and saddle, and rode out of the Barn leaving the door to swing.

"Let us go south, Pepper," said he, "for it is warmer to ride into the sun than away from it, and so we shall visit my Father's lands that might have been mine."

South they went, with the great Downs ahead of them, and who knew what beyond? And first they came to the Hawking Sopers, who when they saw William approaching tumbled out of their dwelling with a great racket, crying to him to come and drink and play with them.

"Not I," said he. "For so I should lose my Barn to you, and such as it is it is a shelter, and my only one. But tell me, if you can, what should a King do in a Barn?"

"He should dance in it," said they, and went laughing and singing back to their cups.

"What sort of advice is this, Pepper?" said the King. "Shall we try elsewhere?"

The nag whinnied with unusual vehemence, and the King, taking this for yea, and not observing that she limped as she went, rode on to the Doves: the gentle gray-gowned Brothers who spent their days in pious works and their nights in meditation. Between the twelve hours of twilight and dawn they were pledged not to utter speech, but the King arriving there at noon they welcomed him with kind words, and offered him a bowl of rice and milk.

He thanked them, and when he had eaten and drink put to them his riddle.

"What should a King do in a Barn?"

They answered, "He should pray in it."

"This may be good advice," said the King. "Pepper, should we go further?"

The little nag whinnied till her sides shook, which the King took, as before, to be an affirmative. However, because it was Sunday he remained with the Doves a day and a night, and during such time as their lips were not sealed they urged him to become one of them, and found a new settlement of Brothers in his Barn. He spent his night in reflection, but by morning had come to no decision.

"To what better use could you dedicate it?" asked the Chief Brother, who was known as the Ringdove because he was the leader.

"None that I can think of," said the King, "but I fear I am not good enough."

"When you have passed our initiation," said the Ringdove, "you will be."

"Is it difficult?" asked William.

"No, it is very easy, and can be accomplished within a month. You have only to ride south till you come to the hills, on the highest of which you will see a Ring of beech-trees. Under the hills lies the little village of Washington, and there you may dwell in comfort through the week. But on each of the four Saturdays of the lunar month you must mount the hill at sunset and keep a vigil among the beeches till sunrise. And you must see that these Saturdays occur on the fourth quarters of the moon—once when she is in her crescent, once at the half, again at the full, and lastly when she is waning."

"And is this all?" said William. "It sounds very simple."

"Not quite all, but the rest is nearly as simple. You have but to observe four rules. First, to tell no living soul of your resolve during the month of initiation. Second, to keep your vigil always between the two great beeches in the middle of the Ring. Third, to issue forth at midnight and immerse your head in the Dewpond which lies on the hilltop to the west, and having done so to return to your watch between the trees. And fourth, to make no utterance on any account whatever from sunset to sunrise."

"Suppose I should sneeze?" inquired the King anxiously.

"There's no supposing about it," said the Ringdove. "Sneezing, seeing that your head will be extremely wet, is practically inevitable. But the rule applies only to such utterance as lies within human control. When the fourth vigil has been successfully accomplished, return to us for a blessing and the gray robe of our Order."

"But how," asked the King, "during my vigils shall I know when midnight is due?"

"In the third quarter after eleven a bird sings. At the beginning of its song go forth from the Ring, and at the ending plunge your head into the Pond. For on these nights the bird sings ceaselessly for fifteen minutes, but stops at the very moment of midnight."

"And is this really all?"

"This is all."

"How easy it is to become good," said William cheerfully. "I will begin at once."

So impatient was he to become a Brother Dove—

(But here Martin Pippin broke off abruptly, and catching the rope of the swing in his left hand he gave it a great lurch.

Joan: Oh! Oh! Oh!

Martin: I perceive, Mistress Joan, that you lose interest in my story. Your mouth droops.

Joan: Oh, no! Oh, no! It is only—it is a very nice story—but—

Martin: What cannot be said aloud can frequently be whispered.

He leaned his ear close to her mouth, and very shyly she whispered into it.

Joan (whispering very shyly): Why must the young King join a Brotherhood? I thought...this was to be a...love story.

Martin smiled and chose an apple from her lap.

"Keep this for me," said he, "until I ask for it; and if you are not then satisfied, neither will I be")

So impatient (resumed Martin) was the King to enter the Brotherhood, that he abandoned his idea of visiting the Huddle Stone and the Wapping Thorp (which would have taken him out of his course), and, without even waiting to break his fast, leaped on to Pepper's back and turned her head southwest towards the hills. And in his eagerness he failed to remark how Pepper stumbled at every second step. Before he had gone a mile he came to the Guess Gate.

Of the Guess Gate, as you may know, all men ask a question in passing through, and in the back-swing of the Gate it creaks an answer. So nothing more natural than that the King, having flung the Gate open, should cry aloud once more:

"Gate, Gate! What should a King do in a Barn?"

"Now at last," thought he, "I shall be told whether to dance or to pray in it." And he stood listening eagerly as the Gate hung an instant on its outward journey and then began to creak home.

"He—should—rule—in—it—he—should—rule—in—it—he—should—" squeaked the Guess Gate, and then latch clicked and it was silent.

This disconcerted William.

"Now I am worse off than ever," he sighed. "Pray, Pepper, can this advice be bettered?"

As usual when he questioned her, the nag pricked up her ears and whinnied so violently that he nearly fell off her back. Nevertheless, he kept Pepper's head in a beeline for Chanctonbury, never noticing how very ill she was going, and presently crossed the great High Road beyond which lay the Bush Hovel. The Wise Woman was at home; from afar the King saw her sitting outside the Hovel mending her broom with a withe from the Bush.

"Here if anywhere," rejoiced William, "I shall learn the truth."

He dismounted and approached the old woman, cap in hand.

"Wise Woman," he said respectfully, "you know most things, but do you know this—whether a King should dance or pray or rule in his Barn?"

"He should do all three, young man," said the Wise Woman.

"But—!" exclaimed William.

"I'm busy," snapped the Wise Woman. "You men will always be chattering, as though pots need never be stewed nor cobwebs swept." So saying, she went into the Hovel and slammed the door.

"Pepper," said the poor King, "I am at my wits' ends. Go where yours lead you."

At this Pepper whinnied in a perfect frenzy of delight, and the King had to clasp both arms round her neck to avoid tumbling off.

Now the little nag preferred roads to beelines over copses and ditches, and she turned back and ambled along the highway so very lamely that it became impossible even for her preoccupied rider not to perceive that she had cast all her four shoes.

"Poor beast!" he cried dismayed, "how has this happened, and where? Oh, Pepper, how could you be so careless? I have not a penny in my purse to buy you new shoes, my poor Pepper. Do you not remember where you lost them?"

The little nag licked her master's hand (for he had dismounted to examine her trouble), and looked at him with great eyes full of affection, and then she flung up her head and whinnied louder than ever. The sound of it was like nothing so much as laughter. Then she went on, hobbling as best she could, and the King walked by her side with his hand on her neck. In this way they came to a small village, and here the nag turned up a by-road and halted outside the blacksmith's forge. The smith's Lad stood within, clinking at the anvil, the smuttiest Lad smith ever had.

"Lad!" cried the King.

The Lad looked up from his work and came at once to the door, wiping his hands upon his leather apron.

"Where am I?" asked the King.

"In the village of Washington," said the Lad.

"What! Under the Ring?" cried the King.

"Yes, sir," said the Lad.

"A blessing on you!" said the King joyfully, and clapped his hand on the Lad's shoulder. "Pepper, you have solved the problem and led me to my destiny."

"Is Pepper your nag's name?" asked the blacksmith's Lad.

"It is," said the King; "her only one."

"Then she has one more name than she has shoes," said the Lad. "How came she to lose them?"

"I didn't notice," confessed the King.

"You must have been thinking very deeply," remarked the Lad. "Are you in love?"

"I am not quite twenty-one," said the King.

"I see. Do you want your nag shod?"

"I do. But I have spent my last penny."

"Earn another then," said the Lad.

"I did not even earn the last one," said the King shamefacedly. "I have never worked in my life."

"Why, where have you lived?" exclaimed the Lad.

"In a Barn."

"But one works in a Barn—"

"Stop!" cried the king, putting his fingers in his ears. "One prays in a Barn."

"Very likely," said the Lad, looking at him curiously. "Are you going to pray in one?"

"Yes," said the King. "When is the New Moon?"

"Next Saturday."

"Hurrah!" cried the King. "That settles it. But what's to-day?"

"Monday, sir."

"Alas!" sighed William, wondering how he should make shift to live for five days.

"I don't know what you mean, sir," said the Lad.

"I would tell you my meaning," said the King, "but am pledged not to."

Then the Lad said, "Let it pass. I have a proposal to make. My father is dead, and for two years I have worked the forge single-handed. Now I am willing to teach you to shoe your nag with four good shoes and strong, if you will meanwhile blow the bellows for whatever other jobs come to the forge; and if the shoes are not done by dinner-time you shall have a meal thrown in."

The King looked at the Lad kindly.

"I shall blow your bellows very badly," he said, "and shoe my nag still worse."

Said the Lad, "You'll learn in time."

"Not before dinner-time, I hope," said the King, "for I am very hungry."

"You look hungry," said the Lad. "It's a bargain then."

The King held out his hand, but the Lad suddenly whipped his behind his back. "It's so dirty, sir," he said.

"Give it me all the same," said the King; and they clasped hands.

The rest of that morning the King spent in blowing the bellows, and by dinner-time not so much as the first of Pepper's hoofs was shod. For a great deal of business came into the forge, and there was no time for a lesson. So the King and the Lad took their meal together, and the King was by this time nearly as black as his master. He would have washed himself, but the Lad said it was no matter, he himself having no time to wash from week's end to week's end. In the afternoon they changed places, and the King stood at the anvil and the Lad at the bellows. He was a good teacher, but the King made a poor job of it. By nightfall he had produced shoes resembling all the letters of the alphabet excepting U, and when at last he submitted to the Lad a shoe like nothing so much as a drunken S, his master shrugged and said:

"Zeal is praiseworthy within its limits, but the best of smiths does not attempt to make two shoes at once. Let us sup."

They supped; and afterwards the Lad showed the King a small bedroom as neat as a new pin.

"I shall sully the sheets," said William, "and you will excuse me if I fetch the kettle, which is on the boil."

"As you please," said the Lad, and took himself off.

In the morning the King came clean to breakfast, but the Lad was as black as he had been.

Tuesday passed as Monday had passed; now William took the bellows, marveling at his youthful master's deftness, and now the Lad blew, groaning at his pupil's clumsiness. By nightfall, however, he had achieved a shoe faintly recognizable as such. For a second time the King washed himself and slept again in the little trim chamber, but the Lad in the morning resembled midnight. In this way the week went by, the King's heart beating a little faster each morning as Saturday approached, and he wondered by what ruse he could explain his absence without creating suspicion or breaking his pledge.

On Saturday morning the Lad said to the King: "This is a half-day. You must make your shoe this morning or not at all. It is my custom at one o'clock to close the forge and go to visit my Great-Aunt. I will be work again on Monday, till when you must shift for yourself."

The King could hardly believe his luck in having matters so well settled, and he spent the morning so diligently that by noon he had produced a shoe which, if not that of a master-craftsman, was at least adaptable to the purpose for which it had been fashioned.

The Lad examined it and said reluctantly, "It will do," and proceeded to show the King how to fasten it to Pepper's hoof.

"Why," said the King, having the nag's off forefoot in his hand, "here's a stone in it. Small wonder she limped."

"It isn't a stone," said the Lad, extracting it, "it is a ruby."

And he exhibited to the King a ruby of such a glowing red that it was as though the souls of all the grapes of Burgundy had been pressed to create it.

"You are a rich man now," said the Lad quietly, "and can live as you will."

But William closed the Lad's fingers over the stone. "Keep it," he said, "for you have filled me for a week, and I have paid you with nothing but my breath."

"As you please," said the Lad carelessly, and, tossing the stone upon a shelf, locked up the forge. "Now I am going to my Great-Aunt. There's a cake in the larder."

So saying, he strolled away, and the King was left to his own devices. These consisted in bathing himself from head to foot till his body was as pure without as he desired his heart to be within; and in donning his fresh suit of linen. He would not break his fast, but waited, trembling and eager, till an hour before sundown, and then at last he set forth to mount the great hill with the sacred crown of trees upon its crest.

When at last he stood upon the boundary of the Ring, his heart sprang for joy in his breast, and his breath nearly failed him with amazement at the beauty of the world which lay outspread for leagues below him.

"Oh, lovely earth!" he cried aloud, "never till now have I known what beauty I lived in. How is it that we cannot see the wonder of our surroundings until we gaze upon them from afar? But if you look so fair from the hilltops, what must you appear from the very sky?" And lost in delight he turned his eyes upward, and was recalled to his senses by the sight of the sinking sun. "Lovely one, how nearly you have betrayed me!" he said, and smiling waved his hand to the dear earth, sealed up his lips, and entered the Ring.

And here between two midmost beeches he knelt down and buried his face in his hands, and prayed the spirits of that place to make him worthy.

The hours passed, quarter by quarter, and the King stayed motionless like one in a dream. Presently, however, the dream was faintly shaken by a little lirrup of sound, as light as rain dropping from leaves above a pool. Again and again the sweet round notes fell on the meditations of the King, and he remembered with entrancement that this was the tender signal by which he was summoned to the Pond. So, rising silently, he wandered through the trees, and keeping his eyes fixed on the soft dim turf, lest some new beauty should tempt him to speech, he went across the open hill the Pond. Here he knelt down again, listening to the childlike bird, until at last the young piping ceased with a joyous chuckle. And at that instant, reflected in the Pond, he saw the silver star that watches the invisible young moon, and dipped his head.

Oh, my dear maids! When he lifted it again, all wet and bewildered, he saw upon the opposite border of the Pond, a figure, the white figure of—a woman! a girl! a child! He could not tell, for she lay three parts in the shadowy water with her back towards him, and his gaze and senses swam; but in that faint starlight one bare and lovely arm, as white as the crescent moon, was clear to him, upcurved to her shadowy hair. So she reclined, and so he knelt, both motionless, and his heart trembled (even as it had trembled at the bird's song) with a wish to go near to her, or at least to whisper to her across the water. Indeed, he was on the point of doing so, when a sudden contraction seized him, his eyes closed in a delicious agony, and he sneezed once vigorously; and in that moment of shattering blackness he recalled his vow, and rising turned his back upon the vision and groped his way again to the shelter of the trees.

Here he remained till dawn in meditation, but as to the nature of his meditations I am, dear maidens, ignorant. Nor do I know in what restless wise he passed his Sunday.

It is enough to know that on Monday when he went into the forge he found the Lad already at work, and if he had been pitch-black at their parting he was no less so at their meeting. He appeared to be out of humor, and for some time regarded his apprentice with dissatisfaction, but only remarked at last:

"You look fatigued."

"My sleep was broken with dreams," said the King. "I am sorry if I am late. Let me to my shoeing. Since Saturday ended in success, I suppose I shall now finish the business without more ado."

He was, however, too hopeful as it appeared, for though he managed to fashion a shoe which was in his eyes the equal of the other, the Lad was captious and would not commend it.

"I should be an ill craftmaster," said he, "if I let you rest content on what you have already done. I made such a shoe as this on my thirteenth birthday, and my father's only praise was, You must do better yet.'"

So particular was the young smith that William spent the whole of another week in endeavoring to please him. This might have chafed the King, but that it agreed entirely with his desires to remain in that place, sleeping and eating at no cost to himself, and working so strenuously that his hands grew almost as hard as the metal he worked in; for the Lad now began to entrust him with small jobs of various sorts, although in the matter of the second shoe he refused to be satisfied.

When Saturday came, however, the King contrived a shoe so much superior to any he had yet made that the Lad, examining it, was compelled to say, "It is better than the other." Then Pepper, who always stood in a noose beside the door awaiting her moment, lifted up her near forefoot of her own accord, and the King took it in his hand.

"How odd!" he exclaimed a moment later. "The nag has a stone in this foot also. It is not strange that she went so ill."

"It is not a stone," said the Lad. "It is a pearl."

And he held out to the King a pearl of such a shining purity that it was as though it had been rounded within the spirit of a saint.

"This makes you a rich man," said the Lad moodily, "and you can journey whither you please."

But the King shook his head. "Keep it," he said, "for you have lodged me for a week, and I have given you only the clumsy service of my hands."

"Very well," said the Lad simply, and put the pearl in his pocket. "My Great-Aunt is expecting me. There's a cake in the larder."

So saying he walked off, and the King was left alone. As before, he bathed himself and changed his linen, and left the contents of the larder untouched; and an hour before sunset he climbed the hill for the second time, and presently stood panting on the edge of the Ring. And again a pang of wonder that was akin to pain shot through his heart at the loveliness of the world below him.

"Beautiful earth!" he cried once more, "how fair and dear you are become to me in your remoteness. But oh, if you appear so beautiful from this summit, what must you appear from the summit of the clouds?" And he glanced from the earth to the sky, and saw the sun running down his airy hill. "Dear Temptress!" he said, "how cunningly you would snare me from my purpose." And he kissed his hand to her thrice, sealed up his lips, and entered the Ring.

Between the two tall beeches he knelt down, and drowned the following hours in thought and prayer; till that deep lake of meditation was divided by the sound of singing, as though a shoal of silver fishes swam and leaped upon its surface, putting all quietness to flight, and troubling its waters with a million lovelinesses. For now it was as though the bird's enchanting song came partly from within and partly from without, and if the fall of its music shattered his dream like falling fish, certain it seemed to him that the fish had first leaped from his own heart, out of whose unsuspected caves darted a shoal of nameless longings. He too leaped up and darted through the trees, and with head bent down, for fear of he knew not what, made his way to the Pond. Here he knelt again, drinking in the tremulous song of the bird, as tremulous as youth and maidenhood, until at last it ceased with a sweet uncompleted cry of longing. And at that instant, in the mirror of the Pond, he saw the uncompleted disc of the half-moon, and dipped his head.

Ah wonder! when he lifted it again, dazzled and dripping, he saw across the Pond a figure rising from the water, the figure, as he could now perceive in the fuller light, of a girl, clear to the waist. Her face was half turned from him, and her hair flowed half to him and half away, but within that cloudy setting gleamed the lines of her lovely neck and one white shoulder and one moonlit breast, whose undercurve appeared to float upon the Pond like the petal of a waterlily. So he knelt on his side and she on hers, both motionless, and he heart leaped (even as it had leaped at the bird's song) with a longing to kneel beside and even touch that loveliness; or, if he could not, at least to call to her across the Pond so that he would turn and reveal to him what still was hidden. He was in fact about to do so, when suddenly his senses were overwhelmed with a sweet anguish, darkness fell on him, and from its very core he sneezed twice, violently. This interruption of the previous spell was sufficient to bring him to a realization of his peril, and rising hastily he ran back to the Ring, where he remained till morning. But to what pious thoughts he then committed himself I cannot tell you; neither in what feverish fashion he got through Sunday.

On Monday morning when he arrived at the forge he found the Lad at work before him, and ebony was not blacker than his face. He glanced at the King with some show of temper, but only said:

"You look worn out."

"I have had bad dreams," said the King. "Excuse me for being behind my time. I will try to make up for it by wasting no more, and fashioning instantly two shoes as good as that I made on Saturday."

But though he handled his tools with more dexterity than he had yet exhibited, the Lad petulantly pushed aside the first shoe he made, which to the King appeared to be, if anything, superior to the one he had made on Saturday. The Lad, however, quickly explained himself, saying:

"A master-smith who intends to make his apprentice his equal will not let him rest at the halfway house. I made a shoe like this when I was fourteen, and all my father said was, I have hopes of you.'"

So for yet another week the King's nose was kept to the grindstone, and it would have irritated most men to find their good work repeatedly condemned; but William was, as you may have observed, singularly sweet-tempered, besides which he desired nothing so much as to remain where he was. And for another five days he slept and ate and worked, until the muscles of his arms began to swell, and he swung the hammer with as much ease as his master, who now left a great part of the work entirely in his hands. Although in this matter of the third shoe he refused to be satisfied.

Nevertheless on Saturday morning the King, making a last effort before the forge was shut, submitted a shoe so far beyond anything he had yet achieved, that the Lad could not but say, "This is a good shoe." And Pepper, seeing them coming, lifted her off hind-foot to be shod.

"Now as I live!" cried the King. "Another stone! And how she contrived to hobble so far is a miracle."

"It isn't a stone," said the Lad, "it is a diamond."

And he presented to the King a diamond of such triumphant brilliance that it might have been conceived of the ambitions of the mightiest monarch of the earth.

"You now own surpassing wealth," said the Lad dejectedly, "and you have no more need to work."

But William would not even touch the stone. "Keep it," he said, "for you have befriended me for a week, and I have given you only the strength of my arms."

"Let it be so," said the Lad gently, and put the diamond in his belt. "I must not keep my Great-Aunt waiting. There's a cake in the larder."

So saying he went his way, and the King went his; which, as you may surmise, was to the bath and his clean clothes. He did not go into the larder, and an hour before sunset made the ascent of the hill, and for the third time stood like a conqueror upon the crest. And as he gazed over the lands below his heart throbbed with a passion for the earth that was half agony and half love, unless indeed it was the whole agony of love.

"Most beautiful earth!" he cried aloud, "only as you recede from me do I realize how necessary it is for me to possess you. How is it that when I possess you I know you not as I know you now? But oh! if you are so wonderful from these great hills, what must you be from the greater hills of air?" And he looked up, and saw the sun descending in the west. "Sweet earth," he sighed, "you would hold me when I should be gone, and never remind me that the moment to depart is due." And he stretched out his arms to her, sealed up his lips, and went into the Ring.

Once more he knelt between the giant beeches, and sank all thoughts in pious contemplation; till suddenly those still waters were convulsed as though with stormy currents, and a wild song beat through his breast, so that he could not believe it was the bird singing from a short distance: it was as though the storm of music broke from his singing heart—yes, from his own heart singing for some unexpressed fulfillment. He was barely conscious of going through the trees, with eyes shut tight against the outer world, but soon he was kneeling at the brink of the Pond, while the surge of joy and pain in the song broke on his spirit like waves upon a shore, or love upon a man and a woman—washed back, towered up, and broke on him again. At last on one full glorious phrase it ceased. And at that instant, deep in the Pond, he saw the full orb of the moon, and dipped his head.

Oh, when he lifted it, startled and illuminated, he saw on the further side of the Pond a woman standing. The moonlight bathed her form from head to foot, her hair was thrown behind her, and she stood facing him, so that in the cold clear light he could see her fully revealed: her strong tender face, her strong soft body, her strong slim legs, her strong and lovely arms. As white as mayblossom she was, and beauty went forth from her like fragrance from the shaken bough. So he knelt on his side and she stood on hers, both motionless, but gazing into each other's eyes, and his heart broke (even as it had broken at the bird's song) with a passion to take her in his arms, for it seemed to him that this alone would mend its breaking. Or if he might not do this, at least to send his need of her in a great cry across the Pond. And as his passion grew she slowly lifted her arms and opened them to him as though to bid him enter; and her lips parted, and she cried out, as though she were uttering the cry of his own soul:

"Beloved!"

All the joy and the pain, fulfilled, of the bird's song were gathered in that word.

Glorified he leaped up, his whole being answering the cry of hers, but before his lips could translate it he was gripped by a mighty agony, and sneeze after sneeze shook all his senses, so that he was utterly helpless. When he was able to look up again he saw the woman moving towards him round the Pond, and suddenly he clapped his hands over his eyes and fled towards the Ring, as though pursued by demons. Here he passed the remainder of the night, but in what sort of prayers I leave you to imagine; as also amid what ravings he passed his Sunday.

On Monday the Lad was again before him at the forge, and a crow's wing had looked milky beside his face. He did not raise his eyes as the King came in, but said:

"You look very ill." He said it furiously.

"I have had nightmares," said the King. "Pardon me if you can. I will get to work and make my final shoe."

But though he now had little more to learn in his craft, the Lad, when the shoe was made, picked it up in his pincers and flung it to the other end of the forge; yet the King now knew enough to know that few smiths could have made its equal. So he looked surprised; at which the Lad, controlling himself, said:

"When I pass your fourth shoe you will need no more masters—I forged a shoe like that one yonder when I was fifteen, and my father said of it, 'You will make a smith one day.'"

And on neither Tuesday nor Wednesday nor Thursday nor Friday could the King succeed in pleasing the Lad; the better his shoes the angrier grew his young master that they were not good enough. Yet between these gusts of temper he was gentle and remorseful, and once the King saw tears in his eyes, and another time the Lad came humbly to ask for pardon. Then William laughed and put out his hand, but, as once before, the Lad slipped his behind his back and said:

"It is so dirty, friend."

And this time he would not let William take it. So the King was forced instead to lay his arm about the Lad's shoulder, and press it tenderly; but the Lad made no response, and only stood hanging his head until the King removed his arm. All the same, when next the King made a shoe he was full of rage, and stamped on it, and ran out of the forge. Which surprised the King all the more because it was so excellent a shoe. Yet he was secretly glad of its rejection, for he felt it would break his heart to go away from that place; and he could think of no good cause for remaining, once Pepper was shod. So there he stayed, eating, sleeping, and working, while the thews of his back became as strong under the smooth skin as the thews of a beech-tree under the smooth bark; and his craft was such that the Lad at last left the whole of the work of the forge in his charge. For there was nothing he could not do surpassingly well. And this the Lad admitted, save only in the case of the fourth shoe.

But on Saturday, just before closing-time, the King set to and made a shoe so fine that when the Lad saw it he said quietly, "I could not make a better." Had he not said so he must have lied, or proved that he did know a masterpiece when he saw it. And he too good a craftsman for that, besides being honest.

Pepper instantly lifted up her near hind-foot.

"Upon my word!" exclaimed the King, "the world is full of stones, and Pepper has found them all. The wonder is that she did not fall down on the road."

"This is not a stone," said the Lad, "it is an opal."

And he displayed an opal of such marvelous changeability, such milk and fire shot with such shifting rainbows, that it was as though it had had birth of all the moods of all the women of all time.

"This enriches you for life," said the Lad gloomily, "and now you are free of masters for ever."

But William thrust his hands into his pockets. "Keep it," he said, "for this week you have given me love, and I have given you nothing but the sinews of my body."

The Lad looked at him and said, "I have given you hard words, and fits of temper, and much injustice."

"Have you?" said William. "I remember only your tenderness and your tears. So keep the opal in love's name."

The Lad tried to answer, but could not; and he slipped the opal under his shirt. Then he faltered, "My Great-Aunt—" and still he could not speak. But he made a third effort, and said, "There is a cake in the larder," and turned on his heel and went away quickly. And the King looked after him till he was out of sight, and then very slowly went to his bath and his fresh linen. But he left the cake where it was.

And he sat by the door of the forge with his face in his hands until the length of his shadow warned him that he must go. And he rose and went for the last time up the hill, but with a sinking heart; and when he stood on the top and gazed upon the beauty of the earth he had left below, in his breast was the ache of loss and longing for one he had loved, and with his eyes he tried to draw that beauty into himself, but the void in him remained unfulfilled. Yet never had her beauty been so great.

"Beloved and lovely earth!" he whispered, "why do you appear most fair and most desirable now that I am about to lose you? Why when I had you did you not hold me by force, and tell me what you were? Only now I discover you from mid-heaven—but oh! in what way should I discover you from heaven itself?" And he looked upward, and lo! a blurred sun shone upon him, swimming to its rest. "Farewell, dear earth!" said the King. "Since you cannot mount to me, and I may not descend to you." And he knelt upon the turf and laid his cheek and forehead to it, and then he rose, sealed up his lips, and passed into the Ring.

Between the two tall beeches he sank down, and all sense and thought and consciousness sank with him, as though his being had become a dead forgotten lake, hidden in a lifeless wood; where birds sang not, nor rain fell, nor fishes played, nor currents moved below the stagnant waters. But presently a wind seemed to wail among the trees, and the sound of it traveled over the King's senses, stirred them, and passed. But only to return again, moan over him, and trail away; and so it kept coming and going till first he heard, then listened to, and at last realized the haunting signal of the bird. And he went forth into the open night, his eyes wide apart but seeing nothing until he stumbled at the Pond and crouched beside it. The bird grew fainter and fainter, and presently the sound, like a ghost at dawn, ceased to exist; and at that instant, under the Pond, he beheld the lessening circle of the moon, and dipped his head.

Alas! when he lifted it, shivering and stunned, he saw the form he longed to see on the other side of the Pond; but not, as he had longed to see it, gazing at him with the love and glory of seven nights ago. Now she stood on the turf, half turned from him, and the wave of her hair blew to and fro like a cloud, now revealing her white side, now concealing it. And he looked, but she would not look. So he knelt on his side and she remained on hers, both motionless. And suddenly the impulse to sneeze arose within him, and at that instant she began to move—not towards him, as before, but away from him, downhill.

At that he could bear no more, and quelling the impulse with a mighty effort, he got upon his feet crying, "Beloved, stay! Beloved, stay, beloved!"

And he staggered round the Pound as quickly as his shaking knees would let him; but quicker still she slid away, and when he came where she had been the place was as empty as the sky in its moonless season. He called and ran about and called again; but he got no answer, nor found what he sought. All that night he spent in calling and running to and fro. What he did on Sunday you may know, and I may know, but he did not. On Sunday night he stayed beside the Pond, but whatever his hopes were they received no fulfillment. On Monday night he was there again, and on Tuesday, and on Wednesday; and between the mornings and the nights he went from hill to hill, seeking her hiding-place who came to bathe in the lake. There was not a hill within a day's march that did not know him, from Duncton to Mount Harry. But on none of them he found the Woman. How he lived is a puzzle. Perhaps upon wild raspberries.

After the sun had set on Chanctonbury on Saturday night, he came exhausted to the Ring again, and stood on that high hill gazing earthward. But there was no light above or below, and he said:

"I have lost all. For the earth is swallowed in blackness, and the Woman has disappeared into space, and I myself have cast away my spiritual initiation. I will sit by the Pond till midnight, and if the bird sings then I will still hope, but if it does not I will dip my head in the water and not lift it again."

So he went and lay down by the Pond in the darkness, and the hours wore away. But as the time of the bird's song drew near he clasped his hands and prayed. But the bird did not sing; and when he judged that midnight was come, he got upon his knees and prepared to put his head under the water. And as he did so he saw, on the opposite side of the Pond, the feeble light of a lantern. He could not see who held it, because even as he looked the bearer blew out the light; but in that moment it appeared to him that she was as black as the night itself.

So for awhile he knelt upon his side, and she remained on hers, both trembling; but at last the King, dreading to startle her away, rose softly and went round the Pond to where he had seen her.

He said into the night in a shaking voice, "I cannot see you. If you are there, give me your hand."

And out of the night a shaking voice replied:

"It is so dirty, beloved."

Then he took her in his arms, and felt how she trembled, and he held her closely to him to still her, whispering:

"You are my Lad."

"Yes," she said in a low voice. "But wait."

And she slipped out of his embrace, and he heard her enter the Pond, and she stayed there as it seemed to him a lifetime; but presently she rose up, and even in that black night the whiteness of her body was visible to him, and she came to him as she was and laid her head on his breast and said:

"I am your Woman."

("I want my apple," said Martin Pippin.

"But is this the end?" cried little Joan.

"Why not?" said Martin. "The lovers are united."

Joscelyn: Nonsense! Of course it is not the end! You must tell us a thousand other things. Why was the Woman a woman on Saturday night and a lad all the rest of the week?

Joyce: What of the four jewels?

Jennifer: Which of the answers to the King's riddle was the right one?

Jessica: What happened to the cake?

Jane: What was her name?

"Please," said little Joan, "do not let this be the end, but tell us what they did next."

"Women will be women," observed Martin, "and to the end of time prefer unessentials to the essential. But I will endeavor to satisfy you on the points you name.")

In the morning William said to his beloved:

"Now tell me something of yourself. How come you to be so masterful a smith? Why do you live as a black Lad all the week and turn only into a white Woman on Saturdays? Have you really got a Great-Aunt, and where does she live? How old are you? Why were you so hard to please about the shoeing of Pepper? And why, the better my shoes the worse your temper? Why did you run away from me a week ago? Why did you never tell me who you were? Why have you tormented me for a whole month? What is your name?"

"Trust a man to ask questions!" said his beloved, laughing and blushing. "Is it not enough that I am your beloved?"

"More than enough, yet not nearly enough," said the King, "for there is nothing of yourself which you must not tell me in time, from the moment when you first stole barley sugar behind your father's back, down to that in which you first loved me."

"Then I had best begin at once," she smiled, "or a lifetime will not be long enough. I am eighteen years old and my name is Viola. I was born in Falmer, and my father was the best smith in all Sussex, and because he had no other child he made me his bellows-boy, and in time, as you know, taught me his trade. But he was, as you also know, a stern master, and it was not until, on my sixteenth birthday, I forged a shoe the equal of your last, that he said I could not make a better.' And so saying he died. Now I had no other relative in all the world except my Great-Aunt, the Wise Woman of the Bush Hovel, and her I had never seen; but I thought I could not do better in my extremity than go to her for counsel. So, shouldering my father's tools, I journeyed west until I came to her place, and found her trying to break in a new birch-broom that was still too green and full of sap to be easily mastered; and she was in a very bad temper. Good day, Great-Aunt,' I said, I am your Great-Niece Viola.' I have no more use for great nieces,' she snapped, than for little ones.' And she continued to tussle with the broomstick and took no further notice of me. Then I went into the Hovel, where a fire burned on the hearth, and I took out my tools and fashioned a bit on the hob; and when it was ready I took it to her and said, This will teach it its manners'; and she put the bit on the broom, which became as docile as a lamb. Great-Niece,' said she, it appears that I told you a lie this morning. What can I do for you?' Tell me, if you please, how I am to live now that my father is dead.' There is no need to tell you,' said she; you have your living at your fingers' ends.' But women cannot be smiths,' said I. Then become a lad,' said she, and ply your trade where none knows you; and lest men should suspect you by your face, which fools though they be they might easily do, let it be so sooted from week's end to week's end that none can discover what you look like; and if any one remarks on it, put it down to your trade.' But Great-Aunt,' I said, I could not bear to go dirty from week's end to week's end.' If you will be so particular,' she said, take a bath every Saturday night and spend your

Sundays with me, as fair as when you were a babe. And before you go to work again on Monday you shall once more conceal your fairness past all men's penetration.' But, dear Great-Aunt,' I pleaded, it may be that the day will come when I might not wish—'"

And here, dear maidens, Viola faltered. And William put his arm about her a little tighter—because it was there already—and said, "What might you not wish, beloved?" And she murmured, "To be concealed past one man's penetration. And my Great-Aunt said I need not worry. Because though men, she said, were fools, there was one time in every man's life when he was quick enough to penetrate all obscurities, whether it were a layer of soot or a night without a moon." And she hid her face on the King's shoulder, and he tried to kiss her but could not make her look up until he said, "Or even a woman's waywardness?" Then she looked up of her own accord and kissed him.

"In this way," she resumed, "it became my custom on each Saturday, after closing the forge, to come here with my woman's raiment, and wait in a hollow until night had fallen, and make myself clean of the week's blackness. For I dared not do this by daylight, or be seen going forth from my forge in my proper person."

"But why did you choose to bathe at midnight?" asked the King.

She was silent for a few moments, and then said hurriedly, "I did not choose to bathe at midnight until a month ago.—For the rest," she resumed, "I was hard to please in the matter of the shoes because I knew that when they were finished you would ride away. And therefore the more you improved the crosser I became. And if I have tormented you for a month it was because you tormented me by refusing to speak when you saw me here, in spite of your hateful vow; and you would not even look at my cake in the larder."

"Women are strange," said the King. "How do you know I did not look at the cake?"

"I do know," she said as hurriedly as before. "And if I would not tell you who I was, it was because I could not bear, on the other hand, to extort from you a love you seemed so reluctant to endure; until indeed it became of its own accord too strong even for the purpose which brought you every week to the Ring. For I knew that purpose, since all dwellers in Washington know why men go up the hill with the new moon."

"But when my love did become too strong for my vow, and opened my lips at last," said the King, "why did you run away?"

Viola said, "Had you not run away the week before? And now I have answered all your questions."

"No," said the King, "not all. You haven't told me yet when you first loved me."

Viola smiled and said, "I first stole barley sugar when my father said This is for the other little girl over the way'; and I first loved you when, seeing you had been too absent-minded to know that Pepper had cast her shoes, I feared you were in love."

"But that was three minutes after we met!" cried the King.

"Was it as much as that!" said she.

Now after awhile Viola said, "Let us get down to the world again. We cannot stay here for ever."

"Why not?" said the King. However, they walked to the brow of the hill, and stood together gazing awhile over the sunlit earth that had never been so beautiful to either of them; for their sight was newly-washed with love, and all things were changed.

"Now I know how she looks from heaven," said the King, "and that is like heaven itself. Let us go; for I think she will still look so at our coming, seeing that we carry heaven with us."

So they went downhill to the forge, and there Viola said to her lover, "I can stay no longer in this place where all men have known me as a lad; and besides, a woman's home is where her husband lives."

"But I live only in a Barn," said William the King.

"Then I will live there with you," said Viola, "and from this very night. But first I will shoe Pepper anew, for she is so unequally shod that she might spill us on the road. And that she may be shod worthily of herself and of us, give me what you have tied up in your blue handkerchief." The King fetched his handkerchief and unknotted it, and gave her his crown and scepter; and she set him at the bellows and made three golden shoes and shod the nag on her two fore-feet and her off hind-foot. But when she looked at the near hind-foot, which the King had shod last of all, she said: "I could not make a better. And therefore, like his father, the Lad must shut his smithy, for he is dead." Then she put the three shoes she had removed into a bag with some other trifles; and while she did so the King took what remained of the gold and made it into two rings. This done, they got on to Pepper's back, and with her three shoes of gold and one of iron she bore them the way the King had come. When they passed the Bush Hovel they saw the Wise Woman currying her broomstick, and Viola cried:

"Great-Aunt, give us a blessing."

"Great-Niece," said the Wise Woman, "how can I give you what you already have? But I will give you this." And she held out a horseshoe.

"Good gracious," said the King, "this was once Pepper's."

"It was," said the Wise Woman. "In her merriment at hearing you ask a silly question, she cast it outside my door."

A little further on they came to the Guess Gate, but when the King, dismounting, swung it open, it grated on something in the road. He stooped and lifted—a horseshoe.

"Wonder of wonders!" exclaimed the King. "This also was Pepper's. What shall we do with it?"

"Hang—it—up—hang—it—up—hang—" creaked the Gate; and clicked home.

In due course they reached the Doves, and at the sound of Pepper's hoofs the Brothers flocked out to meet them.

"Is all well?" cried the Ringdove, seeing the King only. "And have you returned to us for the final blessing?"

"I have," replied the King, "for I bring my bride behind me, and now you must make us one."

The gentle Brothers, rejoicing at the sight of their happiness and their beauty, led them in; and there they were wedded. The Doves offered them to eat, but the King was impatient to reach his Barn by nightfall; so they got again on Pepper's back, and as they were about to leave the Ringdove said:

"I have something of yours which is in itself a thing of no moment; yet, because it is of good augury, take it with you."

And he gave the King Pepper's third shoe.

"Thank you," said the King, "I will hang it over my Barn door."

Now he urged Pepper to her full speed, and they went at a gallop past the Hawking Sopers, who, hearing the clatter, came running into the road.

"Stay, gallopers, stay!" they cried, "and make merry with us."

"We cannot," called the King, "for we are newly married."

"Good luck to you then!" shouted the Sopers, and with huzzas and laughter flung something after them. Viola stretched out her hand and caught it in mid-air, and it was a horseshoe.

"The tale is complete," she laughed, "and now you know where Pepper picked up her stones."

Soon after the King said, "Here is my Barn." And he sprang down and lifted his bride from the nag's back and brought her in.

"It is a poor place," he said gently, "but it is all I have. What can I do for you in such a home?"

"I will tell you," said Viola, and putting her hand into her left pocket, she drew out the ruby winking with the wine of mirth. "You can dance in it." And suddenly they caught each other by the hands and went capering and laughing round the Barn like children.

"Hurrah!" cried William, "now I know what a King should do in a Barn!"

"But he should do more than dance in it," said Viola; and putting her hand into her right pocket she gave him the pearl, as pure as a prayer; "beloved, he should pray in it too."

And William looked at her and knelt, and she knelt by him, and in silence they prayed the same prayer, side by side.

Then William rose and said simply, "Now I know."

But she knelt still, and took from her girdle the diamond, as bright as power, and she put it in his hand, saying very low, "Oh, my dear King! but he should also rule in it." And she kissed his hand. But the King lifted her very quickly so that she stood equal with his heart, and embracing her he said, with tears in his eyes:

"And you, beloved! what will a Queen do in a Barn?"

"The same as a King," she whispered, and drew from her bosom the opal, as lovely and as variable as the human spirit. "With the other three stones you may, if you will, buy back your father's kingdom. But this, which contains all qualities in one, let us keep for ever, for our children and theirs, that they may know there is nothing a King and a Queen may not do in a Barn, or a man and a woman anywhere. But the best thing they can do is to work in it."

Then, going out, she came back with the bag which she had slung on Pepper's back, and took from it her father's tools.

"In three weeks you learned all I learned in three years," said she. "When I shod Pepper this morning I did my last job as a smith; for now I shall have other work to do. But you, whether you choose to get your father's lands again or no, I pray to work in the trade I have given you, for I have made you the very king of smiths, and all men should do the thing they can do best. So take the hammer and nail up the horseshoes over the door while I get supper; for you look as hungry as I feel."

"But there's nothing to eat," said the King ruefully.

However, he went outside, and over the door he hung as many shoes as there are nails in one—the four Pepper had cast on the road, and the three he had first made for her. As he drove the last nail home Viola called:

"Supper is ready."

And the King went into the Barn and saw a Wedding Cake.

And now, if you please, Mistress Joan, I have earned my apple.

FIRST INTERLUDE

Now there was a great munching of apples in the tree, for to tell the truth during the latter part of the story this business had been suspended, and between bites the milkmaids discussed the merits of what they had just heard.

Jessica: What is your opinion of this tale, Jane?

Jane: It surprised me more than anything. For who could have suspected that the Lad was a Woman?

Martin: Lads are to be suspected of any mischief, Mistress Jane.

Joscelyn: It is not to be supposed, Master Pippin, that we are acquainted with the habits of lads.

Martin: I suppose nothing. But did the story please you?

Joscelyn: As a story it was well enough to pass an hour. I would be willing to learn whether the King regained his kingdom or no.

Martin: I think he did, since you may go to this day to the little city on the banks of the Adur which is re-named after his Barn. But I doubt whether he lived there, or anywhere but in the Barn where he and his beloved began their life of work and prayer and mirth and loving-rule. And died as happily as they had lived.

Joan: I am glad they lived happily. I was afraid the tale would end unhappily.

Joyce: And so was I. For when the King roamed the hills for a whole week without success, I began to fear he would never find the Woman again.

Jennifer: I for my part feared lest he should not open his lips during the fourth vigil, and so must become a Dove for the remainder of his days.

Jane: It was but by the grace of a moment he did not drown himself in the Pond.

Jessica: Or what if, by some unlucky chance, he had never come to the forge at all?

Martin: In any of these events, I grant you, the tale must have ended in disaster. And this is the special wonder of love-tales: that though they may end unhappily in a thousand ways, and happily in only one, yet that one will vanquish the thousand as often as the desires of lovers run in tandem. But there is one accident you have left out of count, and it is the worst stumbling-block I know of in the path of happy endings.

All the Milkmaids: What is it?

Martin: Suppose the lovely Viola had been a sworn virgin and a hater of men.

There was silence in the Apple-Orchard.

Joscelyn: She would have been none the worse for that, singer. And the tale would have been none the less a tale, which is all we look for from you. This talk of happy endings is silly talk. The King might have sought the Woman in vain, or kept his vow, or drowned himself, or ridden to the confines of Kent, for aught I care.

Joyce: Or I.

Jennifer: Or I.

Jessica: Or I.

Jane: Or I.

Martin: I am silenced. Tales are but tales, and not worth speculation. And see, the moon is gone to sleep behind a cloud, which shows us nothing save the rainbow of her dreams. It is time we did as she does.

Like shooting-stars in August the milkmaids slid from their leafy heaven and dropped to the grass. And here they pillowed their heads on their soft arms and soon were breathing the breath of sleep. But little Joan sat on in the swing.

Now all this while she had kept between her hands the promised apple, turning and turning it like one in doubt; and presently Martin looked aside at her with a smile, and held his open palm to receive his reward. And first she glanced at him, and then at the sleepers, and last she tossed the apple lightly in the air. But by some mishap she tossed it too high, and it made an arc clean over the tree and fell in a distant corner by the hedge. So she ran quickly to recover it for him, and he ran likewise, and they stooped and rose together, she with the apple in her hands, he with his hands on hers. At which she blushed a little, but held fast to the fruit.

"What!" said Martin Pippin, "am I never to have my apple?"

She answered softly, "Only when I am satisfied, as you promised."

"And are you not? What have I left undone?"

Joan: Please, Master Pippin. What did the young King look like?

Martin: Fool that I am to leave these vital things untold! I shall avoid this error in future. He was more than middle tall, and broad in the shoulders; and he had gray-blue eyes, and a fresh color, and a kind and merry look, and dark brown hair that was not always as sleek as he wished it to be.

"Joan: Oh!

Martin: With this further oddity, that above the nape of his neck was a whitish tuft which, though he took great pains to conceal it, continually obtruded through the darker hair like the cottontail on the back of a rabbit.

Joan: Oh! Oh!

And she became as red as a cherry.

Martin: May I have my apple?

Joan: But had not he a—mustache?

Martin: He fondly believed so.

Joan (with unexpected fire): It was a big and beautiful mustache!

Martin (fervently): There was never a King of twenty years with one so big and beautiful.

She gave him the apple.

Martin: Thank you. Will you, because I have answered many questions, now answer one?

Joan: Yes.

Martin: Then tell me this—what is your quarrel with men?

Joan: Oh, Master Pippin! they say that one and one make two.

Martin: Is this possible? Good heavens, are men such numskulls! When they have but to go to the littlest woman on earth to learn—what you and I well know—that one and one make one, and sometimes three, or four, or even half-a-dozen; but never two. Fie upon these men!

Joan: I am glad you think I am in the right. But how obstinate they are!

Martin: As obstinate as children, and should be birched as roundly.

Joan: Oh! but— You would not birch children.

Martin: You are right again. They should be coaxed.

Joan: Yes. No. I mean— Good night, dear singer.

Martin: Good night, dear milkmaid. Sleep sweetly among your comrades who are wiser than we, being so indifferent to happy endings that they would never unpadlock sorrow, though they had the key in their keeping.

Then he took her hands in one of his, and put his other hand very gently under her chin, and lifted it till he could look into her face, and he said: "Give me the key to Gillian's prison, little Joan, because you love happy endings."

Joan: Dear Martin, I cannot give you the key.

Martin: Why not?

Joan: Because I stuck it inside your apple.

So he kissed her and they parted, and lay down and slept; she among her comrades under the apple-tree, and he under the briony in the hedge; and the moon came out of her dream and watched theirs.

With morning came a hoarse voice calling along the hedge:

"Maids! maids! maids!"

Up sprang the milkmaids, rubbing their eyes and stretching their arms; and up sprang Martin likewise. And seeing him, Joscelyn was stricken with dismay.

"It is Old Gillman, our master," she whispered, "come with bread and questions. Quick, singer, quick! into the hollow russet before he reaches the hole in the hedge."

Swiftly the milkmaids hustled Martin into the russet tree, and concealed him at the very moment when the Farmer was come to the peephole, filling it with his round red face and broad gray fringe of whiskers, like the winter sun on a sky that is going to snow.

"Good morrow, maids," quoth old Gillman.

"Good morrow, master," said they.

"Is my daughter come to her mind yet?"

"No, master," said little Joan, "but I begin to have hopes that she may."

"If she do not," groaned Gillman, "I know not what will happen to the farmstead. For it is six months now since I tasted water, and how can a man follow his business who is fuddled day and night with Barley Wine? Life is full of hardships, of which daughters are the greatest. Gillian!" he cried, "when will ye come into your senses and out of the Well-House?"

But Gillian took no more heed of him than of the quacking of the drake on the duckpond.

"Well, here is your bread," said Gillman, and he thrust a basket with seven loaves in it through the gap. "And may to-morrow bring better tidings."

"One moment, dear master," entreated little Joan. "Tell me, please, how Nancy my Jersey fares."

"Pines for you, pines for you, maid, though Charles does his best by her. But it is as though she had taken a vow to let down no milk till you come again. Rack and ruin, rack and ruin!"

And the old man retreated as he had come, muttering "Rack and ruin!" the length of the hedge.

The maids then set about preparing breakfast, which was simplicity itself, being bread and apples than which no breakfast could be sweeter. There was a loaf for each maid and one over for Gillian, which they set upon the wall of the Well-House, taking away yesterday's loaf untouched and stale.

"Does she never eat?" asked Martin.

"She has scarcely broken bread in six months," said Joscelyn, "and what she lives on besides her thoughts we do not know."

"Thoughts are a fast or a feast according to their nature," said Martin, "so let us feed the ducks, who have none."

They broke the stale bread into fragments, and when the ducks had made a meal, returned to their own; and of two loaves made seven parts, that Martin might have his share, and to this they added apples according to their fancies, red or russet, green or golden.

After breakfast, at Martin's suggestion, they made little boats of twigs and leaves and sailed them on the duckpond, where they met with many adventures and calamities from driftweed, small breezes, and the curiosity of the ducks. And before they were aware of it the dinner hour was upon them, when they divided two more loaves as before and ate apples at will.

Then Martin, taking a handkerchief from his pocket, proposed a game of Blindman's-Buff, and the girls, delighted, counter Eener-Meener- Meiner-Mo to find the Blindman. And Joyce was He. So Martin tied the handkerchief over her eyes.

"Can you see?" asked Martin.

"Of course I can't see!" said Joyce.

"Promise?" said Martin.

"I hope, Master Pippin," said Jane reprovingly, "that you can take a girl's word for it."

"I'm sure I hope I can," said Martin, and turned Joyce round three times, and ran for his life. And Joyce caught Jane on the spot and guessed her immediately.

Then Jane was blindfolded, and she was so particular about not seeing that it was quite ten minutes before she caught Jennifer, but she knew who she was by the feel of her gown; and Jennifer caught Joscelyn, and guessed her by her girdle; and Joscelyn caught Jessica and guessed her by the darn in her sleeve; and Jessica caught Joan, and guessed her by her ribbon; and Joan caught Martin, and guessed him by his difference.

So then Martin was Blindman, and it seemed as though he would never have eyes again; for though he caught all the girls, one after another, he couldn't guess which was which, and gave Jane's nose to Jessica, and Jessica's hands to Joscelyn, and Joscelyn's chin to Joyce, and Joyce's hair to Jennifer, and Jennifer's eyebrows to Joan; but when he caught Joan he guessed her at once by her littleness.

In due course the change of light told them it was supper-time; and with great surprise they ate the last two loaves to the sweet accompaniment of the apples.

"I would never have supposed," said Joscelyn, as they gathered under the central tree at the close of the meal, "that a day could pass so quickly."

"Bait time with a diversion," said Martin, "and he will run like a donkey after a dangled carrot."

"It has nearly been the happiest day of my life," said Joyce with a sly glance at Martin.

"And why not quite?" said he.

"Because it lacked a story, singer," she said demurely.

"What can be rectified," said Martin, "must be; and the day is not yet departed, but still lingers like a listener on the threshold of night. So set the swing in motion, dear Mistress Joyce, and to its measure I will endeavor to swing my thoughts, which have till now been laggards."

With these words he set Joyce in the swing and himself upon the branch beside it as before. And the other milkmaids climbed into their perches, rustling the fruit down from the shaken boughs; and he made of Joyce's lap a basket for the harvest. And he and each of the maids chose an apple as though supper had not been.

"We are listening," said Joscelyn from above.

"Not all of you," said Martin. And he looked up at Joscelyn alert on her branch, and down at Gillian prone on the steps.

"You are here for no other purpose," said Joscelyn, "than to make them listen that will not. I would not have you think we desire to listen."

"I think nothing but that you are the prey of circumstances," said Martin, "constrained like flowers to bear witness to that which is against all nature."

"What do you mean by that?" said Joscelyn. "Flowers are nature itself."

"So men have agreed," replied Martin, "yet who but men have compelled them repeatedly to assert such unnaturalnesses as that foxes wear gloves and cuckoos shoes? Out on the pretty fibbers!"

"Please do not be angry with the flowers," said Joan.

"How could I be?" said Martin. "The flowers must always be forgiven, because their inconsistencies lie always at men's doors. Besides, who does not love fairy-tales?"

Then Martin kicked his heels against the tree and sang idly:

When cuckoos fly in shoes
And foxes run in gloves,
Then butterflies won't go in twos
And boys will leave their loves.

"A silly song," said Joscelyn.

Martin: If you say so. For my part I can never tell the difference between silliness and sense.

Jane: Then how can a good song be told from a bad? You must go by something.

Martin: I go by the sound. But since Mistress Joscelyn pronounces my song silly, I can only suppose she has seen cuckoos flying in shoes.

Joscelyn: You are always supposing nonsense. Who ever heard of cuckoos flying in shoes?

Jane: Or of foxes running in gloves?

Joan: Or of butterflies going in ones?

Martin: Or of boys—

Joscelyn: I have frequently seen butterflies going in ones, foolish Joan. And the argument was not against butterflies, but cuckoos.

Martin: And their shoes. Please, dear Mistress Joan, do not look so downcast, nor you, dear Mistress Joscelyn, so vexed. Let us see if we cannot turn a more sensible song upon this theme.

And he sang—

Cuckoo Shoes aren't cuckoos' shoes,
They're shoes which cuckoos never don;
And cuckoo nests aren't cuckoos' nests,
But other birds' for a moment gone;
And nothing that the cuckoo has
But he does make a mock upon.
For even when the cuckoo sings
He only says what isn't true—
When happy lovers first swore oaths
An artful cuckoo called and flew,
Yes! and when lovers weep like dew
The teasing cuckoo laughs Cuckoo!
What need for tears? Cuckoo, cuckoo!

As Martin ended, Gillian raised herself upon an elbow, and looked no more into the green grass, but across the green duckpond.

"The second song seems to me as irrelevant as the first," said Joscelyn, "but I observe that you cuckooed so loudly as to startle our mistress out of her inattention. So if you mean to tell us another story, by all means tell it now. Not that I care, except for our extremity."

"It is my only object to ease it," said Martin, "so bear with me as well as you may during the recital of Young Gerard."

YOUNG GERARD

There was once, dear maidens, a shepherd who kept his master's sheep on Amberley Mount. His name was Gerard, and he was always called Young Gerard to distinguish him from the other shepherd who was known as Old Gerard, yet was not, as you might suppose, his father. Their master was the Lord of Combe Ivy that lay in the southern valleys of the hills toward the sea; he owned the grazing on the whole circle of the Downs between the two great roads—on Amberley and Perry and Wepham and Blackpatch and Cockhill and Highdown and Barnsfarm and Sullington and Chantry. But the two Gerards lived together in the great shed behind the copse between Rackham Hill and Kithurst, and the way they came to do so was this.

One night in April when Old Gerard's gray beard was still brown, the door of the shed was pushed open, letting in not only the winds of Spring but a woman wrapped in a green cloak, with a lining of cherry-color and a border of silver flowers and golden cherries. In one hand she swung a crystal lantern set in a silver frame, but it had no light in it; and in the other she held a small slip of a cherry-tree, but it had no bloom on it. Her dress was white, or had been; for the skirts of it, and her mantle, were draggled and sodden, and her green shoes stained and torn, and her long fair hair lay limp and dank upon her mantle whose hood had fallen away, and the shadows round her blue eyes were as black as pools under hedgerows thawing after a frost, and her lovely face was as white as the snowbanks they bed in. Behind her came another woman in a duffle cloak, a crone with eyes as black as sloes, and a skin as brown as beechnuts, and unkempt hair like the fireless smoke of Old Man's Beard straying where it will on the November woodsides. She too was wet and soiled, but full of life where the young one seemed full of death.

The Shepherd looked at this strange pair and said surlily, "What want ye?"

"Shelter," replied the crone.

She pushed the lady, who never spoke, into the shed, and took from her shoulders the wet mantle, and from her hands the lantern and the tree; and led her to the Shepherd's bed and laid her down. Then she spread the mantle over the Shepherd's bench and,

"Lie there," said she, "till love warms ye."

Next she hung the lantern up on a nail in the wall, and,

"Swing there," said she, "till love lights ye."

Last she took the Shepherd's trowel and went outside the shed, and set the cherry-slip beside the door. And she said:

"Grow there, till love blossoms ye."

After this she came inside and sat down at the bedhead.

Gerard the Shepherd, who had watched her proceedings without word or gesture, said to himself, "They've come through the floods."

He looked across at the women and raised his voice to ask, "Did ye come through the floods?"

The lady moaned a little, and the crone said, "Let her be and go to sleep. What does it matter where we came from by night? By daybreak we shall both of us be gone no matter whither."

The Shepherd said no more, for though he was both curious and ill-tempered he had not the courage to disturb the lady, knowing by the richness of her attire that she was of the quality; and the iron of serfdom was driven deep into his soul. So he went to sleep on his stool, as he had been bidden. But in the middle of the night he was awakened by a gusty wind and the banging of his door; and he started up rubbing his knuckles in his eyes, saying, "I've been dreaming of strange women, but was it a dream or no?" He peered about the shed, and the crone had vanished utterly, but the lady still lay on his bed. And when he went over to look at her, she was dead. But beside her lay a newborn child that opened its eyes and wailed at him.

Then the Shepherd ran to his open door and stared into the blowing night, but there were no more signs of the crone without than there were within. So he fastened the latch and came back to the bedside, and examined the child.—

(But at this point Martin Pippin interrupted himself, and seizing the rope of the swing set it rocking violently.

Joyce: I shall fall! I shall fall!

Martin: Then you will be no worse off than I, who have fallen already. For I see you do not like my story.

Joyce: What makes you say so?

Martin: Till now you listened with all your ears, but a moment ago you turned away your head a moment too late to hide the disappointment in your eyes.

Joyce: It is true I am disappointed. Because the beautiful lady is dead, and how can a love-story be, if half the lovers are dead?

Martin: Dear Mistress Joyce, what has love to do with death? Love and death are strangers and speak in different tongues. Women may die and men may die, but lovers are ignorant of mortality.

Joyce (pouting): That may be, singer. But lovers are also a man and a woman, and the woman is dead, and the love-tale ended before we have even heard it. You should not have let the woman die. What sort of love-tale is this, now the woman is dead?

Martin: Are not more nests than one built in a spring-time?—Give me, I pray you, two hairs of your head.

She plucked two and gave them to him, turning her pouting to laughing. One of them Martin coiled and held before his lips, and blew on it.

"There it flies," said he, and gave her back the second hair. "Hold fast by this and keep it from its fellow with all your might, for to part true mates baffles the forces of the universe. And when you give me this second hair again I swear I will send it where it will find its fellow. But I will never ask for it until, my story ended, you say to me, I am content.'")

Examining the child (repeated Martin) the Shepherd discovered it to be a lusty boy-child, and this rejoiced him, so that while the baby wept he laughed aloud.

"It is better to weep for something than for nothing," said he, "and to laugh for something likewise. Tears are for serfs and laughter is for freedmen." For he had conceived the plan of selling the child to his master, the Lord of Combe Ivy, and buying his freedom with the purchase money. So in the morning he carried the body of the lady into the heart of the copse, and there he dug a grave and laid her in it in her white gown. And afterwards he went up hill and down dale to his master, and said he had a man for sale. The Lord of Combe Ivy, who was a jovial lord and a bachelor, laughed at the tale he had to tell; but being always of the humor for a jest he paid the Shepherd a gold piece for the child, and promised him another each midnight on the anniversary of its birth; but on the twenty-first anniversary, he said, the Shepherd was to bring back the twenty-one gold pieces he had received, and instead of adding another to them he would take them again, and make the serf a freedman, and the child his serf.

"For," said the Lord of Combe Ivy, "an infant is a poor deal for a man in his prime, as you are, but a youth come to manhood is a good exchange for a graybeard, as you will be. Therefore rear this babe as you please, and if he live to manhood so much the better for you, but if he die first it's all one to me."

The Shepherd had hoped for a better bargain, but he must needs be content with seeing liberty at a distance. So he returned to his shed on the hills and made a leather purse to keep his gold-piece in, and hung it round his neck, touching it fifty times a day under his shirt to be sure it was still there. And presently he sought among his ewes one who had borne her young, saying, "You shall mother two instead of one." And the baby sucked the ewe like her very lamb, and thrived upon the milk. And the shepherd called the child Gerard after himself, "since," he said, "it is as good a name for a shepherd as another"; and from that time they became the Young and Old Gerards to all who knew them.

So the Young Gerard grew up, and as he grew the cherry-tree grew likewise, but in the strangest fashion; for though it flourished past all expectation, it never put forth either leaf or blossom. This bitterly vexed Old Gerard, who had hoped in time for fruit, and the frustration of his hopes became to him a cause of grievance against the boy. A further grudge was that by no manner of means could he succeed in lighting any wick or candle in the silver lantern, of which he desired to make use.

"But if your tree and your lantern won't work," said he, "it's no reason why you shouldn't." So he put Young Gerard to work, first as sheepboy to his own flock, but later the boy had a flock of his own. There was no love lost between these two, and kicks and curses were the young one's fare; for he was often idle and often a truant, and none was held responsible for him except the old shepherd who was selling him piece-meal, year by year, to their master. Because of what depended on him, Old Gerard was constrained to show him some sort of care when he would liever have wrung his neck. The boy's fits exasperated the man; whether he was cutting strange capers and laughing without reason, as he frequently did, or sitting a whole evening in a morose dream, staring at the fire or at the stars, and saying never a word. The boy's coloring was as mingled as his moods, a blend of light and dark—black hair, brown skin, blue eyes and golden lashes, a very odd anomaly.

(Martin: What is it, Mistress Joyce?

Joyce: I said nothing, Master Pippin.

Martin: I thought I heard you sigh.

Joyce: I did not—you did not.

Martin: My imagination exceeds all bounds.)

Because of their mutual dislike, when the boy was put in charge of his own sheep the two shepherds spent their days apart. The Old Gerard grazed his flock to the east as far as Chantry, but the Young Gerard grazed his flock to the west as far as Amberley, whose lovely dome was dearer to him than all the other hills of Sussex. And here he would sit all day watching the cloud-shadows stalk over the face of the Downs, or slipping along the land below him, with the sun running swiftly after, like a carpet of light unrolling itself upon a dusky floor. And in the evening he watched the smoke going up from the tiny cottages till it was almost dark, and a hundred tiny lights were lit in a hundred tiny windows. Sometimes on his rare holidays, and on other days too, he ran away to the Wildbrooks to watch the herons, or to find in the water-meadows the tallest kingcups in the whole world, and the myriad treasures of the river—the giant comfrey, purple and white, meadowsweet, St. John's Wort, purple loose-strife, willowherb, and the ninety-nine-thousand-nine-hundred- and-ninety-five others, or whatever number else you please, that go to make a myriad. He came to know more about the ways of the Wildbrooks than any other lad of those parts, and one day he rediscovered the Lost Causeway that can be traveled even in the floods, when the land lies under a lake at the foot of the hills. He kept this, like many other things, a secret; but he had one more precious still.

For as he lay and watched the play of sun and shadow on the plains, he fancied a world of strange places he had known, somewhere beyond the veils of light and mist that hung between his vision and the distance, and he fell into a frequent dream of tunes and laughter, and sunlit boughs in blossom, and dancing under the boughs; or of fires burning in the open night, and a wilder singing and dancing in the starlight; and often when his body was lying on the round hill, or by the smoky hearth, his thoughts were running with lithe boys as strong and careless as he was, or playing with lovely free-limbed girls with flowing hair. Sometimes these people were fair and bright-haired and in light and lovely clothing, and at others they were dark, with eyes of mischief, and clad in the gayest rags; and sometimes they came to him in a mingled company, made one by their careless hearts.

One evening in April, on the twelfth anniversary, when Young Gerard came to gather his flock, a lamb was missing; so to escape a scolding he waited awhile on the hills till Old Gerard should be gone about his business. What this was Young Gerard did not know, he only knew that each year on this night the old shepherd left him to his own devices, and returned in the small hours of the morning. Not therefore until he judged that the master must have left the hut, did the boy fold his sheep; and this done he ran out on the hills again, seeking the lost lamb. For careless though he was he cared for his sheep, as he did for all things that ran on legs or flew on wings. So he went swinging his lantern under the stars, singing and whistling and smelling the spring. Now and then he paused and bleated like a ewe; and presently a small whimper answered his signal.

"My lost lamb crying on the hills," said Young Gerard. He called again, but at the sound of his voice the other stopped, and for a moment he stood quite still, listening and perplexed.

"Where are you, my lamb?" said he.

"Here," said a little frightened voice behind a bush.

He laughed aloud and went forward, and soon discovered a tiny girl cowering under a thorn. When she saw him she ran quickly and grasped his sleeve and hid her face in it and wept. She was small for her years, which were not more than eight.

Young Gerard, who was big for his, picked her up and looked at her kindly and curiously.

"What is it, you little thing?" said he.

"I got lost," said the child shyly through her tears.

"Well, now you're found," said Young Gerard, "so don't cry any more."

"Yes, but I'm hungry," sobbed the child.

"Then come with me. Will you?"

"Where to?"

"To a feast in a palace."

"Oh, yes!" she said.

Young Gerard set her on his shoulder, and went back the way he had come, till the dark shape of his wretched shed stood big between them and the sky.

"Is this your palace?" said the child.

"That's it," said Young Gerard.

"I didn't know palaces had cracks in the walls," said she.

"This one has," explained Young Gerard, "because it's so old." And she was satisfied.

Then she asked, "What is that funny tree by the door?"

"It's a cherry-tree."

"My father's cherry-trees have flowers on them," said she.

"This one hasn't," said Young Gerard, "because it's not old enough."

"One day will it be?" she asked.

"One day," he said. And that contented her.

He then carried her into the shed, and she looked around eagerly to see what a palace might be like inside; and it was full of flickering lights and shadows and the scent of burning wood, and she did not see how poor and dirty the room was; for the firelight gleamed upon a mass of golden fruit and silver bloom embroidered on the covering of the settle by the hearth, and sparkled against a silver and crystal lantern hanging in the chimney. And between the cracks on the walls Young Gerard had stuck wands of gold and silver palm and branches of snowy blackthorn, and on the floor was a dish full of celandine and daisies, and a broken jar of small wild daffodils. And the child knew that all these things were the treasures of queens and kings.

"Why don't you have that?" she asked, pointing to the crystal lantern as Young Gerard set down his horn one.

"Because I can't light it," said he.

"Let ME light it!" she begged; so he fetched it from its nail, and thrust a pine twig in the fire and gave her the sweet-smoking torch. But in vain she tried to light the wick, which always spluttered and went out again. So seeing her disappointment Young Gerard hung the lantern up, saying, "Firelight is prettier." And he set her by the fire and filled her lap with cones and dry leaves and dead bracken to burn and make crackle and turn into fiery ferns. And she was pleased.

Then he looked about and found his own wooden cup, and went away and came back with the cup full of milk, set on a platter heaped with primroses, and when he brought it to her she looked at it with shining eyes and asked:

"Is this the feast?"

"That's it," said Young Gerard.

And she drank it eagerly. And while she drank Young Gerard fetched a pipe and began to whistle tunes on it as mad as any thrush, and the child began to laugh, and jumped up, spilling her leaves and primroses, and danced between the fitful lights and shadows as though she were, now a shadow taken shape, and now a flame. Whenever he paused she cried, "Oh, let me dance! Don't stop! Let me go on dancing!" until at the same moment she dropped panting on the hearth and he flung his pipe behind him and fell on his back with his heels in the air, crying, "Pouf! d'you think I've the four quarters of heaven in my lungs, or what?" But as though to prove he had yet a capful of wind under his ribs, he suddenly began to sing a song she'd never heard before, and it went like this:

I looked before me and behind,
I looked beyond the sun and wind,
Beyond the rainbow and the snow,
And saw a land I used to know.
The floods rolled up to keep me still
A captive on my heavenly hill,
And on their bright and dangerous glass
Was written, Boy, you shall not pass!
I laughed aloud, You shining seas,
I'll run away the day I please!
I am not winged like any plover
Yet I've a way shall take me over,
I am not finned like any bream
Yet I can cross you, lake and stream.
And I my hidden land shall find
That lies beyond the sun and wind—

Past drowned grass and drowning trees
I'll run away the day I please,
I'll run like one whom nothing harms
With my bonny in my arms.

"What does that mean?" asked the child.

"I'm sure I don't know," said Young Gerard. He kicked at the dying log on the hearth, and sent a fountain of sparks up the chimney. The child threw a dry leaf and saw it shrivel, and Young Gerard stirred the white ash and blew up the embers, and held a fan of bracken to them, till the fire ran up its veins like life in the veins of a man, and the frond that had already lived and died became a gleaming spirit, and then it too fell in ashes among the ash. Then Young Gerard took a handful of twigs and branches, and began to build upon the ash a castle of many sorts of wood, and the child helped him, laying hazel on his beech and fir upon his oak; and often before their turret was quite reared a spark would catch at the dry fringes of the fir, or the brown oakleaves, and one twig or another would vanish from the castle.

"How quickly wood burns," said the child.

"That's the lovely part of it," said Young Gerard, "the fire is always changing and doing different things with it."

And they watched the fire together, and smelled its smoke, that had as many smells as there were sorts of wood. Sometimes it was like roast coffee, and sometimes like roast chestnuts, and sometimes like incense. And they saw the lichen on old stumps crinkle into golden ferns, or fire run up a dead tail of creeper in a red S, and vanish in mid-air like an Indian boy climbing a rope, or crawl right through the middle of a birch-twig, making hieroglyphics that glowed and faded between the gray scales of the bark. And then suddenly it caught the whole scaffolding of their castle, and blazed up through the fir and oak and spiny thorns and dead leaves, and the bits of old bark all over blue-gray-green rot, and the young sprigs almost budding, and hissing with sap. And for one moment they saw all the skeleton and soul of the castle without its body, before it fell in.

The child sighed a little and yawned a little and said:

"How nice it is to live in a palace. Who lives here with you?"

"My friends," said Young Gerard, poking at the log with a bit of stick.

"What are your friends like?" she asked him, rubbing her knuckles in her eyes.

He was silent for a little, stirring up sparks and smoke. Then he answered, "They are gay in their hearts, and they're dressed in bright clothes, and they come with singing and dancing."

"Who else lives in your palace with you?" she asked drowsily.

"You do," said Young Gerard.

The child's head dropped against his shoulder and she said, "My name's Dorothea, but my father calls me Thea, and he is the Lord of Combe Ivy." And she fell fast asleep.

For a little while Young Gerard held and watched her in the firelight, and then he rose and wrapped her in the old embroidered mantle on the settle, and went out. And sure-foot as a goat he carried her over the dark hills by the tracks he knew, for roads there were none, and his arms ached with his burden, but he would not wake her till they stood at her father's gates. Then he shook her gently and set her down, and she clung to him a little dazed, trying to remember.

"This is Combe Ivy," he whispered. "You must go in alone. Will you come again?"

"One day," said Thea.

"One day there'll be flowers on my cherry-tree," said Young Gerard. "Don't forget."

"No, I won't," she said.

He returned through the night up hill and down dale, but did not go back to the shed until he had recovered his lamb. By then it was almost dawn, and he found his master awake and cursing. He had feared the boy had made off, and he had had curt treatment at Combe Ivy, which was in a stir about the loss of the little daughter. Young Gerard showed the lamb as his excuse, nevertheless the old shepherd leathered the young one soundly, as he did six days in seven.

After this when Young Gerard sat dreaming on the hills, he dreamed not only of his happy land and laughing friends, but of the next coming of little Thea. But Combe Ivy was far away, and the months passed and the years, and she did not come again. Meanwhile Young Gerard and his tree grew apace, and the limbs of the boy became longer and stronger, and the branches of the tree spread up to the roof and even began to thrust their way through the holes in the wall; but the boy's life, save for his dreaming, was as friendless as the tree's was flowerless. And of a tree's dreaming who shall speak? Meanwhile Old Gerard thrashed and rated him, and reckoned his gold pieces, and counted the years that still lay between him and his freedom. At last came another April bringing its hour.

For as he sat on the Mount in the early morning, when he was in his seventeenth year, Young Gerard saw a slender girl running over the turf and laughing in the sunlight, sometimes stopping to watch a bird flying, or stooping to pluck one of the tiny Down-flowers at her feet. So she came with a dancing step to the top of the Mount, and then she saw him, and her glee left her and shyness took its place. But a little pride in her prevented her from turning away, and she still came forward until she stood beside him, and said:

"Good morning, Shepherd. Is it true that in April the country north of the hills is filled with lakes?"

"Yes, sometimes, Mistress Thea," said Young Gerard.

She looked at him with surprise and said, "You must be one of my father's shepherds, but I do not remember seeing you at Combe Ivy."

"I was only once near Combe Ivy," said Young Gerard, "when I took you there five years ago the night you were lost on these hills."

"Oh, I remember," she said with a faint smile. "How they did scold me. Is your cherry-tree in flower yet, Shepherd?"

"No, mistress," said Young Gerard.

"I want to see it," she said suddenly.

Young Gerard left his flock to the dog, and walked with her along the hillbrow.

"I have run away," she told him as they went. "I had to get up very early while they were asleep. I shall be scolded again. But travelers come who talk of the lakes, and I wanted to see them, and to swim in them."

"I wouldn't do that," said Young Gerard, hiding a smile. "It's dangerous to swim in the April floods. And it would be rather cold."

"What lies beyond?" she asked.

"I'm not able to know," said Young Gerard.

"Some day I mean to know, shepherd."

"Yes, mistress," he said, "you'll be free to."

She looked at him quickly and reddened a little, it might have been from shame or pity, Young Gerard did not know which. And her shyness once more enveloped her; it always came over her unexpectedly, taking her breath away like a breaking wave. So she said no more, and they walked together, she looking at the ground, he at the soft brown hair blowing over the curve of her young cheek. She was fine and delicate in every line, and in her color, and in the touch of her too, Young Gerard knew. He wanted to touch her cheek with his finger as he would have touched the petal of a flower. Her neck, the back of it especially, was one of the loveliest bits of her, like a primrose stalk. He fell a step behind so that he could look at it. They did not speak as they went. He did not want to, and she did not know what to say.

When they reached the shed she lingered a moment by the tree, tracing a bare branch with her finger, and he waited, content, till she should speak or act, to watch her. At last she said with her faint smile, "I am very thirsty." Then he went into the shed and came out with his wooden cup filled with milk. She drank and said, "Thank you, shepherd. How pretty the violets are in your copse."

"Would you like some?" he asked.

"Not now," she said. "Perhaps another day. I must go now." She gave him back his cup and went away, slowly at first, but when she was at some distance he saw her begin to run like a fawn.

She did not come again that spring. And so the stark lives of the boy and the tree went forward for another year. But one evening in the following April, when the green was quivering on wood and hedgerow, he came to the door of the shed and saw her bending like a flower at the edge of the copse, filling her little basket and singing to herself. She looked up soon and said:

"Good evening, shepherd. How does your cherry-tree?"

"As usual, Mistress Thea."

"So I see. What a lazy tree it is. Have you some milk for me?"

He brought her his cup and she drank of it for the third time, and left him before he had had time to realize that she had come and gone, but only how greatly her delicate beauty had increased in the last year.

However, before the summer was over she came again—to swim in the river, she told him, as she passed him on the hills, without lingering. And in the autumn she came to gather blackberries, and he showed her the best place to find them. Any of these things she might have done as easily nearer Combe Ivy, but it seemed she must always offer him some reason for her small truancies—whether to gather berries or flowers, or to swim in the river. He knew that her chief delight lay in escaping from her father's manor.

Winter closed her visits; but Young Gerard was as patient as the earth, and did not begin to look for her till April. As surely as it brought leaves to the trees and flowers to the grass, it would, he knew, bring his little mistress's question, half shy, half smiling, "Is your cherry-tree in blossom, shepherd?" And later her request, smiling and shy, for milk.

They seldom exchanged more than a few words at any time. Sometimes they did not speak at all. For he, who was her father's servant, never spoke first; and she, growing in years and loveliness, grew also in timidity, so that it seemed to cost her more and more to address her greeting or her question even to her father's servant. The sweet quick reddening of her cheek was one of Young Gerard's chief remembrances of her.

But after a while, when they met by those sly chances which she could control and he could not; and when she did not speak, but glanced and hesitated and passed on; or glanced and passed without hesitation; or passed without a glance; he came to know that she would not mind if he arose and walked with her, if he could control the pretext, which she could not. And he did so quietly, having always something to show her.

He showed her his most secret nests and his greatest treasures of flowers, his because he loved them so much. He would have been jealous of showing these things to any one but her. In a great water-meadow in the valley, he had once shown her kingcups making sheets of gold, enameled with every green grass ever seen in spring— thousands of kingcups and a myriad of milkmaids in between, dancing attendance in all their faint shades of silver-white and rosy-mauve. When a breeze blew, this world of milkmaids swayed and curtsied above the kings' daughters in their glory. Then Gerard and Thea looked at each other smiling, because the same delight was in each, and soon she looked away again at the gentle maids and the royal ladies, but he looked still at her, who was both to him.

In silence he showed her what he loved.

But you must not suppose that she came frequently to those hills. She was to be seen no more often than you will see a kingfisher when you watch for it under a willow. Yet because in the season of kingfishers you know you may see one flash at any instant, so to Young Gerard each day of spring and summer was an expectancy; and this it was that kept his lift alight. This and his young troop of friends in a land of fruit in blossom and a sky in stars. For men, dear maids, live by the daily bread of their dreams; on realizations they would starve.

At last came the winter that preceded Young Gerard's twenty-first year. With the stripping of the boughs he stripped his heart of all thoughts of seeing her again till the green of the coming year. The snows came, and he tended his sheep and counted his memories; and Old Gerard tended his sheep and counted his coins. The count was full now, and he dreamed of April and the freeing of his body. Young Gerard also dreamed of April, and the freeing of his heart. And under the ice that bound the flooded meadows doubtless the earth dreamed of the freeing of her waters and the blooming of the land. The snows and the frosts lasted late that year as though the winter would never be done, and to the two Gerards the days crawled like snails; but in time March blew himself off the face of the earth, and April dawned, and the swollen river went rushing to the sea above the banks it had drowned with its wild overflow. And as Old Gerard began to mark the days off on a tally, Young Gerard began to listen on the hills. When the day came whose midnight was to make the old man a freedman, Thea had not appeared.

On the morning of this day, as the two shepherds stood outside their shed before they separated with their flocks, their ears were accosted with shoutings and halloos on the other side of the copse, and soon they saw coming through the trees a man in gay attire. He had a scalloped jerkin of orange leather, and his shoes and cap were of the same, but his sleeves and hose and feather were of a vivid green, like nothing in nature. He looked garish in the sun. Seeing the shepherds he took off his cap, and solemnly thanked heaven for having after all created something besides hills and valleys. "For," said he, "after being lost among them I know not how many hours, with no other company than my own shadow, I had begun to doubt whether I was not the only man on earth, and my name Adam. A curse of all lords who do not live by highroads!"

"Where are you bound for, master?" asked Old Gerard.

"Combe Ivy," said the stranger, "and the wedding."

Old Gerard nodded, as one little surprised; but to Young Gerard this mention of a wedding at Combe Ivy came as news. It did not stir him much, however, for he was not curious about the doings of the master and the house he never saw; all that concerned him was that to-day, at least, he must cease to listen on the hills, since his young mistress would be at the wedding with the others.

Old Gerard said to the stranger, "Keep the straight track to the south till you come under Wepham, then follow the valley to the east, and so you'll be in time for the feasting, master."

"That's certain," said the stranger, "for the Lord of Combe Ivy and the Rough Master of Coates have had no peers at junketing since Gay Street lost its Lord; and the feast is like to go on till midnight."

With that he went on his way, and Old Gerard followed him with his eyes, muttering,

"Would I also were there! But for you," he said, turning on the young man with a sudden snarl, "I should be! Had ye not come a day too late, I'd be a freedman to-night instead of to-morrow, and junketing at the wedding with the rest."

Young Gerard did not understand him. He was not in the habit of questioning the old man, and if he had would not have expected answers. But certain words of the stranger had pricked his attention, and now he said:

"Where is Gay Street?"

"Far away over the Stor and the Chill," growled Old Gerard.

"It's a jolly name."

"Maybe. But they say it's a sorry place now that it lacks its Lord."

"What became of him?"

"How should I know? What can a man know who lives all his life on a hill with pewits for gossips?"

"You know more than I," said Young Gerard indolently. "You know there's a wedding down yonder. Who's the Rough Master of Coates?"

"The bridegroom, young know-nothing. You've a tongue in your head to-day."

"Why do they call him the Rough Master?"

"Because that's what he is, and so are his people, as rough as furze on a common, they say. Have you any more questions?"

"Yes," said Young Gerard. "Who is the bride?"

"Who should the bride be? Combe Ivy's mother?"

"She's dead," said Young Gerard.

"His daughter then," scoffed Old Gerard.

Young Gerard stared at him.

"Get about your business," shouted the old shepherd with sudden wrath. "Why do ye stare so? You're not drunk. Ah! down yonder they'll be getting drunk without me. Enough of your idling and staring!"

He raised his staff, but Young Gerard thrust it aside so violently that he staggered, and the boy went away to his sheep and they met no more till evening. The whole of that day Young Gerard sat on the Mount, not looking as usual to the busy north dreaming of the unknown land beyond the water, but over the silent slopes and valleys of the south, whose peoples were only birds and foxes and rabbits, and whose only cities were built of lights and shadows. Somewhere beyond them was Combe Ivy, and little Thea getting married to the Rough Master of Coates, in the midst of feasting and singing and dancing. He thought of her dancing over the Downs for joy of being free, he thought of her singing to herself as she gathered flowers in his copse, and he thought of her feasting on wild berries he had helped her to find—that also was a feasting and singing and dancing. All day long his thoughts ran, "She will not come any more in the mornings to bathe in the river over the hill. She will not come with her little basket to gather flowers and berries. She will not stop and ask for a cup of milk, or say, Let me see the young lambs, or say, Is your cherry-tree in flower yet, shepherd? She will not ask me with her eyes to come with her—oh, she will not ask me by turning her eyes away, with her little head bent. You! you Rough Master of Coates, what are you like, what are you like?"

In the evening when he gathered his sheep, one was missing. He had to take the flock back without it. Old Gerard was furious with him; it seemed as though on this last night that separated him from the long fulfillment of his hopes he must be more furious than he had ever been before. He was furious at being thwarted of the fun in the valley, furious at the loss of the lamb, most furious at young Gerard's indifference to his fury. He told the boy he must search on the hills, and Young Gerard only sat down by the side of the shed and looked to the south and made no answer. So he went himself, leaving the boy to prepare the mess for supper; for he feared that if he went to Combe Ivy that night with a bad tale to tell, his master for a whim might say that a young sheep was a fair deal for an old shepherd, and take his gold, and keep him a bondman still. For the Lord of Combe Ivy lived by his whimsies. But Old Gerard could not find the lost sheep, and when he came back the boy was where he had left him, looking over the darkening hills.

"Is the mess ready?" said Old Gerard.

"No," said Young Gerard.

"Why not?"

"Because I forgot."

Old Gerard slashed at him with a rope he had taken in case of need. "That will make you remember."

"No," said Young Gerard.

"Why not?"

Young Gerard said, "You beat me too often, I cannot remember all the reasons."

"Then," said Old Gerard full of wrath, "I will beat you out of all reason."

And he began to thrash Young Gerard will all his might, talking between the blows. "Haven't you been the curse of my life for twenty-one years?" snarled he. "Can I trust you? Can I leave you? Would the sheep get their straw? Would the lambs be brought alive into the world? Bah! for all you care the sheep would go cold and their young would die. And down yonder they are getting drunk without me!"

"Old shepherd," said a voice behind him.

The angry man, panting with his rage and the exertion of his blows, paused and turned. Near the corner of the shed he saw a woman in a duffle cloak standing, or rather stooping, on her crutch. She was so ancient that it seemed as though Death himself must have forgotten her, but her eyes in their wrinkled sockets were as piercing as thorns. Old Gerard, staring at them, felt as though his own eyes were pricked.

"Where have I seen you before, hag?" he said.

"Have you ever seen me before?" asked the old woman.

"I thought so, I thought so"—he fumbled with his memory.

"Then it must have been when we went courting in April, nine-and- ninety years ago," said the old woman dryly, "but you lads remember me better than I do you. Can I sleep by your hearth to-night?"

"Where are you going to?" asked Old Gerard, half grinning, half sour.

"Where I'll be welcome," said she.

"You're not welcome here. But there's nothing to steal, you may sleep by the hearth."

"Thank you, shepherd," said the crone, "for your courtesy. Why were you beating the boy?"

"Because he's one that won't work."

"Is he your slave?"

"He's my master's slave. But he's idle."

"I am not idle," said Young Gerard. "The year round I'm busy long before dawn and long after dark."

"Then why are you idle to-day," sneered Old Gerard, "of all the days in the year?"

"I've something else to think of," said the boy.

"You see," said the old man to the crone.

"Well," said she, "a boy cannot always be working. A boy will sometimes be dreaming. Life isn't all labor, shepherd."

"What else is it?" said Old Gerard.

"Joy."

"Ho, ho, ho!" went Old Gerard.

"And power."

"Ho, ho, ho!"

"And triumph."

"Not for serfs," said Old Gerard.

"For serfs and lords," she said.

"Ho, ho, ho!"

"You were young once," said the crone.

Old Gerard said, "What if I was?"

"Good night," said the crone; and she went into the shed.

The shepherds looked after her, the old one stupidly, the young one with lighted eyes.

"Will you get supper?" growled Old Gerard.

"No," said Young Gerard, "I won't. I want no supper. Put down that rope. I am taller and stronger than you, and why I've let you go on beating me so long I don't know, unless it is that you began to beat me when you were taller and stronger than I. If you want any supper, get it yourself."

Old Gerard turned red and purple. "The boy's mad!" he gasped. "Do you know what happens to servants who defy their masters?"

"Yes," said Young Gerard, "then they're lords." And he too went into the shed.

"Try that on Combe Ivy!" bawled Old Gerard, "and see what you'll get for it. I thank fortune, I'll be quit of you tomorrow— What's that to-do in the valley?" he muttered, and stared down the hill.

Away in the hollows and shadows he saw splashes of moving light, and heard far-off snatches of song and laughter, but the movements and sounds were still so distant that they seemed to be only those of ghosts and echoes.

Nearer they came and nearer, and now in the night he could discern a great rabble stumbling among the dips and rises of the hills.

"They're heading this way," said Old Gerard. "Why, tis the wedding-party," he said amazed, "if it's not witchcraft. But why are they coming here?"

"Hola! hola! hola!" shouted a tipsy voice hard by.

"Here's dribblings from the wineskin," said Old Gerard; and up the track struggled a drunken man, waving a torch above his head. It was the guest whom he had directed in the morning.

"Hola!" he shouted again on seeing Old Gerard.

"Well, racketer?" said the shepherd, with a chuckle.

"Shall a man not racket at another man's wedding?" he cried. "Let some one be jolly, say I!"

"The bridegroom," said Old Gerard.

"Ha, ha!" laughed the other, "the bridegroom! He was first in high feather and last in the sulks."

"The bride, then."

"Ha, ha! ha, ha! during the toasts he tried to kiss her."

"Wouldn't she?"

"She wouldn't."

"Hark!" said Old Gerard, "here they come." The sound of rollicking increased as the rout drew nearer.

"He's taking her home across the river," said the guest. "I wouldn't be she. There she sat, her pretty face fixed and frozen, but a fright in her that shook her whole body. You could see it shake. And we drank, how we drank! to the bride and the groom and their daughters and sons, to the sire and the priest, and the ring and the bed, to the kiss and the quarrel, to love which is one thing and marriage which is another—Lord, how we drank! But she drank nothing. And for all her terror the Rough could do no more with her than with a stone. Something in her turned him cold every time. Suddenly up he gets. We'll have no more of this,' he says, we'll go.' Combe Ivy would have had them stay, but She's where she's used to lord it here,' says Rough, I'll take her where I lord it, and teach her who's master,' And he pushes down his chair and takes her hand and pulls her away; and out we tumble after him. Combe Ivy cries to him to wait for the horses, but no, We'll foot it,' says he, up hill and down dale as the crow flies, and if she hates me now without a cause I swear she'll love me with one at the end of the dance.' We're dancing them as far as the Wildbrooks; on t'other side they may dance for themselves. Here they come dancing—dance, you!" cried the guest, and whirled his torch like a madman. And as he whirled and staggered, up the hill came the wedding-party as tipsy as he was: a motley procession, waving torches and garlands, winecups, flagons, colored napkins, shouting and singing and beating on trenchers and salvers—on anything that they could snatch from the table as they quitted it. They came in all their bravery—in doublets of flame-colored silk and blue, in scarlet leather and green velvet, in purple slashed with silver and crimson fringed with bronze; but their vests were unlaced, their hose sagged, and silk and velvet and leather were stained bright or dark with wine. Some had stuck leaves and flowers in their hair, others had tied their forelocks with ribbons like horses on a holiday, and one had torn his yellow mantle in two and capered in advance, waving the halves in either hand like monstrous banners, or the flapping wings of some golden bird of prey. In the midst of them, pressing forward and pressed on by the riot behind, was the Rough Master of Coates, and with him, always hanging a little away and shrinking under her veil, Thea, whose right wrist he grasped in his left hand. Breathless she was among the breathless rabble, who, gaining the hilltop seized each other suddenly and broke into antics, shaking their napkins and rattling on their plates. Their voices were hoarse with laughter and drink, and their faces flushed with it; only among those red and swollen faces, the bridegroom's, in the flare of the torches, looked as black as the bride's looked white. The night about the newly-wedded pair was one great din and flutter.

Then in a trice the dancers all lost breath, and the dance parted as they staggered aside; and at the door of the shed Young Gerard stood, and gazed through the broken revel at little Thea, and she stood gazing at him. And behind and above him, along the walls of the hut, and over the doorway, and making lovely the very roof, she saw a cloud of snowwhite blossom.

Somebody cried, "Here's a boy. He shall dance too. Boy, is there drink within?"

The others took up the clamor. "Drink! bring us something to drink!"

"The red grape!" cried one.

"The yellow grape!" cried another.

"The sap of the apple!"

"The juice of the pear!"

"Nut-brown ale!"

"The spirit that burns!"

"Bring us drink!" they cried in a breath.

"Will you have milk?" said Young Gerard.

At this the company burst into a roar of laughter. They laughed till they rocked. But when they were silent little Thea spoke. She said in a faint clear voice:

"I would like a cup of milk."

Young Gerard went into the hut and came out with his wooden cup filled with milk, and brought it to her, and she drank. None spoke or moved while she drank, but when she gave him the cup again one of the crew said chuckling, "Now she has drunk, now she's merrier. Try her again, Rough, try her on milk!"

Again the night reeled with their laughter. They surrounded the wedded pair crying, "Kiss her! kiss her! kiss her!" Then the Rough Master of Coates pulled her round to him, dark with anger, and tried to kiss her. But she turned sharply in his arms, bending her head away. And despite his force, and though he was a man and she little more than a child, he could not make her mouth meet his. And the laughter of the guests rose higher, and infuriated him.

Then he who had spoken before said, "By Hymen, the bride should kiss something. If the lord's not good enough, let her kiss the churl!" At this the revelers, wild with delight, beat on their trenchers and shouted, "Ay, let her!"

And suddenly they surged in, parting Thea from the Rough; while some pulled him back others dragged Young Gerard forward, till he stood where the bridegroom had stood; and in that seething throng of mockery he felt her clinging helplessly to him, and his arm went round her.

"Kiss him! kiss him! kiss him!" cried the guests.

She looked up pitifully at him, and he bent his head. And she heard him whisper:

"My cherry-tree's in flower."

She whispered, "Yes."

And they kissed each other.

Then the tumult of laughter passed all bounds, so that it was a wonder if it was not heard at Combe Ivy; and the guests clashed their trenchers one against another, and whirled their torches till the sparks flew, yelling, "The bride's kiss! Ha, ha! the bride's kiss!"

But the Rough Master of Coates had had enough; snarling like a mad dog he thrust his way through the crowd on one side, as Old Gerard, seeing his purpose, thrust through on the other, and both at the same instant fell on the boy, the one with his scabbard, the other with his staff.

"Kisses, will ye?" cried the Rough Master of Coates, "here's kisses for ye!"

"Ha, ha!" cried the guests, "more kisses, more kisses for him that kissed the bride!"

And then they all struck him at once, kicking and beating him without mercy, till he lay prone on the earth. When he had fallen, the Rough shouted, "Away to the Wildbrooks, away!"

And he seized Thea in his arms, and rushed along the brow of the hill, and all the company followed in a confusion, and were swallowed up in the night.

But Young Gerard raised himself a little, and groaned, "The Wildbrooks—are they going to the Wildbrooks?"

"Ay, and over the Wildbrooks," said Old Gerard.

"But they're in flood," gasped Young Gerard. "They'll never cross it in the spring floods."

"They'll manage it somehow. The Rough—did you see his eyes when you—? ho, ho! he'll cross it somehow."

"He can't," the boy muttered. "The April tide's too strong. He will drown in the flood."

"And she," said Old Gerard.

"Perhaps she will swim on the flood," said Young Gerard faintly. And he sighed and sank back on the earth.

"Ay, you'll be sore," chuckled the old man. "You had your salve before you had your drubbing. Lie there. I must be gone on business."

He took up his staff and went down the hill for the last time to Combe Ivy, to purchase his freedom.

But Young Gerard lay with his face pressed to the turf. "And that was the bridegroom," he said, and shook where he lay.

"Young shepherd," said a voice beside him. He looked up and saw the hooded crone, come out of the hut. "Why do you water the earth?" said she. "Have not the rains done their work?"

"What work, dame?"

"You've as fine a cherry in flower," said she, "as ever blossomed in Gay Street in the season of singing and dancing."

"Singing and dancing!" he cried, his voice choking, and he sprang up despite his pains. "Don't speak to me, dame, of singing and dancing. You're old, like the withered branch of a tree, but did you not see with your old eyes, and hear with your old ears? Did you not see her come up the green hillside with singing and dancing? Oh, yes, my cherry's in flower, like a crown for a bride, and the spring is all in movement, and the birds are all in song, and she—she came up the hillside with singing and dancing."

"I saw," said the crone, "and I heard. I'm not so old, young shepherd, that I do not remember the curse of youth."

"What's that?" he said moodily.

"To bear the soul of a master in the body of a slave," said she; "to be a flower in a sealed bud, the moon in a cloud, water locked in ice, Spring in the womb of the year, love that does not know itself."

"But when it does know?" said Young Gerard slowly.

"Oh, when it knows!" said she. "Then the flower of the fruit will leap through the bud, and the moon will leap like a lamb on the hills of the sky, and April will leap in the veins of the year, and the river will leap with the fury of Spring, and the headlong heart will cry in the body of youth, I will not be a slave, but I will be the lord of life, because—"

"Because?" said Young Gerard.

"Because I will!"

Young Gerard said nothing, and they sat together in a long silence in the darkness, and time went by filling the sky with stars.

Now as they sat the hilltop once more began to waver with shadows and voices, but this time the shadows came on heavy feet and weary, and the voices were forlorn. One feebly cried, "Hola!" And round the belt of trees straggled the rout that had left them an hour or so earlier. But now they were sodden and dejected, draggled and woebegone, as sorry a spectacle as so many drowned rats.

"Fire!" moaned one. "Fire! fire!"

"Who's burning?" said Young Gerard, and got quickly on his feet; but he did not see the two he looked for.

"None's burning, fool, but many are drowning. Do we not look like drowned men? How shall we ever get back to Combe Ivy, and warmth and drink and comforts? Would we were burning!"

"What has happened?" the boy demanded.

"We went in search of the ferry," he said, "but the ferry was drowned too."

"We couldn't find the ferry," said a second.

"No," mumbled a third, "the river had drunk it up. Where there were paths there are brooks, and where there were meadows, lakes."

The miserable crew broke out into plaints and questions—"Have you no fire? have you no food? no coverings?"

"None," said Young Gerard. "Where is the bride?"

"Have you do drink?"

"Where is the bride?"

"The groom stumbled," said one. "Let us to Combe Ivy, in comfort's name. There'll be drink there."

He staggered down the hill, and his fellows made after him. But Young Gerard sprang upon one, and gripped him by the shoulder and shook him, and for the third time cried:

"Where is the bride?"

"In the water," he answered heavily, "because—there was—no wine."

Then he dragged himself out of the boy's grasp, and fell down the hill after his companions.

Young Gerard stood for one instant listening and holding his breath. Suddenly he said, "My lost lamb, crying on the hills." He ran into the shed and looked about, and snatched from the settle the green and cherry cloak, and from the wall the crystal and silver lantern. He struck a spark from a flint and lit the wick. It burned brightly and steadily. Then he ran out of the shed. The old woman rose up in his path.

"That's a good light," said she, "and a warm cloak."

"Don't stop me!" said Young Gerard, and ran on. She nodded, and as he vanished in one direction, she vanished in the other.

He had not run far when he saw one more shadow on the hills; and it came with faltering steps, and a trembling sobbing breath, and he held up his lantern and the light fell on Thea, shivering in her wet veil. As the flame struck her eyes she sighed, "Oh, I can't see the way—I can't see!"

Young Gerard hurried to her and said, "Come this way," and he took her hand; but she snatched it quickly from him.

"Go, man!" she said. "Don't touch me. Go!"

"Don't be frightened of me," said Young Gerard gently.

Then she looked at him and whispered, "Oh—it is you—shepherd. I was trying to find you. I'm cold."

Young Gerard wrapped the cloak about her, and said, "Come with me. I'll make you a fire."

He took her back to the shed. But she did not go in. She crouched on the ground under the cherry-tree. Young Gerard moved about collecting brushwood. They scarcely looked at each other; but once when he passed her he said, "You're shivering."

"It's because I'm so wet," said Thea.

"Did you fall in the water?"

She nodded. "The floods were so strong."

"It's a bad night for swimming," said Young Gerard.

"Yes, shepherd." She then said again, "Yes." He could tell by her voice that she was smiling faintly. He glanced at her and saw her looking at him; both smiled a little and glanced away again. He began to pile his brushwood for the fire.

After a short pause she said timidly, "Are you sore, shepherd?"

"No, I feel nothing," said he.

"They beat you very hard."

"I did not feel their blows."

"How could you not feel them?" she said in a low voice. He looked at her again, and again their eyes met, and again parted quickly.

"Now I'll strike a spark," said Young Gerard, "and you'll be warm soon."

He kindled his fire; the branches crackled and burned, and she knelt beside the blaze and held her hands to it.

"I was never here by night before," she said.

"Yes, once," said Young Gerard. "You often came, didn't you, to gather flowers in the morning and to swim in the river at noon. But once before you were here in the night."

"Was I?" said she.

He dropped a handful of cones into her lap, throwing the last on the fire. She threw another after it, and smiled as it crackled.

"I remember," she said. "Thank you, shepherd. You were always kind and found me the things I wanted, and gave me your cup to drink of. Who'll drink of it now?"

"No one," he said, "ever again."

He went and fetched the cup and gave it to her. "Burn that too," said Young Gerard. Thea put it into the fire and trembled. When it was burned she asked very low, "Will you be lonely?"

"I'll have my sheep and my thoughts."

"Yes," said Thea, "and stars when the sheep are folded. The stars are good to be with too."

"Good to see and not be seen by," he said.

"How do you know they don't see you?" she asked shyly.

"One shepherd on a hill isn't much for the eye of a star. He may watch them unwatched, while they come and go in their months. Sometimes there aren't any, and sometimes not more than one pricking the sky near the moon. But to-night, look! the sky's like a tree with full branches."

Thea looked up and said with a child's laugh, "Break me a branch!"

"I'd want Jacob's Ladder for that," smiled Young Gerard.

"Then shake the tree and bring them down!" she insisted.

"Here come your stars," said Young Gerard. Suddenly she was enveloped in a falling shower, white and heavenly.

"The stars—!" she cried. "Oh, what is it?"

"My cherry-tree—it's in flower—" said Young Gerard, and his voice trembled. She looked up quickly and saw that he was standing beside her, shaking the tree above her head. And now their eyes met and did not separate.

He put out his hand and broke a branch from the tree and offered it to her. She took it from him slowly, as though she were in a dream, and laid it in her lap, and put her face in her hands and began to cry.

Young Gerard whispered, "Why are you crying?"

Thea said, "Oh, my wedding, my wedding! Only last year I thought of the night of my wedding and how it would be. It was not with torchlight and shouting and wine, but moonlight and silence and the scent of wild blossoms. And now I know that it was not the night of my wedding I dreamed of."

"What did you dream of?" asked Young Gerard.

"The night of my first love."

"Thea," said Young Gerard, and he knelt beside her.

"And my love's first kiss."

"Oh, Thea," said Young Gerard, and he took her hands.

"Why did you not feel their blows?" she said. "I felt them."

Their arms went round each other, and for the second time that night they kissed.

Young Gerard said, "I've always wondered if this would happen."

And Thea answered, "I didn't know it would be you."

"Didn't you? didn't you?" he whispered, stroking her head, wondering at himself doing what he had so often dreamed of doing.

"Oh," she faltered, "sometimes I thought—it might—be you, darling."

"Thea, Thea!"

"When I came over the Mount to swim in the river, and saw you in the distance among your sheep, there was a swifter river running through all my body. When I came every April to ask for your cherry-tree, what did it matter to me that it was not in bloom? for all my heart was wild with bloom, oh, Gerard, my—lover!"

"Oh, Thea, my love! What can I give you, Thea, I, a shepherd?"

"You were the lord of the earth, and you gave me its flowers and its birds and its secret waters. What more could you give me, you, a shepherd and my lord?"

"The wild white bloom of its fruit-trees that comes to the branches in April like love to the heart. I'll give it you now. Sit here, sit here! I'll make you a bower of the cherry, and a crown, and a carpet too. There's nothing in all April lovely and wild enough for you to-night, your bridal night, my lady and my darling!"

And in a great fit of joy he broke branch after branch from the tree as she sat at its foot, and set them about her, and filled her arms to overflowing, and crowned her with blossoms, and shook the bloom under her feet, till her shy happy face, paling and reddening by turns, looked out from a world of flowers and she cried between laughing and weeping, "Oh, Gerard, oh, you're drowning me!"

"It's the April floods," shouted Young Gerard, "and I must drown with you, Thea, Thea, Thea!" And he cast himself down beside her, and clasped her amid all the blossoming, and with his head on her shoulder kissed and kissed her till he was breathless and she as pale as the flowers that smothered their kisses.

And then suddenly he folded her in the green mantle, blossoms and all, and sprang up and lifted her to his breast till she lay like a child in the arms of its mother; and he picked up the lantern and said, "Now we will go away for ever."

"Where are we going?" she whispered with shining eyes.

"To the Wildbrooks," he said.

"To drown in the floods together?" She closed her eyes.

"There's a way through all floods," said Young Gerard.

And he ran with her over the hills with all his speed.

And Old Gerard returned to a hut as empty as it had been one-and-twenty years ago. And they say that Combe Ivy, having never set eyes on the boy in his life, swore that the shepherd's tale had been a fiction from first to last, and kept him a serf to the end of his days.

("What a night of stars it is!" said Martin Pippin, stretching his arms.

"Good heavens, Master Pippin," cried Joyce, "what a moment to mention it!"

"It is worth mentioning," said Martin, "at all moments when it is so. I would not think of mentioning it in the middle of a snowstorm."

"You should as little think of mentioning it," said Joyce, "in the middle of a story."

"But I am at the end of my story, Mistress Joyce."

Joscelyn: Preposterous! Oh! Oh, how can you say so? I am ashamed of you!

Martin: Dear Mistress Joscelyn, I thank you in charity's name for being that for me which I have never yet succeeded in being for myself.

Joscelyn: What! are you not ashamed to offer us a broken gift? Your story is like a cracked pitcher with half the milk leaked out. What was the secret of the Lantern, the Cloak, and the Cherry-tree?

Joyce: Who was the lovely lady, his mother? and who the old crone?

Jennifer: What was the end of the Rough Master of Coates?

Jessica: Did not the lovers drown in the floods?

Jane: And if they did not, what became of them?

"Please," said little Joan, "tell us why Young Gerard dreamed those dreams. Oh, please tell us what happened."

"Women's taste is for trifles," said Martin. "I have offered you my cake, and you wish only to pick off the nuts and the cherries."

"No," said Joan, "we wish you to put them on. Do you not love nuts and cherries on a cake?"

"More than anything," said Martin.)

A long while ago, dear maidens, there were Lords in Gay Street, and up and down the Street the cherry-trees bloomed in Spring as they bloomed nowhere else in Sussex, and under the trees sang and danced the loveliest lads and lasses in all England, with hearts like children. And on all their holiday clothes they worked the leaf and branch and flower and fruit of the cherry. And they never wore anything else but their holiday clothes, because in Gay Street it was always holidays.

And a long while ago there were Gypsies on Nyetimber Common, the merriest Gypsies in the southlands, with the gayest tatters and the brightest eyes, and the maddest hearts for mirth-making. They were also makers of lanterns when they were anything else but what all Gypsies are.

And once the son of a Gypsy King loved the daughter of a Lord of Gay Street, and she loved him. And because of this there was wrath in Gay Street and scorn on Nyetimber, and all things were done to keep the lovers apart. But they who attempt this might more profitably chase wild geese. So one night in April they were taken under one of her father's own wild cherries by the light of one of his father's own lanterns. And it was her father and his father who found them, as they had missed them, in the same moment, and were come hunting for sweethearts by night with their people behind them.

Then the Lord of Gay Street pronounced a curse of banishment on his own daughter, that she must go far away beyond the country of the floods, and another on his own tree, that it might never blossom more. And there and then it withered. And the Gypsy King pronounced as dark a curse of banishment on his own son, and a second on his own lantern, that it might never more give light. And there and then it went out.

Then from the crowd of gypsies came the oldest of them all, who was the King's great-grandmother, and she looked from the angry parents to the unhappy lovers and said, "You can blight the tree and make the lantern dark; nevertheless you cannot extinguish the flower and the light of love. And till these things lift the curse and are seen again united among you, there will be no Lords in Gay Street nor Kings on Nyetimber."

And she broke a shoot from the cherry and picked up the lantern and gave them to the lady and her lover; and then she took them one by each hand and went away. And the Lord of Gay Street and the Gypsy King died soon after without heirs, and the joy went out of the hearts of both peoples, and they dressed in sad colors for one-and-twenty years.

But the three traveled south through the country of the floods, and on the way the King's son was drowned, as others had been before him, and after him the Rough Master of Coates. But the crone brought the lady safely through, and how she was at once delivered of her son and her sorrow, dear maidens, you know.

And for one-and-twenty years the crone was seen no more, and then of a sudden she re-appeared at daybreak and bade her people put on their bright apparel because their King was coming with a young Queen; and after this she led them to Gay Street where she bade the folk to don their holiday attire, because their Lord was on his way with a fair Lady. And all those girls and boys, the dark and the light, felt the child of joy in their hearts again, and they went in the morning with singing and dancing to welcome the comers under the cherry-trees.

I entreat you now, Mistress Joyce, for the second hair from your head.

SECOND INTERLUDE

The milkmaids put their forgotten apples to their mouths, and the chatter began to run out of them like juice from bitten fruit.

Jessica: What did you think of this story, Jane?

Jane: I did not know what to think, Jessica, until the very conclusion, and then I was too amazed to think anything. For who would have imagined the young Shepherd to be in reality a lord?

Martin: Few of us are what we seem, Mistress Jane. Even chimney- sweeps are Jacks-in-Green on May-Days; for the other three-hundred- and-sixty-four days in the year they pretend to be chimney-sweeps. And I have actually known men who appeared to be haters of women, when they secretly loved them most tenderly.

Joscelyn: It does not surprise me to hear this. I have always understood men to be composed of caprices.

Martin: They are composed of nothing else. I see you know them through and through.

Joscelyn: I do not know anything at all about them. We do not study what does not interest us.

Martin: I hope, Mistress Joscelyn, you found my story worthy of study?

Joscelyn: It served its turn. Might one, by going to Rackham Hill, see this same cherry-tree and this same shed?

Martin: Alas, no. The shed rotted with time and weather, and bit by bit its sides were rebuilt with stone. And the cherry-tree Old Gerard chopped down in a fury, and made firewood of it. But it too had served its turn. For as every man's life (and perhaps, but you must answer for this, every woman's life), awaits the hour of blossoming that makes it immortal, so this tree passed in a single night from sterility to immortality; and it mattered as little if its body were burned the next day, as it would have mattered had Gerard and Thea gone down through the waters that night instead of many years later, after a life-time of great joy and delight.

Joyce: I am glad of that. There were moments when I feared it would not be so.

Jennifer: I too. For how could it be otherwise, seeing that he was a shepherd and she a lord's daughter?

Jessica: And when it was related how she was to wed the Rough Master of Coates, my hopes were dashed entirely.

Jane: And when they beat Young Gerard I was perfectly certain he was dead.

Joan: I rather fancied the tale would end happily, all the same.

Martin: I fancied so too. For though any of these accidents would have marred the ending, love is a divinity above all accidents, and guards his own with extraordinary obstinacy. Nothing could have thwarted him of his way but one thing.

Five of the Milkmaids: Oh, what?

Martin: Had Thea been one of those who are not interested in the study of men.

Nobody said anything in the Apple-Orchard.

Joscelyn: She need not have been condemned to unhappiness on that account, singer. And what does the happiness or unhappiness of an idle story weigh? Whether she wedded another, or whether they were parted by whatever cause, such as her superior station, or even his death, it's all one to me.

Jennifer: And me.

Jessica: And me.

Jane: And me.

Martin: The tale is judged. Let it go hang. For a cloud has dropped over nine-tenths of the moon, like the eyelid of a girl who still peeps through her lashes, but will soon fall asleep for weariness. I have made her lids as heavy as yours with my poor story. Let us all sleep and forget it.

So the girls lay down in the grass and slept. But Joyce went on swinging. And every time she swayed past him she looked at Martin, and her lips opened and shut again, nothing having escaped them but a very little laughter. The tenth time this happened Martin said:

"What keeps your lashes open, Mistress Joyce, when your comrades' lie tangled on their cheeks? Is it the same thing that opens your lips and peeps through the doorway and runs away again?"

"MUST my lashes shut because others' do?" said Joyce. "May not lashes have whims of their own?"

"Nothing is more whimsical," said Martin Pippin. "I have known, for instance, lashes that WILL be golden though the hair of the head be dark. It is a silly trick."

"I don't dislike such lashes," said Joyce. "That is, I think I should not if ever I saw them."

Martin: Perhaps you are right. I should love them in a woman.

Joyce: I never saw them in a woman.

Martin: In a man they would be regrettable.

Joyce: Then why did you give them to Young Gerard?

Martin: Did I? It was pure carelessness. Let us change the color of his lashes.

Joyce: No, no! I will not have them changed. I would not for the world.

Martin: Dear Mistress Joyce, if I had the world to offer you, I would sit by the road and break it with a pickax rather than change a single eyelash in Young Gerard's lids. Since you love them.

Joyce: Oh, did I say so?

Martin: Didn't you?—Mistress Joyce, when you laugh I am ready to forgive you all your debts.

Joyce: Why, what do I owe you?

Martin: An eyelash.

Joyce: I am sure I do not.

Martin: No? Then a hair of some sort. How will you be able to sleep to-night with a hair on your conscience? For your own sake, lift that crowbar.

Joyce: To tell you the truth, I fear to redeem my promise lest you are unable to redeem yours.

Martin: Which was?

Joyce: To blow it to its fellow, who is now wandering in the night like thistledown.

Martin: I will do it, nevertheless.

Joyce: It is easier promised than proved. But here is the hair.

Martin: Are you certain it is the same hair?

Joyce: I kept it wound round my finger.

Martin: I know no better way of keeping a hair. So here it goes!

And he held the hair to his lips and blew on it.

Martin: A blessing on it. It will soon be wedded.

Joyce: I have your word on it.

Martin: You shall have your eyes on it if you will tell me one thing.

Joyce: Is it a little thing?

Martin: It's as trifling as a hair. I wish only to know why you have fallen out with men.

Joyce: For the best of reasons. Why, Master Pippin! they say the world is round!

Martin: Heaven preserve us! was ever so giddy a statement? Round? Why, the world's as full of edges as the dealings of men and women, in which you can scarcely go a day's march without reaching the end of all things and tumbling into heaven. I tell you I have traveled the world more than any man living, and it takes me all my time to keep from falling off the brink. Round? The world is one great precipice!

Joyce: I said so! I said so! I know I was right! I should like to tell—them so.

Martin: Were you only able to go out of the Orchard, you would be free to tell—them so. They are such fools, these men.

Joyce: Not in all matters, Master Pippin, but certainly in this. They are good at some things.

Martin: For my part I can't think what.

Joyce: They whitewash cowsheds beautifully.

Martin: Who wouldn't? Whitewash is such beautiful stuff. No, let us be done with these round-minded men and go to bed. Good night, dear milkmaid.

Joyce: Ah, but singer! you have not yet proved your fable of the two hairs, which you swore were as hard to keep apart as the two lovers in your tale.

"Whom love guarded against accidents," said Martin; and he held out to her the third finger of his left hand, and wound at its base were the two hairs, in a ring as fine as a cobweb. She took his finger between two of hers and laughed, and examined it, and laughed again.

"You have been playing the god of love to my hairs," said Joyce.

"Somebody must protect those that cannot, or will not, be kind to themselves," said Martin. And then his other fingers closed quickly on her hand, and he said: "Dear Mistress Joyce, help me to play the god of love to Gillian, and give me your key to the Well-House, because there were moments when you feared my tale would end unhappily."

She pulled her hand away and began to swing rapidly, without answering. But presently she exclaimed, "Oh, oh! it has dropped!"

"What? what?" said Martin anxiously.

But she only cried again, "Oh, my heart! it has dropped under the swing."

"In love's name," said Martin, "let me recover your heart."

He groped in the grass and found what she had dropped, and then was obliged to fall flat on his back to escape her feet as she swung.

"Well, any time's a time for laughing," said Martin, crawling forth and getting on his knees. "Here's the key to your heart, laughing Joyce."

"Oh, Martin! how can I take it with my hands on the ropes?"

"Then I'll lay it on your lap."

"Oh, Martin! how do you expect it to stay there while I swing?"

"Then you must stop swinging."

"Oh, Martin! I will never stop swinging as long as I live!"

"Then what must I do with this key?"

"Oh, Martin! why do you bother me so about an old key? Can't you see I'm busy?"

"Oh, Joyce! when you laugh I must—I must—"

"Yes?"

"I must!"

And he caught her two little feet in his hands as she next flew by, and kissed each one upon the instep.

Then he ran to his bed under the hedge, and she sat where she was till her laughing turned to smiling, and her smiling to sleeping.

"Maids! maids! maids!"

It was morning.

"To your hiding-place, Master Pippin!" urged Joscelyn. "It's our master come again."

Martin concealed himself with speed, and an instant later the farmer's burly face peered through the gap in the hedge.

"Good morrow, maids."

"Good morrow, master."

"Has my daughter stopped weeping yet?"

"No, master," said Joyce, "but I begin to think that she will before long."

"A little longer will be too long," moaned Gillman, "for my purse is running dry with these droughty times, and I shall have to mortgage the farm to buy me ale, since I am foiled of both water and milk. Who would have daughters when he might have sons? Gillian!" he cried, "when will ye learn that old heads are wiser than young ones?"

But Gillian paid no more attention to him than to the cawing rooks in the elms in the oatfield.

"Take your bread, maids," said Gillman, "and heaven send us grace to-morrow."

"Just an instant, master," said Joyce. "I would like to know if Blossom my Shorthorn is well?"

"As well as a child without its mother, maid, though Michael has turned nurse to her. But she seems sworn to hold back her milk till you come again. Rack and ruin, nothing but rack and ruin!"

And off he went.

Then breakfast was prepared as on the previous day, and Gillian's stale loaf was broken for the ducks. But Joscelyn pointed out that one of the kissing-crusts had been pulled off in the night.

"Your stories, Master Pippin, are doing their work," said she.

"I begin to think so," said Martin cheerfully. And then they fell to on their own white loaves and sweet apples.

When they had breakfasted Martin observed that he could make better and longer daisy-chains than any one else in the world, and his statement was pooh-poohed by six voices at once. For girls' fingers, said these voices, had been especially fashioned by nature for the making of daisy-chains. Martin challenged them to prove this, and they plucked lapfuls of the small white daisies with big yellow eyes, and threaded chains of great length, and hung them about each other's necks. And so deft and dainty was their touch that the chains never broke in the making or, what is still more delicate a matter, in the hanging. But Martin's chains always broke before he had joined the last daisy to the first, and the girls jeered at him for having no necklace to match their necklaces of pearls and gold, and for failing so contemptibly in his boast. And he appeared so abashed by their jeers that little Joan relented and made a longer chain than any that had been made yet, and hung it round his neck. At which he was merry again, and confessed himself beaten, and the girls became very gracious, being in their triumph even more pleased with him than with themselves. Which was a great deal. And by then it was dinner-time.

After dinner Martin proposed that as they had sat all the morning they should run all the afternoon, so they played Touchwood. And Martin was He. But an orchard is so full of wood that he had a hard job of it. And he observed that Jennifer had very little daring, and scarcely ever lifted her finger from the wood as she ran from one tree to another; and that Jane had no daring at all, and never even left her tree. And that Joscelyn was extremely daring when it was safe to be so; and that Jessica was daring enough to tweak him and run away, while Joyce was more daring still, for she tweaked him and did not run. As for little Joan, she puzzled him most of all; for half the time she outdid them all in daring, and then she was uncatchable, slipping through his very fingers like a ray of sunlight a child tries to hold; but the other half of the time she was timidity itself, and crept from tree to tree, and if he were near became like a little frightened rabbit, forgetting, or being through fear unable, to touch safety; and then she was snared more easily than any.

By supper, however, every maid had been He but Jane. For no man can catch what doesn't run.

"How the time has flown," said Joscelyn, when they were all seated about the middle tree after the meal.

"It makes such a difference," said Jennifer, "when there's something to do. We never used to have anything to do till Master Pippin came, and now life is all games and stories."

"The games," said Joscelyn, "are well enough."

"Shall we," said Martin, "forego the stories?"

"Oh, Master Pippin!" said Jennifer anxiously, "we surely are to have a story to-night?"

"Unless we are to remain here for ever," said Martin, "I fear we must. But for my part I am quite happy here. Are not you, Mistress Joscelyn?"

"Your questions are idle," said she. "You know very well that we cannot escape a story."

"You see, Mistress Jennifer," said Martin. "Let us resign ourselves therefore. And for your better diversion, please sit in the swing, and when the story is tedious you will have a remedy at hand."

So saying, he put Jennifer on the seat and her hands on the ropes, and the five other girls climbed into the tree, while he took the bough that had become his own. And all provided themselves with apples.

"Begin," said Joscelyn.

"A story-teller," said Martin, "as much as any other craftsman, needs his instruments, of which his auditors are the chief. And of these I lack one." And he fixed his eyes of the weeper in the Well-House.

"You have six already," said Joscelyn. "The seventh you must acquire as you proceed. So begin."

"Without the vital tool?" cried Martin. "As well might you bid Madam Toad to spin flax without her distaff."

"What folly is this?" said Joscelyn. "Toads don't spin."

"Don't they?" said Martin, much astonished. "I thought they did. What then is toadflax? Do the wildflowers not know?"

And still keeping his eyes fixed on Gillian he thrummed and sang—

Toad, toad, old toad,
  What are you spinning?
Seven hanks of yellow flax
  Into snow-white linen.
What will you do with it
  Then, toad, pray?
Make shifts for seven brides
  Against their wedding-day.
Suppose e'er a one of them
  Refuses to be wed?
Then she shall not see the jewel
  I wear in my head.

As he concluded, Gillian raised herself on her two elbows, and with her chin on her palms gazed steadily over the duckpond.

Joscelyn: Why seven?

Martin: Is it not as good a number as another?

Jennifer: What is the jewel like in the toad's head, Master Pippin?

Martin: How can I say, Mistress Jennifer? There's but one way of knowing, according to the song, and like a fool I refused it.

Jennifer: I wish I knew.

Martin: The way lies open to all.

Joscelyn: These are silly legends, Jennifer. It is as little likely that there are jewels in toads' heads as that toads spin flax. But Master Pippin pins his faith to any nonsense.

Martin: True, Mistress Joscelyn. My faith cries for elbow-room, and he who pins his faith to common-sense is like to get a cramp in it. Therefore since women, as I hear tell, have ceased to spin brides' shifts, I am obliged to believe that these things are spun by toads. Because brides there must be though the wells should run dry.

Joscelyn: I do not see the connection. However, it is obvious that the bad logic of your song has aroused even Gillian's attention, so for mercy's sake make short work of your tale before it flags again.

Martin: I will follow your advice. And do you follow me with your best attention while I turn the wheel of The Mill of Dreams.

THE MILL OF DREAMS

There was once, dear maidens, a girl who lived in a mill on the Sidlesham marshes. But in those days the marshlands were meadowlands, with streams running in from the coast, so that their water was brackish and salt. And sometimes the girl dipped her finger in the water and sucked it and tasted the sea. And the taste made storms rise in her heart. Her name was Helen.

The mill-house was a gaunt and gloomy building of stone, as gray as sleep, weatherstained with dreams. It had fine proportions, and looked like a noble prison. And in fact, if a prison is the lockhouse of secrets, it was one. The great millstones ground day and night, and what the world sent in as corn it got back as flour. And as to the secrets of the grinding it asked no questions, because to the world results are everything. It understands death better than sorrow, marriage better than love, and birth better than creation. And the millstones of joy and pain, grinding dreams into bread, it seldom hears. But Helen heard them, and they were all the knowledge she had of life; for if the mill was a prison of dreams it was her prison too.

Her father the miller was a harsh man and dark; he was dark within and without. Her mother was dead; she did not remember her. As she grew up she did little by little the work of the big place. She was her father's servant, and he kept her as close to her work as he kept his millstones to theirs. He was morose, and welcomed no company. Gayety he hated. Helen knew no songs, for she had heard none. From morning till night she worked for her father. When she had done all her other work she spun flax into linen for shirts and gowns, and wool for stockings and vests. If she went outside the mill-house, it was only for a few steps for a few moments. She wasn't two miles from the sea, but she had never seen it. But she tasted the salt water and smelt the salt wind.

Like all things that grow up away from the light, she was pale. Her oval face was like ivory, and her lips, instead of being scarlet, had the tender red of apple-blossom, after the unfolding of the bright bud. Her hair was black and smooth and heavy, and lay on either side of her face like a starling's wings. Her eyes too were as black as midnight, and sometimes like midnight they were deep and sightless. But when she was neither working nor spinning she would steal away to the millstones, and stand there watching and listening. And then there were two stars in the midnight. She came away from those stolen times powdered with flour. Her black hair and her brows and lashes, her old blue gown, her rough hands and fair neck, and her white face—all that was dark and pale in her was merged in a mist, and seen only through the clinging dust of the millstones. She would try to wipe off all the evidences of her secret occasions, but her father generally knew. Had he known by nothing else, he need only have looked at her eyes before they lost their starlight.

One day when she was seventeen years old there was a knock at the mill-house door. Nobody ever knocked. Her father was the only man who came in and went out. The mill stood solitary in those days. The face of the country has since been changed by man and God, but at that time there were no habitations in sight. At regular times the peasants brought their grain and fetched their meal; but the miller kept his daughter away from his custom. He never said why. Doubtless at the back of his mind was the thought of losing what was useful to him. Most parents have their ways of trying to keep their children; in some it is this way, in others that; not many learn to keep them by letting them go.

So when the knock came at the door, it was the strangest thing that had ever happened in Helen's life. She ran to the door and stood with her hand on the heavy wooden bar that fell across it into a great socket. Her heart beat fast. Before we know a thing it is a thousand things. Only one thing would be there when she lifted the bar. But as she stood with her hand upon it, a host of presences hovered on the other side. A knight in armor, a king in his gold crown, a god in the guise of a beggar, an angel with a sword; a dragon even; a woman to be her friend; her mother...a child...

"Would it be better not to open?" thought Helen. For then she would never know. Yes, then she could run to her millstones and fling them her thoughts in the husk, and listen, listen while they ground them into dreams. What knowledge would be better than that? What would she lose by opening the door?

But she had to open the door.

Outside on the stones stood a common lad. He might have been three years older than she. He had a cap with a hole in it in his hand, and a shabby jersey that left his brown neck bare. He was whistling when she lifted the bar, but he stopped as the door fell back, and gave Helen a quick and careless look.

"Can I have a bit of bread?" he asked.

Helen stared at him without answering. She was so unused to people that her mind had to be summoned from a world of ghosts before she could hear and utter real words. The boy waited for her to speak, but, as she did not, shrugged his shoulders and turned away whistling his tune.

Then she understood that he was going, and she ran after him quickly and touched his sleeve. He turned again, expecting her to speak; but she was still dumb.

"Thought better of it?" he said.

Helen said slowly, "Why did you ask me for bread?"

"Why?" He looked her up and down. "To mend my boots with, of course."

She looked at his boots.

"You silly thing," grinned the boy.

A faint color came under her skin. "I'm sorry for being stupid. I suppose you're hungry."

"As a hunter. But there's no call to trouble you. I'll be where I can get bread, and meat too, in forty minutes. Good-by, child."

"No," said Helen. "Please don't go. I'd like to give you some bread."

"Oh, all right," said the boy. "What frightened you? Did you think I was a scamp?"

"I wasn't frightened," said Helen.

"Don't tell me," mocked the boy. "You couldn't get a word out."

"I wasn't frightened."

"You thought I was a bad lot. You don't know I'm not one now."

Helen's eyes filled with tears. She turned away quickly. "I'll get you your bread," she said.

"You are a silly, aren't you?" said the boy as she disappeared.

Before long she came back with half a loaf in one hand, and something in the other which she kept behind her back.

"Thanks," said the boy, taking the bit of loaf. "What else have you got there?"

"It's something better than bread," said Helen slowly.

"Well, let's have a look at it."

She took her hand from behind her, and offered him seven ears of wheat. They were heavy with grain, and bowed on their ripe stems.

"Is this what you call better than bread?" he asked.

"It is better."

"Oh, all right. I sha'n't eat it though—not all at once."

"No," said Helen, "keep it till you're hungry. The grains go quite a long way when you're hungry."

"I'll eat one a year," said the boy, "and then they'll go so far they'll outlast me my lifetime."

"Yes," said Helen, "but the bread will be gone in forty minutes. And then you'll be where you can get meat."

"You funny thing," said the boy, puzzled because she never smiled.

"Where can you get meat?" she asked.

"In a boat, fishing for rabbits."

But she took no notice of the rabbits. She said eagerly, "A boat? are you going in a boat?"

"Yes."

"Are you a sailor?"

"You've hit it."

"You've seen the sea! you've been on the sea!—sailors do that..."

"Oh, dear no," said the boy, "we sail three times round the duckpond and come home for tea."

Helen hung her head. The boy put his hand up to his mouth and watched her over it.

"Well," he said presently, "I must get along to Pagham." He stuck the little sheaf of wheat through the hole in his cap, and it bobbed like a ruddy-gold plume over his ear. Then he felt in his pocket and after some fumbling got hold of what he wanted and pulled it out. "Here you are, child," he said, "and thank you again."

He put his present into her hand and swung off whistling. He turned once to wave to her, and the corn in his cap nodded with its weight and his light gait. She stood gazing till he was out of sight, and then she looked at what he had given her. It was a shell.

She had heard of shells, of course, but she had never seen one. Yet she knew this was no English shell. It was as large as the top of a teacup, but more oval than round. Over its surface, like pearl, rippled waves of sea-green and sea-blue, under a luster that was like golden moonlight on the ocean. She could not define or trace the waves of color; they flowed in and out of each other with interchangeable movement. One half of the outer rim, which was transparently thin and curled like the fantastic edge of a surf wave, was flecked with a faint play of rose and cream and silver, that melted imperceptibly into the moonlit sea. When she turned the shell over she found that she could not see its heart. The blue-green side of the shell curled under like a smooth billow, and then broke into a world of caves, and caves within caves, whose final secret she could not discover. But within and within the color grew deeper and deeper, bottomless blues and unfathomable greens, shot with such gleams of light as made her heart throb, for they were like the gleams that shoot through our dreams, the light that just eludes us when we wake.

She went into the mill, trembling from head to foot. She was not conscious of moving, but she found herself presently standing by the grinding stones, with sound rushing through her and white dust whirling round her. She gazed and gazed into the labyrinth of the shell as though she must see to its very core; but she could not. So she unfastened her blue gown and laid the shell against her young heart. It was for the first time of so many times that I know not whether when, twenty years later, she did it for the last time, they outnumbered the silver hairs among her black ones. And the silver by then were uncountable. Yet on the day when Helen began her twenty years of lonely listening—

(But having said this, Martin Pippin grasped the rope just above Jennifer's hand, and pulled it with such force that the swing, instead of swinging back and forth, as a swing should, reeled sideways so that the swinger had much ado to keep her seat.

Jennifer: Heaven help me!

Martin: Heaven help ME! I need its help more sorely than you do.

Jennifer: Oh, you should be punished, not helped!

Martin: I have been punished, and the punished require help more than censure, or scorn, or anger, or any other form of righteousness.

Jennifer: Who has punished you? And for what?

Martin: You, Mistress Jennifer. For my bad story.

Jennifer: I do not remember doing so. The story is only begun. I am sure it will be a very good story.

Martin: Now you are compassionate, because I need comfort. But the truth is that, good or bad, you care no more for my story. For I saw a tear of vexation come into your eye.

Jennifer: It was not vexation. Not exactly vexation. And doubtless Helen will have experiences which we shall all be glad to hear. But all the same I wish—

Martin: You wish?

Jennifer: That she was not going to grow old in her loneliness. Because all lovers are young.

Martin: You have spoken the most beautiful of all truths. Does the grass grow high enough by the swing for you to pluck me two blades?

Jennifer: I think so. Yes. What do you want with them?

Martin: I want but one of them now. You shall only give me the other if, at the end of my tale, you agree that its lovers are as green as this blade and that.)

On the day (resumed Martin) when Helen began her lonely listening of heart and ears betwixt the seashell and the millstones of her dreams, there was not, dear Mistress Jennifer, a silver thread in her black locks to vex you with. For a girl of seventeen is but a child. Yet old enough to begin spinning the stuff of the spirit...

"My boy!—

"Oh, how strange it was, your coming like that, so suddenly. Before I opened the door I stood there guessing...And how could I have guessed this? Did you guess too on the other side?"

"No, not much. I thought it might be a cross old woman. What did YOU guess?"

"Oh, such stupid things. Kings and knights and even women. And it was you!"

"And it was you!"

"Suppose I'd been a cross old woman?"

"Suppose I'd been a king?"

"And you were just my boy."

"And you—my sulky girl."

"Oh, I wasn't sulky. Oh, didn't you understand? How could I speak to you? I couldn't hear you, I couldn't see you, even!"

"Can you see me now?"

She was lying with her cheek against his heart, and she turned her face suddenly inwards, because she saw him bend his head, and the sweetness of his first kiss was going to be more than she could bear.

"Why don't you look up, you silly child? Why don't you look at me, dear?"

"How can I yet? Can I ever? It's so hard looking in a person's eyes. But I am looking at you, I AM, though you can't see me."

"Then tell me what color my eyes are."

"They're gray-green, and your hair is dark red, a sort of chestnut but a little redder and rough over your forehead, and your nose is all over freckles with very very snub—"

(Martin: Heaven help you, Mistress Jennifer!

Jennifer: W-w-w-why, Master Pippin?

Martin: Were you not about to fall again?

Jennifer: N-n-n-no. I-I-I-I—

Martin: I see you are as firm as a rock. How could I have been so deceived?)

He shook her a little in his arms, saying: "How rude you are to my nose. I wish you'd look up."

"No, not yet...presently. But you, did you look at me?"

"Didn't you see me look?"

"When?"

"As soon as you opened the door."

"What did you see?"

"The loveliest thing I'd ever seen."

"I'm not really—am I?"

"I used to dream about you at night on my watches. I made you up out of bits of the night—white moonlight, black clouds, and stars. Sometimes I would take the last cloud of sunset for your lips. And the wind, when it was gentle, for your voice. And the movements of the sea for your movements, and the rise and fall of it for your breathing, and the lap of it against the boat for your kisses. Oh, child, look up!..."

She looked up....

"What's your name?"

"Helen."

"I can't hear you."

"Helen. Say it."

"I'm trying to."

"I can't hear YOU now. And I want to hear your voice say my name. Oh, my boy, do say it, so that I can remember it when you're away."

"I can't say it, child. Why didn't you tell me your name?"

"What is yours?"

"I'm trying to tell you."

"Please—please!"

"I'm trying with all my might. Listen with all yours."

"I am listening. I can't hear anything. Yet I'm listening so hard that it hurts. I want to say your name over and over and over to myself when you're away. CAN'T you say it louder?"

"No, it's no good."

"Oh, why didn't you tell me, boy?"

"Oh, child, why didn't you tell me?"

"Is my bread sweet to you?"

"The sweetest I ever ate. I ate it slowly, and took each bit from your hand. I kept one crust."

"And my corn."

"Oh, your corn! that is everlasting. You have sown your seed. I have eaten a grain, and it bore its harvest. One by one I shall eat them, and every grain will bear its full harvest. You have replenished the unknown earth with fields of golden corn, and set me walking there for ever."

"And you have thrown golden light upon strange waters, and set me floating there for ever. Oh, you on my earth and I on your ocean, how shall we meet?"

"Your corn is my waters, my waters are your corn. They move on one wave. Oh, child, we are borne on it together, for ever."

"But how you teased me!"

"I couldn't help it."

"You and your boats and your duckponds."

"It was such fun. You were so serious. It was so easy to tease you."

"Why did you put your hand over your mouth?"

"To keep myself from—"

"Laughing at me?"

"Kissing you. You looked so sorry because sailors only sail round duckponds, when you thought they always sailed out by the West and home by the East. You believed the duckponds."

"I didn't really."

"For a moment!"

"I felt so stupid."

"You blushed."

"Oh, did I?"

"A very little. Like the inside of a shell. I'd always tease you to make you blush like that. Don't you ever smile or laugh, child?"

"You might teach me to. I haven't had the sort of life that makes one smile and laugh. Oh, but I could. I could smile and laugh for you if you wished. I could do anything you wanted. I could be anything you wanted."

"Shall I make something of you? What shall it be?"

"I don't care, so long as it is yours. Oh, make something of me. I've been lonely always. I don't want to be any more. I want to be able to come to you when I please, not only because I need so much to come, but because you need me to come. Can you make me sure that you need me? When no one has ever needed you, how can you believe...? Oh, no, no! don't look sorry. I do believe it. And will you always stand with me here in the loneliness that has been so dark? Then it won't be dark any more. Why do two people make light? One alone only wanders and holds out her hand and finds no one— nothing. Sometimes not even herself. Will you be with me always?"

"Always."

"Why?"

"Because I love you."

"No," said Helen, "but because I love you."

"Tell me—WERE you frightened?"

"Of you? when I saw you at the door?"

"Yes. Were you?"

"Oh, my boy."

"But didn't you think I might be a scamp?"

"I didn't think about it at all. It wouldn't have made any difference."

"Then why were you as mum as a fish?"

"Oh, my boy."

"Why? why? why?—if you weren't frightened? Of course you were frightened."

"No, no, I wasn't. I told you I wasn't. Why don't you believe me?— Oh, you're laughing at me again."

"You're blushing again."

"It's so easy to make me ashamed when I've been silly. Of course you know now why I couldn't speak. You know what took my words away. Didn't you know then?"

"How could I know? How could I dream it would be as quick for you as for me?"

"One can dream anything...oh!"

"What is it, child?" For she had caught at her heart.

"Dreams...and not truth. Oh, are you here? Am I? Where are you— where are you? Hold me, hold me fast. Don't let it be just empty dreams."

"Hush, hush, my dear. Dreams aren't empty. Dreams are as near the truth as we can come. What greater truth can you ever have than this? For as men and women dream, they drop one by one the veils between them and the mystery. But when they meet they are shrouded in the veils again, and though they long to strip them off, they cannot. And each sees of each but dimly the truth which in their dreams was as clear as light. Oh, child, it's not our dreams that are our illusions."

"No," she whispered. "But still it is not enough. Not quite enough for the beloved that they shall dream apart and find their truths apart. In life too they must touch, and find the mystery together. Though it be only for one eternal instant. Touch me not only in my dreams, but in life. Turn life itself into the dream at last. Oh, hold me fast, my boy, my boy..."

"Hush, hush, child, I'm holding you..."

"You wept."

"Oh, did you see? I turned my head away."

"Why did you weep?"

"Because you thought I had misjudged you."

"Then I misjudged you."

"But I did not weep for that."

"Would you, if I misjudged you?"

"It would not be so hard to bear."

"And you went away with tears and brought me the corn of your mill."

"And you took it with smiles, and gave me the shell of your seas."

"Your corn rustled through my head."

"Your shell whispers at my heart."

"You shall always hear it whispering there. It will tell you what I can never tell you, or only tell you in other ways."

"Of your life on the sea? Of the countries over the water? Of storms and islands and flashing birds, and strange bright flowers? Of all the lands and life I've never seen, and dream of all wrong? Will it tell me those things?—of your life that I don't know."

"Yes, perhaps. But I could tell you of that life."

"Of what other life will it tell me?"

"Of my life that you do know."

"Is there one?"

"Look in your own heart."

"I am looking."

"And listen."

"Yes."

"What do you hear?"

"Oh, boy, the whispering of your shell!"

"Oh, child, the rustling of your corn!"

Oh, maids! the grinding of the millstones.

This is only a little part of what she heard. But if I told you the whole we should rise from the story gray-headed. For every day she carried her boy's shell to the grinding stones, and stood there while it spoke against her heart. And at other times of the day it lay in her pocket, while she swept and cooked and spun, and she saw shadows of her mill-dreams in the cobwebs and the rising steam, and heard echos of them in her singing kettle and her singing wheel. And at night it lay on her pillow against her ear, and the voice of the waters went through her sleep.

So the years slipped one by one, and she grew from a girl into a young woman; and presently passed out of her youth. But her eyes and her heart were still those of a girl, for life had touched them with nothing but a girl's dream. And it is not time that leaves its traces on the spirit, whatever it may do to the body. Her father meanwhile grew harder and more tyrannical with years. There was little for him to fear now that any man would come to take her from him; but the habit of the oppressor was on him, and of the oppressed on her. And when this has been many years established, it is hard for either to realize that, to escape, the oppressed has only to open the door and go.

Yet Helen, if she had ever thought of escape into another world and life, would not have desired it. For in leaving her millstones she would have lost a world whose boundaries she had never touched, and a life whose sweetness she had never exhausted. And she would have lost her clue to knowledge of him who was to her always the boy in the old jersey who had knocked at her door so many years ago.

Once he was shipwrecked...

...The waters had sucked her under twice already, when her helpless hands hit against some floating substance on the waves. She could not have grasped it by herself, for her strength was gone; but a hand gripped her in the darkness, and dragged her, almost insensible, to safety. For a long while she lay inert across the knees of her rescuer. Consciousness was at its very boundary. She knew that in some dim distance strong hands were chafing a wet and frozen body...but whose hands?...whose body?...Presently it was lifted to the shelter of strong arms; and now she was conscious of her own heart-beats, but it was like a heart beating in air, not in a body. Then warmth and breath began to fall like garments about this bodiless heart, and they were indeed not her own warmth and breath, but these things given to her by another—the warmth was that of his own body where he had laid her cold hands and breast to take what heat there was in him, and the breath was of his own lungs, putting life into hers through their two mouths....She opened her eyes. It was dark. The darkness she had come out of was bright beside this pitchy night, and her struggle back to life less painful than the fierce labor of the wind and waves. Their frail precarious craft was in ceaseless peril. His left arm held her like a vice, but for greater safety he had bound a rope round their two bodies and the small mast of their craft. With his right arm he clasped the mast low down, and his right hand came round to grip her shaking knees. In this close hold she lay a long while without speaking. Then she said faintly:

"Is it my boy?"

"Yes, child. Didn't you know?"

"I wanted to hear you say it. How long have you been in danger?"

"I don't know. Some hours. I thought you would never come to yourself."

"I tried to come to you. I can't swim."

"The sea brought you to me. You were nearly drowned. You slipped me once. If you had again—!"

"What would you have done?"

"Jumped in. I couldn't have stayed on here without you."

"Ah, but you mustn't ever do that—promise, promise! For then you'd lose me for ever. Promise."

"I promise. But there's no for ever of that sort. There's no losing each other, whatever happens. You know that, don't you?"

"Yes, I do know. When people love, they find each other for ever. But I don't want you to die, and I don't want to die—yet. But if it is to-night it will be together. Will it be to-night, do you think?"

"I don't know, dear. The storm's breaking up over there, but that's not the only danger."

"But nothing matters, nothing matters at all while I'm with you." She lay heavily against him; her eyes closed, and she shook violently.

"Child, you're shuddering, you're as cold as ice." He put his hand upon her chilly bosom, and hugged her more fiercely to his own. With a sudden movement of despair and anger at the little he could do, he slipped his arms from his jacket, and stripping open his shirt pulled her to him, re-fastening his jacket around them both, tying it tightly about their bodies by the empty sleeves. She felt his lips on her hair and heard him whisper, "You're not frightened of me, are you, child? You never will be, will you?"

She shook her head and whispered, "I never have been."

"Sleep, if you can, dear."

"I'll try."

So closely was she held by his coat and his arms, so near she lay to his beloved heart, that she knew no longer what part of that union was herself; they were one body, and one spirit. Her shivering grew less, and with her lips pressed to his neck she fell asleep.

It was noon.

The hemisphere of the sky was an unbroken blue washed with a silver glare. She could not look up. The sea was no longer wild, but it was not smooth; it was a dancing sea, and every small wave rippled with crested rainbows. A flight of gulls wheeled and screamed over their heads; their movements were so swift that the mid-air seemed to be filled with visible lines described by their flight, silver lines that gleamed and melted on transparent space like curved lightnings.

"Oh, look! oh, look!" cried Helen.

He smiled, but he was not watching the gulls. "Yes, you've never seen that, have you, child?" His eyes searched the distance.

"But you aren't looking. What are you looking at?"

"Nothing. I can't see what I'm looking for. But the gulls might mean land, or icebergs, or a ship."

"I don't want land or a ship, or even icebergs," said Helen suddenly.

He looked at her with the fleeting look that had been her first impression of him.

"Why not? Why don't you?"

"I'm so happy where I am."

"That's all very well," said her boy, with his eyes on the distance.

For awhile she lay enjoying the warmth of the sun, watching the gulls sliding down the unseen slopes of the air. Presently high up she saw one hover and pause, settling on nothingness by the swift, almost imperceptible beat of its wings. And suddenly it dropped like a stone upon a wave, and darted up again so quickly that she could not follow what had happened.

"What is it doing?" she asked.

"Fishing," said the boy. "It wanted its dinner."

"So do I," said Helen.

He put his hand in his pocket and pulled out a packet wrapped in oilskin. There was biscuit in it. He gave some to her, bit by bit; though it was soft and dull, she was glad of it. But soon she drew away from the hand that fed her.

"What's the matter?" he asked.

"You must have some too."

"That's all right. I'm not greedy like you birds."

"I'm not a bird. And I'm not greedy. Being hungry's not being greedy. I'd be greedy if I ate while you're hungry."

"I'm not hungry."

"Then neither am I."

To satisfy her he ate a biscuit. Soon after she began to feel thirst, but she dared not ask for water. She knew he had none. He looked at her lying pale in his arms, and said with a smile that was not like a real smile, "It's a pity about the icebergs." She smiled and nodded, and lay still in the heat, watching the gulls, and thinking of ice. Some of the birds settled on the raft. One sat on the mast; another hovered at her knee, picking at crumbs. They played in the sun, rising and falling, and turned in her vision into a whirl of snowflakes, enormous snowflakes....She began to dream of snow, and her lips parted in the hope that some might fall upon her tongue. Presently she ceased to dream of snow....The boy looked down at her closed lids, and at her cheeks, as white as the breasts of the gulls. He could not bear to look long, and returned to his distances.

It was night again.

The circle of the sea was as smooth as silk. Pale light played over it like dreams and ghosts. The sky was a crowded arc of stars, millions of stars, she had never seen or imagined so many. They glittered, glittered restlessly, in an ecstasy that caught her spirit. She too was filled with millions of stars, through her senses they flashed and glittered—a delirium of stars in heaven and her heart....

"My boy!"

"Yes, child."

"Do you see the stars?"

"Yes, child."

"Do you feel them?"

"Yes."

"Oh, can't we die now?"

She felt him move stiffly. "There's a ship! I'm certain of it now— I'm certain! Oh, if it were day!"

The stars went on dazzling. She did not understand about the ship. Time moved forward, or stood still. For her the night was timeless. It was eternity.

But things were happening outside in time and space. By what means they had been seen or had attracted attention she did not know. But the floating dreamlight and the shivering starlight on the sea were broken by a dark movement on the waveless waters. A boat was coming. For some time there had been shouting and calling in strange voices, one of them her boy's. But once again she hovered on the dim verge of consciousness. She had flown from the body he was painfully unbinding from his own. What he had suffered in holding it there so long she never knew. From leagues away she heard him whispering, "Child, can you help yourself a little?" And now for an instant her soul re-approached her body, and looked at him through the soft midnight of her eyes, and he saw in them such starlight as never was in sky or on sea.

"Kiss me," said Helen.

He kissed her.

With a great effort she lifted herself and stood upright on the raft, swaying a little and holding by the mast. The boat was still a little distant.

"Good-by, my boy."

"Child—!"

"Don't jump. You promised not to. You promised. But I can't come with you now. You must let me go."

He looked at her, and saw she was in a fever. He made a desperate clutch at her blue gown. But he was not quick enough. "Keep your promise!" she cried, and disappeared in the dreamlit waters; she disappeared like a dream, without a sound. As she sank, she heard him calling her by the only name he knew....

When she was thirty-five her father died. Now she was free to go where she pleased. But she did not go anywhere.

Ever since, as a child, she had first tasted salt water, she had longed to travel and see other lands. What held her now? Was it that her longing had been satisfied? that she had a host of memories of great mountains and golden shores, of jungles and strange cities of the coast, of islands lost in seas of sapphire and emerald? of caravans and towers of ivory? of haunted caverns and deserted temples? where, a child always, with her darling boy, she had had such adventures as would have filled a hundred earthly lives. They had built huts in uninhabited places, or made a twisted bower of strong green creepers, and lived their primitive paradisal life wanting nothing but each other; sometimes, through accidents and illness, they had nursed each other, with such unwearied tenderness that death himself had to withdraw, defeated by love. Once on a ship there had been mutiny, and she alone stood by him against a throng; once savages had captured her, and he, outwitting them, had rescued her, riding through leagues of prairie-land and forest, holding her before him on the saddle. In nearly all these adventures it was as though they had met for the first time, and were struck anew with the dumb wonder of first love, and the strange shy sweetness of wooing and confession. Yet they were but playing above truth. For the knowledge was always between them that they were bound immortally by a love which, having no end, seemed also to have had no beginning. They quarreled sometimes—this was playing too. She put, now herself, now him, in the wrong. And either reconciliation was sweet. But it was she who was oftenest at fault, his forgiveness was so dear to her. And still, this was but playing at it. When all these adventures and pretenses were done, they stood heart to heart, and out of their only meeting in life built up eternal truth and told each other. They told it inexhaustibly.

And so, when her father left her free to go, Helen lived on still in the mill of dreams, and kept her millstones grinding. Two years went by. And her hard gray lonely life laid its hand on her hair and her countenance. Her father had worn her out before her time.

It was only invisible grain in the mill now. The peasants came no longer with their corn. She had enough to live on, and her long seclusion unfitted her for strange men in the mill, and people she must talk to. And so long was the habit of the recluse on her, that though her soul flew leagues her body never wandered more than a few hundred yards from her home. Some who had heard of her, and had glimpses of her, spoke to her when they met; but they could make no headway with this sweet, shy, silent woman. Yet children and boys and girls felt drawn to her. It was the dream in her eyes that stirred the love in their hearts; though they knew it no more than the soup in the pipkin knows why it bubbles and boils. For it cannot see the fire. But to them she did not seem old; her strength and eagerness were still upon her, and that silver needlework with which time broiders all men had in her its special beauty, setting her aloof in the unabandoned dream which the young so often desert as their youth deserts them. Those of her age, seeing that unyouthful gleam of her hair combined with the still-youthful dream of her eyes, felt as though they could not touch her; for no man can break another's web, he can only break his own, and these had torn their films to tatters long ago, and shouldered their way through the smudgy rents, and no more walked where she walked. But very young people knew the places she walked in, and saw her clearly, for they walked there too, though they were growing up and she was growing old.

At the end of the second year there was a storm. It lasted three days without stopping. Such fury of rain and thunder she had never heard. The gaunt rooms of the mill were steeped in gloom, except when lightning stared through the flat windows or split into fierce cracks on the dingy glass. Those three days she spent by candle-light. Outside the world seemed to lie under a dark doom.

On the third morning she woke early. She had had restless nights, but now and then slept heavily; and out of one dull slumber she awakened to the certainty that something strange had happened. The storm had lulled at last. Through her window, set high in the wall, she could see the dead light of a blank gray dawn. She had seen other eyeless mornings on her windowpane; but this was different, the air in her room was different. Something unknown had been taken from or added to it. As she lay there wondering, but not yet willing to discover, the flat light at the window was blocked out. A seagull beat against it with its wings and settled on the sill.

The flutter and the settling of the bird overcame her. It was as though reality were more than she could bear. The birds of memory and pain flew through her heart.

She got up and went to the window. The gull did not move. It was broken and exhausted by the storm. And beyond it she looked down upon the sea.

Yes, it was true. The sea itself washed at the walls of the mill.

She did not understand these gray-green waters. She knew them in vision, not in reality. She cried out sharply and threw the window up. The draggled bird fluttered in and sank on the floor. A sea-wind blew in with it. The bird's wings shivered on her feet, and the wind on her bosom. She stared over the land, swallowed up in the sea. Wreckage of all sorts tossed and floated on it. Fences and broken gates and branches of trees; and fragments of boats and nets and bits of cork; and grass and flowers and seaweed—She thought—what did she think? She thought she must be dreaming.

She felt like one drowning. Where could she find a shore?

She hurried to the bed and got her shell; its touch on her heart was her first safety. In her nightgown as she was she ran with her naked feet through the dim passages until she stood beside the grinding stones....

"Child! child! child!"

"Where are you, my boy, where are you?"

"Aren't you coming? Must I lose you after all this?—Oh, come!"

"But tell me where you are!"

"In a few hours I should have been with you—a few hours after many years."

"Oh, boy, for pity, tell me where to find you!"

"You are there waiting for me, aren't you, child? I know you are— I've always known you were. What would you have said to me when you opened the door in your blue gown?—"

"Oh, but say only where you are, my boy!"

"Do you know what I should have said? I shouldn't have said anything. I should have kissed you—"

"Oh, let me come to you and you shall kiss me...."

But she listened in vain.

She went back to her room. The gull was still on the floor. Its wing was broken. Her actions from this moment were mechanical; she did what she did without will. First she bound the broken wing, and fetched bread and water for the wounded bird. Then she dressed herself and went out of the mill. She had a rope in her hands.

The water was not all around the mill. Strips and stretches of land were still unflooded, or only thinly covered. But the face of the earth had been altered by one of those great inland swoops of the sea that have for centuries changed and re-changed the point of Sussex, advancing, receding, shifting the coast-line, making new shores, restoring old fields, wedding the soil with the sand.

Helen walked where she could. She had no choice of ways. She kept by the edge of the water and went into no-man's land. A bank of rotting grasses and dry reeds, which the waves had left uncovered, rose from the marshes. She mounted it, and beheld the unnatural sea on either hand. Here and there in the desolate water mounds of gray-green grass lifted themselves like drifting islands. Trees stricken or still in leaf reared from the unfamiliar element. Many of those which were leafless had put on a strange greenness, for their boughs dripped with seaweed. Over the floods, which were littered with such flotsam as she had seen from her window, flew sea-birds and land-birds, crying and cheeping. There was no other presence in that desolation except her own.

And then at last her commanded feet stood still, and her will came back to her. For she saw what she had come to find.

He was hanging, as though it had caught him in a snare, in a tree standing solitary in the middle of a wide waste of water. He was hanging there like a dead man. She could distinguish his dark red hair and his blue jersey.

She paused to think what to do. She couldn't swim. She would not have hesitated to try; but she wanted to save him. She looked about, and saw among the bits of stuff washing against the foot of the bank a large dismembered tree-trunk. It bobbed back and forth among the hollow reeds. She thought it would serve her if she had an oar. She went in search of one, and found a broken plank cast up among the tangled growth of the bank. When she had secured it she fastened one end of her rope around the stump of an old pollard squatting on the bank like a sturdy gnome, and the other end she knotted around herself. Then, gathering all the middle of the rope into a coil, and using her plank as a prop, she let herself down the bank and slid shuddering into the water. But she had her tree-trunk now; with some difficulty she scrambled on to it, and paddled her way into the open water.

It was not really a great distance to his tree, but to her it seemed immeasurable. She was unskillful, and her awkwardness often put her into danger. But her will made her do what she otherwise might not have done; presently she was under the branches of the tree.

She pulled herself up to a limb beside him and looked at him. And it was not he.

It was not her boy. It was a man, middle-aged, rough and weatherbeaten, but pallid under his red-and-tan. His hair was grizzled. And his face was rough with a growth of grizzled hair. His whole body lurched heavily and helplessly in a fork of the tree, and one arm hung limp. His eyes were half-shut.

But they were not quite shut. He was not unconscious. And under the drooping lids he was watching her.

For a few minutes they sat gazing at each other in silence. She had her breath to get. She thought it would never come back.

The man spoke first.

"Well, you made a job of it," he said.

She didn't answer.

"But you don't know much about the water, do you?"

"I've never seen the sea till to-day," said Helen slowly.

He laughed a little. "I expect you've seen enough of it to-day. But where do you live, then, that you've never seen the sea? In the middle of the earth?"

"No," said Helen, "I live in a mill."

His eyelids flickered. "Do you? Yes, of course you do. I might have guessed it."

"How should you guess it?"

"By your blue dress," said the man. Then he fainted.

She sat there miserably, waiting, ready to prop him if he fell. She did not know what else to do. Before very long he opened his eyes.

"Did I go off again?" he asked.

She nodded.

"Yes. Well, it's time to be making a move. I dare say I can now you're here. What's your name?"

"Helen."

"Well, Helen, we'd better put that rope to some use. Will that tree at the other end hold?"

"Yes."

"Then just you untie yourself and we'll get aboard and haul ourselves home."

She unfastened the rope from her body, and helped him down to her makeshift boat.

"You take the paddle," he said. "My arm's damaged. But I can pull on the rope with the other."

"Are you sure? Are you all right? What's your name?"

"Yes, I can manage. My name's Peter. This would have been a lark thirty years ago, wouldn't it? It's rather a lark now."

She nodded vaguely, wondering what she would do if he fell off the log in mid-water.

"Suppose you faint again?"

"Don't look for trouble," said the man. "Push off, now."

Pulling and paddling they got to the bank. He took her helping-hand up it, and she saw by his movements that he was very feeble. He leaned on her as they went back to the mill; they walked without speaking.

When they reached the door Peter said, "It's twenty years since I was here, but I expect you don't remember."

"Oh, yes," said Helen, "I remember."

"Do you now?" said Peter. "It's funny you should remember."

And with that he did faint again. And this time when he recovered he was in a fever. His staying-power was gone.

She put him to bed and nursed him. She sat day and night in his room, doing by instinct what was right and needful. At first he lay either unconscious or delirious. She listened to his incoherent speech in a sort of agony, as though it might contain some clue to a riddle; and sat with her passionate eyes brooding on his countenance, as though in that too might lie the answer. But if there was one, neither his words nor his face revealed it. "When he wakes," she whispered to herself, "he'll tell me. How can there be barriers between us any more?"

After three days he came to himself. She was sitting by the window preparing sheep's-wool for her spindle. She bent over her task, using the last of the light, which fell upon her head. She did not know that he was conscious, or had been watching her, until he spoke.

"Your hair used to be quite brown, didn't it?" he said. "Nut-brown."

She started and turned to him, and a faint flush stained her cheeks.

"Ah, you're not pleased," said Peter with a slight grin. "None of us like getting old, do we?"

Helen put by the question. "You're yourself again."

"Doing my best," said he. "How long is it?"

"Three days."

"As much as that? I could have sworn it was only yesterday. Well, time passes."

He said no more, and fell into a doze. Helen was as grateful for this as she could have been for anything just then. She couldn't have gone on talking. She was stunned with misgivings. How could he ever have thought her hair was brown? Couldn't he see even now that it had once been as black as jet? She put her hand up to her head, and unpinned a coil of her heavy hair, and spread it over her breast and looked at it. Yes, the silver was there, too much and too soon. But there was less silver than black. It was still time's stitchery, not his fabric. The man who was not her boy need never have seen her before to know that once her hair had been black. This was worse than forgetfulness in him; it was misremembrance. She pulled at the silver hairs passionately as though she would pluck them out and make him see her as she had been. But soon she stopped her futile effort to uncount the years. "I am foolish," she whispered to herself, and coiled her lock again and bound it in its place. "There are other ways of making him remember. Presently when he wakes again I will talk to him. I will remind him of everything, yes, and I'll tell him everything. I WON'T be afraid." She waited with longing his next consciousness.

But to her woe she found herself defeated. While he slept she was able, as when he had been delirious or absent, to create the occasion and the talk between them. She dropped all fears, and in frank tenderness brought him her twenty years of dreams. And in her thought he accepted and answered them. But when he woke and spoke to her from the bed, she knew at once that the man who lay there was not the man with whom she had been speaking. His personality fenced with hers; it had barriers she could not pass. She dared not try, for dread of his indifference or his smiles.

"What made you stick on in this place?" he asked her.

"I don't know," said Helen. "Places hold one, don't they?"

"None ever held me. I couldn't have been content to stay the best half of my life in one spot. But I suppose women are different."

"You speak as though all women were the same."

"Aren't they? I thought they might be. I don't know much about them," said Peter, rubbing his chin. "Rough as a porcupine, aren't I? You must have thought me a savage when you found me stuck upside-down in that tree like a sloth. What DID you think?"

She looked at him, longing to tell him what she had thought. She longed to tell him of the boy she had expected to find in the tree. She longed to tell him how the finding had shocked her by bringing home to her her loss—not of the boy, but of something in that moment still more precious to her. Because (she longed to tell him) she had so swiftly rediscovered the lost boy, not in his face but in his glance, not in his words but in the tones of his voice.

But when she looked at him and saw him leaning on his elbow waiting for her answer with his half-shut lids and the half-smile on his lips, she answered only, "I was thinking how to get you back to the bank."

"Was that it? Well, you managed it. I've never thanked you, have I?"

"Don't!" said Helen with a quick breath, and looked out of the window.

He waited for a few moments and then said, "I'm a bad hand at thanking. I can't help being a savage, you know. I'm not fit for women's company. I don't look so rough when I'm trimmed."

"I don't want to be thanked," said Helen controlling her voice; and added with a faint smile, "No one looks his best when he's ill."

"Wait till I'm well," grinned Peter, "and see if I'm not fit to walk you out o' Sundays." He lay back on his pillow and whistled a snatch of tune. Her heart almost stopped beating, because it was the tune he had whistled at the door twenty years ago. For a moment she thought she could speak to him as she wished. But desire choked her power to choose her words; so many rushed through her brain that she had to pause, seeking which of them to utter; and that long pause, in which she really seemed to have uttered them all aloud, checked the impulse. But surely he had heard her? No; for she had not spoken yet. And before she could make the effort he had stopped whistling, and when she looked at him to speak, he was fumbling restlessly about his pillow.

"What is it?" she asked.

"Something I had—where's my clothes?"

She brought them to him, and he searched them till he had found among them a small metal box which he thrust under the pillow; and then he lay back, as though too tired to notice her. So her impulse died in her, unacted on.

And during the next four days it was always so. A dozen times in their talks she tried to come near him, and could not. Was it because he would not let her?

or because the thing she wished to find in him was not really there? Sometimes by his manner only, and sometimes by his words, he baffled her when she attempted to approach him—and the attempt had been so painful to conceive, and its still-birth was such agony to her. He would talk frequently of the time when he would be making tracks again.

"Where to?" asked Helen.

"I leave it to chance. I always have. I've never made plans. Or very seldom. And I'm not often twice in the same place. You look tired. I'm sorry to be a bother to you. But it'll be for the last time, most likely. Go and lie down."

"I don't want to," said Helen under her breath. And in her thoughts she was crying, "The last time? Then it must be soon, soon! I'll make you listen to me now!"

"I want to sleep," said Peter.

She left the room. Tears of helplessness and misery filled her eyes. She was almost angry with him, but more angry with herself; but her self-anger was mixed with shame. She was ashamed that he made her feel so much, while he felt nothing. Did he feel nothing?

"It's my stupidity that keeps us apart," she whispered. "I will break through it!" As quickly as she had left him she returned, and stood by the bed. He was lying with his hand pressed over his eyes. When he was conscious of her being there, his hand fell, and his keen eyes shot into hers. His brows contracted.

"You nuisance," he muttered, and hid his eyes again. She turned and left him. When she got outside the door she leaned against it and shook from head to foot. She hovered on the brink of her delusions and felt as though she would soon crash into a precipice. She longed for him to go before she fell. Yes, she began to long for the time when he should go, and end this pain, and leave her to the old strange life that had been so sweet. His living presence killed it.

After that third day she had had no more fears for his safety, and he was strong and rallied quickly. The gull too was saved. He saved it. It had drooped and sickened with her. She did not know what to do with it. On the fourth day as he was so much better, she brought it to him. He reset its wing and kept it by him, making it his patient and his playfellow. It thrived at once and grew tame to his hand. He fondled and talked to it like a lover. She would watch him silently with her smoldering eyes as he fed and caressed the bird, and jabbered to it in scraps of a dozen foreign tongues. His tenderness smote her heart.

"You're not very fond of birds," he said to her once, when she had been sitting in one of her silences while he played with his pet.

The words, question or statement, filled her with anger. She would not trust herself to protest or deny. "I don't know much about them," she said.

"That's a pity," said Peter coolly. "The more you know em the more you have to love em. Yet you could love them for all sorts of things without knowing them, I'd have thought."

She said nothing.

"For their beauty, now. That's worth loving. Look at this one— you're a beauty all right, aren't you, my pretty? Not many girls to match you." He paused, and ran his finger down the bird's throat and breast. "Perhaps you don't think she's beautiful," he said to Helen.

"Yes, she's beautiful," said Helen, with a difficulty that sounded like reluctance.

"Ah, you don't think so. You ought to see her flying. You shall some day. When her hurt's mended she'll fly—I'll let her go."

"Perhaps she won't go," said Helen.

"Oh, yes, she will. How can she stop in a place like this? This is no air for her—she must fly in her own."

"You'll be sorry to see her go," said Helen.

"To see her free? No, not a bit. I want her to fly. Why should I keep her? I'd not let her keep me. I'd hate her for it. Why should I make her hate me?"

"Perhaps she wouldn't," said Helen, in a low voice.

"Oh, I expect she would. Ungrateful little beggar. I've saved her life, and she ought to know she belongs to me. So she might stay out of gratitude. But she'd come to hate me for it, all the same. Not at first; after a bit. Because we change. Bound to, aren't we?"

"Perhaps."

"I know I do. We can none of us stay what we were. You haven't either."

"You haven't much to go by," said Helen.

"Seven minutes at the door, wasn't it? This time it's been seven days."

"Yes."

"It's a long time for me," said Peter.

"It's not much out of a lifetime."

"No. But suppose it were more than seven days?"

Helen looked at him and said slowly, "It will be, won't it? You won't be able to go to-morrow."

"No," said Peter, "not to-morrow, or next day perhaps. Perhaps I won't be able to go for the rest of my life."

This time Helen looked at him and said nothing.

Peter stroked his bird and whistled his tune and stopped abruptly and said, "Will you marry me, Helen?"

"I'd rather die," said Helen.

And she got up and went out of the room.

("Oh, the green grass!" chuckled Martin like a bird.

"Nobody asked her you to begin a song, Master Pippin," quavered Jennifer.

"It was not the beginning of a song, Mistress Jennifer. It was the epilogue of a story."

"But the epilogue comes at the end of a story," said Jennifer.

"And hasn't my story come to its end?" said Martin.

Joscelyn: Ridiculous! oh, dear! there's no bearing with you. How CAN this be the end? How can it be, with him on one side of the door and her on the other?"

Joyce: And her heart's breaking—you must make an end of that.

Jennifer: And you must tell us the end of the shell.

Jessica: And of the millstones.

Jane: What did he have in his box?

"Please," said little Joan, "tell us whether she ever found her boy again—oh, please tell us the end of her dreams."

"Do these things matter?" said Martin. "Hasn't he asked her to marry him?"

"But she said no," said Jennifer with tears in her eyes.

"Did she?" said Martin. "Who said so?"

"Master Pippin," said Joscelyn, and her voice shook with the agitation of her anger, "tell us immediately the things we want to know!"

"When, I wonder," said Martin, "will women cease to want to know little things more than big ones? However, I suppose they must be indulged in little things, lest—"

"Lest?" said little Joan.

"There is such a thing," said Martin, "as playing for safety.")

Well, then, my dear maids, when Helen ran out of his room she went to her own, and she threw herself on the bed and sobbed without weeping. Because everything in her life seemed to have been taken away from her. She lay there for a long time, and when she moved at last her head was so heavy that she took the pins from her hair to relieve herself of its weight. But still the pain weighed on her forehead, which burned on her cold fingers when she pressed them over her eyes, trying to think and find some gleam of hope among her despairing thoughts. And then she remembered that one thing at least was left her—her shell. During his illness she had never carried it to the millstones. It was as though his being there had been the only answer to her daily dreams, an answer that had failed them all the time. But now in spite of him she would try to find the old answers again. So she went once more to the millstones with her shell. And when she got there she held it so tightly to her heart that it marked her skin.

And the millstones had nothing to say. For the first time they refused to grind her corn.

Then Helen knew that she really had nothing left, and that the home-coming of the man had robbed her of her boy and of the child she had been. Nothing was left but the man and woman who had lost their youth. And the man had nothing to give the woman. Nothing but gratitude and disillusion. And now a still bitterer thought came to her—the thought that the boy had had nothing to give the girl. For twenty years it had been the girl's illusion. The storms in her heart broke out. She put her face in her hands and wept like wild rain on the sea. She wept so violently that between her passion and the speechless grinding of the stones she did not hear him coming. She only knew he was there when he put his arm round her.

"What is it, you silly thing?" said Peter.

She looked up at him through her hair that fell like a girl's in soft masses on either side of her face. There was a change in him, but she didn't know then what it was. He had got into his clothes and made himself kempt. His beard was no longer rough, though his hair was still unruly across his forehead, and under it his gray-green eyes looked, half-anxious, half-smiling, into hers. His face was rather pale, and he was a little unsteady in his weakness. But the look in his eyes was the only thing she saw. It unlocked her speech at last.

"Oh, why did you come back?" she cried. "Why did you come back? If you had never come I should have kept my dream to the end of my life. But now even when you go I shall never get it again. You have destroyed what was not there."

He was silent for a moment, still keeping his arm round her. Then he said, "Look what's here." And he opened his hand and showed her his metal box without its lid; in it were the mummies of seven ears of corn. Some were only husks, but some had grain in them still.

She stared at them through her tears, and drew from her breast her hand with the shell in it. Suddenly her mouth quivered and she cried passionately, "What's the use?" And she snatched the old corn from him and flung it to the millstones with her shell. And the millstones ground them to eternal atoms....

"My boy! my boy! it was you over there in the tree!"

"Oh, child, you came at last in your blue gown!"

"Why didn't you call to me?"

"I'd no breath. I was spent. And I knew you'd seen me and would do your best."

"I'll never forget that sight of you in the tree, with your old jersey and your hair as red as ever."

"I shall always see your free young figure standing on the high bank against the sky."

"Oh, I was desperate."

"I wondered what you'd do. I knew you'd do something."

"I thought I'd never get across the water."

"Do you know what I thought as I saw you coming so bravely and so badly? I thought, I'll teach her to swim one day. Shall I, child?"

"I can't swim without you, my boy," she whispered.

"But you pretended not to know me!"

"I couldn't help it, it was such fun."

"How COULD you make fun of me then?"

"I always shall, you know."

"Oh, yes," she said, "do, always."

"What DID you think when you saw me in the tree? What did you see when you got there? Not what you expected."

"No. I saw twenty years come flying upon me, twenty years I'd forgotten all about. Because for me it has always been twenty years ago."

"And you expected to see a boy, and you saw a grizzled man."

"No," said Helen, her eyes shining with tears, "I expected to see a boy, and I saw a gray-haired woman. I've seen her ever since."

"I've only seen her once," said Peter. "I saw her rise up from the water and sit in my tree. And when she spoke and looked at me, it was a child." He put his hand over her wet eyes. "You must stop seeing her, child," he said.

"When I told you my name, were you disappointed?"

"No. It's the loveliest name in the world."

"You said it at once."

"I had to. I'd wanted to say it for twenty years. But I sha'n't say it often, Helen."

"Won't you?"

"No, child."

"Now and then, for a treat?" she looked up at him half-shy, half-merry.

"Oh, you CAN smile, can you?"

"You were to teach me that too."

"Yes, I've a lot to teach you, haven't I?—I've yet to teach you to say my name."

"Have you?"

"You've never said it once."

"I've said it a thousand times."

"You've never let me hear you."

"Haven't I?"

"Let me hear you!"

"Peter."

"Say it again!"

"Peter! Peter! Peter!"

"Again!"

"My boy!"...

"When we got back to the mill-door the last of the twenty years, that had been melting faster and faster, melted away for ever. And you and I were standing there as we'd stood then; and I wanted to kiss your mouth as I'd wanted to then."

"Oh, why didn't you?—both times!"

"Shall I now, for both times?"

"Oh!—oh, that's for a hundred times."

"Think of all the times I've wanted to, and been without you."

"You've never been without me."

"I know that. How often I came to the mill."

"Did you come to the mill?"

"As often as I ate your grain. Didn't you know?"

"I know how often your sea brought me to you."

"Did it?"

"And, oh, my boy! at last the sea brought you to me."

"And the mill," he said. "Where has that brought us?"

"I thought perhaps you'd die."

"I couldn't have died so close on finding you. I was fighting the demons all the time—fighting my way through to you. And at last I opened my eyes and saw you again, your black hair edged with light against the window."

"My black hair? you mean my brown hair, don't you?"

"Oh, weren't you cross! I loved you for being cross."

"I wasn't cross. Why will you keep on saying I'm things I'm not?"

"You were so cross that you pretended our twenty years were sixty."

"I never said anything about twenty years, OR sixty."

"You did, though. Sixty! why, in sixty years we'd have been very nearly old. So to punish you I pretended to go to sleep, and I saw you take your hair down. It was so beautiful. You've seen the threads spiders spin on blackened furze that gypsies have set fire to? Your hair was like that. You were angry with those lovely lines of silver, and you wanted to get rid of them. I nearly called to you to stop hurting what I loved so much, but you stopped of yourself, as though you had heard me before I called."

"I was ashamed of myself," whispered Helen. "I was ashamed of trying to be again what I was the only other time you saw me."

"You've never stopped being that, child," said Peter.

"You knew, didn't you, why it was I had stayed on at the mill? You knew what it was that held me, and why I could never leave it?"

"Yes, I knew. It held you because it held me too. I wondered if you'd tell me that."

"I longed to, but I couldn't. I've never been able to tell you things. And I never shall."

"Oh, child, don't look so troubled. You've always told me things and always will. Do you think it's with our tongues we tell each other things? What can words ever tell? They only circle round the truth like birds flying in the sun. The light bathes their flight, yet they are millions of miles away from the light they fly in. We listen to each other's words, but we watch each other's eyes."

"Some people half-shut their eyes, Peter."

"Some people, Helen, can't shut their eyes at all. Your eyes will never stop telling me things. And the strangest thing about them is that looking into them is like being able to see in the dark. They are darkness, not light. And in darkness dreams are born. When I look into your eyes I go into your dream."

"I shall never shut my eyes again," she whispered. "I will keep you in my dream for ever."

"Women aren't all the same, Peter."

"Aren't they?"

"And yet—they are."

"Well, I give it up."

"Didn't you know?"

"No. I told you the truth that time. I've not had very much to do with women."

"Then I've something to teach you, Peter."

"I don't know what you can prove," said Peter. "One woman by herself can't prove a difference."

"Can't she?" said Helen; and laughed and cried at once.

"But why did you call me a nuisance?"

"You were one—you are one. You leave a man no peace—you're like the sea. You're full of storms, aren't you?"

"Not only storms."

"I know. But the sea wouldn't be the sea without her storms. They're one of her ways of holding us, too. And there are more storms in her than ever break. I see them in you, big ones and little ones, brooding. Then you're a—nuisance. You always will be, won't you?"

"Not to wreck you."

"You won't do that. Or if you do—I can survive shipwreck."

"I know."

"How do you know? I nearly gave up once, but the thought of you stopped me. I wanted to come back—I'd always meant to. So I held on."

"I know."

"How do you know? I never told you, did I?"

"Oh, Peter, the things we have to tell each other. The times you thought you were alone—the times I thought I was! You've had a life you never dreamed of—and I another life that was not in my dreams."

"You've saved me from death more than once," said Peter.

"You've done more than that," said Helen, "you've given me the only life I've had. But a thing doesn't belong to you because you've saved its life or given it life. It only belongs to you because you love it. I know you belong to me. But you only know if I belong to you."

"That's not true now. You do know. And I know."

"Yes; and we know that as that belonging has nothing to do with death, it can't have anything either to do with the saving or even the giving of life. So you must never thank me, or I you. There are no thanks in love. And that was why I couldn't bear your asking me to marry you to-day. I thought you were thanking me."

"When you played with the seagull..."

"Yes?"

"How you loved it!"

"Yes."

"I looked to see how you felt when you loved a thing. I wanted so much to be the seagull in your hands."

"When I touched it I was touching you."

She put his hand to her breast and whispered, "I love birds."

He smiled. "I knew you loved them; and best free. All birds must fly in their own air."

"Yes," she said. "But their freedom only means their power to choose what air they'll fly in. And every choice is a cage too."

"I shall leave the door open, child."

"I shall never fly out," said Helen.

"You talked of going away."

"Yes. But not from you."

"Am I to go with you always, following chance and making no plans?"

"Will you? You are the only plan I ever made. Will you leave everything else but me to chance? Perhaps it will lead us all over the earth; and perhaps after all we shall not go very far. But I never could see ahead, except one thing."

"What was it?"

"The mill-door and you in your old blue gown. And for seven days I've stopped seeing that. I haven't it to steer by. Will you chance it?"

"Must you be playing with meanings even in dreams? Don't you know—don't you know that for a woman who loves, and is not sure that she is loved, her days and nights are all chances, every minute she lives is a chance? It might be...it might not be...oh, those ghosts of joy and pain! they are almost too much to bear. For the joy isn't pure joy, or the pain pure pain, and she cannot come to rest in either of them. Sometimes the joy is nearly as great as though she knew; yet at the instant she tries to take it, it looks at her with the eyes of doubt, and she trembles, and dare not take it yet. And sometimes the pain is all but the death she foresees; yet even as she submits to it, it lays upon her heart the finger of hope. And then she trembles again, because she need not take it yet. Those are her chances, Peter. But when she knows that her beloved is her lover, life may do what it will with her; but she is beyond its chances for ever."

"Your corn! you kept my corn!"

"Till it should bear. And your shell there—you've kept my shell."

"Till it should speak. And now—oh, see these things that have held our dreams for twenty years! The life is threshed from them for ever—they are only husks. They can hold our dreams no more. Oh, I can't go on dreaming by myself, I can't, it's no use. I thought my heart had learned to bear its dream alone, but the time comes when love in its beauty is too near to pain. There is more love than the single heart can bear. Good-by, my boy—good-by!"

"Helen! don't suffer so! oh, child, what are you doing?—"

"Letting my dear dreams go...it's no use, Peter..."

The millstones took them and crushed them.

She uttered a sharp cry....

His arm tightened round her. "What is it, child?" she heard him say.

She looked at him bewildered, and saw that he too was dazed. She looked into the gray-green eyes of a boy of twenty. She said in a voice of wonder, "Oh, my boy!" as he felt her soft hair.

"Such a fuss about an empty shell and a bit of dead wheat."

She hid her face on his jersey.

"You are a silly, aren't you?" said Peter. "I wish you'd look up."

Helen looked up, and they kissed each other for the first time.

I defy you now, Mistress Jennifer, to prove that your grassblade is greener than mine.

THIRD INTERLUDE

The girls now turned their attention to their neglected apples, varying this more serious business with comments on the story that had just been related.

Jessica: I should be glad to know, Jane, what you make of this matter.

Jane: Indeed, Jessica, it is difficult to make anything at all of matter so bewildering. For who could have divined reality to be the illusion and dreams the truth? so that by the light of their dreams the lovers in this tale mistook each other for that which they were not.

Martin: Who indeed, Mistress Jane, save students of human nature like yourselves?—who have doubtless long ago observed how men and women begin by filling a dim dream with a golden thing, such as youth, and end by putting a shining dream into a gray thing, such as age. And in the end it is all one, and lovers will see to the last in each other that which they loved at the first, since things are only what we dream them to be, as you have of course also observed.

Joscelyn: We have observed nothing of the sort, and if we dreamed at all we would dream of things exactly as they are, and never dream of mistaking age for youth. But we do not dream. Women are not given to dreams.

Martin: They are the fortunate sex. Men are such incurable dreamers that they even dream women to be worse preys of the delusive habit than themselves. But I trust you found my story sufficiently wide-awake to keep you so.

Joscelyn: It did not make me yawn. Is this mill still to be found on the Sidlesham marshes?

Martin: It is where it was. But what sort of gold it grinds now, whether corn or dreams, or nothing, I cannot say. Yet such is the power of what has been that I think, were the stones set in motion, any right listener might hear what Helen and Peter once heard, and even more; for they would hear the tale of those lovers' journeys over the changing waters, and their return time and again to the unchanging plot of earth that kept their secrets. Until in the end they were together delivered up to the millstones which thresh the immortal grain from its mortal husk. But this was after long years of gladness and a life kept young by the child which each was always re-discovering in the other's heart.

Jennifer: Oh, I am glad they were glad. Do you know, I had begun to think they would not be.

Jessica: It was exactly so with me. For suppose Peter had never returned, or when he did she had found him dead in the tree?

Jane: And even after he returned and recovered, how nearly they were removed from ever understanding each other!

Joan: Oh, no, Jane! once they came together there could be no doubt of the understanding. As soon as Peter came back, I felt sure it would be all right.

Joyce: And I too, all along, was convinced the tale must end happily.

Martin: Strange! so was I. For Love, in his daily labors, is as swift in averting the nature of perils as he is deft in diverting the causes of misunderstanding. I know in fact of but one thing that would have foiled him.

Four of the Milkmaids: What then?

Martin: Had Helen not been given to dreams.

Not a word was said in the Apple-Orchard.

Joscelyn: It would have done her no harm had she not been, singer. Nor would your story have suffered, being, like all stories, a thing as important as thistledown. In either event, though Peter had perished, or misunderstood her for ever, it would not have concerned me a whit. Or even in both events.

Jessica: Nor me.

Jane: Nor me.

Martin: Then farewell my story. A thing as important as thistledown is as unimportantly dismissed. And yonder in heaven the moon sulks at us through a cloud with a quarter of her eye, reproaching us for our peace-destroying chatter. It destroys our own no less than hers. To dream is forbidden, but at least let us sleep.

One by one the milkmaids settled in the grass and covered their faces with their hands, and went to sleep. But Jennifer remained where she was. She sat with downcast eyes, softly drawing the grassblade through and through her fingers, and the swing swayed a little like a branch moving in an imperceptible wind, and her breast heaved a little as though stirred with inaudible sighs. She sat so long like that that Martin knew she had forgotten he was beside her, and he quietly put out his hand to draw the grassblade from hers. But before he had even touched it he felt something fall upon his palm that was not rain or dew.

"Dear Mistress Jennifer," said Martin gently, "why do you weep?"

She shook her head, since there are times when the voice plays a girl false, and will not serve her.

"Is it," said Martin, "because the grass is not green enough?"

She nodded.

"Pray let me judge," entreated Martin, and took the grassblade from her fingers. Whereupon she put her face into her two hands, whispering:

"Master Pippin, Master Pippin, oh, Master Pippin."

"Let me judge," said Martin again, but in a whisper too.

Then Jennifer took her hands from her wet face, and looked at him with her wet eyes, and said with great braveness and much faltering:

"I will be nineteen in November."

At this Martin looked very grave, and he got down from the tree and walked to the end of the orchard full of thought. But when he turned there he found that she had stolen after him, and was standing near him hanging her head, yet watching him with deep anxiety.

Jennifer: It is t-t-too old, isn't it?

Martin: Too old for what?

Jennifer: I—I—I don't know.

Martin: It is, of course, extremely old. There are things you will never be able to do again, because you are so old.

Jennifer sobbed.

Martin: You are too old to be rocked in a cradle. You are too old to write pothooks and hangers, and too old, alas, to steal pickles and jam when the house is abed. Yet there are still a few things you might do if—

Jennifer: Oh, if?

Martin: If you could find a friend as old as yourself, or even a little older, to help you.

Jennifer: But think how old h—h—h— the friend would have to be.

Martin: What would that matter? For all grass is green enough if it not near grass that looks greener.

Jennifer: Oh, is this true?

Martin: It is indeed. And I believe too that were your friend's hair red enough, and your friend's freckled nose snub enough, since youth resides long in these qualities, you might even, with such a companion, begin once more to steal pickles and jam by night, to learn your pothooks and hangers, and even in time to be rocked asleep by a cradle.

Jennifer: D-d-dear Master Pippin.

Martin: They look quite green, don't they?

And he laid the two blades side by side on her palm, and Jennifer, whose voice once more would not serve her, nodded and put the two blades in her pocket. Then Martin took out his handkerchief and very carefully dried her eyes and cheeks, saying as he did so, "Now that I have explained this to your satisfaction, won't you, please, explain something to mine?"

Jennifer: I will if I can.

Martin: Then explain what it is you have against men.

Jennifer: I don't know how to tell you, it is so terrible.

Martin: I will try to bear it.

Jennifer: They say women cannot—cannot—

Martin: Cannot?

Jennifer: Keep secrets!

Martin: Men say so?

Jennifer: Yes!

Martin: MEN say so?

Jennifer: They do, they do!

Martin: Men! Oh, Jupiter! if this were true—but it is not—these men would be blabbing the greatest of secrets in saying so. If I had a secret—but I have not—do you think I would trust it to a man? Not I! What does a man do with a secret? Forgets it, throws it behind him into some empty chamber of his brain and lets the cobwebs smother it! buries it in some deserted corner of his heart, and lets the weeds grow over it! Is this keeping a secret? Would you keep a garden or a baby so? I will a thousand times sooner give my secret to a woman. She will tend it and cherish it, laugh and cry with it, dress it in a new dress every day and dandle it in the world's eye for joy and pride in it—nay, she will bid the whole world come into her nursery to admire the pretty secret she keeps so well. And under her charge a little secret will grow into a big one, with a hundred charms and additions it had not when I confided it to her, so that I shall hardly know it again when I ask for it: so beautiful, so important, so mysterious will it have become in the woman's care. Oh, believe me, Mistress Jennifer, it is women who keep secrets and men who neglect them.

Jennifer: If I had only thought of these things to say! But I am not clever at argument like men.

Martin: I suspect these clever arguers. They can always find the right thing to say, even if they are in the wrong. Women are not to be blamed for washing their hands of them for ever.

Jennifer: I know. Yet I cannot help wondering who bakes them gingerbread for Sunday.

Martin: Let them go without. They do not deserve gingerbread.

Jennifer: I know, I know. But they like it so much. And it is nice making it, too.

Martin: Then I suppose it will have to be made till the last of Sundays. What a bother it all is.

Jennifer: I know. Good night, dear Master Pippin.

Martin: Dear milkmaid, good night. There lie your fellows, careless of the color of the grass they lie on, and of the years that lie on them. They have forsworn the baking of cakes, the eating of which begets dreams, to which women are not given. Go lie with them, and be if you can as careless and dreamless as they are.

And then, seeing the tears refilling her eyes, he hastily pulled out his handkerchief again and wiped them as they fell, saying, "But if you cannot—if you cannot (don't cry so fast!)—if you cannot, then give me your key (dear Jennifer, please dry up!) to Gillian's Well-House, because you were glad that my tale ended gladly, and also because all lovers, no matter of what age, are green enough, and chiefly because my handkerchief's sopping."

Then Jennifer caught his hands in hers and whispered, "Oh, Martin! are they? ALL lovers?—are they green enough?"

"God help them, yes!" said Martin Pippin.

She dropped his hands, leaving her key in them, and looked up at him with wet lashes, but happiness behind them. So he stooped and kissed the last tears from her eyes. Since his handkerchief had become quite useless for the purpose.

And she stole back to her place, and he lay down in his, and Jennifer dreamed that she was baking gingerbread, and Martin that he was eating it.

"Maids! maids! maids!"

It was Old Gillman on the heels of dawn.

"A pest on him and all farmers," groaned Martin, "who would harvest men's slumbers as soon as they're sown."

"Get into hiding!" commanded Joscelyn.

"I will not budge," said Martin. "I am going to sleep again. For at that moment I had a lion in one hand and a unicorn in the other—"

"WILL you conceal yourself!" whispered Joscelyn, with as much fury as a whisper can compass.

"And the lion had comfits in his crown, and the unicorn a gilded horn. And both were so sticky and spicy and sweet—"

Joscelyn flung herself upon her knees before him, spreading her yellow skirts which barely concealed him, as Old Gillman thrust his head through the hawthorn gap.

"Good morrow, maids," he grunted.

"—that I knew not, dear Mistress Joscelyn," murmured Martin, "which to bite first."

"Good morrow, master!" cried the milkmaids loudly; and they fluttered their petticoats like sunshine between the man at the hedge and the man in the grass.

"Is my daughter any merrier this morning?"

"No, master," said Jennifer, "yet I think I see smiles on their way."

"If they lag much longer," muttered the farmer, "they'll be on the wrong side of her mouth when they do come. For what sort of a home will she return to?—a pothouse! and what sort of a father?—a drunkard! And the fault's hers that deprives him of the drink he loved in his sober days. Gillian!" he exclaimed, "when will ye give up this child's whim to learn by experience, and take an old man's word for it?"

But Gillian was as deaf to him as to the cock crowing in the barnyard.

"Come fetch your portion," said Old Gillman to the milkmaids, "since there's no help for it. And good day to ye, and a better morrow."

"Wait a bit, master!" entreated Jennifer, "and tell me if Daisy, my Lincoln Red, lacks for anything."

"For nothing that Tom can help her to, maid. But she lacks you, and lacking you, her milk. So that being a cow she may be said to lack everything. And so do I, and the men, and the farm—ruin's our portion, nothing but rack and ruin."

Saying which he departed.

"To breakfast," said Martin cheerfully.

"Suppose you'd been seen," scolded Joscelyn.

"Then our tales would have been at an end," said Martin. "Would this have distressed you?"

"The sooner they're ended the better," said Joscelyn, "if you can do nothing but babble of sticky unicorns."

"It was fresh from the oven," explained Martin meekly. "I wish we could have gingerbread for breakfast instead of bread."

"Do not be sure," said Joscelyn severely, "that you will get even bread."

"I am in your hands," said Martin, "but please be kinder to the ducks."

Joscelyn, all of a fluster, then put new bread in the place of Gillian's old; but her annoyance was turned to pleasure when she discovered that the little round top of yesterday's loaf had entirely disappeared.

"Upon my word!" cried she, "the cure is taking effect."

"I believe you are right," said Martin. "How sorry the ducks will be."

They quickly fed the ducks, and then themselves; and Martin received his usual share, Joscelyn having so far relented that she even advised him as to the best tree for apples in the whole orchard.

After breakfast Martin found six pair of eyes fixed so earnestly upon him that he began to laugh.

"Why do you laugh?" asked little Joan.

"Because of my thoughts," said he. So she took a new penny from her pocket and gave it to him.

"I was thinking," said Martin, "how strange it is that girls are all so exactly alike."

"Oh!" cried six different voices in a single key of indignation.

"What a fib!" said Joyce. "I am like nobody but me."

"Nor am !" cried all the others in a breath.

"Yet a moment ago," said Martin, "you, Mistress Joyce, were wondering with all your might what diversion I had hit upon for this morning. And so were Jane and Jessica and Jennifer and Joan and Joscelyn."

"I was NOT!" cried six voices at once.

"What, none of you?" said Martin. "Did I not say so?"

And they were very provoked, not knowing what to answer for fear it might be on the tip of her neighbor's tongue. So they said nothing at all, and with one accord tossed their heads and turned their backs on him. And Martin laughed, leaving them to guess why. On which, greatly put out, every girl without even consulting one another they decided to have nothing further to do with him, and each girl went and sat under a different apple-tree and began to do her hair.

"Heigho!" said Martin. "Then this morning I must divert myself." And he began to spin his golden penny in the sun, sometimes spinning it very dexterously from his elbow and never letting it fall. But the girls wouldn't look, or if they did, it was through stray bits of their hair; when they could not be suspected of looking.

"I shall certainly lose this penny," communed Martin with himself, quite audibly, "if somebody does not lend me a purse to keep it in." But nobody offered him one, so he plucked a blade of Shepherd's Purse from the grass, soliloquizing, "Now had I been a shepherd, or had the shepherd's name been Martin, here was my purse to my hand. And then, having saved my riches I might have got married. Yet I never was a shepherd, nor ever knew a shepherd of my name; and a penny is in any case a great deal too much money for a man to marry on, be he a shepherd or no. For it is always best to marry on next-to-nothing, from which a penny is three times removed."

Then he went on spinning his penny in the air again, humming to himself a song of no value, which, so far as the girls could tell for the hair over their ears, went as follows:

If I should be so lucky
As a farthing for to find.
I wouldn't spend the farthing
According to my mind,
But I'd beat it and I'd bend it
And I'd break it into two,
And give one half to a Shepherd
And the other half to you.
And as for both your fortunes,
I'd wish you nothing worse
Than that YOUR half and HIS half
Should lie in the Shepherd's Purse.

At the end of the song he spun the penny so high that it fell into the Well-House; and endeavoring to catch it he flung the spire of wild-flower after it, and so lost both. And nobody took the least notice of his song or his loss.

Then Martin said, "Who cares?" and took a new clay pipe and a little packet from his pocket; and he wandered about the orchard till he had found an old tin pannikin, and he scooped up some water from the duckpond and made a lather in it with the soap in the packet, and sat on the gate and blew bubbles. The first bubble in the pipe was always crystal, and sometimes had a jewel hanging from it which made it fall to the earth; and the second was tinged with color, and the third gleamed like sunset, or like peacocks' wings, or rainbows, or opals. All the colors of earth and heaven chased each other on their surfaces in all the swift and changing shapes that tobacco smoke plays at on the air; but of all their colors they take the deepest glow of one or two, and now Martin would blow a world of flame and orange through the trees, or one of blue and gold, or another of green and rose. And, as he might have watched his dreams, he watched the bubbles float away; and break. But one of the loveliest at last sailed over the Well-House and between the ropes of the swing and among the fruit-laden boughs, miraculously escaping all perils; and over the hedge, where a small wind bore it up and up out of sight. And Martin, who had been looking after it with a rapt gaze, sighed, "Oh!" And six other "Ohs!" echoed his. Then he looked up and saw the six milkmaids standing quite close to him, full of hesitation and longing. So he took six more pipes from his pockets, and soon the air was glistening with bubbles, big and little. Sometimes they blew the bubbles very quickly, shaking the tiny globes as fast as they could from the bowl, till the air was filled with a treasure of opals and diamonds and moonstones and pearls, as though the king of the east had emptied his casket there. And sometimes they blew steadily and with care, endeavoring to create the best and biggest bubble of all; but generally they blew an instant too long, and the bubble burst before it left the pipe. Whenever a great sphere was launched the blower cried in ecstasy, "Oh, look at mine!" and her comrades, merely glancing, cried in equal ecstasy, "Yes, but see mine!" And each had a moment's delight in the others' bubbles, but everlasting joy in her own, and was secretly certain that of all the bubbles hers were the biggest and brightest. The biggest and brightest of all was really blown by little Joan: as Martin, in a whisper, assured her. He whispered the same thing, however, to each of her friends, and for one truth told five lies. Sometimes they played together, taking their bubbles delicately from one pipe to another, and sometimes blew their bubbles side by side till they united, and made their venture into the world like man and wife. And often they put all their pipes at once into the pannikin, and blew in the water, rearing a great palace of crystal hemispheres, that rose until it hit their chins and cheeks and the tips of their noses, and broke on them, leaving on their fair skin a trace of glistening foam. And as the six laughing faces bent over the pannikin on his knees, Martin observed that Joscelyn's hair was coiled like two great lovely roses over her ears, and that Joyce's was in clusters of ringlets, and that Jane's was folded close and smooth and shining round her small head, and that Jessica's was tucked under like a boy's, while Jennifer's lay in a soft knot on her neck. But little Joan's was hanging still in its plaits over her shoulders, and one thick plait was half undone, and the loose hair got in her own and everybody's way, and was such a nuisance that Martin was obliged at last to gather it in his hand and hold it aside for the sake of the bubble-blowers. And when they lifted their heads he was looking at them so gravely that Joyce laughed, and Jessica's eyes were a question, and Jane looked demure, and Jennifer astonished, and Joscelyn extremely composed and indifferent. And little Joan blushed. To cover her blushing she offered him another penny.

"I was thinking," said Martin, "how strange it is that girls are so absolutely different."

Then six demure shadows appeared at the very corners of their mouths, and they rose from their knees and said with one accord, "It must be dinner-time." And it was.

"Bread is a good thing," said Martin, twirling a buttercup as he swallowed his last crumb, "but I also like butter. Do not you, Mistress Joscelyn?"

"It depends on who makes it," said she. "There is butter and butter."

"I believe," said Martin, "that you do not like butter at all."

"I do not like other people's butter," said Joscelyn.

"Let us be sure," said Martin. And he twirled his buttercup under her chin. "Fie, Mistress Joscelyn!" he cried. "What a golden chin! I never saw any one so fond of butter in all my days."

"Is it very gold?" asked Joscelyn, and ran to the duckpond to look, but couldn't see because she was on the wrong side of the gate.

"Do I like butter?" cried Jessica.

"Do I?" cried Jennifer.

"Do I?" cried Joyce.

"Do I?" cried Jane.

"Oh, do I?" cried Joan.

"We'll soon find out," said Martin, and put buttercups under all their chins, turn by turn. And they all liked butter exceedingly.

"Do YOU like butter, Master Pippin?" asked little Joan.

"Try me," said he.

And six buttercups were simultaneously presented to his chin, and it was discovered that he liked butter the best of them all.

Then every girl had to prove it on every other girl, and again on Martin one at a time, and he on them again. And in this delicious pastime the afternoon wore by, and evening fell, and they came golden-chinned to dinner.

Supper was scarcely ended—indeed, her mouth was still full—when Jessica, looking straight at Martin, said, "I'm dying to swing."

"I never saved a lady's life easier," said Martin; and in one moment she found herself where she wished to be, and in the next saw him close beside her on the apple-bough. The five other girls went to their own branches as naturally as hens to the roost. Joscelyn inspected them like a captain marshalling his men, and when each was armed with an apple she said:

"We are ready now, Master Pippin."

"I wish I were too," said he, "but my tale has taken a fit of the shivers on the threshold, like an unexpected guest who doubts his welcome."

"Are we not all bidding it in?" said Joscelyn impatiently.

"Yes, like sweet daughters of the house," said Martin. "But what of the mistress?" And he looked across at Gillian by the well, but she looked only into the grass and her thoughts.

"Let the daughters do to begin with," said Joscelyn, "and make it your business to stay till the mistress shall appear."

"That might be to outstay my welcome," said Martin, "and then her appearance would be my discomfiture. For a hostess has, according to her guests, as many kinds of face as a wildflower, according to its counties, names."

"Some kinds have only one name," said Jessica, plucking a stalk crowned with flowers as fine as spray. "What would you call this but Cow Parsley?"

"If I were in Anglia," said Martin, "I would call it Queen's Lace."

"That's a pretty name," said Jessica.

"Pretty enough to sing about," said Martin; and looking carelessly at the Well-House he thrummed his lute and sang—

The Queen netted lace
On the first April day,
The Queen wore her lace
In the first week of May,
The Queen soiled her lace
Ere May was out again,
So the Queen washed her lace
In the first June rain.
The Queen bleached her lace
On the first of July,
She spread it in the orchard
And left it there to dry,
But on the first of August

It wasn't in its place
Because my sweetheart picked it up
And hung it o'er her face.
She laughed at me, she blushed at me,
With such a pretty grace
That I kissed her in September
Through the Queen's own lace.

At the end of the song Gillian sat up in the grass, and looked with all her heart over the duckpond.

Joscelyn: I find your songs singularly lacking in point, singer.

Martin: You surprise me, Mistress Joscelyn. The kiss was the point.

Joscelyn: It is like you to think so. It is just like you to think a—a—a—

Martin: —kiss—

Joscelyn: Sufficient conclusion to any circumstances.

Martin: Isn't it?

Joscelyn: My goodness! You might as soon ask, is a peardrop sufficient for a body's dinner.

Martin: It would suffice me. I love peardrops. But then I am a man. Women doubtless need more substance, being in themselves more insubstantial. Now as to your quarrel with my song—

Joscelyn: It is of no consequence. You raise expectations which you do not fulfill. But it is not of the least consequence.

Martin: Dear Mistress Joscelyn, my only desire is to please you. We will not conclude on a kiss. You shall fulfill your own expectations.

Joscelyn: Mine?—I have no expectations whatever.

Martin: But I have disappointed you. What shall I do with my sweetheart? Shall she be whipped for her theft? Shall she be shut in a dungeon? Shall she be thrown before elephants? Choose your conclusion.

Joan: But, Master Pippin!—why must the poor sweetheart be punished? I am sure Joscelyn never wished her to be punished. There are other conclusions.

Martin: Dunderhead that I am, I can't think of any! What, Mistress Joscelyn, was the conclusion you expected?

Joscelyn: I tell you, I expected none!

Joan: Why, Master Pippin! I should have fancied that, seeing the dear sweetheart had hung the veil over her face, she might—

Martin: Yes?

Joan: Be expected—

Martin: Yes!

Joan: To be about to be—

Joscelyn: I am sick to death of this silly sweetheart. And since our mistress appears to be listening with both her ears, it would be more to the point to begin whatever story you propose to relate to-night, and be done with it.

Martin: You are always right. Therefore add your ears to hers, while I tell you the tale of Open Winkins.

OPEN WINKINS

There were once, dear maidens, five lords in the east of Sussex, who owned between them a single Burgh; for they were brothers. Their names were Lionel and Hugh and Heriot and Ambrose and Hobb. Lionel was ten years of age and Hobb was twenty-two, there being exactly three years all but a month between the birthdays of the brothers. And Lionel had a merry spirit, and Hugh great courage and daring, and Heriot had beauty past any man's share, and Ambrose had a wise mind; but Hobb had nothing at all for the world's praise, for he only had a loving heart, which he spent upon his brothers and his garden. And since love begets love, they all loved him dearly, and leaned heavily on his affection, though neither they nor any man looked up to him because he was a lord. Although he was the eldest, and in his quiet way administered the affairs of the Burgh and of the people of Alfriston under the Burgh, it was Ambrose who was always thinking of new schemes for improvement, and Heriot who undertook the festivities. As for the younger boys, they kept the old place alive with their youth and spirits; and it was evident that later on Hugh would win honor to the Burgh in battle and adventure, and Lionel would draw the world thither with his charm. But Hobb, to whom they all brought their shapeless dreams white-hot, since sympathy helps us to create bodies for the things which begin their existence as souls—Hobb differed from the four others not only in his name, but in his plain appearance and simple tastes. And all these things, as well as his tender heart, he got from his mother, who was the only daughter of a gardener of Alfriston. The gardener, to whom she was the very apple of his eye, had kept her privately in a place on a hill, fearing lest in her youth and inexperience she should fall to the lot of some man not worthy of her; for her knew, or believed, that a young girl of her sweetness and tenderness and devotedness of disposition would by her sweetness attract a lover too early, and by her tenderness respond to him too readily, and by her devotedness follow him too blindly, before she had time to know herself or men. And he also knew, or believed, that first love is as often a will-o'-the-wisp as the star for which all young things take it. Five days in the week he tended the gardens of Alfriston, the sixth he gave to the Lord of the Burgh that lay among the hills, and the seventh he kept for his daughter on the hill a few miles distant, which was afterwards known as Hobb's Hawth. She on her part spent her week in endeavoring to grow a perfect rose of a certain golden species, and her heart was given wholly to her father and her flower. And he watched her efforts with interest and advice, and for the first she thanked him but of the second took no heed. "For," said she, "this is MY garden, father, and MY rose, and I will grow it in my own way or not at all. Have you not had a lifetime of gardens and roses which you have brought to perfection? And would you let any man take your own upon his shoulders, even your own mistakes, and shoulder at last the praise after the blame?" Then Hobb, her father, laughed at her indulgently and said, "Nay, not any man; yet once I let a woman, and without her aid I would never have brought my rarest and dearest flower to perfection. So if I should let a woman help me, why not you a man?"

"Was the woman your mother?" said she. And her father was silent. Then a day came when he trudged up and down the hills from Alfriston, and standing at the gate of her garden saw his child in the arms of a stranger; and her face, as it lay against his heart, seemed to her father also to be the face of a stranger, and not of his child. He recognized in the stranger the Lord of the Burgh. And he saw that what he had feared had come to pass, and that his daughter's heart would be no more divided between her father and her flower, for it was given whole to the lover who had first assailed it. Hobb came into the garden, and they looked up as the gate clicked, and their faces grew as red as though one had caught the reflection from the other. But both looked straight into his eyes. And his daughter, pointing to her bush, said, "Father, my rose is grown at last," and he saw that the bush was crowned with a glorious golden bloom, perfect in every detail. Then it was the turn of the Lord of the Burgh, and he said, "Sir, I ask leave to rob your garden of its rose." "Do robbers ask leave?" said Hobb. And he shook his head, adding, "Nay, when the thief and the theft are in collusion, what say is left to the owner of the treasure? Yet I do not like this. Sir, have you considered that she is a gardener's child? Daughter, have you considered that he is a lord?" And neither of them had considered these questions, and they did not propose to do so. Then Hobb shook his head again and said, "I will not waste words. I know when a plant can drink no more water. And though you pretend to ask my leave, I know that you are prepared to dispense with it. But by way of consent I will say this: whatever you may call your other sons, you shall call your first Hobb, to remind you to-morrow of what you will not consider to-day. For my daughter, when she is a lord's wife, will none the less still be a gardener's daughter, and your children will be grafted of two stocks. And if this seems to you a hard condition, then kiss and bid farewell." And they both laughed with joy at the lightness of the condition; but the gardener did not laugh. And so the Lord of the Burgh married the gardener's daughter, and they called their first son Hobb. He was born on a first of August, and thirty-five months later Ambrose was born on the first of July, and in due course Heriot in June, and Hugh in May, and Lionel in April. And the Lord, loving his sons equally, made them equal possessors of the Burgh when in time it should pass out of his hands. Which, since men are mortal, presently came to pass, and there were five lords instead of one.

It happened on a roaring night of March, when the wind was blustering over the barren ocean of the east Downs, and Lionel was still a boy of ten, but soon to be eleven, that the five brothers sat clustered about the great hearth in the hall, roasting apples and talking of this and that. But their talk was fitful, and had long pauses in which they listened to the gusty night, which had so much more to say than they. And after one of the silences Lionel shuddered slightly, and drawing his little stool close to Hobb he said:

"It sounds like witches." Hobb put his big hand round the child's head and face, and Lionel pressed his cheek against his brother's knee.

"Or lions," said Hugh, jumping up and running to the window, where he flattened his nose to stare into the night. "I wish it were lions coming over the Downs."

"What would you do with them?" said Hobb, smiling broadly.

"Fight them," said Hugh, "and chain them up. I should like to have lions instead of dogs—a red lion and a white one."

"I never heard tell of lions of those colors," said Hobb. "But perhaps Ambrose has with all his reading."

"Not I," said Ambrose, "but I haven't read half the books yet. The wind still knows more than I, and it may be that he knows where red and white lions are to be found. For he knows everything."

"And has seen everything," murmured Heriot, watching a lovely flame of blue and green that flickered among the red and gold on the hearth.

"And has been everywhere," muttered Hugh. "If I could find and catch him, I'd ask him for a red and a white lion."

"I'd rather have peacocks," said Heriot, his eyes on the fire.

"What would you choose, Ambrose?" asked Hobb.

"Nothing," said he, "but it's the hardest of all things to have, and I doubt if I'd get it. But what business have we to be choosing presents? That is Lionel's right before ours, for isn't his birthday next month? What will you ask of the wind for your birthday, Lal?"

Then Lionel, who was getting very drowsy, smiled a sleepy smile, and said, "I'd like a farm of my own in the Downs, a very little farm with pink pigs and black cocks and white donkeys and chestnut horses no bigger than grasshoppers and mice, and a very little well as big as my mug to draw up my water from, and a little green paddock the size of my pocket-handkerchief, and another of yellow corn, and another of crimson trefoil. And I would have a blue farm-wagon no larger than Hobb's shoe, and a haystack half as big as a seed-cake, and a duckpond that I could cover with my platter. And I'd live there and play with it all day long, if only I knew where the wind lives, and could ask him how to get it."

"Don't start till to-morrow," jested Ambrose, "to-night you're too sleepy to find the way."

Then he turned to his book, and Hugh was still at the window, and Heriot gazing into the fire. And as he felt the child's head droop in his hand, Hobb picked him up in his arms and carried him to bed. And he alone of all those brothers had made no choice, nor had they thought to ask him, so accustomed were they to see him jog along without the desires that lead men to their goals—such as Ambrose's thirst for knowledge, and Heriot's passion for beauty, and Hugh's lust for adventure, and Lionel's pursuit of delight. And yet, unknown to them all, he had a heartfelt wish, which, among other things, he had inherited from his mother. For on a height west of the Burgh he had made a garden where, like her, he labored to produce a perfect golden rose. But so far luck was against him, though his height, which was therefore spoken of as the Gardener's Hill, bloomed with the loveliest flowers of all sorts imaginable. But year by year his rose was attacked by a special pest, the nature of which he had not succeeded in discovering. Yet his patience was inexhaustible, and his brothers who sometimes came to his garden when they needed a listener for their achieved or unachieved ambitions, never suspected that he too had an ambition he had not realized, for they saw only a lovely garden of his creating, where wisdom, beauty, adventure, and delight were made equally welcome by the gardener.

Now on the March day following the night of the brothers' windy talk—

(But suddenly Martin, with a nimble movement, stood upright on his bough, and grasping that to which the swing was attached, shook it with such frenzy that a tempest seemed to pass through the tree, and the girls shrieked and clung to the trunk, and leaves and apples flew in all directions; and Jessica, between clutching at her ropes, and letting go to ward off the cannonade of fruit, gasped in a tumult of laughter and indignation.

Jessica: Have you gone mad, Master Pippin? have you gone mad?

Martin: Mad, Mistress Jessica, stark staring mad! March hares are pet rabbits to me!

Jessica: Sit down this instant! do you hear? this instant! That's better. What fun it was! Aha, you thought you could shake me off, but you didn't. Are you still mad?

Martin: Melancholy mad, since you will not let me rave.

Jessica: You are the less dangerous. But I hate you to be melancholy.

Martin: It is no one's fault but yours. How can I be jolly when my story upsets you?

Jessica: How do you know it upsets me?

Martin: You put out your tongue at me.

Jessica: Did I?

Martin: Yes, without reason. So what could I do but whistle mine to the winds?

Jessica: You were too hasty, for I had my reason.

Martin: If it was a good one I'll whistle mine back again.

Jessica: It was this. That no man in a love-tale should be wiser or braver or more beautiful or more happy than the hero; or how can he be the hero? Yet I am sure Hobb is the hero and none of the others, because he is the only one old enough to be married.

Martin: Ambrose in nineteen, and will very soon be twenty.

Jessica: What's nineteen, or even twenty, in a man? Fie! a man's not a man till he comes of age, and the hero's not Ambrose for all his wisdom, though wisdom becomes a hero. Nor Heriot for all his beauty, though a hero should be beautiful. Nor Hugh, who will one day be brave enough for any hero, though now he's but a boy. Nor the happy Lionel, who is only a child—yet I love a gay hero. It's none of these, full though they be of the qualities of heroes. And here is your Hobb with nothing to show but a fondness for roses.

Martin: You deserve to be stood in a corner for that nothing, Mistress Jessica. Your reason was such a bad one that I see I must return to sense if only to teach you a little of it. Did I not say Hobb had a loving heart?

Jessica: But he was plain and simple and patient and contented. Are these things for a hero?

Martin: Mistress Jessica, I will ask you a riddle. What is it—? Oh, but first, I take it you love apple-trees?

Jessica: Who doesn't?

Martin: What is it, then, you love in an apple-tree? Is it the dancing of the leaves in the wind? Is it the boldness of the boughs? Or perhaps the loveliness of the flower in spring? Or again the fruit that ripens of the flower amongst the leaves on the boughs? What is it you love in an apple-tree?

Jessica: All riddles are traps. I must consider before I answer.

Martin: You shall consider until the conclusion of my story, and not till you are satisfied that many things can be contained in one, will I require your solution. And as for traps, it is always the solver of riddles who lays his own trap, by looking all round the question and never straight at it. Put on your thinking-cap, I beg, while I go on babbling.)

On the March day following the brothers' talk (continued Martin) Lionel was missing. It was some time before his absence was noticed, for Hobb was in his distant garden, and Ambrose among his books, and Heriot had ridden north to the market-town to buy stuff for a jerkin, and Hugh had run south to the sea to watch the ships. So Lionel was left to his own devices, and what they were none tried to guess till evening, when the brothers met again and he was not there. Then there was hue and cry among the hills, but to no purpose. The child had vanished like a cloud. And the month wore by, and their hearts grew heavier day by day.

It was in the last week of March that Hugh one morning came red-eyed to his brothers and said, "I am going away, and I will not come back until I have found Lionel. For I can't rest."

"None of us can do that," said Ambrose, "and we have searched and sent messengers everywhere. You are too young to go alone."

"I am nearly fourteen," said Hugh, "and stronger than Heriot, and even than you, Ambrose, and I can take care of myself and Lionel too. There are more ways than one to seek, and I'll go my way while you go yours. But I will find him or die." And he looked with defiance at Ambrose, and then turned to Hobb and said doggedly, "I'm going, Hobb."

Hobb, who himself sought the hills unwearingly day after day, and then sat up three parts of the night attending to the duties of the Burgh, said, "Go, and God bless you."

And Hugh's mouth grew less set, and he kissed his brothers, and put his knife in his belt, and took food in his wallet, and walked out of the Burgh. He followed the grass-track to the north, and had walked less than half-an-hour when the wind took his cap and blew it into the middle of a pond, where it lay soddening out of reach. So he took off his shoes and walked into the pond to fetch it out, stirring up the yellow mud in thick soft clouds. But as he stooped to grab his cap, something else stirred the mud in the middle, and a body heaved itself sluggishly into view. At first Hugh thought it must be the body of a sheep that had tumbled into the water, but to his amazement the sulky head of an old man appeared. He was barely distinguishable from the mud out of which he had risen.

"Drat the boys!" said the muddy man. "Will they never be done with disturbing the newts and me? Drat em, I say!"

"Who are you?" demanded Hugh, staring with all his might.

"Jerry I am, and this is my pond. Why can't you leave me in peace?"

"The wind took my cap," said Hugh.

"Finding's keepings," said the muddy man, taking the cap himself, "and windfalls on this water is mine. So I'll keep your cap, and it's the second wind's brought me this March. And if you're in want of another you'd best go to where Wind lives and ask him for it, like t'other one. But he said he'd ask for a toy farm instead."

"A toy farm?" shouted Hugh.

"Go away and don't deafen a body," said Jerry, and prepared to sink again. But Hugh caught him by the hair and said fiercely, "Keep my cap if you like, but I won't let you go until you tell me where my brother went."

"Your brother was it?" growled the muddy man. "He went to High and Over, dancing like a sunbeam."

"What's High and Over?"

"Where Wind lives."

"Where's that?"

"Find out," mumbled the muddy man; and he wriggled himself out of Hugh's clutch and buried himself like a monstrous newt in the mud. And though Hugh groped and fumbled shoulder-deep he could not feel a trace of him.

"But," said he, "there's at least a name to go on." And he got out of the pond and went in search of High and Over. And his brothers waited in vain for his return. And the heaviness of four hearts was now divided between three, and doubled because of another brother lost.

But on the first of April, which was Lionel's birthday, Lionel came back. Or rather, Hobb found him in a valley north of his garden hill, when he was wandering on one of his forlorn searches. And when he found him Hobb could not believe his eyes. For the child was sitting in the middle of the prettiest plaything in the world. It was a tiny farm, covering perhaps a quarter of an acre, with minute barns and yards and stables, and pigmy livestock in the little pastures, and hand-high crops in the little meadows; and smoke came from the tiny chimney of the farmhouse, and Lionel was drawing water from a well in a bucket the size of a thimble. And all the colors were so bright and painted that the little farmstead seemed to have been conceived of the gayest mind on earth. But through his amazement Hobb had no thought except for the child, and he ran calling him by his name, but Lionel never looked up. And then Hobb lifted him in his arms, and embraced him closely, but the child did not respond.

Then Hobb looked at him anxiously, and was so shocked that he forgot the strange blithe little farm entirely. For Lionel was as wan and wasted as though he had been through a fever, and his rosy face was white, and his merry eyes were melancholy. And suddenly, as Hobb clasped him, he flung his arms round his big brother's neck and buried his face in his bosom and wept bitterly.

Then Hobb tried to soothe and comfort him, asking him little questions in a coaxing voice—"Where has the child been? Why did he run away and leave us? Where did he get this pretty, wonderful toy? Is he hurt, or hungry? Does he remember it is his birthday? There will be presents for him at the Burgh, and a cake for tea. Did Hugh bring him home? Has he seen Hugh? Lal, Lal, where is Hugh?"

But Lionel answered none of these questions, he only sobbed and sobbed, and suddenly slipped out of Hobb's arms, and began to play once more with his farm, while the tears ran down his thin cheeks. Presently he let Hobb take him home, and there Heriot and Ambrose rejoiced and sorrowed over him. For he would scarcely speak or eat, and only shook his head at their questions. At Hugh's name his tears flowed twice as fast, but he would tell them nothing of him. Very soon Hobb carried him to bed, and in undressing him noticed that he had no shirt. This too Lionel would not explain, and Hobb ceased troubling him with talk, and knelt and prayed by him, and laid him down to sleep, hoping that in the morning he would be better. But morning brought no change. Lionel from that day was given up to grief. Each morning he went dejectedly to play with his marvelous toy in the valley, but how he came by it he would not say.

Towards the end of April Heriot came to Hobb and Ambrose and said, "I cannot bear this; Lionel is home and we are none the better for it, and Hugh is gone and we are all the worse. Hugh is capable of looking after himself, yet perhaps danger has befallen him; and even if not, he will roam the country fruitlessly for months, and it may be years; since Lionel is restored and he does not know it. The Burgh can spare me better than it can you, and I will ride abroad and see if I can find him, and return in seven days, whether or no."

So they embraced him, and he departed. But at the end of seven days he did not appear. And Ambrose and Hobb were dismayed at his vanishing like the others, and so heavy a gloom descended on the Burgh that each could scarcely have endured it without the other. And every day they went forth in search of Hugh and Heriot, or of traces of them, but found none.

Then it happened that on the first of May, which was Hugh's birthday, Hobb, wandering further north than usual, to the brow of the great ridge east of the Ouse, heard a wild roaring and bellowing on the Downs; or rather, it was two separate roarings, as you may sometimes hear two separate storms thundering at once over two ranges of hills. And in astonishment he went first to Beddingham, and there, bound by an iron chain to a stake beside a pond, he found a mighty lion, as white as a young lamb. But he had not a lamb's meekness, for he ramped and raved in a great circle around the stake, and his open throat set in his shaggy mane looked like the red sun seen upon white mist. Hobb rubbed his eyes and turned towards Ilford, where the second roaring sought to outdo the first. And there beside another pond he found another stake and chain, and a lion exactly similar, except that he was as red as a rose. But he had not a rose's sweetness, for he snarled and leaped with fury at the end of his chain, and his flashing teeth under his red muzzle looked like the blossom of the scarlet runner.

And then, turning about for an explanation of these wonders, Hobb saw what drove them from his mind—the figure of Hugh crouched in a little hollow, and shaking like a leaf. Hobb ran towards him with a shout, and at the shout Hugh leaped to his feet, with the eyes of a hunted hare, and looked on all sides as though seeking where to hide. But Hobb was soon beside him, with his arm round the boy's shoulder, and gazing earnestly into his face.

"Why, lad," said he, "do you not know me again?"

Hugh stole a glance at him, and suddenly smiled and nodded, and tried to answer, but could not for the chattering of his teeth. And he clung hard to his brother's side, and shuddered from head to foot.

"Are you ill, Hugh?" Hobb asked him, bewildered at the boy's unlikeness to himself.

"No, Hobb," said Hugh, "but need we stay here now?"

"Why, no," said Hobb gently, "we will go when you like. Where do these beasts come from?"

Hugh set his lips and began to move away.

Hobb went beside him and said, "Lionel is home, but Heriot is lost. Have you seen Heriot?"

Hugh hesitated, and then stammered, "No, I have not seen him."

And Hobb knew that he had lied, Hugh who had always been as fearless of the truth as of anything else. So after that he asked no more, fearing to get another lie for an answer; and he led Hugh home, supporting him with his arm, for he was full of fits and starts and shiverings. If a lump of chalk rolled under his shoe he blanched and cried, "What's that?" and once when a field-mouse ran across the path he swooned. Then Hobb, opening his tunic at the neck, saw that nothing was between it and his body; for he, like Lionel, was without his shirt.

They got back to the Burgh, and Hobb found Ambrose and told him how it was. And Ambrose came to Hugh and talked with him, and turned away with knitted brows. For here was a puzzle not dealt with in his books. And May went by in miserable fashion, with Lionel spending the days in playing mournfully beside his farm, and Hugh in cowering abjectly between his lions. And sometimes Ambrose and Hobb, after searching for Heriot or news of him, or spending their spirits in endeavoring to hearten their two brothers, or to elicit from them something that should give them the key to the mystery, would meet in Hobb's hill-garden, where seemed to be the only peace and loveliness left upon earth. And Hobb would weed and tend his neglected flowers, and they bloomed for him as though they knew he loved them—as indeed they did. Only his golden rose-tree would not flourish, but this small sorrow was unguessed by Ambrose.

One evening as they sat in the garden in the last week of May, Ambrose said to his brother, "I have been thinking, Hobb, that at all costs Heriot must be found, and not for his own sake only. He is younger than we, and nearer in spirit to the boys; and he may be able to help them as we cannot. For if this goes on,

Hugh will die of his fears and Lionel of his melancholy. You must stay and administer our affairs as usual, and look after the boys; and I will go further afield in search of Heriot."

Hobb was silent for a moment, and then he sighed and said, "No good has come of these seekings. Our lads returned of themselves, as Heriot may. And their return was worse than anything we feared of their absence, as, if he come back, I pray Heriot's will not be. And for you, Ambrose—" But then he paused, not saying what was in his mind. And Ambrose said, "Do not be afraid for me. These boys are young, and I am older than my years. And though I cannot face danger with a stouter heart than our brothers, I can perhaps see into it a little further than they. And foresight is sometimes a still better tool than courage."

Then he took Hobb's hand in his, and they gripped with the grip of men who love each other; and Ambrose went out of the garden, and Hobb was left alone. For Hugh and Lionel were companions to none but themselves.

But on the first of June Hobb, coming to the gate of his garden, saw with surprise a peacock strutting on the hillbrow, his fan spread in the sun, a luster of green and blue and gold, and behind him was another, and further south three more. So Hobb went out to look at them, and found not five but fifty peacocks sweeping the Downs with their heavy trains, or opening and shutting them like gigantic magical flowers. Following the throng of birds, he came shortly to a barn already known to him, but he had never seen it as he saw it now. For the roof was crowded with peacocks, and peacocks strayed in flocks within and without; and sitting in the doorway was Heriot, the sight of whom so overjoyed his brother that Hobb forgot the thousand peacocks in the one man. And he made speed to greet him, but within a few yards halted full of doubt. For was this Heriot? He had Heriot's air and attitude, yet the grace was gone from his body; and Heriot's features, surely, but the beauty had melted away like morning dew. And his dress, which had always been orderly and beautiful, was neglected; so that under the half-laced jerkin Hobb saw that he was shirtless. Yet after the first moment's shock, he knew this gaunt and ugly youth was Heriot. And Heriot seeing his coming hung his head, and made a shamed movement of retreat into the shadow of the barn. But Hobb hurried to him, and took him by the shoulders, and beheld him with the eyes of love which always find its object beautiful. Then the flush faded from Heriot's haggard cheeks, and he looked as full at Hobb as Hobb at him. And as at the steadfast meeting of eyes men see no longer the physical appearance, but for an eternal instance the appearance of the soul, these brothers knew that they were to each other what they had always been. And Heriot saw that Hobb was full of questions, and he laid his hand over Hobb's mouth and said, "Hobb, do not ask me anything, for I can tell you nothing."

"Neither of yourself nor of Ambrose?" said Hobb.

"Nothing," repeated Heriot.

So Hobb left his questions unspoken, and as they went home together told Heriot of Hugh's return, and what had happened to him. And Heriot heard it without comment. And in the evening, when Lionel and Hugh returned, they had nothing to say to Heriot, nor he to them; and it seemed to Hobb that this was because these three everything was understood.

It was a lonely June for Hobb, with his eldest brother away, and the three others spending all their days beside their strange possessions, which brought them no tittle of joy; and had it not been for his garden he would have felt utterly bereft. Yet here too failure sat heavily on his heart; for an many a night he saw upon his bush a bud that promised perfection to come, and in the morning it hung dead and rotten on its stem.

So the month wore on, and Hobb began to feel that the Burgh, where now his brothers only came to sleep, was a dead shell, too desolate to inhabit if Ambrose did not soon return. And he was impelled to go in search of him, yet decided to remain until Ambrose's birthday had dawned, for had not their birthdays brought his three youngest brothers home? And it might be so with Ambrose. And so it was.

For on the first of July, before going to his garden, he stayed at Heriot's barn to try to induce him to leave his peacocks for once, and spend the day with him in search of Ambrose; but Heriot, who was feeding his fowl, never looked up, and said sadly, "What need to seek Ambrose to-day? Ambrose has returned."

"Have you seen him?" cried Hobb joyfully.

"Early this morning," said Heriot.

"Where?"

"Down yonder in Poverty Bottom," said Heriot, pointing south of his barn to a hollow that went by that name. For there was a dismal habitation that had fallen into decay, a skeleton of a hut with only two rotting walls, and a riddled thatch for a roof. And it was worse than no habitation at all, for what might have been a green and lovely vale was made desolate and rank with disused things, rusting among the lumber of bricks and nettles. It was enough to have been there once never to go again. And Hobb had been there once.

But now, at Heriot's tidings, he ran down the hill a second time as though it led to Paradise, calling Ambrose as he went. And getting no answer he began to fear that either Heriot was mistaken, or Ambrose had gone away. His fears were unfounded, for coming to the Bottom he found Ambrose; yet he had to look twice to make sure it was he. For he was dressed only in rags, and less in rags than nakedness; and his skin was dirty and his hair unkempt. He was stooping about the ground gathering flints dropped through, and a small trail of them marked his passage over the rank grass.

Hobb strode towards him with dread in his bosom, and laid his hand on Ambrose's wild head, saying his name again. And at this his brother looked up and eyed him childishly, and said "Who is Ambrose?" And then the dread in Hobb took a definite shape, and he saw with horror that Ambrose had lost his wits. At that knowledge, and the sight of his neglected body and pitiful foolish smile, Hobb turned away and sobbed. But Ambrose with a little random laugh continued to drop flints in his bottomless bucket. And no word of Hobb's could win him from that place.

Then Hobb went back to the Burgh alone, and buried his face in his hands, and thought. He thought of the evil which had fallen upon his house, the nature of which was past his brothers' telling, and far beyond his guessing. And he said to himself, "I have done the best I could in governing the affairs of the Burgh and of our people, since the others were younger than I; but I see I have been selfish, keeping safety for my portion while they went into danger. And now there is none to set this evil right but I, and if I can I must follow the way they went, and do better than they at the end of it. And if I fail—as how should I succeed where they have not?—and if like them I too must suffer the dreadful loss of a part of myself, let it be so, and I shall at least fare as they have fared, and we will share an equal fate. Though what I have to lose I know not, to match their bright and noble qualities."

Then he called his steward, and gave all the affairs of the Burgh into his hands, and bade him have an eye to his brothers as far as possible, and to consult Heriot in any need, since he was the only one who could in the least be relied on. And then he walked out of the Burgh as he was, and went where his feet took him. He had not been walking half-an-hour when a sudden blast of wind tore the cap from his head, and blew it into the very middle of a pond.

Now the pond was exceedingly muddy, and as it seemed to Hobb rather deep, and he was wondering whether his old cap were worth wading for, and had almost decided to abandon it, when he saw a skinny yellow arm, like a frog's leg, stretch up through the water, and a hand that dripped with slime grope for his cap. With three strides he was in the pond, and he caught the cap and the hand together in his fist. The hand writhed in his, but Hobb was too strong for it; and with a mighty tug he dragged first the shoulder and then the head belonging to the hand into view. They were the shoulder and head of the muddy man whom you, dear maidens, have seen once before in this tale, but whom Hobb had never seen till then. And Jerry said, "Drat these losers of caps! will they NEVER be done with disturbing the newts and me? Tis the fifth in a summer. And first there's one with a step like a wagtail, and next there's one as bold as a hawk, and after him one as comely as a wild swan, and last was one as wise as an owl. And now there's this one with nothing particular to him, but he grips as hard as all the rest rolled into one. Drat these cap-losers!"

Then Hobb who, for all his surprise to begin with, and his increase of excitement as the muddy creature spoke, had never slackened his grasp, said, "Old man, you are welcome to my cap if you will tell me what happened to the wearers of the four other caps after they left you."

"How do I know what happened to em?" growled the muddy man. "For they all went to High and Over, and after that twas nobody's business but Wind's, who lives there."

"Where's High and Over?" said Hobb.

"Find out," said the muddy man, and gave a wriggle that did him no good.

"I will," said Hobb, "for you shall tell me." And he looked so sternly at the muddy man that Jerry cringed, moaning:

"I thought by his voice twas a turtle, but I see by his eye tis an eagle. If you must know you must. And south of Cradle Hill that's south of Pinchem that's south of Hobb's Hawth that's south of the Burgh that's south of this pond is where High and Over is. And I'll thank you to let me go."

Nevertheless, when Hobb released him Jerry forgot the thanks and disappeared into the mud taking the cap with him. But Hobb did not care for his thanks. He hurried south as fast as his feet would carry him, going by the places he knew and then by those he did not, till he came at nightfall to High and Over.

And on High and Over a great wind was blowing from all the four quarters of heaven at once. And Hobb was caught up in the crossways of the wind, and turned about and about till he was dizzy, and all his thoughts were churning in his brain, so that he could not tell one from the other. And at the very crisis of the churning a voice in the wind from the north roared in his ear:

"What do you want that you lack?"

And a voice from the south murmured, "What is the wish of your heart?"

And a voice from the west sighed, "What is it that life has not given you?"

And a voice from the east shrieked, "What will you have, and lose yourself to have?"

And Hobb forgot his brothers and why he was there, he forgot everything but the dream of his soul which had been churned uppermost in that turmoil, and he cried aloud, "A golden rose!"

Then the four voices together roared and murmured and sighed and shrieked, "Open Winkins! Open Winkins! Open Winkins! Open Winkins!" And the tumult ceased with a shock, and the shock of silence overwhelmed Hobb with sickness and darkness, and his senses deserted him. As he became unconscious he seemed to be, not falling to earth, but rising in the air.

When he opened his eyes he was lying on his back in a strange world, a world of trees, whose noble trunks rose up as though they were columns of the sky, but their heaven was a green one, shutting out daylight, yet enclosing a luminous haunted air of its own. Such forests were unknown in Hobb's open barren land, and this alone would have made his coming to his senses appear rather to be a coming away from them. But he scarcely noticed his surroundings, he was only vaguely aware of them as the strange and beautiful setting of the strangest and most beautiful thing he had ever seen. For he was looking into the eyes of the loveliest woman in the world. She was bending above him, tall and slim and supple, her perfect body clad in a deep black gown, the hem and bosom of which were embroidered with celandines, and it had a golden belt and was lined with gold, as he could see when the loose sleeves fell open on her round and slender arms; and the bodice of the gown hung a little away from her stooping body, and was embroidered inside, as well as outside, with celandines, which made reflections on her white neck, as they will on a pure pool where they lean to watch their April loveliness. Her skin was as creamy as the petals of a burnet rose, and her eyes were the color of peat-smoke, and her hair was as soft as spun silk and fell in two great shining waves of the purest gold over her bosom as she bent above him, and lay on the earth like golden grass on green water. A tress of the hair had flowed across his hand. And about her small fine head it was bound with a black fillet, a narrow coil so sleek and glossy that it was touched with silver lights, and this intense blackness made the gold of her head more dazzling. And Hobb lay there bewildered under the spell of her loveliness, asking nothing but to lie and gaze at it for ever.

But presently as he did not move she did, sinking upon her knees and stooping closer so that her breast nearly rested on his own, and she put her white hand softly on his forehead, and the smoke of her eyes was washed with tears that did not fall, and she said in a tremulous voice that fell on his ears like music heard in a dream, "Oh, stranger, if you are not dying, speak and move."

Then Hobb raised himself slowly on his elbow, and as she did not stir their faces were brought very close together; and not for an instant had they taken their eyes from each other. And he said in a low voice, not knowing either his voice or his own words, "I am not dying, but I think I must be dead." And suddenly the woman broke into a rain of tears, and she sank into his arms with her own about his neck, and she wept upon his heart as though her own were breaking. After a few moments she lifted her head and Hobb bent his to meet her quivering mouth. But before his lips touched hers she tore herself from his hold and fled away through the trees.

Hobb leaped to his feet, and scarcely knowing what he said cried, "Love! don't be afraid!" and he made no attempt to follow her, but stood where he was. He saw her halt in the distance, and turn, and hesitate, and struggle with herself as to her coming or going. At last she decided for the former, and came slowly between the pillars of the trees until she stood but a few paces from him with lowered lids. And she said sweetly, "Forgive me, stranger. But I found you here like one dead, and when you opened your eyes the fear was still on me, and when you moved and spoke the relief was too great, and I forgot myself and did what I did."

Then Hobb said gently, but with his heart beating on his ribs as fast as a swallow's wings beat the air, "I thought you did what you did because at that moment you knew, and I knew also, that it was your right for ever to weep and to laugh on my heart, and mine to bear for ever your laughing and weeping. But if it was not with you as with me, say so, and I will go away and not trouble you or your strange woods again."

Then the woman came quickly to him, and seized his hands saying, half agitated, half commanding, "It was with me as with you. And you shall stay with me for ever in these woods, and I will give you the desire of your life."

"And what shall I give you?" said Hobb.

"Whatever is nearest to yourself," she whispered, "the dearest treasure of your soul." And she looked at him with eyes full of passions which he could not fathom, but among them he saw terror. And with great tenderness he drew her once more to his heart, putting his strong and steady arms around her like a shield, and he said:

"Love whose name I do not know, what is nearer to myself than you, what dearer treasure has my soul than you? If I am to give you this, it is yourself I must give you; and I will restore to you whatever it is that you have lost through the agony of your soul. Be at peace, my love whose name I do not know." And holding her closely to him he bent his head and kissed her lips; and a great shudder passed through her, and then she lay still in his arms, with her strange eyes half-closed, and slow tears welling between the lids and hanging on her cheeks like the rain on the rose. And she let him quiet her with his big hands that were so used to care for flowers. Presently she lifted his right hand to her mouth, and kissed it before he could prevent her. Next she drew herself a little away from him, hanging back in his arms and gazing into his face as though her soul were all a question and his was the answer that she could not wholly read. And last she broke away from him with a strange laugh that ended on a sob.

Hobb said, "Will you not tell me what makes you unhappy?"

"I have no unhappiness," she answered, and quenched her sob with a smile as strange as her laugh. "My foolish lover, are you amazed that when her hour comes a woman knows not whether she is happy or unhappy? Oh, when joy is so great that it has come full circle with pain, what wonder that laughter and weeping are one?"

And Hobb believed her, for ever since he had opened his eyes upon her, he had felt in his own heart more joy than he could bear; and he knew that for this there is no remedy except to find a second heart to help in the bearing. And he knew it was the same with her. But now he saw that she was free for awhile from the excess of joy; and indeed these respites must happen even to lovers for their own sakes, lest they sink beneath the heavenly burden of their hearts. And her smile was like the diver's rise from his enchanted deeps to take again the common breath of man; and Hobb also smiled and said, "Come now, and tell me your name. For though love needs none for its object, I think the name itself is eager to be made known and loved beyond all other names for love's sake. As I love yours, whatever it be."

"My name," she said, "is Margaret."

"It is an easy name to love," said Hobb, "for its own sake."

"And what is yours?" asked she.

And Hobb's smile broadened as he answered, "Try to love it, for my sake. For it is Hobb. Yet it is as fitting to me, who am as plain as my name, as your lovely name is fitting to you."

She cast a quick sly look at him and said, "If love knows not how to distinguish between joy and pain, since all that comes from the heart of love is joy, neither can it tell the plain from the beautiful, since all that comes under the eye of love is beauty. And I will find all things beautiful in my lover, from his name to the mole on his cheek."

For I know now, dear maidens, whether in describing him I had mentioned this peculiarity of Hobb's.

(Jessica: You hadn't described him at all.

Martin: Well, now the omission is remedied.

Jessica: Oh fie! as though it were enough to say the man had a mole on his left cheek!

Martin: Dear Mistress Jessica, did I say it was his left cheek?

Jessica: Why—why!—where else would it be?

Martin: Nowhere else, on my honor. It WAS his left cheek.)

Then Hobb said to Margaret, "What place is this?"

"It is called Open Winkins," said she, and at the name he started to his feet, remembering much that he had forgotten. She looked at him anxiously and cajolingly and said, "You are not going away?" But he hardly heard her question. "Margaret," he said, "I have come from a place that may be far or near, for I do not know how I came; but I think it must be far, since I never saw this forest, or even heard of it, till a moment before my coming. But I am seeking a clue to a trouble that has come upon me this year, and I think the clue may be here. And now tell me, have you in these last four months seen in these woods anything of your people that are my brothers?—a child that once was merry, and a boy that once was brave, and a youth that once was beautiful, and a young man that once was wise? Have these ever been to Open Winkins?"

Margaret looked at him thoughtfully and said, "If they have, I have not seen them here. And I think they could not have been here without my knowledge. For no one lives here but I, and I live nowhere else."

Hobb sighed and said, "I had hoped otherwise. For, dear, I cannot rest until I have helped them." Then he told her as much as he knew of his four brothers; and her face clouded as he spoke, and her eyes looked hurt and angry by turns, and her beautiful mouth turned sulky. So then Hobb put his arm round her and said, "Do not be too troubled, for I know I shall presently find the cause and cure of these boys' ills." But Margaret pushed his arm away and rose restlessly to her feet, and paced up and down, muttering, "What do I care for these boys? It is not for them I am troubled, but for myself and you."

"For us?" said Hobb. "How can trouble touch us who love each other?"

At this Margaret threw herself on the grass beside him, and laid her head against his knee, and drew his hands to her, pressing them against her eyes and lips and throat and bosom as though she would never let them go; and through her kisses she whispered passionately, "Do you love me? do you truly love me? Oh, if you love me do not go away immediately. For I have only just found you, but your brothers have had you all their lives. And presently you shall go where you please for their sakes, but now stay a little in this wood for mine. Stay a month with me, only a month! oh, my heart, is a month much to ask when you and I found each other but an hour ago? For this time of love will never come again, and whatever other times there are to follow, if you go now you will be shutting your eyes upon the lovely dawn just as the sun is rising through the colors. And when you return, you will return perhaps to love's high-noon, but you will have missed the dawn for ever." And then she lifted her prone body a little higher until it rested once more in the curve of his arm against his heart, and she lay with her white face upturned to his, and her dark soft eyes full of passion and pleading, and she put up her fingers to caress his cheek, and whispered, "Give me my little month, oh, my heart, and at the end of it I will give you your soul's desire."

And not Hobb or any man could have resisted her.

So he promised to remain with her in Open Winkins, and not to go further on his quest till the next moon. And indeed, with all time before and behind him it did not seem much to promise, nor did he think it could hurt his brothers' case. But the kernel of it was that he longed to make the promise, and could not do otherwise than make the promise, and so, in short, he made the promise.

Then Margaret led him to two small lodges on the skirts of the forest; they were made of round logs, with moss and lichen still upon them, and they were overgrown with the loveliest growths of summer—with blackberry blossoms, a wonderful ghostly white, spread over the bushes like fairies' linen out to dry, and wild roses more than were in any other lovers' forest on earth, and the maddest sweetest confusion of honeysuckle you ever saw. Within, the rooms were strewn with green rushes, and hung with green cloths on which Margaret had embroidered all the flowers and berries in their seasons, from the first small violets blue and white to the last spindle-berries with their orange hearts splitting their rosy rinds. And there was nothing else under each roof but a round beech-stump for a stool, and a coffer of carved oak with metal locks, and a low mattress stuffed with lamb's-fleece picked from the thorns, and pillows filled with thistledown; and each couch had a green covering worked with waterlily leaves and white and golden lilies. "These are the Pilleygreen Lodges," said she, "and one is mine and one is yours; and when we want cover we will find it here, but when we do not we will eat and sleep in the open."

And so the whole of that July Hobb dwelt in the Pilleygreen Lodges in Open Winkins with his love Margaret. And by the month's end they had not done their talking. For did not a young lifetime lie behind them, and did they not foresee a longer life ahead, and between lovers must not all be told and dreamed upon? and beyond these lives in time, which were theirs in any case, had not love opened to them a timeless life of which inexhaustible dreams were to be exchanged, not always by words, though indeed by their mouths, and by the speech of their hands and arms and eyes? Hobb told her all there was to tell of the Burgh and his life with his brothers, both before and after their tragedies, but he did not often speak of them for it was a tale she hated to hear, and sometimes she wept so bitterly that he had ado to comfort her, and sometimes was so angry that he could hardly conciliate her. But such was his own gentleness that her caprices could withstand it no more than the shifting clouds the sun. And Margaret told him of herself, but her tale was short and simple—that her parents had died in the forest when she was young, and that she had lived there all her life working with her needle, twice yearly taking her work to the Cathedral Town to sell; and with the proceeds buying what she needed, and other cloths and silk and gold with which to work. She opened the coffer in Hobb's lodge and showed him what she did: veils that she had embroidered with cobwebs hung with dew, so that you feared to touch them lest you should destroy the cobweb and disperse the dew; and girdles thick-set with flowers, so that you thought Spring's self on a warm day had loosed the girdle from her middle, and lost it; and gowns worked like the feathers of a bird, some like the plumage on the wood-dove's breast, and others like a jay's wing; and there was a pair of blue skippers so embroidered that they appeared and disappeared beneath a flowing skirt with reeds and sallows rising from a hem of water, you thought you had seen kingfishers; and there were tunics overlaid with dragonflies' wings and their delicate jointed bodies of green and black-and-yellow and Chalk-Hill blue; and caps all gay with autumn berries, scarlet rose-hips and wine-red haws, and the bright briony, and spindle with its twofold gayety, and one cap was all of wild clematis, with the vine of the Traveler's Joy twined round the brim and the cloud of the Old Man's Beard upon the crown. And Hobb said, "It is magic. Who taught you to do this?" And Margaret said, "Open Winkins."

Early in their talks he told her of his garden, and of the golden rose he tried to grow there, and of his failures; and Margaret knew by his voice and his eyes more than by his words that this was the wish of his heart. And she smiled and said, "Now I know with what I must redeem my promise. Yet I think I shall be jealous of your golden rose." And Hobb, lifting a wave of her glittering hair and making a rose of it between his fingers, asked, "How can you be jealous of yourself?" "Yet I think I am," said she again, "for it was something of myself you promised to give me presently, and I would rather have something of you." "They are the same thing," said Hobb, and he twisted up the great rose of her hair till it lay beside her temple under the ebony fillet. And as his hand touched the fillet he looked puzzled, and he ran his finger round its shining blackness and exclaimed, "But this too is hair!" Margaret laughed her strange laugh and said, "Yes, my own hair, you discoverer of open secrets!" And putting up her hands she unbound the fillet, and it fell, a slender coil of black amongst the golden flood of her head, like a serpent gliding down the sunglade on a river.

"Why is it like that?" said Hobb simply.

With one of her quick changes Margaret frowned and answered, "Why is the black yew set with little lamps? Why does a black cloud have an edge of light? Why does a blackbird have white feathers in his body? Must things be ALL dark or ALL light?" And she stamped her foot and turned hastily away, and began to do up her hair with trembling hands. And Hobb came behind her and kissed the top of her head. She turned on him half angrily, half smiling, saying, "No! for you do not like my black lock." And Hobb said very gravely, "I will find all things beautiful in my beloved, from her black lock to her blacker temper." Margaret shot a swift look at him and saw that he was laughing at her with an echo of her own words; and she flung her arms about him, laughing too. "Oh, Hobb!" said she, "you pluck out my black temper by the roots!"

So with teasing and talking and quarreling and kissing, and ever-growing love, July came near its close; and as love discovers or creates all miracles in what it loves, Hobb for pure joy grew light of spirit, and laughed and played with his beloved till she knew not whether she had given her heart to a child or a man; and again when the happiness that was in his soul shone through his eyes, he was so transfigured that, gazing on his beauty, she knew not whether she had received the heart of a man or a god. And the truth was that at this time Hobb was all three, since love, dear maidens, commands a region that extends beyond birth and death, and includes all that is mortal in all that is eternal. And as for Margaret, she was all things by turns, sometimes as gay as sunbeams so that Hobb could scarcely follow her dancing spirit, but could only sun himself in the delight of it; and sometimes she was full of folly and daring, and made him climb with her the highest trees, and drop great distances from bough to bough, mocking at all his fears for her though he had none for himself; and sometimes when he was downcast, as happened now and then for thinking on his brothers, she forgot her jealousy in tenderness of his sorrow, and made him lean his head upon her breast, and talked to him low as a mother to her baby, words that perhaps were only words of comfort, yet seemed to him infinite wisdom, as the child believes of its mother's tender speech. And at all times she was lovelier than his dreams of her. Not once in this month did Hobb go out of the forest, which was confined on the north and north-west by big roads running to the world, and on all other sides by sloped of Downland. But whenever in their wanderings they arrived at any of these boundaries, Margaret turned him back and said, "I do not love the open; come away."

But on the last day of the month they came upon a very narrow neck of the treeless down, a green ride carved between their wood and a dark plantation that lay beyond, so close as to be almost a part of Open Winkins, but for that one little channel of space; and Hobb pointed to it and said, "That's a strange place, let us go there."

"No," said Margaret.

"But is it not our own wood?"

"How can you think so?" she said petulantly. "Do you not see how black it is in there? How can you want to go there? Come away."

"What is it called?" asked Hobb.

"The Red Copse," said she.

"Why?" asked Hobb.

"I don't know," said she.

"Have you never been there?" asked Hobb.

"No, never. I don't like it. It frightens me." And she clung to him like a child. "Oh, come away!"

She was trembling so that he turned instantly, and they went back to the Pilleygreen Lodges, getting wild raspberries for supper on the way. And after supper they sang songs, one against the other, each sweeter than the last, and told stories by turns, outdoing each other in fancy and invention; and at last went happily to bed.

But Hobb could not sleep. For in the night a wind came up and blew four times round his lodge, shaking it once on every wall. And it stirred in him the memory of High and Over, and with the memory misgivings that he could not name. And he rose restlessly from his couch and went out under the troubled moon, for a windy rack of clouds was blowing over the sky. But through it she often poured her amber light, and by it Hobb saw that Margaret's door was blowing on its hinges. He called her softly, but he got no answer; and then he called more loudly, but still she did not answer.

"She cannot be sleeping through this," said Hobb to himself; and with an uneasy heart he stood beside the door and looked into the lodge. And she was not there, and the couch had not been slept on. But on it lay her empty dress, its gold and black all tumbled in a heap, and on top of it was an embroidered smock. And something in the smock attracted him, so that he went quickly forward to examine it; and he saw that it was Heriot's shirt, that had been cut and changed and worked all over with peacocks' feathers. And he stood staring at it, astounded and aghast. Recovering himself, he turned to leave the lodge, but stumbled on the open coffer, hanging out of which was a second smock; and this one had two lions worked on the back and front, and one was red and the other white, and the smock had been Hugh's shirt. Then Hobb fell on the coffer and searched its contents till he had found Lionel's little shirt fashioned into a linen vest, with a tiny border of fantastic animals dancing round it, pink pigs, and black cocks, and white donkeys, and chestnut horses. And last of all he found the shirt of Ambrose, tattered and frayed, and every tatter was worked at the edge with a different hue, and here and there small mocking patches of color had been stitched above the holes.

And at each discovery the light in Hobb's eyes grew calmer, and the beat of his heart more steady. And he walked out of the Pilleygreen Lodge and as straight as his feet would carry him across Open Winkins and the green ride, and into the Red Copse. As he went he shut down the dread in his heart of what he should find there, "For," said Hobb to himself, "I shall need more courage now than I have ever had." It was black in the Red Copse, with a blackness blacker than night, and the wild races of moonlight that splashed the floors of Open Winkins were here unseen. But a line of ruddy fireflies made a track on the blackness, and Hobb, going as softly as he might, followed in their wake. Just before the middle of the Copse they stopped and flew away, and one by one, as each reached the point deserted by its leader, darted back as though unable to penetrate with its tiny fire the fearful shadows that lay just ahead. But Hobb went where the fireflies could not go. And he found a dark silent hollow in the wood, where neither moon nor sun could ever come; and at the bottom of it a long straggling pool, with a surface as black as ebony, and mud and slime below. Here toads and bats and owls and nightjars had come to drink, with rats and stoats who left their footprints in the mud. And on the ground and bushes Hobb saw slugs and snails, woodlice, beetles and spiders, and creeping things without number. The gloom of the place was awful, and turned the rank foliage of trees and shrubs black in perpetual twilight. But what Hobb saw he saw by a light that had no place in heaven. For kneeling beside the pool was his love Margaret, her naked body crouched and bowed among the creatures of the mud; and her two waves of gold were flung behind her like a smooth mantle, but the one black lock was drawn forward over her head, and she was dipping and dipping it into the dank waters. And every time she drew the dripping lock from its stagnant bath, it glimmered with an unearthly phosphorescence, that shed a ghostly light upon the hollow, and all that it contained. And at each dipping the lock of hair came out blacker than before.

At last she was done, and she slowly squeezed the water from her unnatural tress, and laid it back in its place among the gold. And then she stretched her arms and sighed so heavily that the crawling creatures by the pool were startled. But less started than she, when lifting her head she saw the eyes of Hobb looking down on her. And such terror came into her own eyes that the look rang on his heart as though it had been a cry. Yet not a sound issued between her lips. And he said to himself, "Now I need more wisdom than I have ever had." And he continued to look steadily at her with eyes that she could not read. And presently he spoke.

"We have some promises to redeem to-night," he said, "and we will redeem them now. You promised me my perfect golden rose, and this night I am going out of Open Winkins and back to my own Burgh. And to-morrow, since I now know something of your power of gifts, I shall find the rose upon my hill, and in exchange for it I will keep my word and give you back yourself. But there is something more than this." And he went a little apart, and soon came back to her with his jerkin undone and his shirt in his hand. "You have my brothers' shirts and here is mine," he said. "To-night when I am gone you shall return to Open Winkins, and spend the hours in taking out the work you have put into their shirts. And in the morning when I meet them at the Burgh I shall know if you have done this. But in exchange for theirs I give you mine to do with as you will. And the only other thing I ask of you is this; that when you have taken out the work in their shirts, you will spend the day in making a white garment for the lady who will one day be my wife. And whatever other embroidery you put upon it, let it bear on the left breast a golden rose. And to-morrow night, if all is well at the Burgh, I will come here for the last time and fetch it from you."

Then Hobb laid his shirt beside her on the ground, and turned and went away. And she had not even tried to speak to him.

When Hobb got out of the Red Copse he presently found a road and followed it, hoping for the best. After awhile he saw a tramp asleep in a ditch, and woke him and asked him the way to the Burgh of the Five Lords. But the tramp had never heard of it. So then Hobb asked the way to Firle, and the tramp said "That's another matter," for Sussex tramps know all the beacons of the Downs, and he told him to go east. Which Hobb did, walking without rest through the night and dawn and day, here and there getting a lift that helped him forward. And in his heart he carried hope like a lovely flower, but under it a quick pain like a reptile's sting that felt to him like death. And he would not give way to the pain, but went as fast and as steadily as he could; and at last, with strained eyes and aching feet, and limbs he could scarcely drag for weariness, and the dust of many miles upon his shoes and clothes, he came to his own bare country and the Burgh. He rested heavily on the gate, and the first thing he saw was Lionel on the steps, laughing and playing with a litter of young puppies. And the next was Hugh climbing the castle wall to get an arrow that had lodged in a high chink. And out of a window leaned Heriot in all his young beauty, picking sweet clusters of the seven-sisters roses that climbed to his room. And in the doorway sat Ambrose, with a book on his knee, but his eyes fixed on the gate. And when he saw Hobb standing there he came quickly down the steps, calling to the others, "Lionel! Hugh! Heriot! our brother has come home." And Lionel rushed through the puppies, and Hugh dropped bodily from the wall, and Heriot leaped through the window. And the four boys clung to Hobb and kissed him and wrung his hands, and seemed as they would fight for very possession of him. And Hobb, with his arms about the younger boys, and Heriot's hand in his, leaned his forehead on Ambrose's cheek, and Ambrose felt his face grow wet with Hobb's tears. Then Ambrose looked at him with apprehension, and said in a low voice, "Hobb, what have you lost?" And Hobb understood him. And he answered in a voice as low, "My heart. But I have found my four brothers." They took him in and prepared a bath and fresh clothes for him, and a meal was ready when he was refreshed. He came among them steady and calm again, and the three youngest had nothing but rejoicing for him. And he saw that all memory of what had happened had been washed from them. But with Ambrose it was different, for he who had had his very mind effaced, in recovering his mind remembered all. And after the meal he took Hobb aside and said, "Tell me what has happened to you."

Then Hobb said, "Some things happen which are between two people only, and they can never be told. And what has passed in this last month, dear Ambrose, is only for her knowledge and mine. But as to what is going to happen, I do not yet know."

After a moment's silence Ambrose said, "Tell me this at least. Has she given you a gift?"

"She has given me you again," said Hobb.

"That is different," said Ambrose. "She has given us ourselves again, and our power to pursue the destiny of our natures. But no man is another man's destiny. And it was our error to barter our own powers to another in exchange for the small goals our natures desired. And so we lost a treasure for a trifle. For every man's power is greater than the thing he achieves by it. But what has she given you in exchange for what she has taken from you?" And as he spoke he looked into Hobb's gentle eyes, and thought that if he had lost his heart it was a loss that had somehow multiplied his possession of it. "What has she given you?" he said again.

"I shall not know," said Hobb, "until I have been to my garden. And I must go alone. And afterwards, Ambrose, I must ride away for another night and day, but then I will return to the Burgh for ever."

So he got his horse, and went to the Gardener's Hill, and his garden was blazing with flowers like a joyous welcome. But when he approached the bush on which his heart was set, he saw a great gold bloom upon it that startled him with its beauty; until coming closer he perceived that all the petals were rotten at the heart, and coiled in the center was a small black snake.

He plucked the rose from its stem, and as he looked at it his face grew bright, and he suddenly laughed aloud for joy; and he ran out of the garden and got on his horse, and rode with all his speed to Open Winkins. When he got there the moon had risen over the Pilleygreen Lodges.

And Margaret sat at the door of her lodge in the moonlight, putting the last stitches into her work.

But when she saw him coming she broke her thread, and rose and averted her head. Then Hobb dismounted and came and stood beside her, and saw that in some way she was changed from the woman he knew. Margaret, still not turning to him, muttered, "Do not look at me, please. For I am ugly and unhappy and afraid and nearly mad. And here are your brothers' shirts." She gave him the four shirts, restored to themselves. He took them silently. "And here," continued Margaret, is her wedding-smock."

And Hobb took it from her, and saw that out of his own shirt, washed and bleached, she had made a lovely garment. And round it, from the hem upward, ran a climbing briar of exquisite delicacy, and with a beautiful design of spines and leaves; but the only flower upon it was a golden rose, worked on the heart of the smock in her own gold hair. And Hobb took it from her and again said nothing.

Then Margaret with a great cry, as though her heart were breaking, gasped, "Go! go quickly! I have done what you wanted. Go!"

"Yes, dear," said Hobb, "but you must come with me."

She turned then, whispering, "How can I go with you? What do you mean?" And she looked in his eyes and saw in them such infinite compassion and tenderness that she was overwhelmed, and swayed where she stood. And then his arms, which she had never expected to feel again, closed round her body, and she lay helplessly against him, and heard him say, "Love Margaret, you are my only love, and you worked the wedding-smock for yourself. Oh, Margaret, did you think I had another love?"

She looked at him blankly as though she could not understand, and her face was full of wonder and joy and fright. And she hung away from him sobbing, "No, no, no! I cannot. I must not. I am not good enough."

"Which of us is good enough?" said Hobb. "So then we must all come to love for help."

And she cried again in an agony, "No, no, no! There is evil in me. And I lived alone and had nothing, nothing that ever lasted, for I was born on High and Over in the crossways of the winds, and they were the godfathers of my birth. And all my life they have blown things to and from me. And I tried to keep what they blew me; and I gave their hearts' desire to all comers, and took in exchange the best they could give me; for I thought that if it was fair for them to take, it was fair for me to take too. But nothing that I took mattered longer than a week or a day or an hour, neither laughter nor courage nor beauty nor wisdom—all, all were unstable till the winds blew me you. And as I looked at you lying there unconscious, something, I knew not what, seemed different from anything I had ever known, but when you opened your eyes I knew what it was, and my heart seemed to fly from my body. And I longed, as I had never longed with the others, to give you your soul's desire, and I have tried and tried, and I could not. I could not give you anything at all, but every hour of the day and night I seemed to be taking from you. And yet what you had to give me was never exhausted. And the evil in me often fought against you, when I dreaded your knowing the truth about me, and would have lied my soul away to keep you from knowing it; and when I was jealous of your love for your brothers. So again and again I failed, when I should have thought of nothing but that you loved me as I loved you. For did I not know of my own love that it could never give you cause to be jealous, nor would ever shrink from any truth it might know of you?—but now—but now!— oh, my heart, had I known, when you spoke last night of your bride, that I was she! I will never be she! I was not good enough. I fought myself in vain." And she drooped in his arms, nearly fainting.

"Love Margaret!" said Hobb, and the tears ran down his face, "I will fight for you, yes, and you will fight for me. And if you have sacrificed joy and courage and beauty and wisdom for my sake, I will give them all to you again; and yet you must also give them to me, for they are things in which without you I am wanting. But together we can make them. And when I went to my garden this morning, I thanked God that my rose was not perfect, and that you had not taken my heart, as you had taken joy and courage and beauty and wisdom, as a penalty for a gift. Their desires you could give them, and take their best in payment, but mine you could not give me in the same way. For in love there are no penalties and no payments, and what is given is indistinguishable from what is received." And he bent his head and kissed her long and deeply, and in that kiss neither knew themselves, or even each other, but something beyond all consciousness that was both of them.

Presently Hobb said, "Now let us go away from Open Winkins together, and I will take you to the Burgh. But you must go as my bride."

And Margaret, pale as death from that long kiss, withdrew herself very slowly from his arms. And her dark eyes looked strange in the moonlight as he had never seen them, and more beautiful, with a beauty beyond beauty; and deep joy too was in them, and an infinite wisdom, and a strength of courage, that seemed more than courage, wisdom and joy, for they had come from the very fountain of all these things. And very slowly, with that unfading look, she took off her black gown and put on the white bridal-smock she had made; and as soon as she had put it on she fell dead at his feet.

("I think," said Martin Pippin, "that you have now had plenty of time, Mistress Jessica, to ponder my riddle."

"Your riddle?" exclaimed Jessica. "But—good heavens! bother your riddle! get on with the story."

"How can I get on with it?" said Martin. "It's got there."

Joscelyn: No, no, no! oh, it's impossible! oh, I can't bear it! oh, how angry I am with you!

Martin: Dear Mistress Joscelyn, why are you so agitated?

Joscelyn: I? I am not at all agitated. I am quite collected. I only wish you were as collected, for I think you must be out of your wits. How DARE you leave this story where it is? How dare you!

Martin: Dear, dear Mistress Joscelyn, what more is there to be told?

Joscelyn: I do not care what more is to be told. Only some of it must be re-told. You must bring that girl instantly to life!

Joyce: Of course you must! And explain why she died, though she mustn't die.

Jennifer: No, indeed! and if it had to do with her black hair, you must pluck it out by the roots.

Jessica: Yes, indeed! and you must do something about the horrible pool in the Red Copse, for perhaps that is what killed her.

Jane: Oh, it is too dreadful not to have a story with a wedding in it!

And little Joan leaned out of her branch and took Martin's hand in hers, and looked at him pleadingly, and said nothing.

"Will women NEVER let a man make a thing in his own way?" said Martin. "Will they ALWAYS be adding and changing this detail and that? For what a detail is death once lovers have kissed. However—!")

Not less than yourselves, my silly dears, was Hobb overwhelmed by that down-sinking of his love Margaret. And he fell on his knees beside her, and took her in his arms, and put his hand over the rose on her heart, that had ceased to beat. Suddenly it seemed to him that his hand had been stung, and he drew it away quickly, his eyes on the golden rose. And where she had left it just incomplete at his coming, he saw a jet-black speck. A light broke over him swiftly, and one by one he broke the strands at the rose's heart, and under it revealed a small black snake; and as the rose had been done from her own gold locks, so the snake had been done from the one black lock in the gold. Then at last Hobb understood why she had cried she was not good enough to be his bride, for she had fought in vain her last dark impulse to prepare death for the woman who should wear the bridal-smock. And he understood too the meaning of her last wonderful look, as she took the death upon herself. And he loved her, both for her fault and her redemption of it, more than he had ever thought that he could love her; for he had believed that in their kiss love had reached its uttermost. But love has no uttermost, as the stars have no number and the sea no rest.

Now at first Hobb thought to pluck the serpent from her breast, but then he said, "Of what use to destroy the children of evil? It is evil itself we must destroy at the roots." And very carefully he undid her beautiful hair, and laid its two gold waves on either side; but the slim black tress he gathered up in his hand until he held every hair of it, and one by one he plucked them from her head. And every time he plucked a hair the pain that had been under his heart stabbed him with a sting that seemed like death, and with each sting the mortal agony grew more acute, till it was as though the powers of evil were spitting burning venom on that steadfast heart, to wither it before it could frustrate them. But he did not falter once; and as he plucked the last hair out, Margaret opened her eyes. Then all pain leapt like a winged snake from his heart, and he forgot everything but the joy and wonder in her eyes as she lay looking up at him, and said, "What has happened to me? and what have you done?" And she saw the tress in his hand

and understood, and she kissed the hand that had plucked the evil from her. Then, her smoky eyes shining with tears, but a smile on her pale lips, she said, "Come, and we will drown that hair for ever." So hand-in-hand they went across Open Winkins and over the way that led to the Red Copse. And as they pushed and scrambled through the bushes, what do you think they saw? First a shimmering light round the edge of the pool, and then a sheet of moon-daisies, the largest, whitest, purest blooms that ever were. And they stood there on their tall straight stems of tender green in hundreds and hundreds, guarding and sanctifying the place. It was like a dark cathedral with white lilies on the high altar. And they saw a cock blackbird wetting his whistle at the pool, and heard two others and a green woodpecker chuckling in the trees close by. And they had no eyes for slimy goblin things, even if there were any. And I don't believe there were.

They bound the black tress about a stone, and it sank among the reflections of the daisies in the water, there to be purified for ever. And the next day he put her behind him on his horse, and they rode to the garden on the eastern hills, and found on his bush a single perfect rose. And as she had given it to him, Hobb straightway plucked and gave it to her. For that is the only way to possess a gift.

And then they went together to the Burgh, and very soon after there was a wedding.

I am now all impatience, Mistress Jessica, to hear you solve my riddle.

FOURTH INTERLUDE

Like contented mice, the milkmaids began once more to nibble at their half-finished apples, and simultaneously nibbled at the just-finished story.

Jessica: Do, pray, Jane, let us hear what conclusions you draw from all this.

Jane: I confess, Jessica, I am all at sea. The good and the evil were so confused in this tale that even now I can scarcely distinguish between black and gold. For had Margaret not done ill, who would have discovered how well Hobb could do? Yet who would wish her, or any woman, to do ill? even for the proof of his, or any man's, good?

Martin: True, Mistress Jane. Yet women are so strangely constructed that they have in them darkness as well as light, though it be but a little curtain hung across the sun. And love is the hand that takes the curtain down, a stronger hand than fear, which hung it up. For all the ill that is in us comes from fear, and all the good from love. And where there is fear to combat, love is life's warrior; but where there is no fear he is life's priest. And his prayer is even stronger than his sword. But men, always less aware of prayers than of blows, recognize him chiefly when he is in arms, and so are deluded into thinking that love depends on fear to prove his force. But this is a fallacy; love's force is independent. For how can what is immortal depend on what is mortal? Yet human beings must, by the very fact of being alive at all, partake of both qualities. And strongly opposed as we shall find the complexing elements of light and darkness in a woman, still more strongly opposed shall we discover them in a man. As I presume I have no need to tell you.

Joscelyn: You presume too much. The elements that go to make a man are not to our taste.

Martin: My story I hope was so.

Joscelyn: To some extent. And this pool in the Red Copse, is it hard to find?

Martin: Neither harder nor easier than all fairies' secrets. And at certain times in summer, when the wood is altogether lovely with centaury and purple loosestrife, you can hardly miss the pool for the fairies that flock there.

Joyce: What dresses do they wear?

Martin: The most beautiful in the world. The dresses of White Admirals and Red, and Silver-Washed Fritillaries and Pearl-Bordered Fritillaries, and Large Whites and Small Whites and Marbled Whites and Green-Veined Whites, and Ringlets, and Azure Blues, and Painted Ladies, and Meadow Browns. And they go there for a Feast Day in honor of some Saint of the Fairies' Church. Which Hobb and Margaret also attended once yearly on each first of August, bringing a golden rose to lay upon the altars of the pool. And the year in which they brought it no more, two Sulphurs, with dresses like sunlight on a charlock-field, came with the rest to the moon-daisies' Feast; because not once in all their years of marriage had the perfect rose been lacking.

Jessica: It relieves me to hear that. For I had dreaded lest their rose was blighted for ever.

Jane: And I too, Jessica. Especially when she died at his feet.

Joan: And yet, Jane, she did not really die, and somehow I was sure she would live.

Joyce: Yes, I was confident that Hobb would be as happy as he deserved to be.

Jennifer: I do not know why, but even at the worst I could not imagine a love-story ending in tears.

Martin: Neither could I. Since love's spear is for woe and his shield for joy. Why, I know of but one thing that could have lost him that battle.

Three of the Milkmaids: What thing?

Martin: Had the elements that go to make a man not been to Margaret's taste.

Conversation ceased in the Apple-Orchard.

Joscelyn: Her taste would have been the more commendable, singer. And your tale might have been the better worth listening to. But since tales have nothing in common with truth, it's a matter of indifference to me whether Hobb's rose suffered perpetual blight or not.

Jane: And to me.

Martin: Then let the tale wilt, since indifference is a blight no story can suffer and live. And see! overhead the moon hangs undecided under a cloud, one half of her lovely body unveiled, the other half draped in a ghostly garment lit from within by the beauties she still keeps concealed; like a maid half-ready for her pillow, turned motionless on the brink of her couch by the oncoming dreams to which she so soon will wholly yield herself. Let us not linger, for her chamber is sacred, and we too have dreams that await our up-yielding.

Like a flock of clouds at sundown, the milkmaids made a golden group upon the grass, and soon, by their breathing, had sunk into their slumbers. All but Jessica, who instead of following their example, pushed the ground with her foot to keep herself in motion; and as she swung she bit a strand of her hair and knitted her brows. And Martin amused himself watching her. And presently as she swung she plucked a leaf from the apple-tree and looked at it, and let it go. And then she snapped off a twig, and flung it after the leaf. And next she caught at an apple, and tossed it after the twig.

"Well?" said Martin Pippin.

"Don't be in such a hurry," said Jessica. She got off the swing and walked round the tree, touching it here and there. And all of a sudden she threw an arm up into the branches and leaned the whole weight of her body against the trunk, and began to whistle.

"Give it up?" said Martin Pippin.

"Stupid!" said Jessica. "I've guessed it."

"Impossible!" said Martin. "Nobody ever guesses riddles. Riddles were only invented to be given up. Because the pleasure of not being guessed is so much greater than the pleasure of having guessed. Do give it up and let me tell you the answer. Even if you know the answer, please, please give it up, for I am dying to tell it you."

"I shall never have saved a young man's life easier," said Jessica, "and as you saved mine before the story, I suppose I ought to save yours after it. How often, by the way, have you saved a lady's life?"

"As often as she thought herself in danger of losing it," said Martin. "It happens every other minute with ladies, who are always dying to have, or to do, or to know—this thing or that."

"I hope," said Jessica, "I shall not die before I know everything there is to know."

"What a small wish," said Martin.

"Have you a bigger one?"

"Yes," said he; "to know everything, there is not to know."

Jessica: Oh, but those are the only things I do know.

Martin: It is a knowledge common to women.

Jessica: How do YOU know?

Martin: I'm sure I don't know.

Jessica: I don't think, Master Pippin, that you know a great deal about women.

And she put out her tongue at him.

Martin: (Take care!) I know nothing at all about women.

Jessica: (Why?) Yet you pretend to tell love-stories.

Martin: (Because if you do that I can't answer for the consequences.) It is only by women's help that I tell them at all.

Jessica: (I'm not afraid of consequences. I'm not afraid of anything.) Who helped you tell this one?

Martin: (Your courage will have to be tested.) You did.

Jessica: Did I? How?

Martin: Because what you love in an apple-tree is not the leaf or the flower or the bough or the fruit—it is the apple-tree. Which is all of the things and everything besides; for it is the roots and the rind and the sap, it is motion and rest and color and shape and scent, and the shadows on the earth and the lights in the air—and still I have not said what the tree is that you love, for thought I should recapitulate it through the four seasons I should only be telling you those parts, none of which is what you love in an apple-tree. For no one can love the part more than the whole till love can be measured in pint-pots. And who can measure fountains? That's the answer, Mistress Jessica. I knew you'd have to give it up. (Take care, child, take care!)

Jessica: (I won't take care!). I knew the answer all the time.

Martin: Then you know what your apple-tree has to do with my story.

Jessica: Yes, I suppose so.

Martin: Please tell me.

Jessica: No.

Martin: But I give it up.

Jessica: No.

Martin: That's not fair. People who give it up must always be told, in triumph if not in pity.

Jessica: I sha'n't tell.

Martin: You don't know.

Jessica: I'll box your ears.

Martin: If you do—!

Jessica: Quarreling's silly.

Martin: Who began it?

Jessica: You did. Men always do.

Martin: Always. What was the beginning of your quarrel with men?

Jessica: They say girls can't throw straight.

Martin: Silly asses! I'd like to see them throw as straight as girls. Did you ever watch them at it? Men can throw straight in one direction only—but watch a girl! she'll throw straight all round the compass. Why, a man will throw straight at the moon and miss it by the eighth of an inch; but a girl will throw at the sun and hit the moon as straight as a die. I never saw a girl throw yet without straightway finding some mark or other.

Jessica: Yes, but you can't convince a man till he's hit.

Martin: Hit him then.

Jessica: It didn't convince him. He said I'd missed. And he said he had hi—he wasn't convinced.

Martin: Did he really say that? These men can no more talk straight than throw straight. Can you talk straight, Jessica?

Jessica: Yes, Martin.

Martin: Then tell me what your apple-tree has to do with my story.

Jessica: Bother. All right. Because wisdom and beauty and courage and laughter can all be measured in pint-pots. And any or all of these things can be dipped out of a fountain. You thought I didn't know, but I do know.

Martin: (Take care!) Where did you get all this knowledge?

Jessica: And that was why Margaret could take what she took from Lionel and Hugh and Heriot and Ambrose, because it was something measurable. Yes, because even a gay spirit can be sad at times, and a strong nerve weak, and a beautiful face ugly, and a clever brain dull. But when it came to taking what Hobb had, she could take and take without exhausting it, and give and give and always have something left to give, because that wasn't measurable. And the tree is the tree, and love is never anything else but love.

Martin: Oh, Jessica! who has been your schoolmaster?

Jessica: And so when she threw away her four pints what did it matter, any more than when the tree loses its leaves, or its flowers, or snaps a twig, or drops its apples? For though nobody else thought them lovely or clever or witty or splendid, she and Hobb were so to each other for ever and ever; because—

Martin: Because?

Jessica: It doesn't matter. I've told you enough, and you thought I couldn't tell you anything, and I simply hated saying it, but you thought I couldn't throw straight and I can, and your riddle was as simple as pie.

Martin: (Look out, I tell you!) You have thrown as straight as a die. And now I will ask you a straight question. Will you give me your key to Gillian's prison?

Jessica: Yes.

Martin: Because you dreaded lest Hobb's rose was blighted for ever?

Jessica: No. Because it's a shame she should be there at all.

And she gave him the key.

Martin: You honest dear.

Jessica: You thought I was going to beg the question—didn't you, Martin?

Martin: Put in your tongue, or—

Jessica: Or what?

Martin: You know what.

Jessica: I don't know what.

Martin: Then you must take the consequences.

And she took the consequences on both cheeks.

Jessica: Oh! Oh, if I had guessed you meant that, do you suppose for a moment that I would have—?

Martin: You dishonest dear.

Jessica: I don't know what you mean.

Martin: How crooked girls throw!

She boxed his ears heartily and ran to her comrades. When she was perfectly safe she turned round and put out her tongue at him.

Then they both lay down and went to sleep.

Martin was wakened by water squeezed on his eyelids. He looked up and saw Joscelyn wringing out her little handkerchief in the pannikin.

"Let us have no nonsense this morning," said she.

"I like that!" mumbled Martin. "What's this but nonsense?" He sat up, drying his face on his sleeve. "What a silly trick," he said.

"Rubbish," said Joscelyn. "Our master is due, and yesterday you overslept yourself and were troublesome. Go to your tree this instant."

"I shall go when I choose," said Martin.

"Maids! maids! maids!"

"This instant!" said Joscelyn, and dipped her handkerchief in the pannikin.

Martin crawled into the tree.

"Is a dog got into the orchard, maids?" said Old Gillman, looking through the hedge.

"What an idea, master," said Joscelyn.

"I thought I seed one wagging his tail in the grass."

The girls burst out laughing; they laughed till the apples shook, and Old Gillman laughed too, because laughter is catching. And then he stopped laughing and said, "Is an echo got into the orchard?"

And the startled girls laughed louder than ever, and they grew red in the face, and tears stood in their eyes, and Joscelyn had to go and lean against the russet tree, where she stood frowning like a stepmother.

" Tis well to be laughing," said Old Gillman, "but have ye heard my daughter laughing yet?"

"No, master," said Jessica, "but I shouldn't wonder if it happened any day."

"Any day may be no day," groaned Gillman, "and though it were some day, as like as not I'd not be here to see the day. For I'm drinking myself into my grave, as Parson warned me yesternight, coming for my receipt for mulled beer. Gillian!" he implored, "when will ye think better of it, and save an old man's life?"

But for all the notice she took of him, he might have been the dog barking in his kennel.

"Bitter bread for me, maids, and sweet bread for you," said the farmer, passing the loaves through the gap. " Tis plain fare for all these days. May the morrow bring cake."

"Oh, master, please!" called Jessica. "I would like to know how Clover, the Aberdeen, gets on without me."

"Gets on as best she can with Oliver," said Gillman, "though that fretty at times tis as well for him she's polled. Yet all he says is Patience.' But I say, will patience keep us all from rack and ruin?"

And he went away shaking his head.

"Why did you laugh?" stormed Joscelyn, as soon as he was out of earshot.

"How could I help it?" pleaded Martin. "When the old man laughed because you laughed, and you laughed for another reason—hadn't I a third reason to laugh? But how you glared at me! I am sorry I laughed. Let us have breakfast."

"You think of nothing but mealtimes," said Joscelyn crossly; and she carried Gillian's bread to the Well-House, where she discovered only the little round top of yesterday's loaf. For every crumb of the bigger half had been eaten. So Joscelyn came away all smiles, tossing the ball of bread in the air, and saying as she caught it, "I do believe Gillian is forgetting her sorrow."

"I am certain of it," agreed Martin, clapping his hands. And she flung the top of the loaf to his right, and he made a great leap to the left and caught it. And then he threw it to Jessica, who tossed it to Joan, who sent it to Joyce, who whirled it to Jennifer, who spun it to Jane, who missed it. And all the girls ran to pick it up first, but Martin with a dexterous kick landed it in the duckpond, where the drake got it. And he and the ducks squabbled over it during the next hour, while Martin and the milkmaids breakfasted on bread and apples with no squabbling and great good spirits.

And after breakfast Martin lay on his back, chewing a grassblade and counting the florets on another, whispering to himself as he plucked them one by one. And the girls watched him. He did it several times with several blades of grass, and always looked disappointed at the end.

"Won't it come right?" asked little Joan.

"Won't what come right?" said Martin.

"Oh, I know what you're doing," said little Joan; and she too plucked a blade and began to count—

Tinker,
Tailor,
Soldier,
Sailor"—

"I'm sure I wasn't," said Martin. "Tailor indeed!"

"Well, something like that," said Joan.

"Nothing at all like that. Oh, Mistress Joan! a tailor. Why, even if I were a maid like yourselves, do you think I'd give fate the chance to set me on my husband's cross-knees for the rest of my life?"

"What would you do then if you were a maid?" asked Joyce.

"If I were a town-maid," said Martin, "I should choose the most delightful husbands in the city streets." And plucking a fresh blade he counted aloud,

Ballad-singer,
Churchbell-ringer,
Chimneysweep,
Muffin-man,
Lamplighter,
King!
Ballad-singer,
Churchbell-ringer,
Chimneysweep"—

"There, Mistress Joyce," said Martin Pippin, "I should marry a Sweep and sit in the tall chimneys and see stars by daylight."

"Oh, let me try!" cried Joyce.

And—"Let me!" cried five other voices at once.

So he chose each girl a blade, and she counted her fate on it, with Martin to prompt her. And Jessica got the Chimney-sweep, and vowed she saw Orion's belt round the sun, and Jennifer got the Lamplighter and looked sorrowful, for she too wished to see stars in the morning; but Martin consoled her by saying that she would make the dark to shine, and set whispering lights in the fog, when men had none other to see by. And Joyce got the Muffin-man, and Martin told her that wherever she went men, women, and children would run to their snowy doorsteps, for she would be as welcome as swallows in spring. And Jane got the Bell-Ringer, and Martin said an angel must have blessed her birth, since she was to live and die with the peals of heaven in her ears. And Joscelyn got the Ballad-Singer.

"What about Ballad-Singers, Master Pippin?" asked Joscelyn.

"Nothing at all about Ballad-Singers," said Martin. "They're a poor lot. I'm sorry for you."

And Joscelyn threw her stripped blade away saying, "It's only a silly game."

But little Joan got the King. And she looked at Martin, and he smiled at her, and had no need to say anything, because a king is a king. And suddenly every girl must needs grow out of sorts with her fate, and find other blades to count, until each one had achieved a king to her satisfaction. All but Joscelyn, who said she didn't care.

"You are quite right," said Martin, "because none of this applies to any of you. These are town-fortunes, and you are country-maids."

And he plucked a new blade, reciting,

Mower,
Reaper,
Poacher,
Keeper,
Cowman,
Thatcher,
Plowman,
Herd."

"How dull!" said Jessica. "These are men for every day."

"So is a husband," said Martin. "And to your town-girls, who no longer see romance in a Chimneysweep, your Poacher's a Pirate and your Shepherd a Poet. Could you not find it in your heart, Mistress Jessica, to put up with a Thatcher?"

"That's enough of husbands," said Jessica.

"Then what of houses?" said Martin. "Where shall we live when we're wed?—

'Under a thatch,
In a ship's hatch,
An inn, a castle,
A brown paper parcel'—

"Stuff and nonsense!" said Joscelyn.

"For the sake of the rime," begged Martin. But the girls were not interested in houses. Yet the rest of the morning they went searching the orchard for the grass of fortune, and not telling. But once Martin, coming behind Jessica, distinctly heard her murmur "Thatcher!" and smile. And at another time he saw Joyce deliberately count her blade before beginning, and nip off a floret, and then begin; and the end was "Plowman." And presently little Joan came and knelt beside him where he sat counting on his own behalf, and said timidly, "Martin."

"Yes, dear?" said Martin absentmindedly.

"Oh. Martin, is it very wicked to poach?"

"The best men all do it," said Martin.

"Oh. Please, what are you counting?"

"You swear you won't tell?" said Martin, with a side-glance at her. She shook her head, and he pulled at his grass whispering—

Jennifer,
Jessica,
Jane,
Joan,
Joyce,
Joscelyn,
Gillian—"

"And the last one?" said little Joan, with a rosy face; for he had paused at the eighth.

"Sh!" said Martin, and stuck his blade behind his ear and called "Dinner!"

So they came to dinner.

"Have you not found," said Martin, "that after thinking all the morning it is necessary to jump all the afternoon?" And he got the ropes of the swing and began to skip with great clumsiness, always failing before ten, and catching the cord round his ankles. At which the girls plied him with derision, and said they would show him how. And Jane showed him how to skip forwards, and Jessica how to skip backwards, and Jennifer how to skip with both feet and stay in one spot, and Joyce how to skip on either foot, on a run. And Joscelyn showed him how to skip with the rope crossed and uncrossed by turns. But little Joan showed him how to skip so high and so lightly that she could whirl the rope twice under her feet before they came down to earth like birds. And then the girls took the ropes by turns, ringing the changes on all these ways of skipping; or two of them would turn a rope for the others, while they skipped the games of their grandmothers: "Cross the Bible," "All in together," "Lady, lady, drop your purse!" and "Cinderella lost her shoe;" or they turned two ropes at once for the Double Dutch; and Martin took his run with the rest. And at first he did very badly, but as the day wore on improved, until by evening he was whirling the rope three times under his feet that glanced against each other in mid-air like the knife and the steel. And the girls clapped their hands because they couldn't help it, and Joan said breathlessly:

"How quick you are! it took me ten days to do that."

And Martin answered breathlessly, "How quick you were! it took me ten years."

"Are you ever honest about anything, Master Pippin?" said Joscelyn petulantly.

"Three times a day," said Martin, "I am honestly hungry."

So they had supper.

Supper done, they clustered as usual about the story-telling tree, and Martin looked inquiringly from Jane to Joscelyn and from Joscelyn to Jane. And Joscelyn's expression was one of uncontrolled indifference, and Jane's expression was one of bridled excitement. So Martin ignored Joscelyn and asked Jane what she was thinking about.

"A great number of things, Master Pippin," said she. "There is always so much to think about."

"Is there?" said Martin.

"Oh, surely you know there is. How could you tell stories else?"

"I never think when I tell stories," said Martin. "I give them a push and let them swing."

"Oh but," said Jane, "it is very dangerous to speak without thinking. One might say anything."

"One does," agreed Martin, "and then anything happens. But people who think before speaking often end by saying nothing. And so nothing happens."

"Perhaps it's as well," said Joyce slyly.

"Yet the world must go round, Mistress Joyce. And swings were made to swing. Do you think, Mistress Jane, if you sat in the swing I should think twice, or even once, before giving it a push?"

Jane considered this, and then said gravely, "I think, Master Pippin, you would have to think at least once before pushing the swing to-night; because it isn't there."

"What a wise little milkmaid you are," said Martin, looking about for the skipping-ropes.

"Yes," said Jessica, "Jane is wiser than any of us. She is extremely wise. I wonder you hadn't noticed it."

"Oh, but I had," said Martin earnestly, fixing the swinging ropes to their places. "There, Mistress Jane, let me help you in, and I will give you a push."

He offered her his hand respectfully, and Jane took it saying, "I don't like swinging very high."

"I will think before I push," said Martin. And when she was settled, with her skirts in order and her little feet tucked back, he rocked the swing so gently that not an apple fell nor a milkmaid slipped, clambering to her place. And Martin leaned back in his and shut his eyes.

"We are waiting," observed Joscelyn overhead.

"So am I," sighed Martin.

"For what?"

"For a push."

"But you're not swinging."

"Neither's my story. And it will take seven pair of arms to set it going." And he fixed his eyes on Gillian in her sorrow, but she did not lift her face.

"Here's six to start the motion of themselves," said Joscelyn, "and it only remains to you to attract the seventh willy-nilly."

"It were easier," said Martin, "to unlock Saint Peter's Gates with cowslips."

"I was not talking of impossibilities, Master Pippin," said Joscelyn.

"Why, neither was I," said Martin; "for did you never hear that cowslips, among all the golden flowers of spring, are the Keys of Heaven?"

And sending a little chime from his lute across the Well-House he sang—

She lost the keys of heaven
  Walking in a shadow,
  Sighing for her lad O
She lost her keys of heaven.
She saw the boys and girls who flocked
Beyond the gates all barred and locked—
And oh! sighed she, the locks are seven
  Betwixt me and my lad O,
And I have lost my keys of heaven
  Walking in a shadow.
    She found the keys of heaven
  All in a May meadow,
  Singing for her lad O
She found her keys of heaven.
She found them made of cowslip gold
Springing seven-thousandfold—
And oh! sang she, ere fall of even
  Shall I not be wed O?
For I have found my keys of heaven
  All in a May meadow.

By the end of the song Gillian was kneeling upright among the mallows, and with her hands clasped under her chin was gazing across the duckpond.

"Well, well!" exclaimed Joscelyn, "cowslips may, or may not, have the power to unlock the heavenly gates. But there's no denying that a very silly song has unlocked our Mistress's lethargy. So I advise you to seize the occasion to swing your tale on its way."

"Then here goes," said Martin, "and I only pray you to set your sympathies also in motion while I endeavor to keep them going with the story of Proud Rosalind and the Hart-Royal."

PROUD ROSALIND AND THE HART-ROYAL

There was once, dear maidens, a man-of-all-trades who lived by the Ferry at Bury. And nobody knew where he came from. For the chief of his trades he was an armorer, for it was in the far-away times when men thought danger could only be faced and honor won in a case of steel; not having learned that either against danger or for honor the naked heart is the fittest wear. So this man, whose name was Harding, kept his fires going for men's needs, and women's too; for besides making and mending swords and knives and greaves for the one, he would also make brooches and buckles and chains for the other; and tools for the peasants. They sometimes called him the Red Smith. In person Harding was ruddy, though his fairness differed from the fairness of the natives, and his speech was not wholly their speech. He was a man of mighty brawn and stature, his eyes gleamed like blue ice seen under a fierce sun, the hair of his head and his beard glittered like red gold, and the finer hair on his great arms and breast overlaid with an amber sheen the red-bronze of his skin. He seemed a man made to move the mountains of the world; yet truth to tell, he was a most indifferent smith.

(Martin: Are you not quite comfortable, Mistress Jane?

Jane: I am perfectly comfortable, thank you, Master Pippin.

Martin: I fancied you were a trifle unsettled.

Jane: No, indeed. What would unsettle me?

Martin: I haven't the ghost of a notion.)

I have heard gossips tell, but it has since been forgotten or discredited, that this part of the river was then known as Wayland's Ferry; for this, it was said, was one of the several places in England where the spirit lurked of Wayland the Smith, who was the cunningest worker in metal ever told of in song or story, and he had come overseas from the North where men worshiped him as a god. No one in Bury had ever seen the shape of Wayland, but all believed in him devoutly, for this was told of him, and truly: that any one coming to the ferry with an unshod steed had only to lay a penny on the ground and cry aloud, "Wayland Smith, shoe me my horse!" and so withdraw. And on coming again he would find his horse shod with a craft unknown to human hands, and his penny gone. And nobody thought of attributing to Harding the work of Wayland, partly because no human smith would have worked for so mean a fee as was accepted by the god, and chiefly because the quality of the workmanship of the man and the god was as dissimilar as that of clay and gold.

Besides his trade in metal, Harding also plied the ferry; and then men would speak of him as the Red Boatman. But he could not be depended on, for he was often absent. His boat was of a curious shape, not like any other boat seen on the Arun. Its prow was curved like a bird's beak. And when folk wished to go across to the Amberley flats that lie under the splendid shell which was once a castle, Harding would carry them, if he was there and neither too busy nor too surly. And when they asked the fee he always said, "When I work in metal I take metal. But for that which flows I take only that which flows. So give me whatever you have heart to give, as long as it is not coin." And they gave him willingly anything they had: a flower, or an egg, or a bird's feather. A child once gave him her curl, and a man his hand.

And when he was neither in his workshop or his boat, he hunted on the hills. But this was a trade he put to no man's service. Harding hunted only for himself. And because he served his own pleasure more passionately than he served others', and was oftener seen with his bow than with hammer or oar, he was chiefly known as the Red Hunter. Often in the late of the year he would be away on the great hills of Bury and Bignor and Houghton and Rewell, with their beech-woods burning on their sides and in their hollows, and their rolling shoulders lifted out of those autumn fires to meet in freedom the freedom of the clouds.

It was on one of his huntings he came on the Wishing-Pool. This pool had for long been a legend in the neighborhood, and it was said that whoever had courage to seek it in the hour before midnight on Midsummer Eve, and thrice utter her wish aloud, would surely have that wish granted within the year. But with time it had become a lost secret, perhaps because its ancient reputation as the haunt of goblin things had long since sapped the courage of the maidens of those parts; and only great-grandmothers remembered how that once their grandmothers had tried their fortunes there. And its whereabouts had been forgotten.

But one September Harding saw a calf-stag on Great Down. There were wild deer on the hills then, but such a calf he had never seen before. So he stalked it over Madehurst and Rewell, and followed it into the thick of Rewell Wood. And when it led him to its drinking- place, he knew that he had discovered one more secret of the hills, and that this somber mere wherein strange waters bubbled in whispers could be no other than the lost Wishing-Pool. The young calf might have been its magic guard. To Harding it was a discovery more precious than the mere. For all that it was of the first year, with its prickets only showing where its antlers would branch in time, it was of a breed so fine and a build so noble that its matchless noon could already be foretold from its matchless dawn; and added to all its strength and grace and beauty was this last marvel, that though it was of the tribe of the Red Deer, its skin was as white and speckless as falling snow. Watching it, the Red Smith said to himself, "Not yet my quarry. You are of king's stock, and if after the sixth year you show twelve points, you shall be for me. But first, my hart-royal, you shall get your growth." And he came away and told no man of the calf or of the pool.

And in the second year he watched for it by the mere, and saw it come to drink, no longer a calf, but a lovely brocket, with its brow antlers making its first two points. And in the third year he watched for it again, no brocket now but a splendid spayade, which to its brows had added its shooting bays; and in the fourth year the spayade had become a proud young staggarde, with its trays above its bays. And in the fifth year the staggarde was a full-named stag, crowned with the exquisite twin crowns of its crockets, surmounting tray and bay and brow. And Harding lying hidden gloried in it, thinking, "All your points now but two, my quarry. And next year you shall add the beam to the crown, and I will hunt my hart."

Now at the time when Harding first saw the calf, and the ruin of the castle across the ferry was only a ruin, not fit for habitation, it was nevertheless inhabited by the Proud Rosalind, who dwelt there without kith or kin. And if time had crumbled the castle to its last nobility, so that all that was strong and beautiful in it was preserved and, as it were, exposed in nakedness to the eyes of men: so in her, who was the ruins of her family, was preserved and exposed all that had been most noble, strong and beautiful in her race. She was as poor as she was friendless, but her pride outmatched both these things. So great was her pride that she learned to endure shame for the sake of it. She had a tall straight figure that was both strong and graceful, and she carried herself like a tree. Her hair was neither bronze nor gold nor copper, yet seemed to be an alloy of all the precious mines of the turning year— the vigorous dusky gold of November elms, the rust of dead bracken made living by heavy rains, the color of beechmast drenched with sunlight after frost, and all the layers of glory on the boughs before it fell, when it needed neither sun nor dew to make it glow. All these could be seen in different lights upon her heavy hair, which when unbound hung as low as her knees. Her thick brows were dark gold, and her fearless eyes dark gray with gold gleams in them. They may have been reflections from her lashes, or even from her skin, which had upon it the bloom of a golden plum. Dim ages since her fathers had been kings in Sussex; gradually their estate had diminished, but with the lessening of their worldly possessions they burnished the brighter the possession of their honor, and bred the care of it in their children jealously. So it came to pass that Rosalind, who possessed less than any serf or yeoman in the countryside, trod among these as though she were a queen, dreaming of a degree which she had never known, ignored or shrugged at by those whom she accounted her equals, insulted or gibed at by those she thought her inferiors. For the dwellers in the neighboring hamlets, to whom the story of her fathers' fathers was only a legend, saw in her just a shabby girl, less worthy than themselves because much poorer, whose pride and very beauty aroused their mockery and wrath. They did not dispute her possession of the castle. For what to them were four vast roofless walls, enclosing a square of greensward underfoot and another of blue air overhead, and pierced with doorless doorways and windowless casements that let in all the lights of all the quarters of the sky? What to them were these traces of old chambers etched on the surface of the old gray stone, these fragments of lovely arches that were but channels for the winds? In the thick of the great towered gateway one little room remained above the arch, and here the maiden slept. And all her company was the ghosts of her race. She saw them feasting in the halls of the air, and moving on the courtyard of the grass. At night in the galleries of the stars she heard their singing; and often, looking through the empty windows over the flats to which the great west wall dropped down, she saw them ride in cavalcade out of the sunset, from battle or hunt or tourney. But the peasants, who did not know what she saw and heard, preferred their snug squalor to this shivering nobility, and despised the girl who, in a fallen fortress, defended her life from theirs.

At first she had kept her distance with a kind of graciousness, but one day in her sixteenth year a certain boor met her under the castle wall as she was returning with sticks for kindling, and was struck by her free and noble carriage; for though she was little more than a child, through all her rags she shone with the grace and splendor not only of her race, but of the wild life she lived on the hills when she was not in her ruins. She was as strong and fine as a young hind, and could run like any deer upon the Downs, and climb like any squirrel. And the dull-sighted peasant, seeing as though for the first time her untamed beauty, on an impulse offered to kiss her and make her his woman.

Rosalind stared at him like one aroused from sleep with a rude blow. The color flamed in her cheek. "YOU to accost so one of my blood?" she cried. "Mongrel, go back to your kennel!"

The lout gaped between rage and mortification, and, muttering, made a step towards her; but suddenly seeming to think better of it, stumbled away.

Then Rosalind, lifting her glowing face, as beautiful as sunset with its double flush, rose under gold, saw Harding the Red Hunter gazing at her. Some business had brought him over the ferry, and on his road he had lit upon the suit and its rejection. Rosalind, her spirit chafed with what had passed, returned his gaze haughtily. But he maintained his steadfast look as though he had been hewn out of stone; and presently, impatient and disdainful, she turned away. Then, and instantly, Harding pursued his way in silence. And Rosalind grew somehow aware that he had determined to stand at gaze until her eyes were lowered. Thereupon she classed his presumption with that of the other who had dared address her, and hated him for taking part against her. Near as their dwellings were, divided only by the river and a breadth of water-meadow, their intercourse had always been of the slightest, for Harding possessed a reserve as great as her own. But from this hour their intercourse ceased entirely.

The boor mis-spread the tale of her overweening pride through the hamlet, and when next she appeared there she was greeted with derision.

"This is she that holds herself unfit to mate with an honest man!" cried some. And others, "Nay, do but see the silken gown of the great lady Rosalind, see the fine jewels of her!" "She thinks she outshines the Queen of Bramber's self!" scoffed a woman. And a man demanded, "What blood's good enough to mix with hers, if ours be not?"

"A king's!" flashed Rosalind. And even as she spoke the jeering throng parted to let one by that elbowed his way among them; and a second time she saw the Red Hunter come to halt and fix her before all the people. Now this time, she vowed silently, you may gaze till night fall and day rise again, Red Man, if you think to lower my eyes in the presence of these! So she stood and looked him in the face like a queen, all her spirit nerving her, and the people knew it to be battle between them. Harding's great arms were folded across his breast, and on his countenance was no expressiveness at all; but a strange light grew and brightened in his eyes, till little by little all else was blurred and hazy in the girl's sight, and blue fire seemed to lap her from her tawny hair to her bare feet. Then she knew nothing except that she must look away or burn. And her eyes fell. Harding walked past her as he had done before, and not till he was out of hearing did the bystanders begin their cruelty.

"A king's blood for the lady that droops to a common smith!" cried they.

"She shall swing his hammer for a scepter!" cried they.

" Shall sit on's anvil for a throne!" cried they.

" Shall queen it in a leathern apron o' Sundays!" cried they.

Rosalind fled amid their howls of laughter. She hated them all, and far beyond them all she hated him who had lowered her head in their sight.

It was after this that the Proud Rosalind—

(But here, without even trouble to finish his sentence, Martin Pippin suddenly thrust with his foot at the seat of the swing, nearly dislodging Jane with the action; who screamed and clutched first at the ropes, and next at the branches as she went up, and last of all at Martin as she came down. She clutched him so piteously that in pure pity he clutched her, and lifting her bodily out of her peril set her on his knee.

Martin: (with great concern): Are you better, Mistress Jane?

Jane: Where are your manners, Master Pippin?

Martin: My mother mislaid them before I was born. But are you better now?

Jane: I am not sure. I was very much upset.

Martin: So was I.

Jane: It was all your doing.

Martin: I could have sworn it was half yours.

Jane: Who disturbed the swing, pray?

Martin: Every effect proceeds from its cause. The swing was disturbed because I was disturbed.

Jane: Every cause once had its effect. What effected your disturbance, Master Pippin?

Martin: Yours, Mistress Jane.

Jane: Mine?

Martin: Confess that you were disturbed.

Jane: Yes, and with good cause.

Martin: I can't doubt it. Yet that was the mischief. I could find no logical cause for your disturbance. And an illogical world proceeds from confusion to chaos. For want of a little logic my foot and your swing passed out of control.

Jane: The logic had only to be asked for, and it would have been forthcoming.

Martin: Is it too late to ask?

Jane: It is never too late to be reasonable. But why am I sitting on— Why am I sitting here?

Martin: For the best of reasons. You are sitting where you are sitting because the swing is so disturbed. Please teach me to be reasonable, dear Mistress Jane. Why were you disturbed?

Jane: Very well. I was naturally greatly disturbed to learn that your heroine hated your hero. Because it is your errand to relate love-stories; and I cannot see the connection between love and hate. Could two things more antagonistic conclude in union?

Martin: Yes.

Jane: What?

Martin: A button and buttonhole. For one is something and the other nothing, and what in the very nature of things could be more antagonistic than these?

So saying, he tore a button from his shirt and put it into her hand. "Don't drop it," said Martin, "because I haven't another; and besides, every button-hole prefers its own button. Yet I will never ask you to re-unite them until my tale proves to your satisfaction that out of antagonisms unions can spring."

"Very well," said Jane; and she took out of her pocket a neat little housewife and put the button carefully inside it. Then she said, "The swing is quite still now."

"But are you sure you feel better?" said Martin.

"Yes, thank you," said Jane.)

It was after this (said Martin) that the Proud Rosalind became known by her title. It was fastened on her in derision, and when she heard it she set her lips and thought: "What they speak in mockery shall be the truth." And the more men sought to shame her, the prouder she bore herself. She ceased all commerce with them from this time. So for five years she lived in great loneliness and want.

But gradually she came to know that even this existence of friendless want was not to be life, but a continual struggle-with- death. For she had no resources, and was put to bitter shifts if she would live. Hunger nosed at her door, and she had need of her pride to clothe her. For the more she went wan and naked, the more men mocked her to see her hold herself so high; and out of their hearts she shut that charity which she would never have endured of them. If she had gone kneeling to their doors with pitiful hands, saying, "I starve, not having wherewithal to eat; I perish, not having wherewithal to cover me"—they would perhaps have fed and clothed her, aglow with self-content. But they were not prompt with the charity which warms the object only and not the donor; and she on her part tried to appear as though she needed nothing at their hands.

One evening when the woods were in full leaf, and summer on the edge of its zenith, Proud Rosalind walked among the trees seeking green herbs for soup. She had wandered far afield, because there were no woods near the castle, standing on its high ground above the open flats and the river beyond. But gazing over the water she could see the groves and crests upon the hills where some sustenance was. The swift way was over the river, but there was no boat to serve her except Harding's; and this was a service she had never asked of old, and lately would rather have died than ask. So she took daily to the winding roads that led to a distant bridge and the hills with their forests. This day her need was at its sorest. When she had gathered a meager crop she sat down under a tree, and began to sort out the herbs upon her knees. One tender leaf she could not resist taking between her teeth, that had had so little else of late to bite on; and as she did so coarse laughter broke upon her. It was her rude suitor who had chanced across her path, and he mocked at her, crying, "This is the Proud Rosalind that will not eat at an honest man's board, choosing rather to dine after the high fashion of the kine and asses!" Then from his pouch he snatched a crust of bread and flung it to her, and said, "Proud Rosalind, will you stoop for your supper?"

She rose, letting the precious herbs drop from her lap, and she trod them into the earth as weeds gathered at hazard, so that the putting of the leaf between her lips might wear an idle aspect; and then she walked away, with her head very high. But she was nearly desperate at leaving them there, and when she was alone her pain of hunger increased beyond all bounds. And she sat down on the limb of a great beech and leaned her brow against his mighty body, and shut her eyes, while the light changed in the sky. And presently the leaves of the forest were lit by the moon instead of the sun, and the spaces in the top boughs were dark blue instead of saffron, and the small clouds were no longer fragments of amber, but bits of mottled pearl seen through sea-water. But Rosalind witnessed none of these slow changes, and when after a great while she lifted her faint head, she saw only that the day was changed to night. And on the other side of the beech-tree, touched with moonlight, a motionless white stag stood watching her. It was a hart of the sixth year, and stood already higher than any hart of the twelfth; full five foot high it stood, and its grand soft shining flanks seemed to be molded of marble for their grandeur, and silk for their smoothness, and moonlight for their sheen. Its new antlers were branching towards their yearly strength, and the triple-pointed crowns rose proudly from the beam that was their last perfection. The eyes of the girl and the beast met full, and neither wavered. The hart came to her noiselessly, and laid its muzzle on her hair, and when she put her hand on its pure side it arched its noble neck and licked her cheek. Then, stepping as proudly and as delicately as Rosalind's self, it moved on through the trees; and she followed it.

The forest changed from beech to pine and fir. It deepened and grew strange to her. She did not know it. And the light of the sky turned here from silver to gray, and she felt about her the stir of unseen things. But she looked neither to the right nor the left, but followed the snow-white hart that went before her. It brought her at last to its own drinking-place, and as soon as she saw it old rumors gathered themselves into a truth, and she knew that this was the lost Wishing-Pool. And she remembered that this night was Midsummer Eve, and by the position of the ghostly moon she saw it was close on midnight. So she knelt down by the edge of the mere, and stretched her hands above it, the palms to the stars, and in a low clear voice she made her prayer.

"Whatever spirit dwells under these waters," said she, "I know not whether you are a power for good or ill. But if it is true that you will answer in this hour the need of any that calls on you—oh, Spirit, my need is very great to-night. Hunger is bitter in my body, and my strength is nearly wasted. A hind cast me his crust to-day, and five hours I have battled with myself not to creep back to the place where it still lies and eat of that vile bread. I do not fear to die, but I fear to die of my hunger lest they sneer at the last of my race brought low to so mean a death. Neither will I die by my own act, lest they think my courage broken by these breaking days. On my knees," said she, "I beseech you to send me in some wise a little money, if it be but a handful of pennies now and then throughout the year, so that I may keep my head unbowed. Or if this is too much to ask, and even of you the asking is not easy, then send some high and sudden accident of death to blot me out before I grow too humble, and the lofty spirits of my fathers deny one whose spirit ends as lowly as their dust. Death or life I beg of you, and I care not which you send."

Then clasping her hands tightly, she called twice more her plea across the mere: "Spirit of these waters, grant me life or death! Oh, Spirit, grant me life or death!"

There was a stir in the forest as she made an end, and she remained stock still, waiting and wondering. But though she knelt there till the moon had crossed the bar of midnight, nothing happened.

Then the white hart, which had lain beside the water while she prayed, rose silently and drank; and when it was satisfied, laid once more its muzzle on her hair and licked her cheek again and moved away. Not a twig snapped under its slender stepping. Its whiteness was soon covered by the blackness.

Faint and exhausted, Rosalind arose. She dragged herself through the wood and presently found the broad road that curled down the deserted hill and over the bridge, and at last by a branching lane to her ruined dwelling. The door of her tower creaked desolately to and fro a little, open as she had left it. She pushed it further ajar and stumbled in and up the narrow stair. But the pale moonlight entered her chamber with her, silvering the oaken stump that was her table; and there, where there had been nothing, she beheld two little heaps of copper coins.

The gold year waned, and the next passed from white to green; and in the gold Harding began to hunt his hart, and by the green had not succeeded in bringing it to bay. Twice he had seen it at a distance on the hills, and once had started it from cover in Coombe Wood and followed it through the Denture and Stammers, Great Bottom and Gumber, Earthem Wood and Long Down, Nore Hill and Little Down; and at Punchbowl Green he lost it. He did not care. A long chase had whetted him, and he had waited so long that he was willing to wait another year, and if need were two or three, for his royal quarry. He knew it must be his at last, and he loved it the more for the speed and strength and cunning with which it defied him. It had a secret lair he could never discover; but one day that secret too should be his own. Meanwhile his blood was heated, and the Red Hunter dreamed of the hart and of one other thing.

And while he dreamed Proud Rosalind grew glad and strong on her miraculous dole of money, that was always to her hand when she had need of it. Fear went out of her life, for she knew certainly now that she was in the keeping of unseen powers, and would not lack again. And little by little she too began to build a dream out of her pride; for she thought, I am all my fathers' house, and there will be no honor to it more except that which can come through me. And whenever tales went about of the fame of the fair young Queen of Bramber Castle, and the crowning of her name in this tourney and in that, or of the great lords and princes that would have died for one smile of her (yet her smiles came easily, and her kisses too, men said), Rosalind knit her brows, and her longing grew a little stronger, and she thought: If arrows and steel might once flash lightnings about my father's daughter, and cleave the shadows that have hung their webs about my fathers' hearth!

She now began to put by a little hoard of pennies, for she meant to buy flax to spin the finest of linen for her body, and purple for sleeves for her arms, and scarlet leather for shoes for her feet, and gold for a fillet for her head; and so, attired at last as became her birth, one day to attend a tourney where perhaps some knight would fight his battle in her name. And she had no other thought in this than glory to her dead race. But her precious store mounted slowly; and she had laid by nothing but the money for the fine linen for her robe, when a thing happened that shattered her last foothold among men.

For suddenly all the countryside was alive with a strange rumor. Some one had seen a hart upon the hills, a hart of twelve points, fit for royal hunting. Kings will hunt no lesser game than this. But this of all harts was surely born to be hunted only by a maiden queen, for, said the rumor, it was as white as snow. Such a hart had never before been heard of, and at first the tale of it was not believed. But the tale was repeated from mouth to mouth until at last all men swore to it and all winds carried it; and amongst others some wind of the Downs bore it across the land from Arun to Adur, and so it reached the ears of Queen Maudlin of Bramber. Then she, a creature of quick whims, who was sated with the easy conquests of her beauty, yet eager always for triumphs to cap triumphs, devised a journey from Adur to Arun, and a great summer season of revelry to end in an autumn chase. "And," said she, "we will have joustings and dancings in beauty's honor, but she whose knight at the end of all brings her the antlers of the snow-white hart shall be known for ever in Sussex as the queen of beauty; since, once I have hunted it, the hart will be hart-royal." For this, as perhaps you know, dear maidens, is the degree of any hart that has been chased by royalty.

However, before the festival was undertaken, the Queen of Bramber must needs know if the Arun could show any habitation worthy of her; and her messengers went and came with a tale of a noble castle fallen into ruins, but with its four-square walls intact, and a sward within so smooth and fair that it seemed only to await the coming of archers and dancers. So the Queen called a legion of workmen and bade them go there and build a dwelling in one part of the green court for her to stay in with her company. "And see it be done by midsummer," said she. "Castles, madam," said the head workman, "are not built in a month, or even in two." "Then for a frolic we'll be commoners," said the Queen, "and you shall build on the sward not a castle, but a farm." So the workmen hurried away, and set to work; and by June they had raised within the castle walls the most beautiful farmhouse in Sussex; and over the door made a room fit for a queen.

But alas for Proud Rosalind!

When the men first came she confronted them angrily and commanded them to depart from her fathers' halls. And the head workman looked at the ruin and her rags and said, "What halls, girl? and where are these fathers? and who are you?"—and bade his men get about the Queen's work. And Rosalind was helpless. The men from the Adur asked the people of the Arun about her, and what rights she had to be where she was. And they, being unfriendly to her, said, "None. She is a beggar with a bee in her bonnet, and thinks she was once a queen because her housing was once a castle. She has been suffered to stay as long as it was unwanted; but since your Queen wants it, now let her go." And they came in a body to drive her forth. But they got there too late. The Proud Rosalind had abandoned her conquered stronghold, and where she lived from this time nobody knew. She was still seen on the roads and hills now and again, and once as she passed through Bury on washing-day the women by the river called to her, "Where do you live now, Proud Rosalind, instead of in a castle?" And Rosalind glanced down at the kneeling women and said in her clear voice, "I live in a castle nobler than Bramber's, or even than Amberley's; I live in the mightiest castle in Sussex, and Queen Maudlin herself could not build such another to live in."

"Then you'll doubtless be making her a great entertainment there, Proud Rosalind," scoffed the washers.

"I entertain none but the kings of the earth there," said Rosalind. And she made to walk on.

"Why then," mocked they, "you'd best seek one out to hunt the white hart in your name this autumn, and crown you queen over young Maudlin, Proud Rosalind."

And Rosalind stopped and looked at them, longing to say, "The white hart? What do you mean?" Yet for all her longing to know, she could not bring herself to ask anything of them. But as though her thoughts had taken voice of themselves, she heard the sharp questions uttered aloud, "What white hart, chatterers? Of what hunt are you talking?" And there in mid-stream stood Harding in his boat, keeping it steady with the great pole of the oar.

"Why, Red Boatman," said they, "did you not know that the Queen of Bramber was coming to make merry at Amberley?"

"Ay," said Harding.

"And that our proud lady Rosalind, having, it seems, found a grander castle to live in, has given hers up to young Maudlin?"

Harding glanced to and from the scornful tawny girl and said, "Well?"

"Well, Red Boatman! On Midsummer Eve the Queen comes with her court, and on Midsummer Day there will be a great tourney to open the revels that will last, so they say, all through summer. But the end of it all is to be a great chase, for a white hart of twelve points has been seen on the hills, and the Queen will hunt it in autumn till some lucky lord kneels at her feet with its antlers; and him, they say, she'll marry."

Then Harding once more looked at Rosalind over the water, and she flung back a look at him, and each was surprised to see dismay on the other's brow. And Harding thought, "Is she angry because SHE is not the Queen of the chase?" And Rosalind, "Would HE be the lord who kneels to Queen Maudlin?" But neither knew that the trouble in each was really because their precious secret was now public, and the white hart endangered. And Rosalind's thought was, "It shall be no Queen's quarry!" And Harding's, "It shall be no man's but mine!" Then Harding plied his way to the ferry, and Rosalind went hers to none knew where; though some had tried vainly to track her.

In due course June passed its middle, and the Queen rode under the Downs from Bramber to Amberley. And early on Midsummer Eve, while her servants made busy about the coming festival, Queen Maudlin went over the fields to the waterside and lay in the grass looking to Bury, and teased some seven of her court, each of whom had sworn to bring her the Crown of Beauty at his sword's point on the morrow. Her four maidens were with her, all maids of great loveliness. There was Linoret who was like morning dew on grass in spring, and Clarimond queenly as day at its noon, and Damarel like a rose grown languorous of its own grace, and Amelys, mysterious as the spirit of dusk with dreams in its hair. But Maudlin was the pale gold wonder of the dawn, a creature of ethereal light, a vision of melting stars and wakening flowers. And she delighted in making seem cheap the palpable prettiness of this, or too robust the fuller beauty of that, or dim and dull the elusive charm of such-an-one. She would have scorned to set her beauty to compete with those who were not beautiful, even as a proved knight would scorn to joust with an unskilled boor. So now amongst her beautiful attendants, knowing that in their midst her greater beauty shone forth a diamond among crystals, she laughed at her seven lovers; and her four friends laughed with her.

"You do well, Queen Maudlin, to make merry," said one of the knights, "for I know none that gains so much service for so little portion. What will you give to-morrow's victor?"

"What will to-morrow's victor think his due?" said she.

The seven said in a breath, "A kiss!" and the five laughed louder than ever.

Then Maudlin said, "For so great an honor as victory, I should feel ashamed to bestow a thing of such little worth."

"Do you call that thing a little worth," said one, "which to us were more than a star plucked out of heaven?"

"The thing, it is true," said Maudlin, "has two values. Those who are over-eager make it a thing of naught, those from whom it is hard-won render it priceless. But, sirs, you are all too eager, I could scatter you baubles by the hour and leave you still desiring. But if ever I wooed reluctance to receive at last my solitary favor, I should know I was bestowing a jewel."

"When did Maudlin ever meet reluctance?" sighed one, the youngest.

A long shadow fell upon her where she lay in the grass, and she looked up to see the great form of Harding passing at a little distance.

"Who is that?" said she.

"It must be he they call the Red Smith," said Damarel idly.

"He looks a rough, silent creature," remarked Amelys. And Clarimond added in loud and insolent tones, "He knows little enough of kissings, I would wager this clasp."

"It's one I've a fancy for," said young Queen Maudlin. "Red Smith!" called she.

Harding turned at the sweet sound of her voice, and came and stood beside her among the group of girls and knights.

"Have you come from my castle?" said she, smiling up at him with her dawn-blue eyes.

"Ay," he answered.

"What drew you there, big man? My serving-wench?"

The Red Smith stared down at her light alluring loveliness. "Serving-wenches do not draw me."

"What metal then? Gold?" Maudlin tossed him a yellow disc from her purse. He let it fall and lie.

"No, nor gold." His eyes traveled over her gleaming locks. "The things you name are too cheap," said he.

Maudlin smiled a little and raised herself, till she stood, fair and slender, as high as his shoulder.

"What thing draws you, Red Smith?"

"Steel." And he showed her a fine sword-blade, lacking its hilt. "I was sent for to mend this against the morrow."

"I know that blade," said Maudlin, "it was snapped in my cause. Have you the hilt too?"

"In my pouch," said Harding, his hand upon it.

Hers touched his fingers delicately. "I will see it."

He brushed her hand aside and unbuttoned his pouch; but as he drew out the hilt of the broken sword, she caught a glimpse of that within which held her startled gaze.

"What jewels are those?" she asked quickly.

"Old relics," Harding said with sudden gruffness.

"Show them to me!"

Reluctantly he obeyed, and brought forth a ring, a circlet, and a girdle of surpassing workmanship, wrought in gold thick-crusted with emeralds. A cry of wonder went up from all the maidens.

"There's something else," said Maudlin; and without waiting thrust her hand into the bottom of the pouch and drew out a mesh of silver. It was so fine that it could be held and hidden in her two hands; yet when it fell apart it was a garment, as supple as rich silk. The four maids touched it softly and looked their longings.

"Are these your handicraft?" said Maudlin.

"Mine?" Harding uttered a short laugh. "Not I or any man can make such things."

"You are right," said Maudlin. "Wayland's self might acknowledge them. Smith, I will buy them of you."

"You cannot give me my price."

"Gold I know does not tempt you." She smiled and came close beside him.

"Then do not offer it."

"Shall it be steel?"

Harding's eyes swept her flower-like beauty. "Not from Queen Maudlin."

"True. My bid is costlier."

"Name it."

"A kiss from my mouth."

At the sound of his laughter the rose flowed into her cheek.

"What, a bauble for my jewel, too-eager lady?" he said harshly. "Do the women of this land hold themselves so light? In mine men carve their kisses with the sword. Hark ye, young Queen! set a better value on that red mouth if you'd continue to have it valued."

"I could have you whipped for this," said Maudlin.

"I do not think so," Harding answered, and stepped down the river- bank into his waiting boat.

"I keep my clasp," said Clarimond.

Seven men sprang hotly to their feet. "What's your will, Queen?"

"Nothing," said Maudlin slowly, as she watched him row over the water. "Let the smith go. This test was between him and me and no man's business else. Well, he is of a temper to come through fire unmelted." She flashed a smile upon the seven that made them tremble. "But he is a mannerless churl, we will not think of him. Which among YOU would spurn my kiss?" She offered her mouth in turn, and seven flames passed over its scarlet. Maudlin laughed a little and beckoned her watching maids. "Well!" she said, taking the path to the castle, "He that had had strength to refuse me might have worn my favor to-morrow and for ever."

And meanwhile by the further river-bank came Rosalind, with mushrooms in her skirt. And as she walked by the water in the evening she looked across to her lost castle-walls, and touched the pennies in her pouch and dreamed, while the sun dressed the running flood in his royalest colors.

"Linen and purple and scarlet and gold," mused she; "and so I might sit there to-morrow among the rest. But linen and purple!" she said in scorn, "what should they profit my fathers' house? It is no silken daughter we lack, but a son of steel."

And as she pondered a shadow crossed her, and out of his boat stepped Harding, new from his encounter with the Queen. He did not glance at her nor she at him; but the gleam of the broken weapon he carried cut for a single instant across her sight, and her hands hungered for it.

"A sword!" thought she. "Ay, but an arm to wield the sword. Nay, if I had the sword it may be I could find an arm to wield it." She dropped her chin on her breast, and brooded on the vanishing shape of the Red Smith. "If I had been my fathers' son—oh!" cried she, shaken with new dreams, "what would I not give to the man who would strike a blow for our house?"

Then she recalled what day it was. A year of miracles and changes had sped over her life; if she desired new miracles, this was the night to ask them.

So close on midnight Proud Rosalind once more crept up to Rewell Wood; and on its beechen skirts the white hart came to her. It came now as to a friend, not to a stranger. And she threw her arm over its neck, and they walked together. As they walked it lowered its noble antlers so cunningly that not a twig snapped from the boughs; and its antlers were as beautiful as the boughs with their branches and twigs, and to each crown it had added not one, but two more crockets, so that now its points were sixteen. Safe under its guard the maiden ventured into the mysteries of the hour, and when they came to the mere the hart lay down and she knelt beside it with her brow on its soft panting neck, and thought awhile how she would shape her wish. And feeling the strength of its sinews she said aloud, "Oh, champion among stags! were there a champion among men to match you, I think even I could love him. Yet love is not my prayer. I do not pray for myself." And then she stood upright and stretched her hands towards the water and said again, less in supplication than command:

"Spirit, you hear—I do not pray for myself. Of old it may be maidens often came in sport or fear, to make a mid-summer pastime of their love-dreams. Oh, Spirit! of love I ask nothing for myself. But if you will send me a man to strike one blow in my name that is my fathers' name, he may have of me what he will!"

Never so proudly yet had the Proud Rosalind held herself as when she lifted her radiant face to the moon and sent her low clear call thrice over the mystic waters. Gloriously she stood with arms extended, as though she would give welcome to any hero stepping through the night to consummate her wish. But none came. Only the subdued rustling that had stirred the woods a year ago whispered out of the dark and died to silence.

The arms of the Proud Rosalind dropped to her sides.

"Is the time not yet?" said she, "and will it never be? Why, then, let me belong for ever to the champion that strikes for me to-morrow in the lists. A sorry champion," said she a wan smile, "yet I will hold me bound to him according to my vow. But first I must win him a sword."

Then she kissed the white hart between the eyes and said, "Go where you will. I shall be gone till daylight." And it rose up to run the moonlit hills, and she went down through the trees, and left the Wishing-Pool to its unruffled peace.

Straight down towards sleeping Bury Rosalind went, full of her purpose; and after an hour passed through the silent village.

Her errand was not wholly easy to her, but she thought, "I do not go to ask favors, but plain dealings; and it must be done secretly or not at all." As she came near the ferry a red glow broke on her vision.

"Does the water burn?" she said, and quickened her steps. To her surprise she saw that Harding's forge was busy; the light she had seen sprang from it. She had expected to find it locked and silent, but now the little space it held in the night was lit with fire and resounded with the stroke of the Red Smith's hammer.

Proud Rosalind stood fast as though he were fashioning a spell to chain her eyes. And so he was, for he hammered on a sword.

He did not turn his head at her approach; but when at last she stood beside his door, and did not move away, he spoke to her.

"You walk late," said he.

"May not people walk late," said she, "as well as work late?"

Without answering he set himself to his task again and heeded her no more. "Smith!" she cried imperiously.

"What then?"

"I came to speak with you."

"Even so?" She barely heard the words for the din of his great hammer.

"You are unmannerly, Smith."

"Speak then," said he, dropping his tools, "and never forget, maid, that it is not I invited this encounter."

At that she cried out hotly, "Does not your shop invite trade?"

"Ay; but what's that to you?"

"My only purpose in talking with you," she said in a flame of wrath. "I require what you have, but I would rather buy it of any man than you."

"What do you require?"

"That!" She pointed to the sword.

"I cannot sell it. It is a young knight's blade I am mending against the jousting."

"Have you no other?"

"You cannot give me my price," said the Red Smith.

She took from her girdle the little purse containing all her store. "Do you think I am here to bargain? There's more than your price."

"However much it be," said Harding, "it is too little."

"Then say no more that I cannot buy of you, but rather that you will not sell to me."

"And yet that is as the Proud Rosalind shall please."

She flushed deeply, and as though in shame of seeming ashamed said firmly, "No, Smith, it is not in my hands. For I have offered you every penny I possess."

"I do not ask for pence." Harding left his anvil and stepped outside and stood close, gazing hard upon her face. "You have a thing I will take in exchange for my sword, a very simple thing. Women part with it most lightly, I have learned. The loveliest hold it cheap at the price of a golden gawd. How easily then will you barter it for an inch or so of steel!"

"What need of so many words?" she said with a scornful lip, that quivered in her own despite at his nearness. "Name the thing you want."

"A kiss from your mouth, Proud Rosalind."

It was as though the request had turned her into ice. When she could speak she said, "Smith, for your inch of steel you have asked what I would not part with to ransom my soul."

She turned and left him and Harding went back to his work and laughed softly in his beard. "Dream on, my gold queen up yonder," said he, and blew on his waning fires. "You are not the metal I work in," said he, and the river rang again to his hammer on the steel.

But Rosalind went rapidly down to the waterside saying in her heart, "Now I will see whether I cannot get me a lordlier weapon of a better craftsman than you, and at my own price, Red Smith." And when she had come to the ferry she laid her full purse on the bank and cried softly into the night:

"Wayland Smith, give me a sword!"

And then she went away for awhile, and paced the fields till the first light glimmered on the east; and not daring to wait longer for fear of encountering early risers, she turned back to the ferry. And there, shining in the dawn, she found such a blade as made the father in her soul exult. In all its glorious fashioning and splendid temper the hand of the god was manifest. And in the grass beside it lay her purse, of its full store lightened by one penny-piece.

Now to this tale of legends revived and then forgotten, gossips' tales of Wishing-Pools and Snow-white Harts and a God who worked in the dark, we must begin to add the legend of the Rusty Knight. It lasted little longer than the three months of that strange summer of sports within the castle-walls of Amberley. It was at the jousting on Midsummer Day that he first was seen. The lists were open and the roll of knights had answered to their names, and cried in all men's ears their ladies' praises; and nine in ten cried Maudlin. And as the last knight spoke, there suddenly stood in the great gateway an unknown man with his vizard closed, and his coming was greeted with a roar of laughter. For he was clothed from head to foot in antique arms, battered and rusted like old pots and pans that have seen a twelvemonths' weather in a ditch. Out of the merriment occasioned by his appearance, certain of the spectators began to cry, "A champion! a champion!" And others nudged with their elbows, chuckling, "It is the Queen's jester."

But the newcomer stood his ground unflinchingly, and when he could be heard cried fiercely, "They who call me jester shall find they jest before their time. I claim by my kingly birth to take part in this day's fray; and men shall meet me to their rue!"

"By what name shall we know you?" he was asked.

"You shall call me the Knight of the Royal Heart," he said.

"And whose cause do you serve?"

"Hers whose beauty outshines the five-fold beauty in the Queen's Gallery," said he, "hers who was mistress here and wrongly ousted— the most peerless lady of Sussex, Proud Rosalind."

With that the stranger drew forth and flourished a blade of so surpassing a kind that the knights, in whom scorn had vanquished mirth, found envy vanquishing scorn. As for the ladies, they had ceased to smile at the mention of Rosalind, whom none had seen, though all had heard of the girl who had been turned from her ruin at Maudlin's whim; and that this ragged lady should be vaunted over their heads was an insult only equaled by the presence among their shining champions of the Rusty Knight. For by this name only was he spoken thereafter.

Now you may think that the imperious stranger who warned his opponents against laughing before their time, might well have been warned against crowing before his. And alas! it transpired that he crowed not as the cock crows, who knows the sun will rise; for at the first clash he fell, almost unnoticed. And when the combatants disengaged, he had disappeared. He was a subject for much mirth that evening; though the men rankled for his sword and the women for a sight of his lady.

But from this day there was not a jousting held in Maudlin's revels at which the Rusty Knight did not appear; and none from which he bore away the crown. The procedure was always the same: at the last instant he appeared in his ignominious arms, and stung the mockers to silence by the glory of his sword and his undaunted proclamation of his lady. So ardent was his manner that it was difficult not to believe him a conqueror among men and her the loveliest of women, until the fray began; when he was instantly overcome, and in the confusion managed to escape. He was so cunning in this that though traps were laid to catch him he was never traced. By degrees he became, instead of a joke, a thorn in the flesh. It was the women now who itched to see his face, and the men who desired to find out the Proud Rosalind; for by his repeated assertion her beauty came to be believed in, and if the ladies still spoke slightingly of her, the lords in their thoughts did not. But the summer drew to its close without unraveling the mystery. The Rusty Knight was never followed nor the Proud Rosalind found. And now they were on the eve of a different hunting.

For now all the days were to be given up to the pursuit of the rumored hart, whom none had yet beheld; and Queen Maudlin said, "For a month we will hunt by day and dance by night, and if by that time no man can boast of bringing the hart to bay and no woman of owning his antlers, we will acknowledge ourselves outwitted; and so go back to Adur. And it may prove that we have been brought to Arun by an idle tale, to hunt a myth; but be that as it may, see to your bowstrings, for to-morrow we ride forth."

And the men laid by their swords and filled their quivers.

And in the midnight Rosalind came once more from her secret lair to Bury, and laying her purse by the ferry called softly:

"Wayland Smith, give me a bow!"

And in the dawn, before people were astir, she found a bow the unlike of any fashioned by mortal craft, and a quiverful of true arrows; and for these the god had taken his penny fee.

On a lovely day of autumn the chase began. And the red deer and the red fox started from their covers; and the small rabbits stopped their kitten-play on the steep warrens of the Downs, and fled into their burrows; and birds whirred up in screaming coveys, and the kestrel hovered high and motionless on the watch. There was game in plenty, and many men were tempted and forgot the prize they sought. The hunt separated, some going this way and some that. And in the evening all met again in Amberley. And some had game to show and some had none. And one had seen the hart.

When he said so a cry went up from the company, and they pressed round to hear his tale, and it was a strange one.

"For," said he, "where Great Down clothes itself with the North Wood I saw a flash against the dark of the trees, and out of them bounded the very hart, taller than any hart I ever dreamed of, and, as the tale has told, as pure as snow; and the crockets spring from its crowns like rays from a summer cloud. I could not count them, but its points are more than twelve. When it saw me it stood motionless, and trembling with joy I fitted my arrow to the string; but even as I did so out of the trees ran another creature, as strange as the white hart. It was none other than the Rusty Knight; I knew him by his battered vizard, which was closed. But for the rest he wore now, not rust, but rags—a tattered jerkin in place of battered mail. Yet in his hands was a bow which among weapons could only be matched by his sword. He took his stand beside the snow-white hart, and cried in that angry voice we have all heard, These crowns grow only to the glory of the Proud Rosalind, the most peerless daughter of Sussex, and no woman but she shall ever boast of them!' And before I could move or answer for surprise, he had set his arrow to his bow, and drawn the string back to his shoulder, and let fly. It was well I did not start aside, or it might have hit me; for I never saw an arrow fly so wild of its mark. But the whole circumstance amazed me too much for quick action, and before I could come up and chastise this unskillful archer, or even aim at the prize which stood beside him, he and the hart had plunged through the wood again, the man running swiftfoot as the beast; and when I followed I could not find them, and unhappily my dogs were astray."

The strange tale stung the tempers of all listeners, both men and women.

"Well, now," laughed Maudlin, "it has at least been seen that the hart is the whitest of harts."

"But it has not yet been seen," fumed Clarimond, "that this Rosalind is the most beautiful of women."

"Nor have we seen," said the knight who told the tale, "who it is that insults our manhood with valiant words and no deeds to prove them. Yet with such a sword and such a bow a man might prove anything."

The next day all rode forth on fire with eagerness. And at the end of it another knight brought back the selfsame tale. He sword that in the tattered archer was no harm at all but his arrogance, since he was clearly incapable of hitting where he aimed. But his very presence and his swift escape, running beside the hart, made failure seem double; for the derision he excited recoiled on the deriders, who could not bring this contemptible foe to book. After that day many saw him, sometimes at a great distance, sometimes near enough to be lashed by his insolent tongue. He always kept beside the coveted quarry, as though to guard it, and ran when it ran, with incredible speed; but once when he flagged after a longer chase than usual, he had been seen to leap on its back, and so they escaped together. From dawn to dusk through that bright month of autumn the man and the hart were hunted in vain; and in all that while their lair was never discovered. It was now taken for granted that where one would be the other would be; and in all likelihood Proud Rosalind also.

At last the final day of the month and the chase arrived, and Maudlin spoke to her mortified company. Among them all she was the only one who laughed now, for her nature was like that of running water, reflecting all things, retaining none; she could never retain her disappointments longer than a day, or her affections either.

"Sirs and dames," said she, "I see by your clouded faces it is time we departed, but we will depart as we came in the sun. If this day bring no more fruit than its fellows, neither victory to a lord nor sovereignty to his lady, we will to-morrow hold the mightiest tourney of the year, and he who wins the crown shall give it to his love, and she shall be called for ever the fairest of Sussex; but for that, if her lord desire it, she shall wed him—yes, though it be myself she shall!"

And at this the hearts of nine men in ten leapt in their breasts for longing of her, and in the tenth for longing of Linoret or Clarimond or Damarel or Amelys; and all went to the chase thinking as much of the morrow as of the day.

It was the day when the forests burned their brightest. The earth was fuller of color than in the painted spring; the hedgerows were hung with brilliant berries in wreaths and clusters, luminous briony and honeysuckle, and the ebony gloss of the privet making more vivid the bright red of the hips and the dark red of the haws. The smooth flat meadows and smooth round sides of the Downs were not greener in June; nor in that crystal air did the river ever run bluer than under that blue sky. The elms were getting already their dusky gold and the beeches their brighter reds and golds and coppers; where they were young and in thin leaf the sun-flood watered them to transparent pinks and lemons, as bright, though not as burning, as the massed colors of the older trees. That day there was magic on the western hills, for those who could see it, and trees that were not trees.

So Rosalind who, like all the world, was early abroad, though not with all the world, saw a silver cloud pretending to be white flowers upon a hawthorn; never in spring sunlight had the bush shone whiter. But when Maudlin rode by later she saw, not a cloud in flower, but a flowerless tree, dressed with the new-puffed whiteness of wild clematis, its silver-green tendrils shining through their own mist.

Then Rosalind saw a sunset pretending to be a spindle-tree, scattering flecks of red and yellow light upon the ground, till the grass threw up a reflection of the tree, as a cloud in the east will reflect another in the west. But when Maudlin came riding the spots of light upon the ground were little pointed leaves, and the sunset a little tree as round as a clipped yew, mottled like an artist's palette with every shade from primrose to orange and from rose to crimson.

And last, in a green glade under a steep hollow overhung with ash, Rosalind saw a fairy pretending to be a silver birch turned golden. For her leaves hung like the shaking water of a sunlit fountain, and she stood alone in the very middle of the glade as though on tip-toe for a dance; and all the green trees that had retreated from her dancing-floor seemed ready to break into music, so that Rosalind held her breath lest she should shatter the moment and the magic, and stayed spell-bound where she was. But an hour afterwards Maudlin, riding the chalky ledge on the ash-grown height, looked down on that same sight and uttered a sharp cry; for she saw, no fairy, but a little yellowing birch, and under it the snow-white hart with the Rusty Knight beside him. Then all the company with her echoed the cry, and the forest was filled with the round sounds of horns and belling hounds. And while in great excitement men sought a way down into the steep glen, the hart and his ragged guard had started up, and vanished through the underworld of trees.

The hue and cry was taken up. Not one or two, but fifty had now seen the quarry, and panted for the glory of the prize. And so, near the very beginning of the day, the chase began.

The scent was found and lost and found again. The stag swam the river twice, once at South Stoke, and once at Houghton Bridge, and the man swam with it; and then, keeping over the fields they ran up Coombe and went west and north, over Bignor Hill and Farm Hill, through the Kennels and Tegleaze. They were sighted on Lamb Lea and lost in Charlton. They were seen again on Heyshott and vanished in Herringdean Copse. They crossed the last high-road in Sussex and ran over Linch Down and Treyford nearly into Hampshire; and there the quarry turned and tried to double home by Winden Wood and Cotworth Down. The marvel was that the Rusty Knight was always with it, sometimes beside it, often on its back; and even when he bestrode it, it flew over the green hills like a white sail driven by a wind at sea, or a cloud flying the skies. When it doubled it had shaken off the greater part of the hunt. But through Wellhanger and over Levin some followed it still. In the woods of Malecomb only the seven knights who most loved Maudlin remained staunch; and they were spurred by hope, because when they now sighted it it seemed as though the hart began to tire, and its rider drooped. Their own steeds panted, and their dogs' tongues lolled; but over the dells and rises, woods and fields, they still pressed on, exulting that they of all the hunt remained to bring the weary gallant thing to bay.

Once more they were in the home country, and the day was drawing to a glorious close. In the great woods of Rewell the hart tried to confuse the scent and conceal itself with its spent comrade, but it was too late; for it too was nearly spent. Yet it plunged forward to the ridge of Arundel with its high fret of trees like harp-strings, filled with the music of the evening sky. And here again among the dipping valleys, the quarry sought to shake off the pursuit; but as vainly as before. In that exhausted close for hunters and hunted, the first had triumph to spur the last of their strength, and the second despair to eke out theirs. At Whiteways the hart struck down through a secret dip, into the loveliest hidden valley of all the Downs; and descending after it the knights saw suddenly before them a great curve of the steely river, lying under the sunset like a scimitar dyed with blood. And in a last desperate effort the hart swerved round a narrow footway by the river, and disappeared.

The knights followed shouting with their baying dogs, and the next instant were struck mute with astonishment. For the narrow wooded path by the water suddenly swung open into a towering semi-circle of dazzling cliffs, uprising like the loftiest castle upon earth: such castles as heaven builds of gigantic clouds, to scatter their solid piles with a wind again. But only the hurricanes of the first day or the last could bring this mighty pile to dissolution. The forefront of the vast theater was a perfect sward, lying above the water like a green half-moon; beyond and around it small hills and dells rose and fell in waves until they reached the brink of the great cliffs. At the further point of the semi-circle the narrow way by the river began again, and steep woods came down to the water cutting off the north.

And somewhere hidden in the hemisphere of little hills the hart was hidden, without a path of escape.

The men sprang from their horses, and followed the barking dogs across the sward. At the end of it they turned up a neck of grass that coiled about a hollow like the rim of a cup. It led to a little plateau ringed with bushes, and smelling sweet of thyme. At first it seemed as though there were no other ingress; but the dogs nosed on and pointed to an opening through the thick growth on the left, and disappeared with hoarse wild barks and yelps; and their masters made to follow.

But at the same instant they heard a voice come from the bushes, a voice well known to them; but now it was exhausted of its power, though not of its anger.

"This quarry and this place," it cried, "are sacred to the Proud Rosalind and in her name I warn you, trespassers, that you proceed at your peril!"

At this the seven knights burst into laughter, and one cried, "Why, then, it seems we have brought the lady to bay with the hart—a double quarry, friends. Come, for the dogs are full of music now, and we must see the kill."

As they moved forward an arrow sped far above their heads.

Then a second man cried, "We could shoot into the dark more surely than this clumsy marksman out of it. Let us shoot among the trees and give him his deserts. And after that let nothing hold us from the dogs, for their voices turn the blood in me to fire."

So each man plucked an arrow from his quiver.

And as he fitted it, lo! with incredible swiftness seven arrows shot through the air, and one by one each arrow split in two a knight's yew-bow. The men looked at their broken bows amazed. And as they looked at each other the dogs stopped baying, one by one.

One of the knights said, breathing heavily, "This must be seen to. The man who could shoot like this has been playing with us since midsummer. Let us come in and call him to account, and make him show us his Proud Rosalind."

They made a single movement towards the opening; at the same moment there was a great movement behind it, and they came face to face with the hart-royal. It stood at bay, its terrible antlers lowered; its eyes were danger-lights, as red as rubies. And the seven weaponless men stood rooted there, and one said, "Where are the dogs?"

But they knew the dogs were dead.

So they turned and went out of that place, and found their horses and rode away.

And when they had gone the hart too turned again, and went slowly down a little slipping path through the bushes and came to the very inmost chamber of its castle, a round and roofless shrine, walled half by the bird-haunted cliffs and half by woods. Within on the grass lay the dead hounds, each pierced by an arrow; and on a bowlder near them sat the Rusty Knight, with drooping head and body, regarding them through the vizard he was too weary to raise. He was exhausted past bearing himself. The hart lay down beside him, as exhausted as he.

But a sound in the forest that thickly clothed the cliff made both look up. And down between the trees, almost from the height of the cliff, climbed Harding the Red Hunter, bow in hand. He strode across the little space that divided them still, and stood over the Rusty Knight and the white Hart-Royal. And both might have been petrified, for neither stirred.

After a little Harding began to speak. "Are you satisfied, Rusty Knight," said he, "with what you have done in Proud Rosalind's honor?"

The Rusty Knight did not answer.

"Did ever lady have a sorrier champion?" Harding laughed roughly. "She would have beggared herself to get you a sword. And she got you a sword the like of which no knight ever had before. And how have you used it? All through a summer you have brought laughter upon her. She would have beggared herself again to get you a bow that only a god was worthy to draw. And how have you drawn it? For a month you have drawn it to men's scorn of her and of you. You have cried her praises only to forfeit them. You have vaunted her beauty and never crowned it. And what have you got for it?" The Rusty Knight was as dumb as the dead. Harding stepped closer. "Shall I tell you, Rusty Knight, what you have got for it? Last Midsummer Eve by the Wishing-Well the Proud Rosalind forswore love if heaven would send her a man to strike a blow in her name for her fathers' sake. She did not say what sort of man or what sort of blow. She asked in her simplicity only that a blow should be struck. And like a woman she was ready to find it enough, and in gratitude repay it with that which could only in honor be exchanged for what honored her. Yet I myself heard her swear to hold herself bound to the sorry champion who should strike for her in the tourney. And you struck and fell. Did you tell her you fell when you came to her, crownless? And how did she crown you for your fall, Rusty Knight?"

The Knight sprang to his feet and stood quivering.

"That moves you," said Harding, "but I will move you more. The Proud Rosalind is not your woman. She is mine. She was mine from the moment her eyes fell. She was only a child then, but I knew she was mine as surely as I knew this hart was mine and no other's, when first I saw it as a calf drink at its pool.

But I was patient and waited till he, my calf, should become a king, and she, my heifer, a queen. And I am her man because I am of king's stock in my own land, and she of king's stock in hers. And I am her man because for a year I have kept her, without her knowledge, with the pence I earned by my sweat, that were earned for a different purpose. And I am her man because the hart you have defended so ill, and hampered for a month, was saved to-day by my arrows, not yours. It was my arrows slew the hounds from the top of the cliff. It was my arrows split the bows of the seven knights. And it is my arrow now that will kill the White Hart that in all men's sight I may give her the antlers to-morrow, and hear my Proud Rosalind called queen among women."

And as he spoke Harding drew back suddenly, and fitted a shaft to his string as though he would shoot the hart where it lay.

But the Rusty Knight sprang forward and caught his hands crying, "Not my Hart! you shall not shoot my Hart!" And he tore off his casque, and the great tawny mantle of Rosalind's hair fell over her rags, and her face was on fire and her bosom heaving; and she sank down murmuring, "I beg you to spare my Hart."

But Harding, uttering a great laugh of pride and joy, caught her up before she could kneel, saying, "Not even to me, my Proud Rosalind!" And without even kissing her lips, he put her from him and knelt before her, and kissed her feet.

("Will you be so good, Mistress Jane," said Martin, "as to sew on my button?"

"I will not knot my thread, Master Pippin," said Jane, "till you have snapped yours."

"It is snapped," said Martin. "The story is done."

Joscelyn: It is too much! it is TOO much! You do it on purpose!

Martin: Oh, Mistress Joscelyn! I never do anything on purpose. And therefore I am always doing either too much or too little. But in what have I exceeded? My story? I am sorry if it is too long.

Joscelyn: It was too short—and you are quibbling.

Martin: I?—But never mind. What more can I say? It is a fault, I know; but as soon as my lovers understand each other I can see no further.

Joscelyn: There are a thousand things more you can say. Who this Harding was, for one.

Joyce: And what he meant by saying his pennies had kept her, for another.

Jennifer: And for what other purpose he had intended them.

Jessica: And you must describe all that happened at the last tourney.

Jane: And what about the ring and the girdle and the circlet and the silver gown?

"I would so like to know," said little Joan, "if Harding and Rosalind lived happily ever after. Please won't you tell us how it all ended?"

"Will women NEVER see what lies under their noses?" groaned Martin. "Will they ALWAYS stare over a wall, and if they're not tall enough to try to stare through it? Will they ONLY know that a thing has come to its end when they see it making a new beginning? Why, after the first kiss all tales start afresh, though they start on the second, which is as different from the first as a garden rose from a wild one. Here have I galloped you to a conclusion, and now you would set me ambling again."

"Then make up your mind to it," said Joscelyn, "and amble."

"Dear heaven!" went on Martin, "I begin to believe that when a woman is being kissed she doesn't even notice it for thinking, How sweet it will be when he kisses me next Tuesday fortnight!"

"Then get on to Tuesday fortnight," scolded Joscelyn, "if that be the end."

"The end indeed!" said Martin. "On Tuesday fortnight, at the very instant, the slippery creature is thinking, How delicious it was when he kissed me two weeks ago last Saturday! There's no end with a woman, either backwards or forwards!"

"For goodness' sake," cried Joscelyn, "stop grumbling and get on with it!"

"There's no end to a man's grumbling either," said Martin; "but I'll get on with it.")

The tale that Harding had to tell Proud Rosalind was a long one, but I will make as short of it as I can. He told her how in his own country he was sprung of the race of Volundr, who was a God and a King and a Smith all in one; but he had been ill-used and banished, and had since haunted England where men knew him as Wayland, and he did miracles. But in his own northern land his strain continued, until Harding's father, a king himself, was like his ancestor defeated and banished, and crossed the water with his young son and a chest of relics of Old Wayland's work—a ring, a girdle, a crown, and a silver robe; a sword and bow which Rosalind knew already; and other things as well. And the boy grew up filled with the ancient wrongs of his ancestor, and he went about the country seeking Wayland's haunts; and wherever he found them he found a mossy legend, neglected and unproved, of how the god worked, or had worked, for any man's pence, and put his divine craft to laborers' service. And as in Rosalind the dream had grown of building up her fathers' honor again, so Harding had from boyhood nursed his dream of establishing that of the half-forgotten god. And he, who had inherited his ancestor's craft in metal, coming at last through Sussex settled at Bury, where the legend lay on its sick-bed; and he set up his shop by the ferry so that he might doctor it. And there he did his work in two ways; for as the Red Smith he did such work as might be done better by a hundred men, but as Wayland he did what could only have been done better by the god. And the toll he collected for that work he saved, year-in-year-out, till he should have enough to build the god a shrine. And, leaving this visible evidence behind him, he meant to depart to his own land, and let the faith in Wayland wax of itself. And then Harding told Rosalind how he had first seen the hart when it was a calf six years before at midsummer, and how it had led him to the Wishing-Well; and he had marked it for his own. And how in the same year he had first noticed Rosalind, a girl not yet sixteen, and, for the fire of kings in her that all her poverty could not extinguish, chosen her for his mate.

"And year by year," said Harding, "I watched to see whether the direst want could bring you to humbleness, and saw you only grow in nobleness; and year by year I lay in wait for my four-footed quarry each Midsummer Eve beside the Wishing-Pool, and saw it grow in kingliness. And last year, as you know, I saw you come to the Pool beside the hart, and heard you make your high prayer for life or death. And if I had not been able to give you the life, I would have given you the death you prayed for. But I went before you, and going by the ferry put my old god's money in your room before you could be there. And from time to time I robbed his store to keep you. But when in spring they drove you from the castle I did not know where to find you; and I hunted for your lair as I hunted for the hart's, and never knew they were the same. Then this year came the wishing- time again, and lying hidden I heard you cry for a man to strike for you. And I was tempted then to reveal myself and make you know to what man you were committed. But I decided that I would wait and strike for you in the tourney, and come to you for the first time with a crown. And so I went back to the ferry and set to work; and to my amazement you followed me, and for the first time of your own will addressed me. I wondered whether you had come to be humble before your time, and if you had been I would have let you go for ever; but when you spoke with scorn as to a servant who had once forgotten himself so far as to play the man to you, I laughed in my heart and prized your scorn more dearly than your favor; and said to myself, To-morrow she shall know me for her man. But when you went down to the water and made your demand of Wayland, for his sake and yours I was ready to give you a weapon worthy of your steel. So I gave you the god's own sword and waited to see what use you would make of it. And you made as ill an use as after you made of the god's bow. And while men spoke betwixt wrath and mockery of the Rusty Knight, I loved more dearly that champion who was doing so ill so bravely for a championless lady." Then Harding looked her steadily in the eyes, and though her face was all on fire again as he alone had power to make it, she did not flinch from his gaze, and he took her hand and said, "No man has ever struck a blow for you yet, Proud Rosalind, but the Rusty Knight will strike for you to-morrow; and as to-day there was no marksman, so to-morrow there shall be no swordsman who can match him. And when he has won the crown of Sussex for you, you shall redeem your pledge of the Wishing-Well and give him what he will. Till then, be free." And he dropped her hand again and let her go.

She turned and went quickly into the bushes and soon she came out bearing the miserable arms of the Rusty Knight and the glorious sword.

"These are all that were in my fathers' castle for many years," she said, "and I took them when I went away and the white hart brought me to his own castle. But though these are big for me, they will be small for you."

And Harding looked at them and laughed his short laugh. "The casque alone will serve," he said. "By that and the sword men shall know me. I have my own arms else; and I will take on myself the shame of this ludicrous casque, and redeem it in your name. And you shall have these in exchange." And he handed her his pouch and bade her what to do in the morning, and went away. He still had not kissed her mouth, nor had she offered it.

Now there is very little left to tell. On the morrow, when the roll of knights had been called, all eyes instinctively turned to the great gateway, by which the Rusty Knight had always come at the last moment. And as they looked they saw whom they expected, but not what they expected. For though his head was hidden in the rusty casque, and though he held the sword which all men covet, he was clad from neck to foot in arms and mail so marvelously chased and inwrought with red gold that his whole body shone ruddy in the sunshaft. And men and women, dazzled and confused, wondered what trick of light made him appear more tall and broad than they remembered him; so that he seemed to dwarf all other men. The murmur and the doubt went round, "Is it the Rusty Knight?"

Then in a voice of thunder he replied, "Ay, if you will, it is the Rusty Knight; or the Red Knight, or the Knight of the Royal Heart, or of the Hart-Royal; but by any name, the knight of the Proud Rosalind, who is the proudest and most peerless of all the maids of Sussex, as this day's work shall prove."

And none laughed.

The joust began; and before the Rusty Knight the rest went down like corn beaten by hail. And all men marveled at him, and all women likewise. And the young Queen Maudlin of Bramber, a prey to her whims, loved him as long as the tourney lasted. And when it was ended, and he alone stood upright, she rose in her seat and held out to him the crown of gold and flowers upon a silken pillow, crying, "You have won this, you unknown, unseen champion, and it is your right to give it where you will; and none will dispute her supremacy in beauty for ever." And as he strode and knelt to receive the crown she added quickly, "And I know not whether the promise has reached your ears which yesterday was made—that she who accepts the crown is to wed the victor, although he choose the Queen herself to wear it."

And she smiled down at him like morning smiling out of the sky; and her beauty was such as to make a man forget all other beauty and all resolutions. But Harding took the crown from her and touched her hand with the rusty brow of his casque and said, "A Queen will wear it, for my lady's fathers were once Kings of Amberley."

Then Maudlin stamped her foot as a butterfly might, and cried, "Where is this lady whom you keep as hidden as your face?"

And Harding rose and turned towards the gateway, and all turned with him; and into the arch rode Rosalind on the white hart. And she was clothed from her neck to the soles of her naked feet in a sheath of silver that seemed molded to her lovely body; and about her waist a golden girdle hung, set with green stones, and from her finger a great emerald shot green fire, and on her head a golden fillet lay in the likeness of close-set leaves with clusters of gleaming green berries that were other emeralds; and under it her glory of hair fell like liquid metal down her back and over the hart's neck, as low as her silver hem. And the hart with its splendid antlers stood motionless and proud as though it knew it carried a young Queen. But indeed men wondered whether it were not a young goddess. And so for a very few moments this carven vision of gold and silver and ivory and molten bronze and copper and green jewels stood in their gaze. And then Harding bore the crown to her and knelt, and stood up again and crowned her before them all; and laying his hand upon the white hart's neck, moved away with it and its beautiful rider through the gateway. And no one moved or spoke or tried to stop them. But by the footway over the water-meadows they went, and at the river's edge found Harding's broad flat boat with the bird's beak. And Harding said, "Will you come over the ferry with me, Proud Rosalind?"

And Rosalind answered, "What is your fee, Red Boatman?"

Then Harding answered, "For that which flows I take only that which flows."

And Rosalind, stooping of her own accord from the white hart's back, kissed him.

I shall be very uncomfortable, Mistress Jane, till you have sewed on my button.

FIFTH INTERLUDE

The milkmaids had not thought of their apples for the last hour, but now, remembering them, they fell to refreshing their tongues with the sweet flavors of fruit and talk.

Jessica: I cannot rest, Jane, till you have pronounced upon this story.

Jane: I never found pronouncement harder, Jessica. For who can pronounce upon anything but a plain truth or a plain falsehood? and I am too confused to extricate either from such a hotch-potch of magic as came to pass without the help of any real magician.

Martin: Oh, Mistress Jane! are you sure of that? Did not Rosalind's wishes come true, and can there be magic without a magician?

Jane: Her wishes came true, I know, both by the pool and by the ferry; but that the pool and the ferry were supernatural remains unproved. Because in both cases her wishes were brought about by a man. And if there was any other magician at all, you never showed him to us.

Martin: Dear Mistress Jane, where were your eyes? I showed you the greatest of all the magicians that give ear to the wishes of women; and when it is necessary to bring them about, he puts his power on a man and the man makes them come true. Which is a magic you must often have noticed in men, though you may never have known the magician's name.

Joscelyn: We have never noticed any magic whatever in men. And we don't want to know the magician's name. We don't believe in anything so silly as magic.

Martin: I hope, Mistress Joscelyn, there were moments in my story not too silly to be believed in.

Joscelyn: Silliness in stories is more or less excusable, since they are not even supposed to be believed. And is there still a Wishing- Pool on Rewell and a ferry at Bury?

Martin: The ferry is there, but Harding's hammer is silent. And where his shop stood is a little cottage where children live, who dabble in summer on the ferry-step. And their mother will run from her washing or cooking to take you over the water for the same fee that Wayland asked for shoeing a poor man's donkey or making a rich man's sword. And this is the only miracle men call for from those banks to-day; and if ever you tried to take a boat across the Bury currents, you would not only believe in miracles but pray for one, while your boat turned in mid-stream like a merry-go-round. So there's no doubt that the ferry-wife is a witch. But as for the Wishing-Pool, it is as lost as it was before the white hart led two lovers to discover it at separate times, and having brought them together passed with them and its secret out of men's knowledge. For neither it nor Harding nor Rosalind was seen again in Sussex after that day. And yet I can tell you this much of their fortunes: that whatever befell them wherever they wandered, he was a king and she a queen in the sight of the whole world, which to all lovers consists of one woman and one man; and their lives were crowned lives, and they carried their crown with them even when they came in the same hour to exchange one life for another. But this was only a long and cloudless reign on earth.

Jane: Well, it is a satisfaction to know that. For at certain times your story seemed so overshadowed with clouds that I was filled with doubts.

Joan: Oh, but Jane! even when we walk in the thickest clouds on the Downs, we are certain that presently some light will melt them, or some wind blow them away.

Joyce: Yes, it never once occurred to me to doubt the end of the story.

Jennifer: Nor to me. And so the clouds only kept one in a delicious palpitation, at which one could secretly smile, without having to stop trembling.

Jessica: Was it possible, Jane, that YOU could be deceived as to the conclusion of this love-story? Why, even I saw joy coming as plain as a pikestaff.

Martin: And I, with love for its bearer. For that magician, who touches the plainest things with a radiance, makes plain girls and boys look queens and kings, and plain staves flowering branches of joy. And in this case I can think of only one catastrophe that could have obscured or distorted that vision.

Two of the Milkmaids: What catastrophe, pray?

Martin: If Rosalind had refused to believe in anything so silly as magic.

The silence of the Seven Sleepers hung over the Apple-Orchard.

Joscelyn: Then she would have proved herself a girl of sense, singer, and your tale would have gained in virtue. As it stands, I should not have grieved though the clouds had never been dispersed from so foolish a medley of magic and make-believe.

Martin: So be it, if it must be so. We will push back our lovers into their obscurities, and praise night for the round moon above us, who has pushed three parts of her circle clear of all obstacles, and awaits only some movement of heaven to blow the last remnant of cloud from her happy soul. And because more of her is now in the light than in the dark, she knows it is only a question of time. But the last hours of waiting are always the longest, and we like herself can do no better than spend them in dreams, where if we are lucky we shall catch a glimpse of the angels of truth.

Like the last five leaves blown from an autumn branch, the milkmaids fluttered from the apple-tree and couched their sleepy heads on their tired arms, and went each by herself into her particular dream; where if she found company or not she never told. But Jane sat prim and thoughtful with her elbow in her hand and her finger making a dimple in her cheek, considering deeply. And presently Martin began to cough a little, and then a little more, and finally so troublesomely that she was obliged to lay her profound thoughts aside, to attend to him with a little frown. Was even Euclid impervious to midges?

"Have you taken cold, Master Pippin?" said Jane.

"I'm afraid so," he confessed humbly; "for we all know that when we catch cold the grievance is not ours, but our nurse's."

"How did it happen?" demanded Jane, rightly affronted. "Have you been getting your feet wet in the duckpond again?"

"The trouble lies higher," murmured Martin, and held his shirt together at the throat.

Jane looked at him and colored and said, "That is the merest pretense. It was only one button and it is a very warm night. I think you must be mistaken about your cold."

"Perhaps I am," said Martin hopefully.

"And you only coughed and coughed and kept on coughing," continued Jane, "because I had forgotten all about you and was thinking of something quite different."

"It is almost impossible to deceive you," said Martin.

"Oh, Master Pippin," said Jane earnestly, "since I turned seventeen I have seen into people's motives so clearly that I often wish I did not; but I cannot help it."

Martin: You poor darling!

Jane: You must not say that word to me, Master Pippin.

Martin: It was very wrong of me. The word slipped out by mistake. I meant to say clever, not poor.

Jane: Did you? I see. Oh, but—

Martin: Please don't be modest. We must always stand by the truth, don't you think?

Jane: Above all things.

Martin: How long did it take you to discover my paltry ruse? How long did you hear me coughing?

Jane: From the very beginning.

Martin: And can you think of two things at once?

Jane: Of course not.

Martin: No? I wish two was the least number of things I ever think of at once. Mine's an untidy way of thinking. Still, now we know where we are. What were you thinking about me so earnestly when I was coughing and you had forgotten all about me?

Jane: I—I—I wasn't thinking about you at all.

And she got down from the swing and walked away.

Martin: Now we DON'T know where we are.

And he got down from the branch and walked after her.

Martin: Please, Mistress Jane, are you in a temper?

Jane: I am never in a temper.

Martin: Hurrah.

Jane: Being in a temper is silly. It isn't normal. And it clouds people's judgments.

Martin: So do lots of things, don't they? Like leapfrog, and mad bulls, and rum punch, and very full moons, and love—

Jane: All these things are, as you say, abnormal. And I have no more use for them than I have for tempers. But being disheartened isn't being in a temper; and I am always disheartened when people argue badly. And above all, men, who, I find, can never keep to the point. Although they say—

Martin: What do they say?

Jane: That girls can't.

Martin began to cough again, and Jane looked at him closely, and Martin apologized and said it was that tickle in his throat, and Jane said gravely, "Do you think I can't see through you? Come along, do!" and opened her housewife, and put on her thimble, and threaded her needle, and got out the button, and made Martin stand in a patch of moonlight, and stood herself in front of him, and took the neck of his shirt deftly between her left finger and thumb, and began to stitch. And Martin looking down on the top of her smooth little head, which was all he could see of her, said anxiously, "You won't prick me, will you?" and Jane answered, "I'll try not to, but it is very awkward." Because to get behind the button she had to lean her right elbow on his shoulder and stand a little on tiptoe. So that Martin had good cause to be frightened; but after several stitches he realized that he was in safe hands, and drew a big breath of relief which made Jane look up rather too hastily, and down more hastily still; so that her hand shook, and the needle slipped, and Martin said "Ow!" and clutched the hand with the needle and held it tightly just where it was. And Jane got flustered and said, "I'm so sorry."

Martin: Why should you be? You've proved your point. If I knew any man that could stick to his so well and drive it home so truly, I would excuse him for ever from politics and the law, and bid him sit at home with his work-basket minding the world's business in its cradle. It is only because men cannot stick to the point that life puts them off with the little jobs which shift and change color with every generation. But the great point of life which never changes was given from the first into woman's keeping because, as all the divine powers of reason knew, only she could be trusted to stick to it. I should be glad to have your opinion, Jane, as to whether this is true or not.

Jane: Yes, Martin, I am convinced it is true.

Martin: Then let the men shilly-shally as much as they like. And so, as long as the cradle is there to be minded, we shall have proved that out of two differences unions can spring. My buttonhole feels empty. What about my button?

Jane: I was just about to break off the thread when you—

Martin: When I what?

Jane: Sighed.

Martin: Was it a sigh? Did I sigh? How unreasonable of me. What was I sighing for? Do you know?

Jane: Of course I know.

Martin: Will you tell me?

Jane: That's enough. (And she tried to break off the thread.)

Martin: Ah, but you mustn't keep your wisdom to yourself. Give me the key, dear Jane.

Jane: The key?

Martin: Because how else can the clouds which overshadow our stories be cleared away? How else can we allay our doubts and our confusions and our sorrows if you who are wise, and see motives so clearly, will not give us the key? Why did I sigh, Jane? And why does Gillian sigh? And, oh, Jane, why are you sighing? Do you know?

Jane: Of course I know.

Martin: And won't you give me the key?

Jane: That's quite enough.

And this time she broke off the thread. And she put the needle in and out of the pinked flannel in her housewife, and she tucked the thimble in its place. And then she felt in a little pocket where something clinked against her scissors, and Martin watched her. And she took it out and put it in his hand. And his hand tightened again over hers and he said gravely, "Is it a needle?"

"No, it is not," said Jane primly, "but it's very much to the point."

"Oh, you wise woman!" whispered Martin (and Jane colored with satisfaction, because she was turned seventeen). "What would poor men do without your help?"

Then he kissed very respectfully the hand that had pricked him: on the back and on the palm and on the four fingers and thumb and on the wrist. And then he began looking for a new place, but before he could make up his mind Jane had taken her hand and herself away, saying "Good night" very politely as she went. So he lay down to dream that for the first time in his life he had made up his mind. But Jane, whose mind was always made up, for the first time in her life dreamed otherwise.

It happened that by some imprudence Martin had laid himself down exactly under the gap in the hedge, and when Old Gillman came along the other side crying "Maids!" in the morning, the careless fellow had no time to retreat across the open to safe cover; so there was nothing for it but to conceal himself under the very nose of danger and roll into the ditch. Which he hurriedly did, while the milkmaids ran here and there like yellow chickens frightened by a hawk. Not knowing what else to do, they at last clustered above him about the gap, filling it so with their pretty faces that the farmer found room for not so much as an eyelash when he arrived with his bread. And it was for all the world as though the hedge, forgetting it was autumn, had broken out at that particular spot into pink-and-white may. So that even Old Gillman had no fault to find with the arrangement.

"All astir, my maids?" said he.

"Yes, master, yes!" they answered breathlessly; all but Joscelyn, who cried, "Oh! oh! oh!" and bit her lip hard, and stood suddenly on one foot.

"What's amiss with ye?" asked Gillman.

"Nothing, master," said she, very red in the face. "A nettle stung my ankle."

"Well, I'd not weep for t," said Gillman.

"Indeed I'm not weeping!" cried Joscelyn loudly.

"Then it did but tickle ye, I doubt," said Gillman slyly, "to blushing-point."

"Master, I AM not blushing!" protested Joscelyn. "The sun's on my face and in my eyes, don't you see?"

"I would he were on my daughter's, then," said Gillman. "Does Gillian still sit in her own shadow?"

"Yes, master," answered Jane, "but I think she will be in the light very shortly."

"If she be not," groaned Gillman, "it's a shadow she'll find instead of a father when she comes back to the farmstead; for who can sow wild oats at my time o' life, and not show it at last in his frame? Yet I was a stout man once."

"Take heart, master," urged Joyce eyeing his waistcoat. But he shook his head.

"Don't be deceived, maid. Drink makes neither flesh nor gristle; only inflation. Gillian!" he shouted, "when will ye make the best of a bad job and a solid man of your dad again?"

But the donkey braying in its paddock got as much answer as he.

"Well, it's lean days for all, maids," said Gillman, and doled out the loaves from his basket, "and you must suffer even as I. Yet another day may see us grow fat." And he turned his basket upside down on his head and moved away.

"Excuse me, master," said Jane, "but is Nellie, my little Dexter Kerry, doing nicely?"

"As nicely as she ever does with any man," said Gillman, "which is to kick John twice a day, mornings and evenings. He say he's getting used to it, and will miss it when you come back to manage her. But before that happens I misdoubt we'll all be plunged in rack and ruin."

And he departed, making his usual parrot-cry.

"I'm getting fond of old Gillman," said Martin sitting up and picking dead leaves out of his hair; "I like his hawker's cry of Maids, maids, maids!' for all the world as though he had pretty girls to sell, and I like the way he groans regrets over his empty basket as he goes away. But if I had those wares for market I'd ask such unfair prices for them that I'd never be out of stock."

"What's an unfair price for a pretty girl, Master Pippin?" asked Jessica.

"It varies," said Martin. "Joan I'd not sell for less than an apple, or Joyce for a gold-brown hair. I might accept a blade of grass for Jennifer and be tempted by a button for Jane. You, Jessica, I rate as high as a saucy answer."

"Simple fees all," laughed Joyce.

"Not so simple," said Martin, "for it must be the right apple and the particular hair; only one of all the grass-blades in the world will do, and it must be a certain button or none. Also there are answers and answers."

"In that case," said Jessica, "I'm afraid you've got us all on your hands for ever. But at what price would you sell Joscelyn?"

"At nothing less," said Martin, "than a yellow shoe-string."

Joscelyn stamped her left foot so furiously that her shoe came off. And little Joan, anxious to restore peace, ran and picked it up for her and said, "Why, Joscelyn, you've lost your lace! Where can it be?" But Joscelyn only looked angrier still, and went without answering to set Gillian's bread by the Well-House; where she found nothing whatever but a little crust of yesterday's loaf.

And surprised out of her vexation she ran back again exclaiming, "Look, look! as surely as Gillian is finding her appetite I think she is losing her grief."

"The argument is as absolute," said Martin, "as that if we do not soon breakfast my appetite will become my grief. But those miserable ducks!"

And he snatched the crust from Joscelyn's hand and flung it mightily into the pond; where the drake gobbled it whole and the ducks got nothing.

And the girls cried "What a shame!" and burst out laughing, all but Joscelyn who said under her breath to Martin, "Give it back at once!" But he didn't seem to hear her, and raced the others gayly to the tree where they always picnicked; and they all fell to in such good spirits that Joscelyn looked from one to another very doubtfully, and suddenly felt left out in the cold. And she came slowly and sat down not quite in the circle, and kept her left foot under her all the time.

As soon as breakfast was over Jennifer sighed, "I wish it were dinner-time."

"What a greedy wish," said Martin.

"And then," said she, "I wish it were supper-time."

"Why?" said he.

"Because it would be nearer to-morrow," said Jennifer pensively.

"Do you want it to be to-morrow so much?" asked Martin. And five of the milkmaids cried, "oh, yes!"

"That's better than wanting it to be yesterday," said Martin, "yet I'm always so pleased with to-day that I never want it to be either. And as for old time, I read him by a dial which makes it any hour I choose."

"What dial's that?" asked Joyce. And Martin looked about for a Dandelion Clock, and having found one blew it all away with a single puff and cried, "One o'clock and dinner-time!"

Then Jennifer got a second puff and blew on it so carefully that she was able to say, "Seven o'clock and supper-time!"

And then all the girls hastened to get clocks of their own, and make their favorite time o'day.

"When I can't make it come right," confided little Joan to Martin, "I pull them off and say six o'clock in the morning."

"It's a very good way," agreed Martin, "and six o'clock in the morning is a very good hour, except for lazy lie-abeds. Isn't it?"

"Nancy always looked for me at six of a summer morning," said little Joan.

"Yes," said Martin, "milkmaids must always turn their cows in before the dew's dry. And carters their horses."

"Sometimes they get so mixed in the lane," said Joan.

"I am sure they do," said Martin. "How glad your cows will be to see you all again."

"Are you certain we shall be out of the orchard to-morrow, Master Pippin?" asked Jane.

"Heaven help us otherwise," said he, "for I've but one tale left in my quiver, and if it does not make an end of the job, here we must stay for the rest of our lives, puffing time away in gossamer."

Then Jessica, blowing, cried, "Four o'clock! come in to tea!"

And Joyce said, "Twelve o'clock! baste the goose in the oven."

"Three o'clock! change your frock!" said Jane.

"Eight o'clock! postman's knock!" said Jennifer.

"Ten o'clock! to bed, to bed!" cried Jessica again.

"Nine o'clock!—let me run down the lane for a moment first," begged little Joan.

Then Martin blew eighteen o'clock and said it was six o'clock tomorrow morning. And all the girls clapped their hands for joy—all except Joscelyn, who sat quite by herself in a corner of the orchard, and neither blew nor listened. And so they continued to change the hour and the occupation: now washing, now wringing, now drying; now milking, now baking, now mending; now cooking their meal, now eating it; now strolling in the cool of the evening, now going to market on marketing-day:—till by dinner they had filled the morning with a week of hours, and the air with downy seedlings, as exquisite as crystals of frost.

At dinner the maids ate very little, and Jessica said, "I think I'm getting tired of bread."

"And apples?" said Martin.

"One never gets tired of apples," said Jessica, "but I would like to have them roasted for a change, with cream. Or in a dumpling with brown sugar. And instead of bread I would like plum-cake."

"What wouldn't I give for a bowl of curds and whey!" exclaimed Joyce.

"Fruit salad and custard is nice," sighed Jennifer.

"I could fancy a lemon cheesecake," observed Jane, "or a jam tart."

"I should like bread-and-honey," said little Joan. "Bread-and- honey's the best of all."

"So it is," said Martin.

"You always have to suck your fingers afterwards," said Joan.

"That's why," said Martin. "Quince jelly is good too, and treacle because if you're quick you can write your name in it, and picked walnuts, and mushrooms, and strawberries, and green salad, and plovers' eggs, and cherries are ripping especially in earrings, and macaroons, and cheesestraws, and gingerbread, and— "

"Stop! stop! stop! stop! stop!" cried the milkmaids.

"I can hardly bear it myself," said Martin. "Let's play See-Saw."

So the maids rolled up a log from one part of the orchard, and Martin got a plank from another part, because the orchard was full of all manner of things as well as girls and apples, and he straddled one end and said, "Who's first?" And Jessica straddled the other as quick as a boy, and went up with a whoop. But Joyce, who presently turned her off, sat sideways as gay and graceful as a lady in a circus. And Jennifer crouched a little and clung rather hard with her hands, but laughed bravely all the time. And Jane thought she wouldn't, and then she thought she would, and squeaked when she went up and fell off when she came down, so that Martin tumbled too, and apologized to her earnestly for his clumsiness; and while he rubbed his elbows she said it didn't matter at all. But little Joan took off her shoes, and with her hands behind her head stood on the end of the see-saw as lightly as a sunray standing on a wave, and she looked up and down at Martin, half shyly because she was afraid she was showing off, and half smiling because she was happy as a bird. And Joscelyn wouldn't play. Then the girls told Martin he'd had more than his share, and made him get off, and struggled for possession of the see-saw like Kings of the Castle. And Martin strolled up to Joscelyn and said persuasively, "It's such fun!" but Joscelyn only frowned and answered, "Give it back to me!" and Martin didn't seem to understand her and returned to the see-saw, and suggested three a side and he would look after Jane very carefully. So he and Jane and Jennifer got on one end, and Jessica, Joyce and Joan sat on the other, and screaming and laughing they tossed like a boat on a choppy sea: until Jessica without any warning jumped off her perch in mid-air and destroyed the balance, and down they all came helter-skelter, laughing and screaming more than ever. But Jane reproved Jessica for her trick and said nobody would believe her another time, and that it was a bad thing to destroy people's confidence in you; and Jessica wiped her hot face on her sleeve and said she was awfully sorry, because she admired Jane more than anybody else in the world. Then Martin looked at the sun and said, "You've barely time to get tidy for supper." So the milkmaids ran off to smooth their hair and their kerchiefs and do up ribbons and buttons or whatever else was necessary. And came fresh and rosy to their meal, of which not one of them could touch a morsel, she declared.

"Dear, dear, dear!" said Martin anxiously. "What's the matter with you all?"

But they really didn't know. They just weren't hungry. So please wouldn't he tell them a story?

"This will never do," said Martin. "I shall have you ill on my hands. An apple apiece, or no story to-night."

At this dreadful threat Joan plucked the nearest apple she could find, which was luckily a Cox's Pippin.

"Must I eat it all, Martin?" she asked. (And Joscelyn looked at her quickly with that doubtful look which had been growing on her all day.)

"All but the skin," said Martin kindly. And taking the apple from her he peeled it cleverly from bud to stem, and handed her back nothing but the peel. And she twirled the peel three times round her head, and dropped it in the grass behind her.

"What is it? what is it?" cried the milkmaids, crowding.

"It's a C," said Martin. And he gave Joan her apple, and she ate it.

Then Joyce came to Martin with a Beauty of Bath, and he peeled it as he had Joan's, and withheld the fruit until she had performed her rite. And her letter was M. Jennifer brought a Worcester Pearmain, and threw a T. And Jessica chose a Curlytail and made a perfect O. And Jane, who preferred a Russet, threw her own initial, and Martin said seriously, "You're to be an old maid, Jane." (And Joscelyn looked at him.) And Jane replied, "I don't see that at all. There are lots of lots of J's, Martin." (And Joscelyn looked at her.) Then Martin turned inquiringly to Joscelyn, and she said, "I don't want one." "No stories then," said

Martin as firm as Nurse at bedtime. And she shook her shoulders impatiently. But he himself picked her a King of Pippins, the biggest and reddest in the orchard, and peeled it like the rest and gave her the peel. And very crossly she jerked it thrice round her head, so that it broke into three bits, and they fell on the grass in the shape of an agitated H. And Martin gave her also her Pippin.

"But what about your own supper?" said little Joan.

And Martin, glancing from one to another, gathered a Cox, a Beauty, a Pearmain, a Curlytail, a Russet, and a King of Pippins; and he peeled and ate them one after another, and then, one after another, whirled the parings. And every one of the parings was a J.

Then, while Martin stood looking down at the six J's among the clover-grass, and the milkmaids looked anywhere else and said nothing: little Joan slipped away and came back with the smallest, prettiest, and rosiest Lady Apple in Gillman's Orchard, and said softly, "This one's for you."

So Martin pared it slenderly, and the peel lay in his hand like a ribbon of rose-red silk shot with gold; and he coiled it lightly three times round his head and dropped it over his left shoulder. And as suddenly as bubbles sucked into the heart of a little whirlpool, the milkmaids ran to get a look at the letter. But Martin looked first, and when the ring of girls stood round about him he put his foot quickly on the apple-peel and rubbed it into the grass. And without even tasting it he tossed his little Lady Apple right over the wicket, and beyond the duckpond, and, for all the girls could see, to Adversane.

Then Jane and Jessica and Jennifer and Joyce and little Joan, as by a single instinct, each climbed to a bough of the center apple-tree, and left the swing empty. And Martin sat on his own bough and waited for Joscelyn. And very slowly she came and sat on the swing and said without looking at him:

"We're all ready now."

"All?" said Martin. And he fixed his eyes on the Well-House, where it made no difference.

"Most of us, anyhow," said Joscelyn; "and whoever isn't ready is—nearly ready."

"Yet most is not all, and nearly is not quite," said Martin, "and would you be satisfied if I could only tell you most of my story, and was obliged to break off when it was nearly done? Alas, with me it must be the whole or nothing, and I cannot make a beginning unless I can see the end."

"All beginnings must have endings," said Joscelyn, "so begin at once, and the end will follow of itself."

"Yet suppose it were some other end than I set out for?" said Martin. "There's no telling with these endings that go of themselves. We mean one thing, but they mistake our meaning and show us another. Like the simple maid who was sent to fetch her lady's slippers and her lady's smock, and brought the wrong ones."

"She must have been some ignorant maid from a town," said Jane, "if she did not know lady-smocks and lady's-slippers when she saw them."

"It was either her mistake or her lady's," said Martin carelessly. "You shall judge which." And he tuned his lute and, still looking at the Well-House, sang:

The Lady sat in a flood of tears
All of her sweet eyes' shedding.
"To-morrow, to-morrow the paths of sorrow
Are the paths that I'll be treading."
So she sent her lass for her slippers of black,
But the careless lass came running back
  With slippers as bright
  As fairy gold
  Or noonday light,
  That were heeled and soled
  To dance in at a wedding.

The Lady sat in a storm of sighs
Raised by her own heart-searching.
"To-morrow must I in the churchyard lie
Because love is an urchin."
So she sent her lass for her sable frock,
But the silly lass brought a silken smock
  So fair to be seen
  With a rosy shade
  And a lavender sheen,
  That was only made
  For a bride to come from church in.

Now as Martin sang, Gillian got first on her elbow, and then on her knees, and last upright on her two feet. And her face was turned full on the duckpond, and her eyes gazed as though she could see more and further than any other woman in the world, and her two hands held her heart as though but for this it must follow her eyes and be lost to her for ever.

"So far as I can see," said Joscelyn, "there's nothing to choose between the foolishness of the maid and that of the mistress. But since Gillian appears to have risen to some sense in it, for goodness' sake, before she sinks back on her own folly, tell us your tale and be done with it!"

"It is ready now," said Martin, "from start to finish. Glass is not clearer nor daylight plainer to me than the conclusion of the whole, and if you will listen for a very few instants, you shall see as certainly as I the ending of The Imprisoned Princess."

THE IMPRISONED PRINCESS

There was once, dear maidens, a Princess who was kept on an island.

(Joscelyn: There are no islands in Sussex.

Martin: This didn't happen in Sussex.

Joscelyn: But I thought it was a true story.

Martin: It is the only true story of them all.)

She was kept on the island locked up in a tower, for the best of all the reasons in the world. She had fallen in love. She had fallen in love with her father's Squire. So the King banished him for ever and locked up his daughter in a tower on an island, and had it guarded by six Gorgons.

(Joscelyn: It's NOT a true story!

Martin: It IS a true story! If you don't say so at the end I'll give you—

Joscelyn: What?—I don't want you to give me anything!

Martin: All right then.

Joscelyn: What will you give me?

Martin: A yellow shoe-string.)

By six Gorgons (repeated Martin) who had the sharpest claws and the snakiest hair of any Gorgons there ever were. And their faces—

(Joscelyn: Leave their faces alone!

Martin: You're being a perfect nuisance!

Joscelyn: I simply HATE this story!

Martin: Tell it yourself then!

Joscelyn: What ABOUT their faces?)

Their faces (said Martin) were as beautiful as day and night and the four seasons of the year. They were so beautiful that I must stop talking about them or I shall never talk about anything else. So I'd better talk about the young Squire, who was a great deal less interesting, except for one thing: that he was in love. Which is a big advantage to have over Gorgons, who never are. The only other noteworthy thing about him was that his voice was breaking because he was merely fifteen years old. He was just a sort of Odd Boy about the King's court.

(Martin: Mistress Joscelyn, if you keep on wiggling so much you'll get a nasty tumble. Kindly sit still and let me get on. This isn't a very long story.)

One morning in April this Squire sat down at the end of the world, and he sobbed and he sighed like any poor soul; and a sort of wandering fellow who was going by had enough curiosity to stop and ask him what was the matter. And the Squire told him, and added that his heart was breaking for longing of the flower that his lady wore in her hair. So this fellow said, "Is that all?" And he got into his boat, which had a painted prow, and a light green pennon, and a gilded sail, and called itself The Golden Truant, and he sailed away a thousand leagues over the water till he came to the island where the princess was imprisoned; and the six Gorgons came hissing to the shore, and asked him what he wanted. And he said he wanted nothing but to play and sing to them; so they let him. And while he did so they danced and forgot, and he ran to the tower and found the Princess with her beautiful head bowed on the windowsill behind the bars, weeping like January rain. And he climbed up the wall and took from her hair the flower as she wept, in exchange for another which—which the Squire had sent her. And she whispered a word of sorrow, and he another of comfort, and came away. And the Gorgons suspected nothing; except perhaps the littlest Gorgon, and she looked the other way.

So in the summer the Squire told the Wanderer that he would surely die unless he had his lady's ring to kiss; and the fellow went again to the island. The Gorgons were not sorry to see him, and were willing to dance while he played and sang as before; and as before he took advantage of their pleasure, and stole the gold ring from the Princess's hand as she lay in tears behind her bars. But in place of the gold ring he left a silver one which had belonged to— to the Squire. And the voice of her despair spoke through her tears, and he answered it as best he could with the voice of hope. And went away as before, leaving the Gorgons dancing.

Then in the autumn the Squire said to the Wanderer, "Who can live on flowers and rings? If you do not get me my lady herself, let me lie in my grave." So the Wanderer set sail for the third time, though he knew that the dangers and difficulties of this last adventure were supreme; and once more he landed on the island of the Imprisoned Princess. And this time the Gorgons even appeared a little pleased to see him, and let him stay with them six days and nights, telling them stories, and singing them songs, and inventing games to keep them amused. For he was very sorry for them.

(Joscelyn: Why? Why? Why?

Martin: Because he discovered that they were even unhappier than the Princess in her tower.

Joscelyn: It isn't true! It isn't true!

Martin: Look out! you're losing your slipper.)

Of course the Gorgons were unhappier than the Princess. She was only parted from her lover; but they were parted from love itself.

But as the week wore on, miracles happened; for every night one of the Gorgons turned into the beautiful girl she used to be before the Goddess of Reason, infuriated with the Irrational God who bestows on girls their quite unreasonable loveliness, had made her what she was. And night by night the Wanderer rubbed his eyes and wondered if he had been dreaming; for the guardians of the tower no longer hissed, but sighed at love, and instead of claws for the destructions of lovers had beautiful kind hands that longed to help them. Until on the sixth night only one remained this fellow's enemy. But alas! she was the strongest and fiercest of them all.

(Joscelyn: How dare you!)

And her case (said Martin) was hopeless, because she alone of them all had never known what love was, and so had nothing to be restored to.

(Joscelyn: How DARE you!)

And without her (said Martin) there was nothing to be done. She had always had the others under her thumb, and by this time she had the Wanderer in exactly the same place. And so—and so—

And so here is your shoe-string, Mistress Joscelyn; and I am sorry the want of it has been such an inconvenience to you all day, so that you could not make merry with us. But I must forfeit it now, for the story is ended, and I think you must own it is true.

(Joscelyn: I won't take it! The story is NOT true! The story is NOT ended! Finish it at once! None of the others ended like this.

Martin: The others weren't true.

Joscelyn: I don't care. You are to say what happened to the Gorgons.

Joyce: And to the Squire.

Jennifer: And to the Princess.

Jessica: And what she looked like.

Jane: And what happened to the King.

"Please, Martin," said little Joan, "please don't let the story come to an end before we know what happened to the Wanderer."

"I'm tired of telling stories," said Martin, "and I'll never tell another as long as I live. But I suppose I must add the trimmings to this one, or I shall get no peace.")

All these things, dear maidens, are very quickly told, except what the Princess looked like, for that is impossible. No man ever knew. He never got further than her eyes, and then he was drowned. But what does it matter how she looked? She died a thousand years ago of a broken heart. And her Squire, hearing of her death, died too, a thousand leagues away. And the King her father expired of remorse, and his country went to rack and ruin. And the five kind Gorgons had to pay the penalty of their regained humanity, and wilted into their maiden graves. Only the Sixth Gorgon lived on for ever and ever. I dare not think of her solitary eternity. But as for the Wanderer, he is of no importance. A little while he still went wandering, singing these lovers' sorrows to the world, and what became of him I never knew.

That's the end.

And now, dear Mistress Joscelyn, let me lace up your shoe.

(Joscelyn buried her face in her hands and burst out crying.)

POSTLUDE

PART I

There was consternation in the Apple-Orchard.

All the milkmaids came tumbling from their perches to run and comfort their weeping comrade. And as they passed Martin, Joyce cried, "It's a shame!" and Jennifer murmured "How could you?" and Jessica exclaimed "You brute!" and Jane said "I'm surprised at you!" and even little Joan shook her head at him, and, while all the others fondled Joscelyn, and petted and consoled her, took her hand and held it very tight. But with her other hand she took Martin's and held it just as tight, and looked a little anxious, with tears in her blue eyes. Yet she looked a little smiling too. And there were tears also in the eyes of all the milkmaids, because the story had ended so badly, and because they did not in the least know what was going to happen, and because a man had made one of them cry. And Martin suddenly realized that all these girls were against him as much as though it were six months ago. And he swung his feet and looked as though he didn't care, so that Joan knew he was feeling rather sheepish inside, and held his hand a little tighter.

Then Joscelyn, who had the loveliest brown, as Joan had the loveliest blue, eyes in England, lifted her young head and looked at Martin so defiantly through her tears that he knew she had given up the game at last; and he pressed Joan's hand for all he was worth, and began to look ashamed of himself, so that Joan knew he had stopped feeling sheepish in the least. And Joscelyn, in a voice that shook like birch-leaves, said, "I don't want it to end like that."

Martin: Dear Mistress Joscelyn, is it my fault? I promised you the truth, and with your help I have told it.

Joscelyn: How dare you say it's with my help? If I had my way—!

Martin: You shall have it. We will leave the end of the story in your hands.

Joscelyn: I won't have anything to do with it!

Martin: Then I'm afraid it's your fault.

Joscelyn: That's what a man always says!

Martin: Did he?

Joscelyn: Yes, he did! he said it was Eve's fault.

Martin: So it was.

Joscelyn: How dare you!

Martin: He said nothing but the truth. And what did you say?

Joscelyn: I said it was Adam's fault.

Martin: So it was. YOU said nothing but the truth.

Joscelyn: How could it be two people's fault?

Martin: How could it be anything else? Oh, Joscelyn! there are two things in this world that one person alone cannot bring to perfection. And one of them is a fault. It takes two people to make a perfect fault. Eve tempted Adam; and Adam was jolly glad to get tempted if he was half as sensible as he ought to have been. And Eve knew it. And Adam let her know it. And if after that she had not tempted him he would never have forgiven her. When it came to fault-making they understood each other perfectly. And between them they made the most perfect fault in the world.

Joscelyn: (after a very long pause): You said there were two things.

Martin: Two things?

Joscelyn: That one person alone can't bring to perfection.

Martin: Did I?

Joscelyn: What is the other thing?

Martin: Love. Isn't it?

Joscelyn: How dare you ask me?

Martin: I dare ask more than that. Joscelyn, how old are you?

Joscelyn: I sha'n't tell you.

Martin: Joscelyn, you are the tallest of the milkmaids, but you can't help that. How old are you?

Joscelyn: Mind your own business.

Martin: Joscelyn, the first three times I saw you, you had your hair down your back. But ever since I told you my first story you have done it up, like beautiful dark flowers, on each side of your head. And it is my belief that you have no business to have it up at all.

Joscelyn (very angrily): How dare you! Of course I have! Am I not nearly sixteen?

Martin: Nearly?

Joscelyn: Well, next June.

Martin: Oh, Hebe! it's worse than I thought. How dare I? You whipper-snapper! How dare YOU have us all under your thumb? How dare YOU play the Gorgon to Gillian? How dare YOU cry your eyes out because my lovers had an unhappy ending? Go back to your dolls'- house! What does sixteen next June know about Adam? What does sixteen next June know about love?

Joscelyn: Everything! how dare you? everything!

Martin: Am I to believe you? Then by all you know, you baby, give me the sixth key of the Well-House!

And he took from his pocket the five keys he already had, and held out his hand for the last one. Joscelyn's eyes grew bigger and bigger, and the doubt that had troubled her all day became a certainty as she looked from the keys to her comrades, who all got very red and hung their heads.

"Why did you give them up?" demanded Joscelyn.

"Because," Martin answered for them, "they know everything about love. But then they are all more than sixteen years of age, and capable of making the right sort of ending which is so impossible to children like you and me."

Then Joscelyn looked as old as she could and said, "Not so impossible, Master Pippin, if—if—"

But all of a sudden she began to laugh. It was the first time Martin had ever heard her laugh, or her comrades for six months. Their faces cleared like magic, and they all clapped their hands and ran away. And Martin got down from his bough, because when Joscelyn laughed she didn't look more than fourteen.

"If what, Joscelyn?" he said.

"If you'd stolen the right shoe-string, Martin," said she. And she stuck out her right foot with its neatly-laced yellow slipper. Then Martin knelt down, and instead of lacing the left shoe unlaced the right one, and inside the yellow slipper found the sixth key just under the instep. "Is that the right ending?" said Joscelyn. And Martin held the little foot in his hands rubbing it gently, and said compassionately, "It must have been dreadfully uncomfortable."

"It was sometimes," said Joscelyn.

"Didn't it hurt?" asked Martin, beginning to lace up her shoes for her.

"Now and then," said Joscelyn.

"It was an awfully kiddish place to hide it in," said Martin finishing, and as he looked up Joscelyn laughed again, rubbing her tear-stained cheeks with the back of her hand, and for all the great growing girl that she was looked no more than twelve. So he slid under the swing and stood up behind her and kissed her on the back of the neck where babies are kissed.

Then all the milkmaids came back again.

PART II

To every girl Martin handed her key. "This is your business," said he. And first Joan, and next Joyce, and then Jennifer, and then Jessica, and then Jane, and last of all Joscelyn, put her key into its lock and turned. And not one of the keys would turn. They bit their lips and held their breath, and turned and turned in vain.

"This is dreadful," said Martin. "Are you sure the keys are in the right keyholes?"

"They all fit," said little Joan.

"Let me try," said Martin. And he tried, one after another, and then tried each key singly in each lock, but without result. Jane said, "I expect they've gone rusty," and Jessica said, "That must be it," and Jennifer turned pale and said, "Then Gillian can never get out of the Well-House or we out of the orchard." And Martin sat down in the swing and thought and thought. As he thought he began to swing a little, and then a little more, and suddenly he cried "Push me!" and the six girls came behind him and pushed with all their strength. Up he went with his legs pointed as straight as an arrow, and back he flew and up again. The third time the swing flew clean over the Well-House, and as true as a diving gannet Martin dropped from mid-air into the little court, and stood face to face with Gillian.

She was not weeping. She was bathed in blushes and laughter. She held out her hands to him, and Martin took them. She had golden hair of lights and shadows like a wheatfield that fell in two thick plaits over her white gown, and she had gray eyes where smiles met you like an invitation, but you had to learn later that they were really a little guard set between you and her inward tenderness, and that her gayety, like a will-o'-the-wisp, led you into the flowery by-ways of her spirit where fairies played, but not to the heart of it where angels dwelled. Few succeeded in surprising her behind her bright shield, but sometimes when she wasn't thinking it fell aside, and what men saw then took their breath from them, for it was as though they were falling through endless wells of infinite sweetness. And afterwards they could have told you nothing further of her loveliness; when they got as far as her eyes they were drowned. Her features, the curves of her cheeks and lips and chin and delicate nostrils, were as finely-turned as the edge of a wild-rose petal, and her skin had the freshness of dew. The sight of her brought the same sense of delight as the sight of a meadow of cowslips. As sweet and sunny a scent breathed out from her beauty.

But all this Martin only felt without seeing, for he was drowned. Gillian, I suppose, wasn't thinking. So they held each other's hands and looked at each other.

Presently Martin said, "It's time now, Gillian, and you can go."

"Yes, Martin," said Gillian. "How shall I go?"

"As I came," said he.

"Before I go," said she, "I am going to ask you a question. You have asked my friends a lot of questions these six nights, which they have answered frankly, and you have twisted their answers round your little finger. Now you must answer my question as frankly."

"And what will you do?" asked Martin.

"I won't twist your answer," said Gillian gently. "I'll take it for what it is worth. You have been laughing up your sleeve a little at my friends because, having a quarrel with men, they were sworn to live single. But you live single too. Tell me, if you please, what is your quarrel with girls?"

Martin dropped her hands until he held each by the little finger only, and then he answered, "That they are so much too good for us, Gillian."

"Thank you, Martin," said Gillian, taking her hands away. "And now please ask them to send over the swing, for it is time for me to go to Adversane." And as she spoke the light played over her eyes again and floated him up to the surface of things where he could swim without drowning. He saw now the flowers of her loveliness, but no longer the deeps of those gray pools where the light shimmered between herself and him. So he turned and climbed to the pent roof of the Well-House, and looked towards the group of shadows clustered under the apple-tree around the swing; and they understood and launched it through the air, and he caught it as it came. And Gillian in a moment was up beside him.

"Are you ready?" said Martin.

"Yes," she answered getting on the swing, "thank you. And thank you for everything. Thank you for coming three times this year. Thank you for the stories. Thank you for giving their happiness again to my darling friends. Thank you for all the songs. Thank you for drying my tears."

"Are they all dried up?" said Martin.

"All," said Gillian.

"If they were not," said he, "you shall find Herb-Robert growing along the roadside, and the Herbman himself in Adversane."

And holding the swing fast as he sat on the roof, Martin sang her his last song, not very loud, but so clearly that the shadows under the apple-tree heard every note and syllable.

Good morrow, good morrow, dear Herbman Robert!
Good morrow, sweet sir, good morrow!
Oh, sell me a herb, good Robert, good Robert,
To cure a young maid of her sorrow.
And hath her sorrow a name, sweet sir?
No lovelier name or purer,
With its root in her heart and its flower in her eyes,
Yet sell me a herb shall cure her.
Oh, touch with this rosy herb of spring
Both heart and eyes when she's sleeping,
And joy will come out of her sorrowing,
And laughter out of her weeping.

"Good-by, Martin."

"Good-by, Gillian."

"I want to ask you a lot more questions, Martin."

"Off you go!" cried he. And let the swing fly. Back it came.

"Martin! why didn't—"

"Jump when you're clear!" called Martin. But back it came.

"Why didn't the young Squire in the story—"

"Jump this time!" And back it came.

"—come to fetch her himself, Martin?"

"Jump!" shouted Martin; and shut his eyes and put his hands over his ears. But it was no use; again and again he felt the rush of air, and questions falling through it like shooting-stars about his head.

"Martin! what was the name on the eighth floret of grass?"

"Martin! what was the letter you threw with the Lady-peel?"

"Martin! why is my silver ring all chased with little apples?"

"Martin! do you—do you—do you—?"

"Shall I never be rid of this swing?" cried Martin. "Jump, you nuisance, jump when I tell you!"

And she jumped, and was caught and kissed among the shadows.

"Gillian!"

"Gillian!"

"Gillian!"

"Gillian!"

"Gillian!"

"Dear Gillian!"

And then like a golden wave and she the foam, they bore her over the moonlit grass to the green wicket, and they threw it open, and she went like a skipping stone across the duckpond and over the fields to Adversane.

When she had vanished Martin slid down the roof, walked across to the coping, put one leg over, and stepped out of the Well-House.

PART IV

The six milkmaids were waiting for him in the apple-tree—no; Joscelyn was in the swing.

"And so," said Martin, sitting down on the bough, "on the sixth night the sixth Gorgon also became a maiden as lovely as her fellows, and gave the Wanderer the sixth key to the Tower. And they let out the Princess and set her in The Golden Truant, and she sailed away to her Squire a thousand leagues over the water. And everybody lived happily ever after."

"What a beautiful story!" said Jane. And they all thought so too.

"I knew from the first," said Joscelyn, "that it would have a happy ending."

"And so did I," said Joyce.

"And I." said Jennifer,

"And I." said Jessica,

"And I," said Jane and

"And I." said little Joan.

"The verdict is passed," said Martin. "And look! over our heads hangs the moon, as round and beautiful as a penny balloon, with an eye as wide awake as a child's at six in the morning. If she will not go to sleep in heaven to-night, why on earth should we? Let's have a party!"

The girls looked at one another in amazement and delight. "A party? Oh!" cried they. "But who will give it?"

"I will," said Martin.

"And who will come to it?"

"Whoever luck sends us," said Martin. "But we'll begin with ourselves. Joan and Joyce and Jennifer and Jessica and Jane and Joscelyn, will you come to my party in the Apple-Orchard?"

"Yes, thank you, Martin!" cried they. And ran away to change. But the only change possible was to take the kerchiefs off their white necks, and the shoes and stockings off their little feet, and let down their pretty hair. So they did these things, and made wreaths for one another, and posies for their yellow dresses. And it is time for you to know that Jennifer's dress was primrose and Jane's cowslip yellow, and that Joyce looked like buttercups and Jessica like marigolds; and Joscelyn's was the glory of the kingcups that rise like magic golden isles above the Amberley floods in May. But little Joan had not been able to decide between the two yellows that go to make wild daffodils, so she had them both. Under their flowerlike skirts their white ankles and rosy heels moved as lightly as windflowers swaying in the grass. And just when they were ready they heard Martin Pippin's lute under the apple-tree, so they came to the party dancing. Round and round the tree they danced in the moonlight till they were out of breath. But when they could dance no more they stood stock still and stared without speaking; for spread under the trees was such a feast as they had not seen for months and months.

In the middle was a great heap of apples, red and brown and green and gold; but besides these was a dish of roasted apples and another of apple dumplings, and between them a bowl of brown sugar and a full pitcher of cream. The cream had spilled, and you could see where Martin had run his finger up the round of the pitcher to its lip, where one drip lingered still. Near these there was a plum-cake of the sort our grannies make. It is of these cakes we say that twenty men could not put their arms round them. There were nuts in it too, and spices. And there was a big basin of curds and whey, and a bigger one of fruit salad, and another of custard; and plates of jam tarts and lemon cheesecakes and cheesestraws and macaroons; and gingerbread in cakes and also in figures of girls and boys with caraway comfits for eyes, and a unicorn and a lion with gilded horn and crown; and pots of honey and quince jelly and treacle; and mushrooms and pickled walnuts and green salads. Even Mr. Ringdaly did not provide a bigger feast when he married Mrs. Ringdaly. For there were also all the best sorts of sweets in the world: sugar- candy on a string, and twisted barley-sticks, and bulls'-eyes, and peardrops, and licorice shoe-strings, and Turkish Delight, and pink and white sugar mice; besides these there was sherbet, not to drink of course, but to dip your finger in. There were a good many other things, but these were what the milkmaids took in at a glance.

"OH!"cried six voices at once. "Where did they come from?"

"Through the gap," said Martin.

"But who brought them?"

"Don't ask me," said Martin.

At first the girls were rather shy—you can't help that at parties. But as they ate (and you know what each ate first) they got more and more at their ease, and by the time they were licking their sticky fingers were in the mood for any game. So they played all the best games there are, such as "Cobbler! Cobbler!" (Joscelyn's shoe), and Hunt the Thimble (Jane's thimble), and Mulberry Bush, and Oranges and Lemons, and Nuts in May. And in Nuts in May Martin insisted on being a side all by himself, and one after another he fetched each girl away from her side to his. And Joan came like a bird, and Joyce pretended to struggle, and Jennifer had no fight in her at all, and Jessica really tried, and Jane didn't like it because it was undignified and so rough. But when Joscelyn's turn came to be fetched as she stood all alone on her side deserted by her supporters, she put her hands behind her back, and jumped over the handkerchief of her own accord, and walked up to Martin and said, "All right, you've won." For when it comes to fetching away it is a game that boys are better at than girls.

"In that case," said Martin, "it's time for Hide-and-Seek." And he sat down on the swing and shut his eyes.

At the same moment the moon went behind a cloud.

And as he waited a light drop fell on Martin's cheek, and another, and another, like the silent weeping of a girl; so that he couldn't help opening his eyes quickly and looking by instinct toward the empty Well-House. It was still empty, for wherever the girls had hidden themselves, it was not there.

Then through the shadowed raining orchard a low voice called "Cuckoo!" and "Cuckoo! Cuckoo!" called another. And softly, clearly, laughingly, mockingly, defiantly, teasingly, sweetly, caressingly, "Cuckoo! Cuckoo! Cuckoo!"

they called on every side. Martin stood up and stole among the trees. At first he went quietly, but soon he ran and darted. And never a girl could he find. For this after all is the game that girls are better at than boys, and when it comes to hiding if they will not be found they will not. And if they will they will. But their will was not for Martin Pippin. Through the pattering moonless orchard he hunted them in vain; and the place was full of slipping shadows and whispers. And every now and then those cuckooing milkmaids called him, sometimes at a distance, sometimes at his very ear. But he could not catch a single one.

And now it seemed to Martin that there were more of these elusive shadows than he could have believed, and whisperings that needed accounting for.

For once he heard somebody whisper, "Oh, you were right! the world IS flat—for six months it's been as flat as a pancake!" And a second voice whispered, "Then I was wrong! for pancakes are round." And Martin said to himself, "That's Joyce!" but the first voice he couldn't recognize. And then followed a sound that was not exactly a whisper, yet not exactly unlike one; and Martin darted towards it, but touched only air.

And again he heard a mysterious voice whisper, "How could you keep yourself so secret all these months? I couldn't have. However can girls keep secrets so long?" And the answer was, "They can't keep them a single instant if you come and ask them—but you didn't come!" "What a fool I was!" whispered the first voice, but whose Martin could not for the life of him imagine. Yet he was sure that the other was Jennifer's. And again he heard that misleading sound which seemed to be something, yet, when he sought it, was nothing.

And now he heard another unknown whisperer say, "You should have seen my drills in the wheatfield last April! How the drill did wobble! Why, I was that upset, any girl could have thrown straighter than I drilled that wheat." And a second whisperer replied, "It MUST have been a sight, then, for girls throw crookeder than swallows fly!" This was surely Jessica; but who was the first speaker?

He was as strange to Martin as another one who whispered, "It was the silence got on my nerves most—it was having nobody to listen to of an evening. Of course there were the lads, but they never talk to the point." "I often fear," whispered a second voice, "that I talk too much at random." "Good Lord! you couldn't, if you talked for ever!" Each of these two cases ended as the first two had ended; and for Martin in as little result.

He hastened to another part of the orchard where the whispers were falling fast and fierce. "It was Adam's fault after all!" "No, I've found out that it was Eve's fault!" "But I've been looking it up." "And I've been thinking it over." "Rubbish! it WAS Adam's fault." "It was NOT Adam's fault. What can a stupid little boy know about it?" "I'm a month older than you are." "I don't care if you are. It was Eve's fault." "Well, don't make a fuss if it was." "Wasn't it?" "Stuff!" "WASN'T it?" "Oh, all right, if you like, it was Eve's fault." "Here's an apple for you," said Joscelyn quite distinctly. "Oh, ripping! but I'd rather have a—" "Sh-h! RUN!" Martin was just too late. "Rather have a what?" said Martin to himself.

He was beginning to feel lonely. His hair was wet with rain. He hadn't seen a milkmaid for an hour. He prowled low in the grass hoping to catch one unawares. In the swing he saw a shadow—or was it two shadows? It looked like one. And yet—

One half of the shadow whispered, "Do you like my new corduroys?" "Ever so much," whispered the other half. "I'm rather bucked about them myself," whispered the first half, "or ought I to say about IT?" "I think it's them," said the second half. The first half reflected, "It might be either one thing or two. But arithmetic's a nuisance—I never was good at it." The second half confessed, "I always have to guess at it myself. I'm only really sure of one bit." "Which bit's that?" whispered the first half, and the second half whispered, "That one and one make two." "Oh, you darling! of course they don't, and never did and never will." "Well, I don't really mind," said little Joan. And then there was a pause in which the two shadows were certainly one, until the second half whispered, "Oh! oh, you've shaved it off!" And this delighted the first half beyond all bounds; because even in the circumstances it was clever of the second half to have noticed it.

But Martin could bear no more. He sprang forward crying "Joan!"—and he grasped the empty swing. And round the orchard he flew, his hands before him, calling now "Joyce!" now "Jane!" now "Jessica!" "Jennifer!" "Joscelyn!" and again "Joan! Joan! Joan!" And all his answer was rustlings and shadows and whispers, and faint laughter like far-away echoes, and empty air.

All of a sudden the light rain stopped and the moon came out of her cloud. And Martin found himself standing beside the Well-House, and nobody near him. He gazed all around at the familiar things, the apple-trees, the swing, the green wicket, the broken feast in the grass. And then at the far end of the orchard he saw an unfamiliar thing. It was a double ladder, arched over the hawthorn. And up the ladder, like a golden shaft of the moon, went six quick girls, and ahead of each her lad.* And on the topmost rung each took his milkmaid by the hand and vanished over the hedge.

Martin Pippin was left alone in the Apple-Orchard.

*It is not important, but their names were Michael, Tom, Oliver, John, Henry, and Charles. And Michael had dark hair and light lashes, and Tom freckles and a snub-nose, and Oliver a mole on his left cheek, and John fine red-gold hair on his bronzed skin; and Henry was merely the Odd-Job Boy whose voice was breaking, so he imagined that it was he alone who ran the farm. But Charles was a dear. He had a tuft of white hair at the back of his dark head, like the cotton-tail of a rabbit, and as well as corduroy breeches he wore a rabbit-skin waistcoat, and he was a great nuisance to gamekeepers, who called him a poacher; whereas all he did was to let the rabbits out of the snares when it was kind to, and destroy the snares. And he used the bring "bunny-rabbits" (which other people call snapdragons) of the loveliest colors to plant in the little garden known as Joan's Corner. I should like to tell you more about Charles (but there isn't time) because I am fond of him. If I hadn't been I shouldn't have let him have Joan.

EPILOGUE

At cockcrow came the call which in that orchard was now as familiar as the rooster's.

"Maids! Maids! Maids!"

Martin Pippin was leaning over the green wicket throwing jam tarts to the ducks. Because in the Well-House Gillian had not left so much as a crumb. But when he heard Old Gillman's voice, he flicked a bull's-eye at the drake, getting it very accurately on the bill, and walked across to the gap.

"Good morning, master," said Martin cheerfully. "Pray how does Lemon, Joscelyn's Sussex, fare?"

Old Gillman put down his loaves with great deliberation, and spent a few minutes taking Martin in. Then he answered, "There's scant milk to a Sussex, and allus will be. And if there was not, there'd be none to Joscelyn's Lemon. And if there was, it would take more than Henry to draw it. And so that's you, is it?"

"That's me," said Martin Pippin.

"Well," said Old Gillman, "I've spent the best of six mornings trying not to see ye. And has my daughter taken the right road yet?"

"Yes, master," said Martin, "she has taken the road to Adversane."

"Which SHE'S spent the best of six months trying not to see," said Old Gillman. "Women's a nuisance. Allus for taking the long cut round."

"I've known many a short cut," said Martin, "to end in a blind alley."

"Well, well, so long as they gets there," grunted Gillman. "And what's this here?"

"A pair of steps," said Martin.

"What for?" said Gillman.

"Milkmaids and milkmen," said Martin.

"So they maids have cut too, have they?"

"It was a full moon, you see."

"I dessay. But if they'd gone by the stile they could have hopped it in the dark six months agone," said Old Gillman. And he got over the stile, which was the other way into the orchard and has not been mentioned till now, and came and clapped Martin on the shoulder.

"Women's more trouble," said he, "than they're worth."

"They're plenty of trouble," said Martin; "I've never discovered yet what they're worth."

"We'll not talk of em more. Come up to the house for a drink, boy," said Old Gillman.

Martin said pleasantly, "You can drink milk now, master, to your heart's content. Or even water." And he walked over to the Well-House, and pointed invitingly to the bucket.

Old Gillman followed him with one eye open. "It's too late for that, boy. When you've turned toper for six months, after sixty sober years, it'll take you another six to drop the habit. That's what these daughters do for their dads. But we'll not talk of em." He stood beside Martin and stared down at the padlock. "How did the pretty go?"

"In the swing, like a swift."

"Why not through the gate like a gal?"

"The keys wouldn't turn."

"Which way?"

"The right way."

"You should ha' tried em the wrong way, boy."

"That would have locked it," said Martin.

"Azactly," said Old Gillman; and slipped the padlock from the staple and put it in his pocket. "Come along up now."

Martin followed him through the orchard and the paddock and the garden and the farmyard to the house. He noticed that everything was in the pink of condition. But as he passed the stables he heard the cows lowing badly.

The farm-kitchen was a big one. It had all the things that go to make the best farm-kitchens: such as red bricks and heavy smoke- blackened beams, and a deep hearth with a great fire on it and settles inside, from which one could look up at the chimney-shaft to the sky, and clay pipes and spills alongside, and a muller for wine or beer; and hams and sides of bacon and strings on onions and bunches of herbs; much pewter, and a copper warming-pan, and brass candlesticks, and a grandfather clock; a cherrywood dresser and wheelback chairs polished with age; and a great scrubbed oaken table to seat a harvest-supper, planed from a single mighty plank. It was as clean as everything else in that good room, but all the scrubbing would not efface the circular stains wherever men had sat and drunk; and that was all the way round and in the middle. There were mugs and a Toby jug upon it now. Old Gillman filled two of the mugs, and lifted one to Martin, and Martin echoed the action like a looking-glass. And they toasted each other in good Audit Ale.

"Well," said Old Gillman stuffing his pipe, "it's been a peaceful time, and now us must just see how things go."

"They look shipshape enough at the moment," said Martin.

"Ah," said Old Gillman shaking his head, "that's the lads. They're good lads when you let em alone. But what it'll be now they maids get meddling again us can't foretell. It were bad enough afore, wi' their quarrelsomeness and their shilly-shally. It sends all things to rack and ruin."

"What does?" said Martin.

"This here love." Old Gillman refilled his mug. "We'll not talk of it. She were a handy gal afore Robin began unmaking her mind along of his own. Lord! why can't these young things be plain and say what they want, and get it? Wasn't I plain wi' her mother?"

"Were you?" said Martin.

"Ah, worse luck!" said Gillman, "and me a happy bachelor as I was. What did I want wi' a minx about the place?" He filled his mug again.

"What do any of us?" said Martin. "These women are the deuce."

"They are," said Gillman. "We'll not talk of em."

"There are a thousand better things to talk of," agreed Martin. "There is Sloe Gin."

Old Gillman's eye brightened. "Ah!" said Old Gillman, and puffed at his pipe. "Her name," he said, "was Juniper, but as oft as not I'd call her June, for she was like that. A rose in the house, boy. Maybe you think my Jill has her share of looks? She has her mother's leavings, let me tell ye. So you may judge. But what's this Robin to dilly-dally with her daughter, till the gal can't sleep o' nights for wondering will he speak in the morning or will he be mum? And so she becomes worse than no use in kitchen and dairy, and since sickness is catching the maids follow suit. It's all off and on wi' them and their lads. In the morning they will, in the evening they won't. Ah, twas a tarrible life. And all along o' Robin Rue. Young man, the farm, I tell ye, was going to fair rack and ruin."

"You seem to have found a remedy," said Martin.

"If they silly maids couldn't make up their minds," said Old Gillman, "there was nothing for it but to turn em out neck and crop till they learned what they wanted. And Robin into the bargain. He's no better than a maid when it comes to taking the bull by the horns. Yet that's the man's part, mark ye. Don't I know? Smockalley she come from, the Rose of Smockalley they called her, for a Rose in June she were. There weren't a lass to match her south of Hagland and north of Roundabout. And the lads would ha' died for her from Picketty to Chiltington. But twas a Billinghurst lad got her, d'ye see?" Old Gillman filled his mug.

"How did that come about?" asked Martin, filling his.

"All along o' the Murray River."

"WHAT'S that!" said Martin Pippin. But Old Gillman thought he said, "What's THAT?"

" Tis the biggest river in Sussex, young man, and the littlest known, and the fullest of dangers, and the hardest to find; because nobody's ever found it yet but her and me. And she'd sworn to wed none but him as could find it with her. Don't I remember the day! Twas the day the Carrier come, and that was the day o' the week for us folk then. He had a blue wagon, had George, with scarlet wheels and a green awning; and his horse was a red-and-white skewbald and jingled bells on its bridle. A small bandy-legged man was George, wi' a jolly face and a squint, and as he drives up he toots on a tin trumpet wi' red tassels on it. Didn't it bring the crowd running! and didn't the crowd bring HIM to a standstill, some holding old Scarlet Runner by the bridle, and others standing on the very axles. And the hubbub, young man! It was Where's my six yards of dimity?' from one, and Have you my coral necklace?' from another. Where's my bag of comfits? where's my hundreds and thousands?' from the children; and I can't wait for my ivory fan?' My bandanna hanky!' My two ounces of snuff!' My guitar!' My clogs!' My satin dancing-shoes!' My onion-seed!' My new spindle!' My fiddle-bow!' My powder-puff!' And some little un would lisp, I'm sure you've forgotten my blue balloon!' And then they'd cry, one-and-all, in a breath, George! what's the news?' And he'd say, Give a body elbow- room!' and handing the packages right and left would allus have something to tell. But on this day he says, News? There BE no news excepting THE News.' And what's THE News?' cries one-and-all. Why,' says George, that the Rose of Smockalley consents to be wed at last.' The Rose!' they cries, and me the loudest, to whom?' To him,' says George, as can find her the Murray River. For a sailor come by last Tuesday wi' a tale o' the Murray River where he'd been wrecked and seen wonders; and a woman tormented by curiosity will go as far as a man tormented by love. And so she's willing to be wed at last. But she's liker to die a maid.' Then I ups and asks why. And George he says, For that the sailor breathed such perils that the lasses was taken wi' the trembles and the lads with the shudders. For, he says, the river's haunted by spirits, and a mystery at the end of it which none has ever come back from. And no man dares hazard so dark and dangerous an adventure, even for love of the Rose.' That pricks a man's pride to hear, boy, and Shame,' says I, on all West Sussex if that be so. Here be one man as is ready, and here be fifty others. What d'ye say, lads?' But Lord! as I looks from one to another they trickles away like sand through an hourglass, and before we knows it me and George has the road to ourselves. So he says, I must be getting on to Wisboro', but first I'll deliver ye your baggage.' You've no baggage o' mine,' says I. Yes, if you'll excuse me,' says he; and wi' that he parts the green awning and says, There she be.' And there she were, sitting on a barrel o' cider."

"What was she like to look at?" asked Martin.

"Yaller hair and gray eyes," said Gillman. "And me a bachelor."

"It was hopeless," said Martin.

"It were," said Old Gillman. "And it were the end o' my peace of life. She looks me straight in the eye and she says, Juniper's my name, but I'm June to them as loves me. And June I'll be to you. For I have traveled his rounds wi' this Carrier for a week, and sat behind his curtain while he told men my wishes. And you be the only one of them all as is willing to do a difficult thing for an idle whim, if what is the heart's desire can ever be idle. So I will sit behind the curtain no longer, and if you will let me I will follow you to the ends of Sussex till the Murray River be found, or we be dead.' And I says Jump, lass!' and down she jumps and puts up her mouth." Gillman filled his mug.

Martin filled his. "Well," said he, "a man must take his bull by the horns. And did you ever succeed in finding the Murray River?"

"Wi' a child's help. It can only be found by a child's help. Tis the child's river of all Sussex. Any child can help you to it."

"Yes," said Martin, "and all children know it."

Old Gillman put down his mug. "Do YOU know it, boy?"

"I live by it," said Martin Pippin, "when I live anywhere."

"Do children play in it still?" asked Gillman.

"None but children," said Martin Pippin. "And above all the child which boys and girls are always rediscovering in each other's hearts, even when they've turned gray in other folks' sight. And at the end of it is a mystery."

"She were a child to the end," said Old Gillman. "A fair nuisance, so she were. And Jill takes after her."

"Well, SHE'S off your hands anyhow," said Martin getting up. "She's to be some other body's nuisance now, and your maids have come back to their milking."

"Ah, have they?" grunted Gillman. "The lads did it better. And they cooked better. And they cleaned better. There is nothing men cannot do better than women."

"I know it," said Martin Pippin, "but it would be unkind to let on."

"Then we'll wash our hands of em. But don't go, boy," said Old Gillman. "Talking of Sloe Gin—"

Martin sat down again.

They talked of Sloe Gin for a very long time. They did not agree about it. They got out some bottles to see if they could not manage to agree. Martin thought one bottle hadn't enough sugar-candy in it, so they put in some more; and Old Gillman thought another bottle hadn't enough gin in it, so they also put in some more. But they couldn't get it right, though they tried and tried. Old Gillman thought it should be filtered drop by drop seventy times through seven hundred sheets of blotting-paper, but Martin thought seven hundred times through seventy sheets was better; and Martin thought it should then be kept for seven thousand years, but Old Gillman thought seven years sufficient. But neither of these points had ever been really proved, and was not that day.

After this, as they couldn't reach an agreement, they changed the subject to rum punch, and argued a good deal as to the right quantities of lemon and sugar and nutmeg; and whether it was or was not improved by the addition of brandy, and how much; and an orange or so, and how many; and a tangerine, if you had it; and a tot of gin, if you had it left. Yet in this case too the most repeated practice proved as inadequate as the most confirmed theory.

So after a bit Old Gillman said, "This is child's play, boy. After all, there's but one drink for kings and men. Give us a song over our cup, and I'll sing along o' ye."

"Right," said Martin, "if you can fetch me the only cup worthy to sing over."

"What cup's that, boy?"

"What but a kingcup?" said Martin.

"A king once drank from this," said Gillman, fetching down a goblet as golden as ale. "He looked like a shepherd, and had a fold just across the road, but he was a king for all that. So strike up."

"After me, then," said Martin; and they pushed the cup between them, and the song too.

Martin: What shall we drink of when we sup?
Gillman: What d'ye say to the King's own cup?
Martin: What's the drink?
Gillman: What d'ye think?
Martin: Farmer, say!
Water?
Gillman: Nay!

Martin: Wine?
Gillman: Aye!
Martin: Red wine?
Gillman: Fie!
Martin: White wine?
Gillman: No!
Martin: Yellow wine?
Gillman: Oh!
Martin: What in fine,
What wine then?
Gillman: The only wine
That's fit for men
Who drink of the King's Cup when they dine,
And that is the Old Brown Barley Wine!
]From This   I'll drink ye high,
Point I   I'll drink ye low,
Don't Know   Till the stars run dry
Which Of   Of their juices oh!
Them Was   I'll drink ye up,
Singing;   I'll drink ye down,
And No More   Till the old moon's cup
Did They: Is cracked all round,
And the pickled sun
Jumps out of his brine,
And you cry Done!
To the Barley Wine.
Come, boy, sup! Come, fill up!
Here's King's own drink for the King's own cup!

What happened after this I really don't know. For I was not there, though I should like to have been.

I only know that when Martin Pippin stepped out of Gillman's Farm with his lute on his back, Old Gillman was fast asleep on the settle. But Martin had never been wider awake.

It was late in the afternoon. There was no sign of human life anywhere. In their stables the cows were lowing very badly.

"Oh, maids, maids, maids!" sighed Martin Pippin. "Rack and ruin, my dears, rack and ruin!"

And he fetched the milkpails and went into the stalls, and did the milkmaids' business for them. And Joyce's Blossom, and Jennifer's Daisy, and Jessica's Clover stood as still for him as they stand in the shade of the willows on Midsummer Day. And Jane's Nellie whisked her tail over his mouth, but seemed sorry afterwards. And Joscelyn's Lemon kicked the bucket and would not let down her milk till he sang to her, and then she gave in. But little Joan's little

Jersey Nancy, with her soft dark eyes, and soft dun sides, and slender legs like a deer's, licked his cheek. And this was Martin's milking-song.

You Milkmaids in the hedgerows,
  Get up and milk your kine!
The satin Lords and Ladies
  Are all dressed up so fine,
But if you do not skim and churn
  How can they dine?
Get up, you idle Milkmaids,
  And call in your kine.

You milkmaids in the hedgerows,
  You lazy lovely crew,
Get up and churn the buttercups
  And skim the milkweed, do!
But the Milkmaids in their country prints
  And faces washed with dew,
They laughed at Lords and Ladies
  And sang "Cuckoo! Cuckoo!"
And if you know their reason
  I'm not so wise as you.

When he had done, Martin carried the pails to the dairy and turned his back on Gillman's. For his business there was ended. So he went out at the gate and lifted his face to the Downs.

It was a lovely evening. Half the sky was clear and blue, and the other half full of silky gold clouds—they wanted to be heavy and wet, but the sun was having such fun on the edge of the Downs, somewhere about Duncton, that they had to be gold in spite of themselves.

CONCLUSION

One evening at the end of the first week in September, Martin Pippin walked along the Roman Road to Adversane. And as he approached he said to himself, "There are many sweet corners in Sussex, but few sweeter than this, and I thank my stars that I have been led to see it once in my life."

While he was thanking his stars, which were already in the sky waiting for the light to go out and give them a chance, he heard the sound of weeping. It came from the malthouse, which is the most beautiful building in Sussex. So persistent was it that after he had listened to it for six minutes it seemed to Martin that he had been listening to it for six months, and for one moment he believed himself to be sitting in an orchard with his eyes shut, and warm tears from heaven falling on his face. But knowing himself to be too much given to fancies he decided to lay those ghosts by investigation, and he went up to the malthouse and looked inside.

There he found a young man flooring the barley. As he turned and re-turned it with his spade he wept so copiously above it that he was frequently obliged to pause and wipe away his tears with his arm, for he could no longer see the barley he was spreading. When the maltster had interrupted himself thus for the third occasion, Martin Pippin concluded that it was time to address him.

"Young master," said Martin, "the bitters that are brewed from your barley will need no adulterating behind the bar, and that's flat."

The maltster leaned on his spade to reply.

"There are no waters in all the world," said he, "plentiful enough to adulterate the bitterness of my despair."

"Then I would preserve these rivers for better sport," said Martin. "And if memory plays me no tricks, your name was once Robin Rue."

"And Rue it will be to my last hour," said Robin, "for a man can no more escape from his name than from his nature."

"Men," observed Martin, "have been in this respect worse served than women. And when will Gillian Gillman change her name?"

"No sooner than I," sighed Robin Rue; "a maid she must die, as I a bachelor. And if she do not outlive me, we shall both be buried before Christmas."

"Heaven forbid!" exclaimed Martin. And stepping into the malthouse he offered Robin six keys.

"How will these help us?" said Robin Rue.

"They are the keys of your lady's Well-House," said Martin Pippin, "and how I have outpaced her I cannot imagine, for she was on the road to you twenty hours ago."

"This is no news," said Robin. "There she is."

And he turned his face to the dark of the malthouse, and there, sitting on a barrel, with a slice of the sunset falling through a slit on her corn-colored hair, was Gillian.

"In love's name," cried Martin Pippin, putting his hands to his head, "what more do you want?"

"A husband worthy of her," moaned Robin Rue, "and how can I suppose that I am he? Oh, that I were only good enough for her! oh, that she could be happily mated, as after all her sorrows she deserves to be!"

Then Martin looked down at the patch on his shoe saying, "And tell me now, if you knew Gillian happily wed, would you ask nothing more of life?"

"Oh, sir," cried Robin Rue, "if I knew any man who could give her all I cannot, I would contrive at least to live long enough to drown my sorrows in the beer brewed from this barley."

"It is a solace," said Martin, "that must be denied to no man. It seems that I must help you out to the last. And if you will take one glance out of doors, you will see that the working-day is over."

Robin Rue looked out of doors, saw by the sun that it was so, put down his spade, and went home to supper.

"Gillian," said Martin Pippin, "the Squire did not come himself to fetch her away because he was a young fool. There was no eighth floret on the grass-blade, so the rime stayed at the seventh. The letter I threw with the Lady-peel was a G. There are apples all round your silver ring because it was once my ring. I do, you dear, I do, I do. And now I have answered your many questions, answer me one. Why did you sit six months in the Well-House weeping for love?"

"Oh, Martin," said Gillian softly, "could you tell my friends so much they did not know, and not know this?—girls do not weep for love, they weep for want of it." And she lifted her heavenly eyes, and out of the last of the sunlight looked at him without thinking. And Martin, like a drowning man catching at straws, caught her corn-colored plaits one in either hand, and drawing himself to her by them, whispered, "Do girls do that? But they are so much too good for us, Gillian."

"I know they are," whispered Gillian, "but if all men were like Robin Rue, what would become of us? Must we be punished for what we can't help?"

And she put her little finger on his mouth, and he kissed it.

Then Martin himself sat down on the barrel where there was only room for one; but it was Martin who sat on it. And after a while he said, "You mightn't think it, but I have got a cottage, and there is nothing whatever in it but a table which I made myself, and I think that is enough to begin with. On the way to it we shall pass Hardham, where in the Priory Ruins lives a Hermit who is sometimes in the mood. Beyond Hardham is the sunken bed of the old canal that is a secret not known to everybody; all flowering reeds and plants that love water grow there, and you have to push your way between water-loving trees under which grass and nettles in their season grow taller than children; but at other times, when the pussy- willows bloom with gray and golden bees, the way is clear. Beyond this presently is a little glade, the loveliest in Sussex; in spring it is patterned with primroses, and windflowers shake their fragile bells and show their silver stars above them. Some are pure and colorless, like maidens who know nothing of love, and others are faintly stained with streaks of purple-rose. So exquisite is the beauty of these earthly flowers that it is like a heavenly dream, but it is a dream come true; and you will never pass it in April without longing to turn aside and, kneeling among all that pallid gold and silver, offer up a prayer to the fairies. And I shall always kneel there with you. But beyond this is a land of bracken and undiscovered forests that hides a special secret. And you may run round it on all sides within fifty yards, yet never find it; unless you happen to light upon a land where grass springs under your feet among deep cart-ruts, and blackberry branches scramble on the ground from the flowery sides. The lane is called Shelley's Lane, for a reason too beautiful to be told; since all the most beautiful reasons in the world are kept secrets. And this is why, dear Gillian, the world never knows, and cannot for the life of it imagine, what this man sees in that maid and that maid in this man. The world cannot think why they fell in love with each other. But they have their reason, their beautiful secret, that never gets told to more than one person; and what they see in each other is what they show to each other; and it is the truth. Only they kept it hidden in their hearts until the time came. And though you and I may never know why this lane is called Shelley's, to us both it will always be the greenest lane in Sussex, because it leads to the special secret I spoke of. At the end of it is an old gate, clambered with blue periwinkle, and the gate opens into a garden in the midst of the forest, a garden so gay and so scented, so full of butterflies and bees and flower-borders and grass-plots with fruit- trees on them, that it might be Eden grown tiny. The garden runs down a slope, and is divided from a wild meadow by a brook crossed by a plank, fringed with young hazel and alder and, at the right time, thick-set with primroses. Behind the meadow, in a glimpse of the distance full of soft blue shadows and pale yellow lights, lie the lovely sides of the Downs, rounded and dimpled like human beings, dimpled like babies, rounded like women. The flow of their lines is like the breathing of a sleeper; you can almost see the tranquil heaving of a bosom. All about and around the garden are the trees of the forest. Crouched in one of the hollows is my cottage with the table in it. And the brook at the bottom of the garden is the Murray River."

Gillian looked up from his shoulder. "I always meant to find that some day," she said, "with some one to help me."

"I'll help you," said Martin.

"Do children play there now?"

"Children with names as lovely as Sylvia, who are even lovelier than their names. They are the only spirits who haunt it. And at the source of it is a mystery so beautiful that one day, when you and I have discovered it together, we shall never come back again. But this will be after long years of gladness, and a life kept always young, not only by our children, but by the child which each will continually rediscover in the other's heart."

"What is this you are telling me?" whispered Gillian, hiding her face again.

"The Seventh Story."

"I'm glad it ends happily," said Gillian. "But somehow, all the time, I thought it would."

"I rather thought so too," said Martin Pippin. "For what does furniture matter as long as Sussex grows bedstraw for ladies to sleep on?"

And tuning his lute he sang her his very last song.

My Lady sha'n't lie between linen,
My Lady sha'n't lie upon down,
She shall not have blankets to cover her feet
Or a pillow put under her crown;
But my Lady shall lie on the sweetest of beds
That ever a lady saw,
For my Lady, my beautiful Lady,
My Lady shall lie upon straw.
Strew the sweet white straw, he said,
Strew the straw for my Lady's bed—
Two ells wide from foot to head,
Strew my Lady's bedstraw.
My Lady sha'n't sleep in a castle,
My Lady sha'n't sleep in a hall,
She shall not be sheltered away from the stars
By curtain or casement or wall;
But my lady shall sleep in the grassiest mead
That ever a Lady saw,
Where my Lady, my beautiful Lady,
My Lady shall lie upon straw.
Strew the warm white straw, said he,
My arms shall all her shelter be,
Her castle-walls and her own roof-tree—
Strew my Lady's bedstraw.

When he had done Martin Said, "Will you go traveling, Gillian?"

And Gillian answered, "With joy, Martin. But before I go traveling, I will sing to you." And taking the lute from him she sang him her very first song.

I saw an Old Man by the wayside
Sit down with his crutch to rest,
Like the smoke of an angry kettle
Was the beard puffed over his breast.
But when I tugged at the Old Man's beard
He turned to a beardless boy,
And the boy and myself went traveling,
Traveling wild with joy.
With eyes that twinkled and hearts that danced
And feet that skipped as they ran—
Now welcome, you blithe young Traveler!
And fare you well, Old Man!

When she had done Martin caught her in his arms and kissed her on the mouth and on the eyes and on both cheeks and on her two hands, and on the back of the neck where babies are kissed; and standing her up on the barrel and himself on the ground, he kissed her feet, one after the other. Then he cried, "Jump, lass! jump when I tell you!" and Gillian jumped. And as happy as children they ran hand-in-hand out of the Malthouse and down the road to Hardham.

Overhead the sun was running away from the clouds with all his might, and they were trying to catch hold of him one by one, in vain; for he rolled through their soft grasp, leaving their hands bright with gold-dust.

Echo Library

www.echo-library.com

Echo Library uses advanced digital print-on-demand technology to build and preserve an exciting world class collection of rare and out-of-print books, making them readily available for everyone to enjoy.

Situated just yards from Teddington Lock on the River Thames, Echo Library was founded in 2005 by Tom Cherrington, a specialist dealer in rare and antiquarian books with a passion for literature.

Please visit our website for a complete catalogue of our books, which includes foreign language titles.

The Right to Read

Echo Library actively supports the Royal National Institute of the Blind's Right to Read initiative by publishing a comprehensive range of large print and clear print titles.

Large Print titles are in 16 point Tiresias font as recommended by the RNIB.

Clear Print titles are in 13 point Tiresias font and designed for those who find standard print difficult to read.

Customer Service

If there is a serious error in the text or layout please send details to feedback@echo-library.com and we will supply a corrected copy. If there is a printing fault or the book is damaged please refer to your supplier.

Printed in the United States
98741LV00003B/127/A

9 781406 863666